WARRIOR PRIEST

WOLFF WAS STILL at the head of the charge, smashing through the thick press of bodies like a vision of Sigmar Himself. He was stood high in the stirrups, swinging his warhammer from left to right in great sweeping arcs, leaving a trail of splintered limbs and shattered armour in his wake. 'Sigmar absolves you,' he cried repeatedly, slamming his hammer into faces and shields with such force that his broad shoulders jolted back with the impact of each blow. Hastily fired arrows whirred towards him, clanging against his breastplate, but he rode on oblivious, dealing out Sigmar's judgement with ten pounds of bloody, tempered steel.

A WARHAMMER NOVEL

WARRIOR PRIEST

DARIUS HINKS

BLACK LIBRARY

For Kathryn – with love and eyeballs.

A BLACK LIBRARY PUBLICATION

First published in Great Britain in 2010 by
The Black Library,
Games Workshop Ltd.,
Willow Road, Nottingham,
NG7 2WS, UK

10 9 8 7 6 5 4 3 2 1

Cover illustration by Clint Langley.

Map by Nuala Kinrade.

A CIP record for this book is available from the British Library.

ISBN: 978 1 84970 003 0

Distributed in the US by Simon & Schuster
1230 Avenue of the Americas, New York, NY 10020.

See the Black Library on the Internet at
www.blacklibrary.com

Find out more about Games Workshop
and the world of Warhammer at
www.games-workshop.com

Printed and bound in the US.

THIS IS A dark age, a bloody age, an age of daemons and of sorcery. It is an age of battle and death, and of the world's ending. Amidst all of the fire, flame and fury it is a time, too, of mighty heroes, of bold deeds and great courage.

AT THE HEART of the Old World sprawls the Empire, the largest and most powerful of the human realms. Known for its engineers, sorcerers, traders and soldiers, it is a land of great mountains, mighty rivers, dark forests and vast cities. And from his throne in Altdorf reigns the Emperor Karl Franz, sacred descendant of the founder of these lands, Sigmar, and wielder of his magical warhammer.

BUT THESE ARE far from civilised times. Across the length and breadth of the Old World, from the knightly palaces of Bretonnia to ice-bound Kislev in the far north, come rumblings of war. In the towering Worlds Edge Mountains, the orc tribes are gathering for another assault. Bandits and renegades harry the wild southern lands of the Border Princes. There are rumours of rat-things, the skaven, emerging from the sewers and swamps across the land. And from the northern wildernesses there is the ever-present threat of Chaos, of daemons and beastmen corrupted by the foul powers of the Dark Gods. As the time of battle draws ever nearer, the Empire needs heroes like never before.

CHAPTER ONE
TANNHAUSER'S GIFT

CAPTAIN KURDT TANNHAUSER was dead. His heart was still hammering fiercely beneath his breastplate, but he knew that each powerful thud only took him closer to the grave. As his charger tore onwards through a blur of steel and fire, the screams of his dying men trailed after him. There would be no triumphant homecoming tonight.

Most of the soldiers who had struck out from Mercy's End had fallen far behind; or just fallen. Bergolt and Gelfrat were still alive, but they were mired in a forest of axes and swords. The panthers emblazoned on their banners were scorched and torn and their sword strikes grew weaker with each desperate blow. Within minutes, they would be dead. The artillery had fallen silent and even the roguish Ditmarus and his pistoliers had vanished from view. Tannhauser could only assume they had finally achieved the glorious end they had always joked about.

Turning away from the bloodbath that surrounded him, he steered his mount towards a single glittering point. Perched on a nearby hilltop, surveying the carnage was a dazzling figure: a sliver of light in the darkness, sat calmly amidst the shadowy hordes with six shimmering wings arching upwards from its back.

Freed from the twin constraints of fear and hope, Captain Tannhauser charged up the hill towards this beautiful horror. Axes and spears hurtled towards him, but his speed confounded even the most practised aim. He rose up in his saddle and held his sword aloft, so that the light of the moons ran along its battered edge. With his other hand he removed his helmet and cast it down onto the mud, revelling in the wind, rain and blood that lashed into his face. 'Join me, Mormius,' he whispered, as he raced towards the gleaming figure. 'Join me in death.'

At the brow of the hill, a wall of tusks and muscle barred his way. Towering men in greasy animal furs and crude iron armour charged to meet him as he neared their champion. The pounding rain blurred their forms, making iridescent ghosts of them, but even the terrible weather could not shield Tannhauser from the extent of their deformity. Elongated arms reached out towards him through the downpour; arms contorted beyond all recognition, ending in cruel, serrated beaks. As he bore down on them, Tannhauser struggled to distinguish one shape from another: arachnid limbs, twisted muscles and gnarled tusks all merged into a nightmarish whole.

The marauders held fast as the captain's mount slammed into them, ripping through the horse's chest with their strange claws and cutting its legs from beneath it. As the animal toppled, screaming to the ground, Tannhauser flew from the saddle, tumbling through the air over the marauders' heads and slamming into the muddy hillside.

Behind him, the grotesque figures struggled up from beneath the dying horse, but they were too slow. Despite his burning lungs, Tannhauser climbed awkwardly to his feet and ran towards Mormius, grunting with pain and exertion as he stumbled through the rain and filth.

As the captain approached his foe, he saw the reason for the pale light playing across his armour. Mormius was clad entirely in faceted crystals that shifted and whirred mechanically as he raised his sword to defend himself. He towered over Tannhauser, at nearly seven feet tall, and as his wings spread out behind him in the moonlight, the captain felt as though he were facing a god. Hatred carried him through his doubt though. He grinned with triumph as he finally swung his sword at the monster that had robbed him of life.

Mormius parried and with the dull *clang* of steel on steel, the fight began.

The captain knew he had precious seconds before the champion's guards pulled him apart, so he attacked with breathtaking speed, landing a flurry of blows on his opponent and leaving him reeling in the face of the onslaught. As Mormius staggered backwards, the captain called out the names of his fallen comrades in a furious roll call for the dead.

Mormius's huge wings began to beat frantically as he slipped through the mud and corpses. Finally, the captain smashed the champion's blade aside and Mormius stumbled back over a broken cannon, his chest exposed. Tannhauser raised his sword for the deathblow.

Then he froze.

He found himself face to face with a proud knight of the Empire. The man's skin was drawn and pale with passion; blood and filth covered his armour and his dark, rain-sodden hair was plastered across his ivory brow. It was the knight's eyes that most arrested him, knifing into Tannhauser with a terrible look of despair.

With dawning horror, the captain realised that this lost soul was his own reflection, trapped like a caged animal in the glimmering plates of Mormius's armour. He was so shocked by his appearance that his sword slipped from his fingers. The war had made a ghoul of him. He was a monster. For a few seconds he forgot all about the battle as he studied the tortured lines of his own face; then, a hot bolt of pain snapped him out of his reverie. As the searing heat grew he looked down to see Mormius's sword, embedded deep in his belly.

The champion began to laugh as Tannhauser dropped silently into the mud.

Mormius's huge command tent was sewn from the hides of fallen soldiers, and as he lit a brazier in its centre, a dozen eyeless faces leered down at him, reanimated in the flickering green light. The champion sat down, cross-legged at the captain's feet and removed his helmet, allowing a shock of lustrous ginger ringlets to roll down over his shoulders. Tannhauser struggled against the tiredness that threatened to overcome him, but a great weight seemed to be pressing him into his chair. He struggled to rise, but found his limbs paralysed, all traces of strength gone from them. He stared curiously into Mormius's face. 'You're a child,' he said, through a mouthful of blood.

It was true. The face before him was that of a youth barely out of his teens. Mormius looked like a pampered aristocrat, or maybe the son of a wealthy merchant. His soft white skin was flawless and his languid blue eyes gazed out from beneath long, feminine lashes. His plump lips were so glossy and pink, that the captain wondered if he were wearing make-up.

'It would appear so to you, I suppose,' replied Mormius with a voice like velvet. He moistened his lips and revealed his perfect ivory teeth in a warm smile. 'I was born in the time of your forefathers, Kurdt, way back when Sigmar's progeny were still little more than beasts, crawling around in their own filth.'

Tannhauser grimaced. 'I would take a quick death over a life such as yours.' He managed to raise a hand and wipe away the blood that was muffling his words. 'What use is an eternity of life, if it's spent in the service of such wretched masters?'

'A commendable sentiment, Kurdt,' replied Mormius as his smile turned into a giggle. 'In fact, now I hear it put like that, I might be forced to reconsider my position.' His laughter grew until his whole body was rocking back and forth and his eyes filled with tears. He lurched to his feet and whirled around the tent, carelessly knocking over furniture of incredible antiquity. Gilt-edged mirrors and crystal bowls smashed across the ground as Mormius's mirth grew, becoming a succession of hiccupping yelps. Then the laughter shifted seamlessly into a scream of rage and the champion flew at Tannhauser, his face contorted with fury. 'What would you know of eternity?' he screamed, slapping the knight with such force that the chair toppled beneath him and he sprawled on the floor. 'You're nothing but an unwitting slave. Since the day you were born you've been ensnared, a plaything of The Great Conspirator.' He crouched down, grabbed Tannhauser's head and howled into his face. 'You're the child! Don't you see? All of you strutting soldiers, celebrating your petty, ridiculous victories. You're just pawns. Not even that. You're a punchline to a joke you couldn't even understand.' He screamed again, but his rage was now so intense it strangled his words into a garbled whine.

As Mormius's anger increased, his features began to change, shifting and sliding in and out of view. Tannhauser saw a bewildering series of faces flash before him: old men, children and crones, all wailing with fury. Then, as suddenly as it began, the screaming ceased.

Mormius covered his mouth and flushed with embarrassment. 'Forgive me, Kurdt,' he whispered, loosing his grip on Tannhauser's head. His voice was gentle again and his face was his own once more. He helped the captain back up onto the chair and dusted him down with his soft white hands. He smiled apologetically. 'I've spent so long with these creatures,' – he gestured to the walls of the tent and the shadows of marauders passing by outside – 'I sometimes forget my manners.' The cheerful smile returned and he stepped over to a table laden with food. 'I haven't even offered you a drink,' he said, filling a silver goblet with wine and bringing it to the captain. 'You must think me quite the heathen.'

Tannhauser simply stared at him in mute horror, so Mormius placed the drink on the floor next to him and returned to the brazier in the centre of the room. 'It's a good vintage,' he muttered, as he measured out an assortment of coloured powders and dropped them into the green flames, filling the tent with thick, heady smoke. 'It would ease your suffering,' he added, with a note of apology in his voice.

As the clouds of smoke grew, the captain strained to follow Mormius's movements. His willowy shape slipped back and forth through the cloying fumes, dropping tinctures and leaves into the brazier like a master chef, humming merrily to himself as he worked. The walls of the tent gradually slipped away behind a haze of coloured smoke. Tannhauser felt himself falling into a realm of shadows. He wondered if his tired heart had finally released him.

A shape caught his eye, to the left of the brazier. It was a large net of some kind and at first he thought it was full of animal carcasses. He saw ribs, gristle and strands of wet meat. To his horror, he noticed the mass of flesh was moving slightly, as though breathing. He looked closer and saw that the organs and limbs were melded together into one grotesque being, layered with glistening viscera and dark, pulsing tumours. As he watched, the pile of meat shifted and several eyes suddenly peered out at him. The sack's thick cords strained as it started to slide across the ground in his direction. Tannhauser gasped as a grey, elongated face looked from beneath the folds of flesh. Then he noticed rows of hands, all reaching towards him from the mass of body parts.

Mormius heard Tannhauser's gasp and rolled his eyes in irritation. He strode across the tent and gave the meat a series of fierce kicks, until the struggling shape crawled back into the shadows. 'Family,' he said, shaking his head despairingly. 'What's to be done with them?' He stooped to wipe some blood from his boot. 'Still, I suppose they have sacrificed much on my behalf.'

Mormius gently fanned the smoke with his broad, silver wings, and Tannhauser sensed another presence, watching him intently. He peered through the fug, trying to spot the new arrival but, to his dismay, he realised that it was not in the tent, but in his mind, a strange sentience, spreading at the back of his thoughts like a shadow, tentatively probing the recesses of his consciousness. Images arrived unbidden in his head: glimpses of places and people he could never have seen. A range of mountains reared up before him, with peaks so sheer that they defied all logic. Then came vast armies of creatures so warped and grotesque he wanted to shield his eyes from the awfulness of them, but the visions were deep within him and however he squirmed, he could not escape them.

Tannhauser realised Mormius was crouched before him again, watching eagerly. The knight looked down at his hands and saw that they were rippling and swelling as the presence exerted its influence over his body. The bones in his back cracked as they stretched and elongated, arching up in a long curve. His head jolted back and with a shocking flash of pain he felt his head rearrange itself into a long beak-like curve.

Tannhauser opened his mouth to cry out, but another sound entirely emerged; a hoarse scraping that ripped through his throat. He was vaguely aware of Mormius, giggling with delight. The alien screech began to form words from Tannhauser's protesting vocal chords. At first it was no more than a jumble of screeched vowels, but then a distinct word filled the tent: 'Mormius.'

'Yes, master,' cried the champion, his voice wavering with emotion. 'You're so kind to spare me your–'

'Failure,' shrieked the hideous voice, forcing Tannhauser's head back even further.

Mormius's smile faltered. 'Failure, master?' He gestured to the door of the tent. 'We're in the very heart of Ostland. I've killed so many in your name, they're already writing songs about me. The province is on its knees.'

A furious chorus of screeches greeted Mormius's words. 'What of the capital? What of Wolfenburg? What of von Raukov? Why are you here? Your idleness is treachery.' As the words grew more enraged, the flames in the brazier began to gut and flicker, plunging the tent in and out of darkness. 'Do you wish to serve me, or make a fool of me?' cried the voice. 'Have you forsaken me? Are you enamoured of another master?'

Fear twisted Mormius's chubby face into a grimace. 'Master,' he gasped. 'Please understand – I've marched ceaselessly for weeks, but I need to gather my strength before I move on. The Ostlanders have refortified an old castle, called Mercy's End. It has already been ruined once by Archaon and we'll easily sweep it away, as surely as everything else, but I must wait for the rest of my army before heading south.'

'No!' screamed the voice, with such force that Tannhauser's throat burst. His whole body began to spasm and twist, like a broken marionette, and blood started rushing quickly from his exposed vocal cords. 'Strike now, or betray me.'

Mormius pawed pathetically at Tannhauser's jerking limbs and began to whine. 'Don't say such things, master. Of course I haven't betrayed you. Strendel, Wurdorf and Steinfeld are already in ruins. The north of the province is overrun with my men and they're all marching to meet me here. The surviving Ostlanders are massing in that crumbling old wreck, but they've picked a poor place to make their stand. We'll be there within days and we'll smash through those old walls like firewood. Then the whole province will be ours.' There was no reply, so he grabbed his sword from the ground and lifted it up over his head. 'As you wish then. We'll leave now. The stragglers will just have to catch up with us as best they can. I won't betray you, master.' There was still no reply and Mormius dashed to the captain's side, falling on his knees and grabbing Tannhauser's bloody hands in his own. 'Master?'

The captain lay slumped in the chair and however much Mormius pleaded and shook him, no more words came. 'Of course,' muttered the champion, rising to his feet and looking anxiously around the room. 'Of course, I must strike now. You're right.' He dashed from the tent and left Tannhauser to bleed alone.

The flames in the brazier flickered and finally died, plunging the tent into darkness. The captain's body was twisted beyond all recognition, but as the after-image of the fire played over his retina, a faint smile spread across his torn lips. His heart finally accepted the truth of his death and gratefully ceased to drum. As his last breath slipped from his lungs, Tannhauser looked down at a sharpened ring on his finger, glistening with a jewel of Mormius's blood. He wondered how long it would be before the champion discovered the gift he had left him.

THE KEEP REARED up from the hillside like a broken tooth. Firelight flickered from its narrow windows and above its crumbling battlements a banner was flying in the moonlight: a single bull, glowering defiantly from a black and white field.

All around the building, a great army was massing, swelling like waves beneath the quickly moving clouds. Mormius mounted a white, barded warhorse and rode to the brow of a hill to look down at the ranks flooding the valley. A grotesque figure shambled out of the darkness and stood at his side. Mormius looked down at his captain with distaste. The thing's serpentine limbs dragged behind him through the mud and silvery mites rushed over his scaled, eyeless face as he grinned up at his general. 'Your army is almost ready, lord,' he said, in a retching, gurgling voice. He lifted one of his writhing arms and gestured at the scene below. 'I've never seen such a gathering. No one could stop it. By tomorrow night we will have a force like nothing they've ever seen.'

'We must leave now,' said Mormius. 'We've rested long enough.'

The creature's smile faltered and a strange hissing noise came from deep in his throat. 'Now, my lord?'

'Yes, now. For every day we spend waiting, Mercy's End grows a little stronger. I have no desire to spend a week tussling over that backwater. I should be within sight of the capital by now, not wasting my time on these parochial skirmishes.'

'Well, master,' the marauder said, shrugging helplessly. 'I'm not sure that will be possible. Many of the troops are still fighting their way through Kislev. Ivarr Kolbeinn has gathered a great number of ogres and they're just a few days north of here. And Ingvarr the Changed has hundreds of men marching with him.' He grimaced with all four of his mouths. 'We should at least wait for Freyviòr Sturl and his horsemen.'

'Didn't you hear me?' said Mormius. 'We attack in the morning.' He grinned. 'Or do you think my skills as a strategist are insufficient?' His shoulders began to shake with amusement. 'Maybe it would be better if you made the tactical decisions from now on?'

At the sound of Mormius's laughter, the colour drained from the marauder's face. He backed away, shaking his head. 'No, of course not, you're absolutely right.' He waved at the keep. 'These fools won't see the dawn. I'll see to it.' He lurched awkwardly away through the rain. 'We'll be marching south within the hour.'

With some difficulty, Mormius managed to stifle his laughter. Once he was calm, he smiled with satisfaction at the great army arrayed before him. The standard bearers had unfurled their crude colours to the wind: the eight pointed star of Chaos, daubed in the blood of their enemies. It was a terrifying sight and his heart swelled with pride.

As he watched the endless stream of troops swarming out of the darkness, Mormius noticed a small hole on his left gauntlet. As he watched, a spidery, black patina began to spread over the crystals that surrounded it. He peered at the dark stain for a moment, then promptly forgot all about it as he turned his attention to the battle ahead.

CHAPTER TWO
MERCIFUL JUSTICE

'ENVY NEVER DIES,' said the old man, leaning in towards the assembled crowd. His voice was low, but his whole body was twisted with hate. Spittle was hanging from his cracked lips and his gaunt face was flushed with emotion. 'The old gods are always there, waiting for revenge; waiting to rise again.' His frenzied, bony arms snaked back and forth across his chest as he spoke and a sheen of sweat glistened over his ribs. A blistered symbol was scorched across his belly: a single flaming hammer.

Anna was torn between fascination and disgust. From her vantage point, up on top of the pyre, she could see how easily he manipulated the mob. Some of these people had recently trusted her with their lives; only the night before, most of them had still doubted her guilt. Now, they could smell blood on the morning air and they would not rest until more of it was spilled. As the old man continued his tirade, she saw life slipping from her grasp. Scarlet tears began to roll down over her bruised, swollen cheeks and she prepared herself for death.

'Their obscure plots always surround us,' continued the old man. 'A tide of unholy filth hides behind the most innocent of faces. Even the most vigilant of Sigmar's servants can struggle to spot the signs.' The crowd murmured their assent, beginning to warm to his theme. 'Look at her,' he hissed, stretching his frail body to its full height and pointing theatrically at Anna. 'See how this "priestess" whimpers for forgiveness. See the cold tears that run from her pitiless eyes. Even now, with judgement at hand, she is unrepentant. If you hesitate, if you falter even for a moment, she will worm her way out of justice. Trust me, my friends, that pretty young face hides an old, terrible evil; there's murder in her heart.' The crowd's murmurs grew louder and many of them cast nervous, furtive glances up at the priestess.

Anna shivered. Dawn light was spreading quickly over the village, but the witch hunter's henchman had torn her white robes as he fastened her to the pyre. Her exposed flesh was wet with dew and the autumn breeze knifed into her. She prayed that one way or another, her ordeal would soon be over. As the crowd began to chant along with the old man's liturgy, she looked out across their heads to the fields beyond the village; out towards the distant forest. Crows were hopping across the ploughed fields and heading towards her. She took a strange comfort in the sight. As mankind acted out its bloody rituals, nature continued unabated. The world marched on, blind to her fate. Even as the crows picked at her charred remains, she would become part of a timeless cycle of rebirth. There was solace in such things, she decided.

'Riders,' she muttered, surprised by the hoarse croak that came from her throat. The blood in her eyes had painted the horizon as a crimson blur, and for a while she doubted herself, but as the shapes grew nearer she was sure: it wasn't crows, but men who were moving towards her. Two horsemen had emerged from the distant trees and were slowly crossing the fields towards the village. She looked down to see if anyone else had noticed, but the old man had the mob in the palm of his sweaty hand. As he lurched back and forth, singing and cursing ecstatically, they cheered him on, waving knives and pitchforks in approval and edging towards the pyre.

'Look around,' he continued, gesturing towards the ruined houses. 'These truly are the end times. Judgement is finally at hand. Only the most pious will survive. Corruption and decay is crawling across our blessed homeland and only those with the faith to stare it down can escape damnation.' The villagers nodded eagerly at each other, unable to dispute the logic of his words. Life had always been hard, out here on the very edge of the Empire, but in recent months even the most hardened Ostlanders had begun to know doubt. Streams of blank-eyed refugees passed through almost daily now, bringing news of terrible defeats in the north. There wasn't a young man left in the village who wasn't fighting for his life in the war, or already cold in the ground.

The old man scampered, spider-like onto the remains of a barn wall and slapped the crumbling stone. 'Bricks and mortar can no longer keep you safe, my friends. The creatures that watch from the trees do not care about walls or doors. They're filled with mindless, animal hate. No mortal protection can stop them. They'll soon be back to finish the job. Yes! And burn down the rest of your homes.' He scratched frantically at his thin beard. 'And if you don't show the strength of your faith, you'll burn along with them.' He levelled a trembling finger at Anna. 'And *she* has brought this upon you!'

The crowd erupted into raucous cheers. 'She must die,' screamed an old woman, grabbing a lit firebrand and holding it aloft.

'It's true,' cried a blacksmith, nervously twisting his leather apron as he rushed to the old woman's side. 'Before the priestess came, we were safe, but now the creatures come almost nightly. I've heard her singing songs in a foreign language.' He looked around at the other villagers. 'I think she's calling to them.'

The old man nodded encouragement as the crowd began hurling a stream of evidence at Anna.

'She cured old Mandred with nothing more than a garland of flowers.'

'She goes into the forest alone, unafraid of the creatures.'

Anna was barely conscious of the accusations. A steady stream of blood was flowing from her head and reality kept slipping in and out of grasp. Visions of her childhood blurred into view and she whispered the name of her abbess, begging her to forgive her for the miserable end she had come to. She still could not be sure if the two horsemen were even real. Certainly none of the villagers seemed to have noticed them. The men's silhouettes were now quite clear as they trotted through the morning mist, but the mob was fixated on the old man. She blinked away her tears. Yes, she was sure now, it was two men, both mounted on powerful warhorses. Admittedly, the first was little more than a boy. His wiry body barely filled the saddle and his limbs flapped around clumsily as he steered the horse over the furrows; but even at this distance she could see the determined frown on his face as he strained to control his mount.

The second rider was another matter altogether. He was a little further back and still partly shrouded in mist, but from his posture Anna could tell this was no travelling merchant or itinerant farmer. He handled his horse with the calm surety of a veteran soldier, his chin raised disdainfully as he surveyed the scene before him. He was a shaven-headed giant, with a broad chest clad in thick, iron armour that glinted dully in the morning light. A great warhammer was slung nonchalantly over his wide shoulders. Anna felt a thrill of hope. Was this her saviour? Her pulse quickened and for the first time she tested the strength of the bonds that held her. She was strapped to a stout post with her hands above her head. The witch hunter's henchman had done his job well, but maybe if she just twisted a little…

'You are wise people,' said the old man, hopping back down from the barn wall. 'I can see it in your eyes.' He hugged and patted those nearest to him, blind to the grimaces his sour odour induced. As he moved amongst the crowd, he handed out small wooden hammers, muttering a blessing to each recipient in turn. The villagers grasped the icons with joy, pressing them to their chests and muttering prayers of thanks. The old man stroked the hammer emblazoned across his puckered belly. 'This symbol is no gaudy badge of honour. No shallow boast. The hammer is a mark of our heavy burden. It's no easy thing to hand out unerring judgement.' He gave the old woman a toothy, yellow grin as he took the flaming brand from her hand. 'Believe me,' he said, as he approached the pyre and looked up at the desperately struggling Anna, 'mercy would often seem the easier path.'

The crowd fell silent as he raised the brand and closed his eyes, as though in prayer. For a few minutes, the crackling of the flames was the only sound, and then, when he spoke again, it was in a dull monotone. 'It is to the merciful justice of Sigmar that I commit you, servant of the Ruinous Powers. May your soul find peace at last in the cleansing flame of his forgiveness.' Then the old man opened his eyes and Anna saw again how unusual they were; the irises were of such a pale grey that his pupils seemed to be floating in a pair of clear, white pools. He gave Anna a kind smile as he thrust the fire into the kindling at her feet.

The crowd gasped and backed away from the pyre, as though suddenly realising the magnitude of their treachery. The kindling was still damp with morning dew and for a while nothing happened; but then, to Anna's horror, thin trails of smoke began to snake around her feet.

'Don't be afraid,' said the old man, signalling for the mob to approach. 'The punishment of Sigmar only falls on his most errant children. You've all done well to reveal this woman's heresy. Now be stout of heart, and see the task through to its end.' He plucked a scroll from his robes and, as Anna began to moan in fear, he started to pray. He left the pyre and scampered back up onto the barn wall, proudly lifting his chin and addressing his words to the indifferent sky. One by one, the villagers stepped nervously back towards the growing fire, murmuring along with his prayers. Soon, the old man's passion started to infect them. Their doubt passed as quickly as it had come and they pressed closer, eager to see the witch burn.

Anna strained at her bonds, but they simply bit into her slender wrists all the more, until fresh blood began to flow down her arms. The smoke was quickly growing thicker and she felt the first glow of warmth under her feet. She strained, trying to stretch herself away from the fire, but it was useless. She wondered desperately whether she should try to inhale the smoke and escape into unconsciousness, but the thought appalled her; she was not ready to give up on life yet. She looked out through the cinders and heat haze and felt a rush of excitement. The two riders had almost reached the square and they were heading straight for her.

Now that she saw the larger of the two men at close hand, he looked even more impressive. The lower part of his face was hidden behind an iron gorget, but the battered metal could not hide the fierce intensity in his dark, brooding eyes. He was obviously a priest of some importance. Crimson robes hung down from beneath his thick, plate armour and the cloth was decorated with beautiful gold embroidery. Religious texts were chained to his cuirass and around his regal, shaven head he wore a studded metal band, engraved with images of a flaming hammer. Anna's heart swelled as he steered his horse towards the baying mob and looked her straight in the eye.

The crowd stumbled over their words and fell silent as they finally noticed the two horsemen. As the priest and his young acolyte approached, the villagers looked nervously towards the old witch hunter for reassurance. He was lost in prayer, swaying back and forth on the wall and muttering garbled words to the heavens. 'Banish, O Sigmar, this Servant of Change. Dispel her unholy form. I invoke Your Name. Let me end this Heresy. Let *me* be the instrument of Your wrath!'

The warrior priest dismounted and lifted his warhammer from over his shoulders. He surveyed the scene, taking in the wide-eyed villagers and the quickly growing fire. As his metal-clad fingers drummed on the haft of his weapon, a scowl crossed his face. Then he spotted the babbling old man, crouched on the barn wall. With a nod of satisfaction he marched straight past the priestess, pausing only to pick up a long wooden stake from the pyre. As the gangly youth tumbled awkwardly from his horse, he gave Anna an apologetic frown, before rushing after his master.

Anna gasped. They had no intention of saving her. They were bloodthirsty Sigmarites, just like the old man; blind to anything but their own hunger for war. She groaned with the horror of it. 'Have you no compassion?' she tried to say, but her lips were thick with dried blood and the words came out as a mumbled croak. She spat into the growing flames, cursing the hammer god and all his witless minions. Let the fire take her. There was no hope for a world ruled by such monsters. She would rather take her chances with the creatures of the forest than face another holy man.

The old man finally noticed the priest striding purposefully towards him. He tugged excitedly at his straggly hair as he saw the holy texts and hammer icons. A broad grin spread across his face. 'Brother,' he cried, skipping down from the wall, 'you've joined us at a crucial moment.' He spread his arms in a greeting and rushed towards him.

The priest remained silent as he approached. Upon reaching the old man he lifted him from the ground, as easily as if he were a small child and carried him back to the wall. Before the witch hunter could mutter a word of protest, the priest raised his great hammer and with one powerful blow pounded the wooden stake through the old man's chest, pinning him to the wall and leaving him dangling, puppet-like a few feet from the ground. Cries of dismay exploded from the crowd as a bright torrent of blood rushed from the old man and began drumming across the dusty earth. For a few seconds he was mute with shock, staring at the priest in confusion, then, he too began to scream, clutching desperately at the splintered wood and trying to stem the flow of blood.

The priest seemed oblivious to the pandemonium he had triggered. He calmly wiped the old man's warm blood from his armour and stepped back to survey his handiwork.

'What have you done?' screamed the old man in disbelief, thrashing his scrawny limbs like an over-turned beetle. 'You've killed me!' He looked over at the crowd. 'Somebody stop him. He's a murderer.'

The crowd backed away, suddenly afraid, as the warrior priest turned to face them. His black eyes flashed dangerously from beneath thick grey eye-brows and when he spoke it was with the quiet surety of a man used to being obeyed. 'Leave us,' he growled.

The villagers looked around for support, but only met the same fear in each other's faces. With a last disappointed look at Anna, they shuffled back towards their homes, muttering bitterly at being deprived of their sport.

The priest turned back towards his prey, who was still howling with pain and fury. 'Adelman,' cried the old man, scouring the upturned carts and ruined houses, 'where are you, you dog? I'm injured.' But however much he called, no one came to the witch hunter's aid.

The priest and the boy watched in silence as the old man continued his frenzied attempts to remove the stake. After a few minutes, he realised that each movement simply quickened the blood flow. At last, as his face began to drain of colour, he realised death was at hand and fell silent, looking over at the priest in wide-eyed terror. 'Who are you?' he said, shaking his head in dismay. 'Why've you done this to me?'

The priest nodded. 'Greetings, Otto Sürman. My name is Jakob Wolff.' He stepped closer to the old man. 'You may remember murdering my parents.'

Sürman's face twisted into a grimace of horror. 'What? I've never met you before, I...' His voice trailed off into a confused silence. 'Wait,' he said, peering at the priest, 'did you say Wolff? I *do* know that—' A fit of choking gripped him and a fresh torrent blood ran from between his crooked teeth. When the fit had passed, he sneered dismissively and spat a thick red gobbet onto the floor. 'Oh, yes, it all comes back to me now. I remember your wretched family, Jakob.' He shook his head at the towering warrior before him. 'And I don't regret a thing. Corruption runs in your people like the rot. I'm only sad I let you live.'

The acolyte flinched at Sürman's words and looked up at his master to see his response. The priest remained calm. The only outward sign of his anger was a slight tightening of his jaw.

'You're a liar,' he replied. 'It has taken me thirty years of false penitence to realise my mistake, but finally I understand. My parents weren't guilty, any more than I was guilty for accusing them.' Colour rushed to his cheeks and he suddenly gripped the stake. The wood was embedded just below the old man's shoulder and with a grunt the priest shoved it even deeper. The noise that came from Sürman's throat sounded barely human. 'You murdered them, knowing my accusations were wrong. I was an innocent child. You knew they weren't occultists.' His voice rose to a roar. 'Admit it, you worm!'

'Save me,' whimpered Sürman reaching out to the young acolyte. 'Don't let him do this to me, I beg–'

'Admit it!' cried Wolff again, ramming the wood even deeper into the ragged wound.

'Yes,' wailed Sürman, arching his back in agony and beginning to weep. 'Yes, yes, yes, you're right, I knew it wasn't them.' He grabbed the priest's arm and gave out a strange keening noise that echoed around the village streets. 'But *you* summoned me. You made the accusation, and someone had to pay the price.' He gave the priest a look of desperation. 'Once the wheels have begun to turn, it's hard to stop these things. I can't...' His words disintegrated into incoherent sobs.

Wolff stepped back and looked up at the sky, considering the old man's words. 'I understand your methods, Sürman.' He shook his head. 'It's to my eternal shame that I did not then. It still haunts me to think that I betrayed my own parents to a villain such as you. Even after a lifetime of penance I can't come to terms with it.'

The witch hunter looked down at the blood that was pooling beneath him, and groaned with fear. 'What do you want with me?' he pleaded, reaching out to the priest. 'It's been thirty years, Jakob, what can I do now? I'm an old man, for Sigmar's sake!'

The priest lowered his gaze and looked back at him. 'We both know my parents were innocent of the crimes they died for; but there's another lie here; one that can't be left to fester.'

The witch hunter's eyes bulged and he shook his head frantically. 'What? What lie? What could you want to know after all these years?'

'Who was the true guilty party, Sürman? Who was the real occultist?'

Sürman gave a strangulated choke of laughter. 'What?' he said, sneering in disbelief. 'You don't even know?' He began to jerk back and forth with deep shuddering laughter, baring his bloody teeth in a feral grin. 'He doesn't know who it was.' Tears continued to flow over his cheeks as he giggled hysterically and pointed at the priest. 'It's almost worth dying, just to see what an ass you've grown into. And to think your parents thought so highly of you. How could you not spot corruption in the face of your own brother?'

Wolff moved to strike the old man, but then the strength seemed to go out of him. He stumbled and leant heavily on the wall next to Sürman.

The old man's face was now just inches from the priest's and he whispered gleefully in his ear. 'Yes, you pompous oaf, you know it's the truth. Fabian was the only occultist in the Wolff household, and he's let you carry his guilt around all these years while he spreads his poison over the Empire; praying to the same unspeakable horrors you've spent your life trying to destroy.'

'Fabian?' whispered Wolff, as he slumped against the wall. 'My own brother?'

'Your life's a joke, Wolff,' spat Sürman. 'You've wasted thirty years in penance for another man's crime.'

Jakob finally gave into his fury and grabbed Sürman by the throat, raising his hammer to dash the old man's brains out. 'It can't be true,' he snarled. 'If Fabian was worshipping the Dark Powers, why would you let him go free? You may be a filthy, deluded monster, but you imagine yourself to be some kind of witch hunter. You even fooled me into believing you were a priest. Even by your own twisted logic you should have wanted Fabian dead. If he were a cultist, why would you let him go free?'

Sürman shook his head and grinned slyly at the priest. 'You're no wiser now than you were at fifteen, Jakob.' He gestured wildly to the pyre. Anna had finally slipped into unconsciousness as the flames rose around her. 'I burned your parents, you fool,' he said in a thin, agonised whisper. 'Do you think I'd be such an idiot as to admit my mistake?' He slapped the hammer on his belly and looked up at the sky. 'I still had important work to do, Jakob. I couldn't risk execution for the sake of one deluded conjurer. Just a few days after you left Berlau, Fabian signed up with the Ostland Black Guard. Sigmar knows what mischief he was planning to wreak there, but three decades have passed since then. I imagine he's long dead.' He shook his head imploringly. 'What can I do about it now, after all this time?'

'The Black Guard?' said Wolff, tightening his grip on Sürman's throat. 'What else do you know of him? Speak quickly, if you—'

An explosion echoed around the village, drowning out the priest's words. Wolff whirled around to see his young acolyte perched awkwardly on top of the flaming pyre, reaching desperately for Anna as the burning wood collapsed beneath his feet. 'Master,' he cried, pathetically, as he lurched through the smoke and attempted to grab onto the lifeless priestess.

Jakob grimaced, looking from the bleeding old man to the pyre and back again. 'I'm not finished,' he said, freeing Sürman's throat and dashing towards the fire.

While the priest had been interrogating Sürman, villagers had gradually been creeping back out of doorways and alleyways to witness the spectacle. Wolff had to barge his way through the growing crowd to reach the pyre. Once there he paused. The flames had now fully taken hold and the heat needled into his eyes. The acolyte cried out again, stranded next to Anna as sparks and embers whirled around him.

Wolff shook his head at the boy's foolishness. Then, clutching his warhammer tightly in both hands, he strode into the fire. Charred wood and cinders erupted all around him as he scrambled through the blaze. At first he made good progress, moving quickly towards the stranded couple. Then, his foot dropped through a hole and he found himself waist deep in flaming wood. Wolff howled with impotent fury at his predicament. Try as he might he could not climb

37

any further. Smoke engulfed him and he felt the stubble on his head begin to shrivel as fire washed over him. He realised the horror of his situation. History was on the verge of repeating itself: another Wolff, burned alive on Sürman's pyre. Hot fury burst from his lungs in an incoherent roar. He lifted his warhammer and, swinging it in a great arc, slammed it into the pyre's central pillar.

The acolyte's eyes widened with fear. 'Master,' he shouted, struggling to keep his footing as the pyre shifted beneath him. 'You'll kill us.'

Wolff was deaf to his cries and swung the hammer again. The pyre belched great gouts of flame but he kept swinging, striking it repeatedly and enveloping himself in an inferno of heat and smoke. Finally, with a sharp *crack*, the priest smashed through the post. The whole structure teetered for a second, swaying drunkenly, then it collapsed in on itself, hurling blazing wood spinning across the village square.

Finally free, Wolff patted himself down, extinguishing the fires that covered his robes. Then, slinging his hammer back over his shoulder he strode through the scattered flames. He lifted the dazed acolyte from beneath the wreckage and with his other hand he grabbed Anna. Then, as the astonished villagers backed away from him, he emerged from the fire, dragging the two bodies behind him like sacks of corn. He dropped Anna and the boy to the ground and collapsed to his knees, gulping clean air into his scorched lungs.

'She's a witch,' cried a fat old militiaman, rushing forward and kicking Anna's prone shape. 'The witch hunter found her guilty.' He grabbed Anna's blistered body and lifted her head from the ground. 'It's all her fault. Everything that's happened to the village these last months.' His voice grew thin with hysteria. 'She *has* to die.'

The other villagers stepped back from the man, nervously eyeing the priest's warhammer. Most were not as keen to pit themselves against someone who had just walked so calmly through fire.

As the militiaman's vengeful screams continued, Wolff stayed on his knees, with his hands pressed into the earth and his eyes closed as he struggled for breath.

With a retching cough, the young acolyte sat up. His hair was twisted and black and his face was flushed with heat. He had the look of a wild-eyed prophet. He saw the villager grappling with Anna and leapt towards him. 'Leave her alone, you brute,' he cried, landing a punch on the man's face and sending him sprawling across the ground. He followed after him, windmilling his arms and landing blow after blow on the militiaman's head. 'You don't know anything. You're listening to the words of a murderer. Sürman's no priest. He's not even a witch hunter; he's just insane.'

The militiaman recovered his composure and rose to his feet. He took a cudgel from his belt and slammed it into the boy's stomach. As the acolyte fell to the ground, doubled up in pain, the militiaman kicked him viciously in the side and looked up at the other villagers. 'The boy's in league with the witch,' he announced, calmly.

The other villagers shuffled towards him, still looking nervously at the choking priest.

'Stop,' gasped Wolff, glaring at the militiaman. 'You're making a mistake. Sürman isn't to be trusted. Let the boy go.'

The militiaman's jowly face grew red with anger and he grabbed the boy by his blackened hair. 'What right do you people have to stop us defending ourselves?' He gestured to the pitiful ruins that surrounded them. 'Look at us. We're barely surviving. Year after year we've fought back monsters you can't even imagine. What do you know of our lives? And now, when we have a minion of Chaos in our very midst, you would free her.' He threw the acolyte back to the floor and levelled a finger at the gasping priest. 'In fact, how do we know you're not in league with her? How is it that you arrived, just as we were about to rid ourselves of this evil?'

Angry mutterings came from the crowd and a few of them nervously fingered their clubs and sticks as they stepped up behind the militiaman.

Wolff took a deep, rasping breath and rose from the ground. He dusted the soot from his armour, lifted his hammer from his back and turned to face the villagers. 'Let the boy go,' he repeated quietly.

'She must burn,' cried the militiaman, pointing at the unconscious priestess. 'And the boy with her. He was clearly trying to save her. I won't let you bring a curse on what's left of this village.'

Jakob gave a rattling cough and stepped forward, straightening up to his full height and lifting his hammer to strike.

The militiaman fled with a yell, leaping over the smouldering remains of the pyre and disappearing from view. The other villagers quickly backed away from the priest and hid their weapons as Wolff helped the acolyte back to his feet.

'Are you hurt?' asked the priest gruffly, dusting the boy down.

'No,' replied the acolyte, with an embarrassed smile. 'I'll think twice about leaping into another fire though.'

The priest nodded and gave a disapproving grunt, before turning to the crumpled priestess.

The boy rushed to the woman's side and lifted her head from the ground. Her long hair had shrivelled to a blackened frizz and her tattered robes crumbled to ash in his fingers, but her chest was still rising and falling as she took a series of quick, shallow breaths. 'She's alive,' he whispered and took a flask of water from his belt, pouring a little into her mouth. At first the liquid just ran over her chin unheeded, but then she gave a hoarse splutter and opened her eyes, pushing the boy away in fear. 'She's alive,' he repeated, helping her to sit up.

'Stay back,' gasped the priestess, shoving the boy away and attempting to stand. Her legs immediately gave way and she toppled to the floor, but she was now fully awake and looked around in confusion. 'The pyre,' she said, looking at the smouldering ruin. 'Did you save me?' she asked, grabbing the boy's arm.

'Well, not exactly,' he replied, blushing. 'It was more–'

'Yes,' snapped Wolff, striding forward and lifting her to her feet. 'If it wasn't for this foolish child, you'd be dead.'

Anna flinched from the priest's grasp, looking nervously of his brutal demeanour and Sigmarite garb. 'Who are you?' she asked, staggering away from him. Then her hand shot to her mouth and she looked around in a panic. 'Where's the witch hunter?'

Wolff spun around to find that barn wall was empty, apart from a dark crimson stain where he had left Sürman. He cursed under his breath and ran across the village square to investigate. 'Sürman,' he cried, dashing in and out of the houses. 'Come back, you wretch.' His face grew purple with rage. 'Where's my brother?'

Wolff tore through the village, turning over carts and barrels, but a fit of coughing overtook him and after a few minutes he dropped to his knees again. With a strangled bark of despair he slammed his hammer into the ground and spat sooty phlegm into the earth. 'Where's my brother, you murdering dog?'

CHAPTER THREE
SIGMAR'S HEIRS

'RATBOY?' ASKED ANNA, laughing as she dragged a knife over her scalp, 'what kind of a name is that?'

'I've grown used to it,' replied the acolyte, with a shrug. He looked around. They were sat on the bank of a small stream and Ratboy couldn't help but smile at the unexpected beauty of the scene. As the morning sun cleared the distant blue hills of Kislev, it gilded the shallow waters, transforming the blasted valley into a memory of happier times. They were in a small clearing, and the scorched trees and shrubs that surrounded them took on a kind of grandeur as they bathed in the dawn glow. Even the rain seemed reluctant to mar the idyllic scene, coming down in a fine, warm drizzle that hissed gently across the stream's surface.

'I can barely remember my childhood,' he said. 'I'm not even sure if this was originally my homeland.

Truth is, I can't remember much at all before Master Wolff took me in. He found me scavenging for food and rescued me from a bunch of meat-headed halberdiers from Nordland.' His eyes glazed over for a moment as he sank into his memories, then he shook his head with a laugh and ran his fingers through the water. 'They weren't quite as sympathetic as my master. I think they might have been the ones who named me. I'm quite happy to be a Ratboy though.' His smile grew and he briefly met the priestess's eye. 'Rats are survivors.'

Anna dipped the knife in the water and continued shaving her head, frowning with concentration as she followed her undulating reflection. The crisp remnants of her flaxen hair fell away easily in little clumps that drifted off in the current. As Ratboy watched her discreetly from the corner of his eye, he couldn't help noticing that even without hair she had an ethereal beauty.

The events of the previous day had left her bruised and weak; so weak, in fact, that he had practically carried her down to the water's edge. But despite her terrible ordeal, there was something noble in Anna's piercing, grey-green eyes. They had been chatting for a few hours now, and Ratboy had never met anyone quite like her. There was such intensity in her gaze that he found it hard to meet her eye. He guessed she was only a few years older than he was – early twenties at most – but he felt childlike in her presence. He wondered how he must look to her. A ridiculous figure, probably, with his gangly limbs and tatty clothes. Not the kind of man to turn her head, certainly. He suddenly felt ashamed of himself for thinking such thoughts about a priestess and looked down into the palms of his hands, trying not to think about how full and red her lips were. Anna continued shaving her head, oblivious to his admiring glances. 'So, tell me about Wolff,' she said.

'Jakob Wolff,' sighed Ratboy. 'He's a bit of mystery to me, I'm afraid. He's not what you might call a great talker, so even after three years in his service, I don't know too much about him.' As the topic of conversation shifted onto another person, Ratboy's confidence grew, and he met Anna's eye with a little more surety. 'Although, that said, I've seen him turn the tide of a whole battle with nothing more than words.' His face lit up with enthusiasm as he warmed to his subject. 'I've seen dying men claw their way up from beneath mounds of the dead, just to fight by his side.' He shook his head in wonder. 'Despite his hatred of sorcery, there's a kind of magic in Brother Wolff.'

'Really?' asked Anna, wiping the knife on her tattered robes and looking at Ratboy with a bitter expression. 'I've met many of these Sigmarites. In my experience their faith seems little more than glorified bloodlust.' She shuddered. 'Is he really so different from the man who tried to burn me yesterday?'

'Sürman? He's no priest. He's just a cheap fraud, exploiting people's fear to pursue his own tawdry ends.' Ratboy shuddered at the thought of the man. 'He calls himself a witch hunter, but the title's just a mask he hides behind. And he's certainly no templar. I think he may once have been a catechist – a lay brother that is – but Wolff told me Sürman has no connection with the church at all now. He's just a very dangerous man.' He paused and looked around the valley, to make sure they were alone. 'He killed Wolff's parents,' he whispered.

Anna's eyes widened and she handed Ratboy's knife back to him. 'Killed them?' She shook her head. 'That would explain things, I suppose. I thought at first he'd come to spare me from the flames, but I quickly realised that he had other priorities.'

'He did save you, eventually.'

'Really? It was you I saw fighting through the flames. After that I can't really remember too much.' She placed a hand on Ratboy's arm and smiled. 'You risked your life for me. I won't forget it. Maybe Wolff played his part, but I'm not sure I'd still be here if I had relied on the compassion of a warrior priest.'

Ratboy blushed and withdrew his arm. 'My master's a devout man. He would've saved you, I'm sure. You must understand though, his thoughts haven't been clear of late. He became a wondering mendicant when he was very young, as a kind of penance. But he was tricked. It's only very recently that he's learned the truth. He'd always believed he had blood on his hands.' Ratboy paused, unsure whether to continue. 'Everyone looks to the priesthood for guidance. When things seem this hopeless, they're the only ones we can really trust. We all rely on them so heavily to revive our faith when it flags, but what if...' his voice trailed off and he looked awkwardly at Anna.

She continued his thought for him. 'What if a priest begins to know doubt?'

Ratboy nodded and leaned towards her, speaking in a low voice. 'Nothing made sense to me until I met Wolff. Everyone else is so twisted and broken. Everyone I ever met seemed damaged, one way or another, but not Wolff. His faith was always so unshakable. So bottomless. All I've ever wanted was to become more like him.' He frowned and looked at Anna with fear in his eyes. 'But recently, he seems unsure of himself. Maybe after witnessing so many horrors, even he could lose his faith?'

Anna smiled and shook her head. 'Anyone can feel afraid, Ratboy, but with such a devoted friend as you by his side, I think he will find his way.'

Ratboy's eyes widened. 'Friend? I'm not sure he'd–'

'Ratboy,' called a voice from further down the valley.

They looked around and saw the towering figure of Wolff, shielding his eyes from the light as he walked out from beneath the blackened trees.

'Yes, master,' replied Ratboy, leaping to his feet and stepping nervously away from Anna. 'I'm just here with the priestess. She needed to use my knife.'

'I'm sure she has little use for your weapons, my boy.'

Anna rose to her feet and made a futile effort to dust down her robes. She barely reached Wolff's chest, but sounded undaunted as she addressed him. 'Apparently, I'm in your debt, Brother Wolff,' she said brusquely. 'Sürman was quite determined to make charcoal of me.'

Wolff massaged his scarred jaw as he studied her. 'Sürman's a clever man, sister, but I doubt he could've turned a whole village against you. Not without some cause.' He peered intently into her eyes. 'What might that cause have been I wonder?'

Colour rushed into Anna's face and she laughed incredulously as she turned to Ratboy. 'What did I tell you? These hammer hurlers are all alike: sanctimonious killers, the lot of them.'

'I merely asked you a question, sister.'

Anna shook her head. 'Questions lead to bonfires, Brother Wolff. At least where you and your brethren are concerned.' She turned to leave. 'I'd be better taking my chances with the damned.'

Wolff placed one hand on her shoulder and the other on the haft of his warhammer. 'An answer please, sister.'

There was an awkward silence as Anna looked from Wolff to Ratboy. Then her shoulders dropped and she nodded. 'My crime was a simple one, Brother Wolff. I've been working my way around this province for months now, trying to salvage a little hope from the chaos.' She sat down heavily on the grass and sighed. 'It's been a losing battle. The woods are crawling with...' she shook her head in despair, '*unspeakable* things. I was travelling with a regiment of halberdiers from Wendorf, but even they weren't safe: with all their armour and weapons they were powerless to stop the awful things we saw. They were heading to the capital, but I decided to stay here and see if I could help these poor people. I suppose I'm deluding myself though. What could I really do? The whole of Ostland seems on the verge of collapse.'

'Believe me, sister, we're well acquainted with the situation,' replied Wolff.

'Really? Do you know how scared these people are? Those villagers were so glad to see me when I arrived. They were terrified of their own shadows. They begged me for help, so I gave it to them. Healing those I could and praying for those I couldn't. The Weeping Maiden doesn't make petty distinctions though. I found a man, dressed in mockery of the creatures that haunted his nightmares. He was covered in his own filth and praying to his livestock, so I attempted to help him.'

'Was the man corrupted?' asked Wolff, crouching next to her.

Anna's eyes filled with tears as she gestured at the smouldering ruins that surrounded them. 'Look around, Brother Wolff. *Everything* is corrupted. This province has been ripped apart. Such terms have lost their meaning. Living or dead. Sane or mad. They're the only distinctions worth making nowadays.' She took a slow breath to calm herself.

'I don't think he was worshipping the Ruinous Powers, if that's what you mean. I think he'd lost his reason in the face of all this madness, but who could blame him for that? The villagers didn't agree though. They found me trying to help him and added me to their long list of suspicions. The witch hunter arrived the following day and happily took matters out of their hands.' She looked up at Wolff with a sneer of disdain. 'I imagine you'd have done much the same.'

The priest shook his head. 'Maybe not, sister. I've seen a good many things I'd rather forget, but I don't think my mind has become quite as twisted as Sürman's. Not yet, at least.' He stood up and looked out across the glittering water. 'You're not the first Sister of

Shallya to fall foul of an overzealous witch hunter and I'm sure you won't be the last. Sürman's no brother of mine. Monsters like him are a stain on the good name of my order.' Wolff removed one of his gloves and held out a hand. 'If there's anything I can do that would give you a better opinion of us, I'd be glad to help.'

Anna looked at Wolff's open hand with suspicion. His broad fingers were misshapen with calluses and scars and there was dried blood beneath his splintered fingernails. Finally, she placed a hesitant hand in his and gave a reluctant nod. 'I think I should return to my temple. I imagine they're quite overwhelmed by now, but I think I may need a little healing myself. It's just a few miles north of Lubrecht. If you're heading that way, maybe we could travel together?' She gave a hollow laugh, and looked down at her scorched, battered limbs. 'I'm not sure I'd make it very far on my own.'

'Gladly,' replied Wolff, and helped her to her feet.

OSTLAND WAS A land long accustomed to war. From as far back as Ratboy could remember, the province had been fighting for its life, but recently the stout hearts of its people had begun to falter. As the trio rode north he looked out over its gloomy forests and meadows. To the west reared the ragged outline of the Middle Mountains. He had never ventured any closer than the heavily-wooded foothills, but even Ratboy knew the legends associated with those towering peaks. The myriad caves and crevices all sheltered some terrifying abomination: ogres, beastmen, every kind of monstrosity that could keep an honest man awake at night. Then he looked east, to the distant realm of Kislev, Realm of the Ice Queen, with her fierce fur-clad hordes; and then, covering everything in between, the Forest of Shadows. The woods of Ostland had always been a fearsome place, but until now the villages and homesteads had stood firm: staking their claims with axes, muscle and sheer bloody-mindedness. Over the last few months, however, Ratboy had seen his countrymen driven from their homes by a foe so numerous, and terrifying, that even the province's cities were now in ruins. Only the capital, Wolfenburg, was still fully intact. Every face he saw, from infantryman to farmer, was filled with the same terrible questions: how much longer can we hold out against this onslaught? How long before I am trampled under the cloven hooves of the enemy?

'This must be the village you were looking for,' called Anna, from further up the trail. The ancient trees leant wearily over the path, making it hard to see through the arboreal gloom, but Ratboy could clearly hear the concern in Anna's voice.

He turned to Wolff, who was riding beside him, and grimaced. 'That sounds like bad news to me.' The warrior priest's only reply was a stern nod, as he spurred his horse onwards.

The village of Gotburg sat in a small clearing, not far from the road to Bosenfels. Wolff had insisted they make a slight detour so that he could visit the place, but Ratboy struggled to see why. It was a pitiful sight. Like every other village they had encountered, its stockade was breached and burned, and several of the houses had been levelled. Unlike some of the others, however, it still boasted a few signs of life. As the trio arrived at the ruined gate, they saw a crowd gathered in the village square.

Ratboy gasped in dismay as he saw what they were doing.

Several dozen villagers were on their knees, thrashing their naked torsos with barbed strips and chanting frantically as blood poured from their scarred flesh. As the rest of the crowd looked on, the penitents were gradually whipping themselves to death. It was not just this that made Ratboy gasp; it was also the man who was the focus of their prayers. They seemed to be worshipping a corpse. A skeletal body was strapped to a broken gatepost with a sign hung around its neck. Its pale, naked flesh was lacerated all over with countless knife wounds, many of which were in the shape of a hammer. Scrawled on the sign, in dark, bloody letters, was a single word: REPENT.

Ratboy realised that slurred, feeble words were coming from the body's cracked mouth. He looked up at Wolff in horror. 'Is that some kind of revenant?'

Wolff scowled back at him as he dismounted. 'Don't mention such things, boy. These are Sigmar's children.'

Anna had already tied her horse to a fence and rushed over to one of the spectators. It was a ruddy-faced old woodcutter with a chinstrap beard. As she approached him, the man waved her away furiously. 'Stay back, healer. We don't need your meddling hands here. The flagellants will save us from further attacks.' He gestured to the emaciated figure that was leading the prayers. 'Raphael has foretold it. But only if they sacrifice themselves in our place.' He grabbed her by the arm and pulled her close. 'It's what Sigmar demands! There's nothing you can do for them now.'

Ratboy noticed several of the villagers blanched at the woodcutter's words. They looked anxiously at Anna as their friends and family spilled themselves across the dusty ground; but none of them seemed brave enough to contradict him. As the priestess looked to them for support, they turned away, blushing with shame at the horror being perpetrated on their behalf.

'"He that cleaves his flesh in my name, abideth in me,"' quoted the man strapped to the post, raising his voice to regain the crowd's attention and rolling his bloodshot eyes at the heavens.

Ratboy stepped a little closer to the gruesome display and realised the man was repeating the same words over and over again: 'He that cleaves his flesh in my name, abideth in me.' He couldn't understand how such a skeletal wretch could still breathe, never mind drive dozens of normal people to such a sickening death.

'Wait,' cried a deep powerful voice, and Ratboy saw that Wolff had strode up to the front of the group.

The skeletal man faltered, stumbling over his words as he tried to focus on Wolff's thick claret robes and ornate, burnished armour. As the man's words slowed, so did the frantic, jerking movements of the crowd. They lowered their whips and looked up expectantly at Wolff from beneath sweaty, matted hair.

The priest unclasped a small leather-bound book from a strap on his forearm. A confused silence descended over the square, as Wolff began to leaf through the text, frowning as he searched for the right passage. Finally, he paused, and smiled to himself, before looking out over the panting, bleeding congregation and addressing them in a voice that boomed around the square. 'The quote is from the *Book of Eberlinus*,' he cried. It reads thus: "He that cleaves flesh and blood in my name, abideth in me, and I in him."'

The crowd looked at him open mouthed, uncomprehending.

Wolff nodded, willing them to understand. 'Your faith is a glorious gesture. A gesture of defiance. I heard tales of your devotion as far away as Haundorf. It's a wonder to behold such belief in the face of the countless evils that assail us.' He gestured towards the surrounding forest. 'Your very survival hinges on it. So many have fallen by the wayside, but you, my pious children of Sigmar have survived everything, simply by the virtue of your faith.' He closed the little book with a *snap* and when he spoke again, his voice trembled with emotion. 'If I had an army of men with hearts like yours, the war would over by nightfall.'

The flagellants began to nod and smile at each other, revelling in the priest's praise. A few of them climbed unsteadily to their feet, wiping the blood from their eyes, and trying to calm their breathing enough to speak. 'Priest,' gasped a middle-aged woman, with tears welling in her eyes. 'I don't understand. What you said about the quote – are we doing wrong?'

Wolff shook his head. 'You're not doing wrong, child, far from it. This man…' He turned to the skeletal figure slumped behind him.

The man's eyes bulged in their sunken sockets and he trembled in awe as Wolff addressed him. 'Raphael,' he whispered.

'Raphael,' repeated Wolff, 'has filled you with the light of Sigmar, and none of you will ever be the same again.'

The congregation gasped and moaned with delight. Several of them crawled forwards and pawed at the hem of Wolff's robes, sobbing in ecstasy and pressing their faces into the embroidered cloth.

Ratboy and Anna watched in amazement at how quickly Wolff had entranced the crowd. Even the spectators began to fall to their knees, muttering prayers of thanks and crossing their chests with the sign of the hammer.

'No,' continued Wolff, 'you're very far from doing wrong, my children.' Wolff paused and strapped the book back onto his arm. 'However…' he allowed the word to echo around the square, 'if you have the strength for the task, I would ask a favour of you.'

Raphael strained to free himself from the post. 'Anything, father,' he gasped, pulling at his bonds until fresh streams of blood erupted from his wounds. 'Let us serve you, I beg.'

'Aye,' cried the middle-aged woman, rushing over to Wolff and falling at his feet. 'Let us serve you, lord. What would you ask?' She waved a trembling, bleeding arm at the assembled crowd. 'We've tried to be penitent.' She grabbed a knife from her belt and held it to her own throat. 'Should we try harder?'

Wolff placed a hand on her arm and lowered the blade. 'Wait, daughter of Sigmar. Eberlinus's words were not "He that cleaves *his* flesh in my name," they were "He that cleaves flesh in my name". The difference is subtle, but important.'

The woman frowned. 'Then whose flesh should we cleave?'

'The enemy's,' gasped Raphael, finally freeing himself and tumbling to the ground at Wolff's feet. 'You wish us to march with you.'

Wolff gave Raphael a paternal smile.

CHAPTER FOUR
BLOOD SPORTS

MUSIC WAS DRIFTING across the ruined landscape. As a merciful dusk fell over the crumbling farms and villages, chords echoed through the smoking wreckage and as the three riders steered their mounts north, ghostly harmonies drifted out of the dark to meet them.

Wolff rode up the side of a hill to find the source of the strange noise. 'Hired swords,' he said, beckoning to Anna and Ratboy to come and see. They rode up beside him and saw a merry trail of lights snaking through the hills towards them. Several regiments of soldiers were travelling north. Proud, armoured knights on barded mounts. Over their heads fluttered banners bearing a symbol Ratboy didn't recognise: a pair of bright yellow swords, emblazoned on a black background. The men wore the most incredible uniforms Ratboy had ever seen. Huge, plumed hats and elaborately frilled collars, all dyed with a yellow pigment so bright that even the chill gloom of an Ostland evening failed to dampen its cheeriness.

'Who are they?' he asked, turning to his master.

Wolff wrinkled his nose with distaste. 'Southerners,' he muttered.

'Southerners?' asked Ratboy. 'From Reikland?'

Wolff shook his head. 'No. They're a long way from home, by the looks of them. Averland, maybe, although half of them look like Tilean freelancers. Sigmar knows what would drag them so far north, but I'm glad to see them here – whatever the reason.' He leant forward in his saddle and peered through the darkness. 'Although, I fear their general may have already been injured. See how he rolls in his saddle?'

Ratboy and Anna followed Wolff's gaze. Near to the front of the regiment, surrounded by standard bearers and musicians rode a knight whose armour was even more ornate than the others. His winged helmet was trimmed with gold, and as he lolled back and forth on his horse, the metal flashed in the moonlight, drawing attention to his lurching movements.

'Strange music for times such as these,' said Anna.

The drummers and pipers that surrounded the general were skipping merrily through the long grass, oblivious to the gentle Ostland rain that was banking over the hills. They were playing a jig and the snatches of song that reached Wolff and the others sounded oddly raucous. In the face of the shattered homes and towers that covered the landscape, it seemed almost disrespectful.

Wolff nodded. 'Indeed.' He turned his horse around to face the shambling figures that were staggering up the hillside behind them. Raphael was too weak to walk, so the rest of the flagellants had fashioned a makeshift litter to drag him along on. As they climbed slowly towards the priest, the sound of their whips could be clearly heard, along with their frantic prayers. 'Just a little further,' he called out to them. 'There's an army ahead. I must speak with the general. Wait here and I'll send word if it's safe to approach.'

Raphael waved weakly in reply.

Anna watched as the penitents stumbled towards them. She shook her head in dismay at the awful violence they were inflicting on their own flesh. 'At a word from you they would drop those whips,' she said, glaring at Wolff. 'Have you no pity?'

Ratboy flinched at the venom in her voice, but Wolff simply ignored her.

As the three of them rode down the hill towards the troops, they saw the injured general summon an officer to his side, who then rode out to meet them. As he approached, they saw he was rake-thin with a long aristocratic face that sneered disdainfully at them as he approached. He carried a brightly polished shield, engraved with the same yellow swords as the banners, and as he reached the top of the hill Ratboy marvelled at the fine, gold embroidery that covered his clothes. He'd never seen such a flamboyantly dressed man. He wore a wide drooping hat, topped with ostrich feathers and studded with pearls, and his slashed leather jerkin was stretched tightly over a bright yellow silk doublet that shimmered as he moved. His short cloak was edged with lace and even his elaborate codpiece was stitched with gold thread. With his fine attire and twirled, waxed moustaches, Ratboy imagined he would be more at home on an elegant, sunlit boulevard than a muddy Ostland battlefield.

'Good evening, father,' he said, with a curt nod to Wolff. 'I'm Obermarshall Hugo von Gryphius's adjutant. He sends you his regards and offers you his hospitality.' The valet looked less than hospitable however, and his thickly accented voice was cool as he continued. 'We'll be making camp soon and Obermarshall von Gryphius would be interested to hear news of the war, especially from a senior priest such as yourself.'

'We'd be glad of the general's protection,' replied Wolff, 'but I'm afraid we're only just heading north ourselves. I doubt we know much more than your lord.'

The valet pursed his lips in irritation, but gave a stiff bow all the same. 'Very well, I'm sure my lord would still be keen to speak to you.' He looked briefly at Anna and then waved his frilled sleeve down the hill, signalling for them to lead the way. 'He generally takes pleasure in good company.'

'I have a group of followers with me—' began Wolff.

'I'll see to them,' snapped the valet, and gestured towards the army again.

As they followed the soldier down the hill, Ratboy felt as though he were entering a strange dream. The musicians were dancing in and out of the horses, dressed in elaborate animal costumes and banging tambourines as they whirled back and forth through the rain. The swarthy soldiers eyed the new arrivals suspiciously from beneath their sallet helmets, but they seemed too exhausted to give them much attention and soon looked back down at their mud-splattered horses, riding onwards through the valley with a slow determination that hinted at months of travel.

The Obermarshall was as unlike his adjutant as he could possibly be: a short, pot-bellied lump, with a soft, ebullient face that seemed quite out place in his finely wrought helmet. His small, ebony eyes sparkled with pleasure as he saw Anna, and his olive skin fractured into a network of wrinkles. 'What a joy to encounter friendly faces in such grim surroundings,' he said in a thin, piping voice.

Ratboy frowned. The general seemed barely able to stay in his saddle, but bore no obvious signs of injury and he wondered what ailed the man. As they reached his side, however, he had his answer: rather than wielding weapons, the general had a bottle of sherry in one hand and a large glass in the other. As he enthusiastically hugged each of his guests in turn, they winced at the thick stench of garlic and alcohol that surrounded him.

'You poor things – what's happened to you?' he asked, noticing their scorched, bloody clothes.

Wolff studied the wine and food stains that covered the general's armour, before replying. 'We're at war, Obermarshall, like the rest of this forsaken province.'

The general seemed oblivious to the disapproving tone in Wolff's voice. His eyes lit up with excitement and he leant forward in his saddle. 'Ah, yes, the war. That's exactly why we're here.' He took a swig of sherry, spilling most of it down his tunic. 'In fact, once we've made camp, I'd like to pick your brains. I believe it's all happening north of here somewhere? Is that right?' He chuckled and slapped Wolff's armour. 'These things usually happen somewhere in the north, don't they?'

Wolff's nostrils flared and he drew a breath to answer, but then he seemed to think better of it and simply nodded.

'Christoff,' cried the general. 'Pitch my tent over there, near that willow tree. I think it would make a pleasant subject for a sketch or two.'

The old valet gave a little bow and backed away, snapping orders to the surrounding guards and stewards as he went.

The general tumbled awkwardly from his warhorse, and gestured for Wolff and the others to sit next to him on the grass. 'So,' he continued, once they had dismounted, 'tell me about yourselves. What are your names?'

'I'm Brother Jakob Wolff, and this is my acolyte, Anselm, although he goes by the name of Ratboy.'

Gryphius took in Ratboy's scrawny frame and tattered tunic and burst into laughter. 'Ratboy! Of course he is! That's wonderful.' He grabbed Ratboy's shoulder and gave it a firm squeeze. 'Ratboy,' he repeated, 'that's why I love you country folk. Always so quick to laugh at yourselves.'

Wolff raised his eyebrows and remained silent until the general managed to stifle his mirth.

'And this is Anna...' he looked over at her enquiringly.

'Fleck,' she snapped, glaring at the priest. 'I'm a Sister of Shallya, lord,' she continued, softening her voice and turning to the general, 'and I'm trained in the healing arts, so if any of your men have injuries, I'd be happy to assist them.'

'Of course,' replied the general, taking another swig of his sherry. 'There'll be plenty of time for that kind of thing later though. You all look quite ravenous.' He lurched to his feet and looked out over a teetering mass of tent poles, flaming torches and ascending banners. 'Christoff,' he cried. 'People are starving over here. Bring food for my guests, man. Where are you?'

'On my way, lord,' came a reply from out of the darkness.

'You look as though you may need medical assistance yourself,' said Gryphius, sitting down again and looking at Anna's scorched, shaven head. 'And I'm sure we could find you some more feminine clothes.'

'These will be fine,' she replied, clutching her tatty white robes protectively. 'Although a needle and thread would be appreciated.'

'Christoff,' bawled the general, 'bring the seamstress too.'

'I don't recognise your heraldry, Obermarshall,' said Wolff, gesturing to the swords on Gryphius's ornate chest armour. 'Where have you travelled from? Averland?'

'Averhiem,' replied the general.

Wolff nodded, but Ratboy gave the general a look of helpless confusion.

Gryphius frowned. 'It's the home of the artists Tilmann and Donatus, and the composer, Ortlieb. You must have heard of the playwright Eustacius at least?'

Ratboy shook his head.

Colour flushed into the general's round cheeks and he gave an embarrassed cough. 'Well, I can assure you, he's quite a talent. Prince Eustacius enjoys the patronage of the Emperor himself.'

'But what brings you so far from home?' asked Wolff, keen to change the subject. 'Of all the provinces in the Empire, Ostland's not the safest place to be at the moment. These are dangerous times to be abroad, Obermarshall. You're lucky to have got this far without encountering the enemy.'

The general grinned, revealing a row of small, uneven teeth. 'But that's exactly why I'm here.' He patted the rapier on his lap. 'I wish to test my mettle against the minions of the Dark Gods.' He puffed out his chest and attempted to suck in his paunch. 'In Averheim, the name von Gryphius is a byword for fearless heroism. There are few foes I have yet to pit myself against: greenskins, dragons, necromancers; all have learned to fear my name.' He leant forward and spoke in a conspiratorial tone. 'I've heard there's a great champion leading this new incursion into your Empire – even greater than the one called Archaon who preceded him.' He drew his sword, narrowly missing Ratboy's face as he waved it at the sky.

'Imagine the glory of slaying such a monster! The name von Gryphius would echo down the centuries.'

'But my lord,' replied Anna, 'the whole province is overrun with marauders and bandits. Even the capital's half ruined. Those who can have fled south, to Reikland. Is it wise for you to risk your men in such a campaign?'

The smile slipped from von Gryphius's face. 'I can assure you, Anna, I'm not one to avoid danger. Your Elector Count needs brave men at his side in times such as these, and mine are amongst the bravest. If there's anything we can do to help von Raukov repel these fiends, then we'll do it.' He sheathed his sword and smiled again, picturing his glorious, impending victory. Then, remembering his guests, he patted Ratboy's leg. 'But enough about me, what drags you three so far north?'

'We're looking for a regiment named the Ostland Black Guard,' Wolff replied. 'I believe they're engaged in the same conflict you're heading towards. And, of course, I wish to lend my support to the army. They will need great spiritual fortitude in the face of such foes. "By Sigmar's light may we know what is to be done; and only through his strength may we avoid the abyss."'

'Indeed,' replied Gryphius, winking at Anna and taking another swig of sherry. 'My thoughts exactly.' He offered the bottle to his guests and when they declined, he shrugged and drank a little more. 'I can see that you would wish to join the army as quickly as possible, but what is the importance of this Black Guard? Is that a regiment you have connections with?'

Wolff paused before replying. 'Of a sort,' he said, making it clear he did not wish to discuss the matter further.

'I see.' Gryphius slapped his thigh and lurched to his feet. 'Well, I believe that's my tent ready,' he said, offering Anna his hand. 'Let's go and make ourselves a little more comfortable. I'll see if Christoff has found you some food yet.'

A grand pavilion had appeared behind them, and as Gryphius staggered towards its black and yellow domes, he regaled them with tales of his chef's wonderful creations.

'I feel it's important to maintain one's standards, even during times of hardship,' he explained. 'At all times I include in my entourage a chef of the very best quality,' – he waved at the musicians dancing around the growing campsite – 'as well as entertainers and artists of renown.' He paused and looked earnestly at Anna. 'I'm something of a patron of the arts,' he said. 'In fact, I'm more than just a patron.' As a bowing Christoff opened the door of the tent, Gryphius strode inside and gestured to an array of canvases that were scattered across the silk cushions within. 'Many of these are my own work.'

'Really?' replied Anna, feigning interest. They all paused to look at a large canvas that Gryphius held up to them. It was a seemingly random collection of black brushstrokes.

'As you can see, it's after Vridel,' he explained, looking at them eagerly. 'Are you admirers of the Heinczel school?'

Anna turned to Wolff and Ratboy for support.

'Generally, Ostlanders don't have a lot of time to study paintings,' answered Wolff.

'Is that so?' replied the general, shaking his head sadly. He dropped the canvas to the floor and waved at the cushions that filled the tent. 'Well, make yourselves comfortable, please.'

'Did you mention food,' asked Ratboy, eyeing up a heavily laden table at the back of the tent.

'Of course,' exclaimed the general, 'tuck in, my boy, tuck in!'

Ratboy and the others hesitated for a moment, daunted by the exotic array of strange dishes. Brightly coloured fruits with thick rubbery skins and unfamiliar cuts of meat were arrayed in a fantastically gaudy display. None of them had ever seen anything like it before; but Ratboy's hunger soon overcame all other concerns and he began to wolf down the strange food, murmuring with pleasure as he devoured the rich morsels on offer.

'Please, I insist,' said von Gryphius, nodding encouragingly to the two hesitant priests.

'Well, maybe a little bread,' replied Wolff and began to eat.

Anna followed suit and all conversation ceased for a few minutes as the grinning general watched them eating.

A little while later, sprawled sleepily on silk cushions and surrounded by the soft glow of a dozen candles, the three travellers finally began to relax. They stretched out their aching, bruised limbs and massaged their stiff joints as von Gryphius's servants flitted discreetly back and forth.

The general was slumped on an ornate throne and the sherry was finally starting to take effect; every few minutes he would make himself jump with a little snore, and then gradually nod off to sleep again. At the far end of the tent, a harpist played a gentle lament while a dancer twirled back and forth, dressed as a signet.

'Obermarshall,' said Wolff, causing the general to snort in surprise and sit bolt upright.

'Yes?' he replied, giving the priest a bleary eyed grin. 'Make yourself at home,' he muttered. 'Christoff has seen to your men. You can sleep here in my tent tonight. We'll sort out your own accommodation tomorrow.'

'I just wondered, lord. If we might make a slight detour tomorrow.' He looked at Anna, struggling to stay awake at his side. 'Sister Fleck's hospital is not far from here. Could we escort her home? I'm sure she has little desire to travel any further in my company.'

'Of course,' replied the general with a dismissive wave of his hand. He looked at Anna with heavy, half-lidded eyes. 'I should be glad to assist her in any way possible. We can leave most of the troops to rest for the morning and head out by ourselves.' He grinned toothily at Anna. 'In a more intimate group.'

'I WAS A foundling – like many of the sisters,' explained Anna as her horse picked its way through a grey smudge of clinging mist and drooping, dew-laden boughs. 'The matriarch is a wonderful, inspirational woman – an abbess, called Sister Gundram – and she made me a ward of temple. It's a very isolated existence, as you can imagine. For the first ten years of my life I never so much as laid eyes on a man.'

At this, Gryphius looked up from the churned muddy path they were following and gave her a sly smile, but Anna was lost in her reverie and carried on oblivious.

'I couldn't have wished for a more caring family – the sisters even taught me to read and write.' She nodded at Wolff, who was riding a few feet ahead, talking to some of Gryphius's guards. 'And, unlike other priesthoods, the Shallyan faith is not above explaining the beliefs of the other churches, so I gained an understanding of the less,' she paused, searching for the right word, 'open-minded faiths.'

'It sounds like an idyllic childhood,' said Gryphius, nodding his head and adopting a more serious expression.

Anna nodded. 'Having seen the conditions of other children in the province, I think I was probably very lucky.' She looked Gryphius in the eye. 'You must understand though, the abbey is a working hospital, so from as soon as I was able to hold a pail of water, I've been helping the sick and the injured. It wasn't always the easiest place to grow up. My childhood prayers were often drowned out by the screams of the dying.'

Gryphius leant a little closer and placed a comforting hand on Anna's arm.

'Obermarshall,' called one of the soldiers and Anna and Gryphius followed the man's finger to see an even darker smudge up ahead.

'I think that's the abbey,' muttered Anna, peering through the morning mist and frowning, 'but I'm not sure. There's something not right. Why does it look so dark?'

Wolff's heavy brow knotted in a frown as he led his warhorse towards the building.

As they moved closer, the explanation for the darkness was clear: the Temple of the Bleeding Heart had been put to the torch.

Ratboy felt Anna's pain, as he saw that the simple, white-washed building was now little more than a blackened ruin.

'What kind of monsters could do this?' Anna groaned, pawing desperately at her pale scalp as she rode closer. 'What of my sisters? What of the children?'

Wolff shook his head in anger, before steering his horse up the hill at a quick canter. Ratboy rode quickly after him, along with von Gryphius and his guardsmen.

'We must find Sister Gundram. She's the abbess,' gasped Anna, looking around desperately as they rode closer. The fear in her voice made Ratboy wince. 'I beg you, help me find her.'

The temple must once have been an impressive complex, thought Ratboy as they approached it: infirmaries, chapels and a domed chapterhouse in the centre, all surrounded by a low wall in the shape of a teardrop, but almost all of it had been razed to the ground. The violence went beyond mere vandalism, though. As they reached the top of the hill, they began to notice charred human remains littered throughout the ruins.

The colour drained from von Gryphius's face and he turned to Anna. 'Wait here,' he snapped, signalling for his men to guard her. 'Let us scout ahead first.'

Anna's eyes were wide with shock and she seemed too dazed to disagree. She gave a mute nod as Gryphius rode ahead.

As they entered the central courtyard, Wolff dismounted and approached one of the corpses. The blackened bodies were barely recognisable as human, but as the priest crouched next to them, he gave a little sigh of relief. 'These aren't children,' he breathed through gritted teeth. 'State troops by the looks of them.' He gestured to a broken sword lying on the ground. 'There was some kind of defence here at least. The priestesses didn't meet their fate alone.'

'Maybe the children were evacuated then?' said Ratboy, dismounting and rushing to his master's side.

Wolff nodded. 'It's possible. We must look inside.' He looked up at the general in surprise as he realised he was unaccompanied. 'We might need at least a few of your men, Obermarshall.'

Von Gryphius gave a loud, slightly forced laugh. 'What, and share all the fun? Is that wise, priest?' he asked. He gestured to the swords and pistols that hung from his belt. 'I'm sure we can handle a few cowardly temple thieves.'

'Obermarshall, the minions of the Dark Gods may not be the easy prey you're expecting. These creatures are unlike anything you will have faced before.'

The general grinned. 'Of course, Brother Wolff – that's why I'm here.' He looked at the shattered buildings. 'I can't imagine there's anyone alive in there anyway.' He toppled from his charger and drew his rapier, swaying slightly as he squinted into the smoke-filled ruins. 'Lead the way, priest.'

More bodies were scattered around the cloistered pathways within. Ratboy tried to avert his gaze, but couldn't help noticing that some of the shapes were clad in white robes and were clearly not soldiers. He pictured Anna, waiting on the hillside below, and felt his eyes prickle with tears. Who could do such a thing, he wondered?

'It looks like we've found your prey, Obermarshall,' snapped Wolff, kicking one of the corpses.

They rushed to his side and saw a large, smouldering body lying at his feet. It was as scorched and broken as everything else, but even the ravages of the fire couldn't hide the thing's monstrous shape. Ratboy grimaced at the stink emanating from it, but stepped closer nonetheless, curious to study the monster. It was vaguely man-shaped, but its shoulders and limbs were grotesquely swollen and muscled, and covered with a thick, greasy hide. Wolff used his iron-clad boot to roll the thing over onto its back, revealing a head that was bloated and distorted into a roughly bovine shape, with great gnarled horns sprouting from its face.

'What is it?' whispered von Gryphius, his eyes wide with shock.

Wolff looked up at him in surprise. 'This is the evil that plagues us, Obermarshall; *this* is the great prize you've been seeking.' He ground his boot into the thing's hide and grimaced. 'This is the embodiment of corruption. "By the simple undividedness of

Sigmar's being, the faithful will find truth; as surely as the deceiver's form will reveal that which his words would hide."'

He shrugged and led the way towards the chapterhouse, which was the only building not to have been completely destroyed by the flames. As they approached it, the number of bodies increased, as did the awful stench that came from the fallen beastmen.

'The fighting seems to have been fiercest here,' commented Wolff as he stepped up to the shattered door that led into the building. As the others gathered behind him, weapons at the ready, Wolff used his warhammer to shove the door open. The splinted wood screeched noisily as it swung inwards, but the darkness inside was complete. The pale grey sun seemed afraid to cross the threshold and illuminate the bloodshed within.

Wolff gripped his hammer tightly in both hands, and then disappeared into the blackness.

After a second's hesitation, Ratboy followed.

At first the gloom seemed impenetrable, but as his eyes grew accustomed to the dark, vague shapes began to emerge and he saw that the floor was littered with overturned tables and chairs. It looked like the scene of some final defence, with the priestesses and soldiers barricaded inside the chapterhouse. From the shattered state of the door and the broken furniture, Ratboy guessed that some kind of battering ram must have been used to smash the barricades aside. He looked around but could find no sign of such a weapon.

Movement caught his eye, and he saw a towering shape rush towards him out of the darkness. He lifted his knife, and then lowered it again as he recognised Wolff's chiselled features glowering down at him.

'They're all dead,' muttered the priest, shaking his head and gesturing to the white shapes slumped on the floor around them. 'I believe I just found the Abbess.' He held up a ring. It was hard to make out in the darkness, but as the metal rolled between the priest's fingers, Ratboy realised it was decorated with a white dove carrying a golden key. There was an unusual note of emotion in Wolff's voice as he continued. 'These women desired only to help. They bore no allegiance to any army or lord. They didn't deserve to meet their end in this way.' He closed his fist around the ring and secreted it within his robes. 'Come,' he said, stepping back towards the door.

The light vanished before either of them could reach the doorway, plunging them into a darkness even more profound than before. A colossal shape had blocked their way, towering over even Wolff. Ratboy heard the deep, rattling breath of a large animal.

Wolff shoved the acolyte violently across the room and as he tumbled over the broken furniture, Ratboy heard a great weapon slam into the ground where he had just been standing. He gasped in pain, winded by a chair leg that jabbed him in the stomach as he landed. As he rolled onto his back, groaning, shapes whirled around him in the darkness, crashing into walls and tables and grunting with exertion.

Sparks flew as weapons collided and in the brief flashes of light, Ratboy saw Wolff fighting desperately against a creature so big it had to stoop beneath the chapterhouse's vaulted ceiling. The light was gone too fast for him to be sure of the monster's shape, but he was left with a vague impression of massive, coiled muscle and long, curved horns.

Ratboy tried to draw breath, but retched instead, powerless to call for help. As he felt around in the dark for his knife, he heard Wolff muttering something nearby. Then, as the priest uttered a final, fierce syllable, glittering light flooded the chamber and the creature looming over them was revealed in all its monstrous glory. It was obviously the same species as the bodies outside, but even more grotesquely oversized. As holy light poured from Wolff's hammer, shimmering and flashing off the whitewashed walls, the creature bellowed and swung an axe at the priest's head. The weapon was almost as big as the priest himself, and as he leapt out of the way it smashed into the wall, cutting into the stone with such force that the whole building shook, sending masonry tumbling from the ceiling. The priest's warhammer slipped from his grip as he landed, clattering across the flagstones and disappearing from view.

The room plunged into darkness once more.

The grunting and smashing sounds continued until Ratboy heard Wolff cry out with pain. As the monster moved back and forth, brief bursts of light crept in from the outside, and in one such flash he suddenly saw the beast lifting Wolff from the ground, about to smash him against the wall, swinging him as easily as a straw doll.

Ratboy tried desperately to rise, but he was still unable to breathe and fell to his knees again, whimpering pathetically as he crawled towards the two combatants.

There was a final, deafening *bang* and then silence filled the chapterhouse.

As Ratboy crawled painfully towards the doorway, the acrid stink of saltpetre filled his nose and he saw another figure stood just inside the doorway, with a thin trail of smoke drifting from its raised hand.

'I told you we didn't need more men,' said von Gryphius, lowering his flintlock pistol with a high-pitched laugh. The colour had drained from his face and his eyes were rolling with fear. As he helped Ratboy to his feet his thin voice sounded slightly hysterical. 'What exactly was that?' he asked, gesturing to the huge mound that lay at his feet.

'Good work, Obermarshall,' came Wolff's voice from the darkness. He stepped into the shaft of light coming through the doorway and looked down at the monster's body in confusion. 'I'm amazed your shot could pierce such a thick skull.'

Von Gryphius nodded slowly, still staring at the huge corpse in amazement. 'I'm a regular at the Giselbrecht hunt,' he muttered. 'And that fellow's left eye was conveniently large.'

The ghost of a smile played around Wolff's lips as he studied the general, then he took Ratboy's arm. Once outside, they both fell to the ground, exhausted. When he had caught his breath, Wolff took the ring from his robes and looked at it thoughtfully as it glittered in the sunlight. The dove was stained with the blood of its previous owner.

'I must talk with Anna,' he said.

CHAPTER FIVE
THE RESTLESS DEAD

RECENTLY, ERASMUS HAD begun to speak to the bodies as he worked. He knew it was a little odd, but with each passing day, he found the mortal world harder to understand and had come to think of these waxy, shrouded shapes as his friends. Their stillness comforted him and sometimes he would give them voices; replying to himself as though the dead were answering. His talk was endless and anodyne: the changing of the seasons and the consistency of his porridge were the most regular topics. He doubted the corpses minded though. After all, his were the last mortal thoughts that would ever be directed at these poor, lost souls.

The garden of Morr at Elghast was a humble temple, but its crypt was a bewildering maze of tunnels and chambers. The priest's flickering lamps had only ever illuminated a small fraction of it. Four generations of his family had tended the dead in this place, but as far as he knew, no one had ever attempted to map out the full extent of the catacombs. The limestone arches had once been ornately carved in the likeness of skulls and black rose petals, but over the centuries the pillars and cornices had shrugged off their sculpted edges, reasserting their natural, ragged shapes.

A more inquisitive mind might have wished to explore the distant, ancient chambers, but not Erasmus. As he performed the funerary rites, he sometimes heard movements from deeper inside the network of tunnels, and felt obliged to investigate, but it usually turned out to be nothing more than rats, feasting on the dead. The rest of the time, he left the rows of crumbling mausoleums alone.

The clapping of large wings announced the arrival of Udo, fluttering in through the half open door that led back up to the temple. As the raven settled on her perch, she cawed repeatedly at the black-robed priest, tilting her head to watch him as he shuffled from corpse to corpse.

'Really?' replied Erasmus, pausing in the act of cleaning a knife to look up at the bird. 'That's most unfortunate, old girl, but owls have as much right to eat mice as you do. All creatures have a right to live.' He carefully lifted a shroud and plunged the knife into something soft and yielding, causing a thin arc of fluid to patter gently across the stone floor. 'At least, for a while they do.'

He chopped and sliced in silence for a few minutes, frowning in concentration. Then he paused. 'Now then friend, what's this?' he muttered, tugging an

arrowhead from his subject's chest with a moist pop-
ping sound. He held the bent piece of metal closer to
his lamp and peered at it. 'I don't think you'll need
this in the afterlife.' He dabbed at the wound with a
cloth and muttered a quick, sonorous prayer, before
dropping the arrowhead in a little copper bowl with a
clang. 'Was it really worth it, I wonder,' he said, taking
a jug of oil from a nearby table and tipping a little
onto the corpse's chest. As the chamber filled with the
scent of rosewater, he shook his head. 'What cause
was worth losing everything for, at your age? How old
were you exactly?'

'*Early thirties*,' he replied to himself in a deep voice.
'*Thirty-five at most.*'

'I see. Old enough to have a family then, maybe,
and people who loved you, but that wasn't enough –
you had to look for something more. Something
exciting.'

'*There's no love out there anymore, father: covetousness,
maybe; the desire for other men's land; bloodlust perhaps,
but no love.*'

Erasmus sighed as he continued to anoint the body.
'Yes, I suppose you might be right.' He paused, frowning at something. Then, with another wet *pop*, he
removed a second arrowhead. 'There certainly doesn't
seem to have been much love for you.'

He wiped down the second wound and finished
applying the scented oil. Then, placing the knife back
in a leather roll, he shuffled across the chamber to a
small recess in the damp rock, filled with a collection
of bottles, jugs and mildewed books. He selected one
of the texts and returned to the body, where he began

to pray. He wished the deceased a quick journey to the afterlife and begged Morr to grant him safe passage.

Natural light hardly reached down into the crypt, but after a few more hours' work, Erasmus's stomach announced quite clearly that it was midday. He stroked his tonsured head and gave a little yawn. 'Oh, Udo, I think it might be time for some lunch.'

The raven gave no reply.

He extinguished all the lamps apart from the one in his hand and fully opened the door that led back up to the temple, allowing a little more distant, grey sunlight to penetrate the immemorial gloom. He extinguished his final lamp and began to climb the rounded steps, holding out his arm for Udo to perch on. 'Bless me!' he exclaimed, slapping his head with his hand and turning around. 'I'm such a doddering old fool. I forgot all about our new guest.' He climbed back down, relit his small, iron lantern and closed the door again, shuffling back towards the furthest recesses of the chamber. The single flickering light picked out a corpse that was such a recent arrival the priest had yet to find a shroud for it. 'I can't leave you like this all afternoon, now can I?'

'*No,*' he replied to himself. '*You should at least show a little respect for a fellow priest.*'

'I know. I know. I'm sorry, brother,' he muttered, lifting some muslin from a shelf as he approached the body. 'Are you actually a priest though?' he wondered aloud, holding the lantern over the remains. The body was that of a wiry old man, with thin, greasy hair and puckered, weather-beaten skin. 'This certainly seems to suggest you were a man of faith,' he said, holding the light over a symbol on the old man's stomach. The sagging folds of skin below his ribs were branded with the shape of a flaming hammer. 'But there's something about your expression that makes me wonder.' He stooped until his clouded, myopic eyes were just an inch or two from the corpse's face. 'There's something a little wild about you.'

'*I'm a mendicant,*' Erasmus said to himself in the same sonorous voice he gave all the dead. '*That's why I look so emaciated.*'

'Well, yes, that would explain the sunburned skin too, I suppose, but what about this injury? It looks to me more like the wound of a soldier, or a fanatic even. You certainly didn't get this in a temple.' He moved the lantern across the body, illuminating a large, ragged hole, just beneath the man's left shoulder. 'And I suppose this must have been the work of your servant,' he said, fingering the crude attempts at bandaging.

'*You're a naïve old fool,*' Erasmus replied to himself in a deep voice. '*Hiding away in the dark for all these years, as the world turns on its head. You think that priests don't get murdered? No one's safe anymore. Violence is the only currency people understand in these dark times. You remember what Ernko said, when he delivered his brother's remains. The whole of Gumprecht is consumed with madness – they've turned on each other, hunting down their own families like dogs. They've burned their own houses to the ground. All because they think there's a heretic somewhere in their midst – someone who might draw the gaze of the Ruinous Powers in their direction. And remember that ferryman from*

Hürdell? He said the people from his village had begun dressing as goats and eating grass, in the hope it would appease the creatures of the forest and spare them from attacks. And if that merchant from Ferlangen was correct, half the cities in the province have fallen to the enemy.'

Erasmus shook his head in surprise as he peeled back the dark, damp rags that covered the wound. 'What kind of weapon did this to you?' he muttered. In truth though, after the horrors of the last few years, there was little that could shock the priest anymore, and he began to hum a little ditty to himself as he worked. He reopened his roll of tools and fetched another bottle of ointment. Then, he paused. 'Looks like you've still got something in there, friend,' he said, peering into the bloody hole. 'Is that a splinter of wood?' He took a small scythe-shaped tool from his roll and slid it into the wound.

The corpse gave out a deafening, tremulous scream.

Its eyes opened wide in terror and one of its sinewy hands shot up, grabbing Erasmus's shoulder in a tight grip.

Erasmus dropped the knife to the floor with a clatter and stared back at the animated corpse in confusion; then he began to scream too. He tried to pull back from its grasp, but the corpse's second hand shot up, grabbing him firmly by the other shoulder.

The corpse's face was twisted in horror and confusion as it looked from Erasmus to the surrounding darkness. The vague shapes of the other bodies were just visible, and the corpse shook its head wildly, before turning back to the priest. 'I'm not dead,' it breathed in a croaky whisper. 'For Sigmar's sake, I'm alive!'

'I WORK HERE mostly on my own,' said Erasmus, shuffling cheerfully in and out of his bedchamber. 'My brother, Bertram, visits occasionally.' His lips twisted into a grimace. 'He only comes to help when he has to, thankfully – only when there's too much embalming for me to handle alone. Mind you, that seems to be more often than not lately.' He lifted Sürman up into a sitting position and handed him a cup of water. 'Lately it seems like the dead outnumber the living.' He chuckled as he pulled open the shutters, filling the small room with flat grey light. 'Another cheerful Ostland day,' he said, watching the autumn rain slanting across the forest below.

Sürman watched him carefully over the top of the cup as he took a gulp of the water. He immediately spat the liquid out and burst into a series of hacking coughs, spraying flecks of blood all over the bed's woollen sheets.

'Be careful,' said Erasmus, dashing to his side and snatching the cup from him. 'You need to drink it slowly.' He shook his head and gently patted Sürman's bony, hunched back. 'It's a miracle you're alive. That wound must have missed your heart by an inch.' Once the coughing fit had passed, he handed the cup back and sat on a stool next to the window. 'Your man brought you to me certain that you were dead.' Erasmus looked at the floor to hide his embarrassment. 'There are various tests I would have performed before beginning the embalming, of course. I was just going to remove a couple of the splinters.'

Sürman sipped the water again, carefully this time, and he managed to hold it down. His hollow, stubbly cheeks were still as grey as the rain clouds rushing past the window, but his breath was coming a little easier now, and he was beginning to think he might even survive. 'Who brought me here?' he asked in a strained whisper.

Erasmus's long, pale face lit up with a smile. 'You sound so much better!' He clasped his tapered fingers together and muttered a prayer. 'My skills as a healer are rarely called upon. It's been a long time since I practiced herb lore. I wasn't sure if that poultice would be powerful enough to draw out the illness.' He shook his head in amazement. 'You're made of sterner stuff than you look, old man.'

No hint of emotion crossed Sürman's face. He took a slow breath and then repeated his words a little louder. 'Who brought me here?'

The eager smile remained on Erasmus's face as he replied. 'As I said, it was your man.' He looked up at the ceiling and drummed his fingers on his knees. 'I think he said his name was Albrecht or Adolphus, or–'

'Adelman,' interrupted Sürman, with a note of impatience in his voice.

'Yes! That's the one. He'd travelled with you for days, trying to find help, but he'd finally given up hope of reviving you.' Erasmus narrowed his eyes and looked back at Sürman. 'He seemed eager to leave. As though he were worried I would ask him the reasons for your condition.' He shrugged. 'But the truth is, my friend, the actions of the living are rarely Morr's concern. Whatever we do in life, we all reach the same destination.'

'There are many different routes to that destination,' muttered Sürman, looking down at his ruined body.

'Aye,' replied Erasmus, finally letting the smile slip from his face. 'That there are.' He gestured to the hammer on Sürman's stomach. 'Are you some kind of priest then, friend?'

'My name's Otto Sürman, and yes, I'm a High Priest of Sigmar.'

Erasmus raised his eyebrows and smiled. 'A *High* Priest, you say? I'd have expected a little more finery.'

'Adelman has robbed me, you idiot,' snapped Sürman, rising up from the bed and twisting the sheets in his bony fists. He looked up at the ceiling of the priest's cell and groaned with frustration. 'That witch did this to me. She must have summoned Wolff somehow – knowing he would save her. And now she goes free and Adelman has taken everything.' He flopped back onto the bed and glared at Erasmus.

Erasmus looked appalled. 'Your servant hasn't robbed you. At least, I don't think so.'

'Idiot. Do you think I travel the province naked and penniless? Adelman's taken my robes and my books too.' His eyes bulged as a terrible thought hit him. 'And all of my relics – my priceless relics.' Sürman drew a breath to hurl more insults at the priest, but before he could speak, the bed dropped away from beneath him and his stomach lurched horribly. He groaned with nausea and clamped his eyes shut in fear. When he opened them again, he was still lying in the priest's bed and Erasmus was watching over him with a concerned expression on his face.

'You should calm yourself,' urged the priest. 'You're not through the worst of it yet. The wound was full of illness and spores of corruption. I was forced to use a more powerful mixture than I would've liked.'

Sürman's vision blurred and his temples began to throb. He tried to focus on the priest, but as he peered at him, Erasmus's long, patrician features began to stretch and elongate: sliding from his face to reveal vivid pits of red flesh beneath his eyes that gradually drooped down towards his mouth. Sürman tried to reach out and push the flesh back into place, but his limbs refused to obey and he groaned in fear. 'Your face...' he murmured, as the walls closed in around him.

'What is it?' asked Erasmus, leaning forward, so that the remaining flesh peeled back from his head and revealed the glistening skull beneath. 'You should rest,' he said, splashing thick blood all over the bed, but Sürman's eyes were already closing as sleep washed over him.

ANNA HAD SPROUTED great, black, oily wings and as she stepped towards Sürman she croaked in a harsh, inhuman voice. She drew a knife from beneath her feathers and brandished it playfully at him. Catching the candlelight on the edge of its curved, serrated blade.

Sürman was sprawled on a mortuary slab and all his strength had gone from him. As the witch approached he was powerless to move and he felt impotent fury rising from deep within him. 'You'll die, Anna,' he said, glaring into her black, lidless eyes. 'Your wound is full of the spores of corruption.'

The witch spread her wings and laughed, before flying up onto the slab and crouching low over him, so that her mouth was almost touching his. She twisted her screeching voice into words he could understand. 'What are you talking about Otto?' she said, holding the knife up to his face. 'How could you ever find me without your eyes?'

'I have eyes!' cried Sürman, straining to twist his head out of her reach.

'You did have,' replied the witch, smiling as she brought the knife down towards him.

Sürman cried out in fear and clamped his eyes shut. 'I'll still find you, witch!' he cried.

Anna's only reply was harsh, bird-like squawks of laughter.

The expected pain never arrived and after a few moments Sürman opened his eyes to find he was back in the priest's cell. It was still morning, but the sky outside was clear and bright, and he guessed this was not the same day. He reached up to feel his eyes, and sighed with relief.

A loud cawing filled the room and Sürman screamed with terror.

He looked around and saw a large raven, sat on an old chest at the foot of the bed, eyeing him warily.

Erasmus burst into the room with a bloody, curved knife in his hand and a look of dismay on his face. 'What's happened?' he cried, placing the knife on the chair and clutching Sürman's hand. 'Are you alright?'

'There's a bird in here!' exclaimed Sürman, crawling fearfully beneath the sheets. 'She tried to steal my eyes.'

The priest laughed gently and patted Sürman's arm. 'That's just Udo. She won't hurt you.' He held out his arm, and the bird flew across the room and perched on its master. 'Come on, old girl. You're scaring our guest.' With another smile at Sürman, he left the room, taking his bird with him.

Sürman shivered. His body was covered with cold sweat. 'He's poisoned me,' he muttered to himself, pulling the sheets up to his chin, and looking warily around the room. 'Another witch. Just like Anna Fleck.' He heard a distant door slam and the sound of voices talking somewhere on the floor below. 'They're all trying to kill me,' he moaned. 'In league with the witch.' He noticed Erasmus's knife on the chair and smiled. He pulled himself to the edge of the bed. His limbs trembled with the effort, but he wasn't sure how long he had and his fear gave him strength. With one hand on the cold stone floor, he reached out to the chair. 'Got it,' he gasped, clutching the knife in his hand. With a grunt, he pushed himself back onto the bed and hid the blade beneath the blankets. With a smile of relief, he lowered his head onto the pillow, and quickly slipped back into his strange dreams.

'Otto,' said Erasmus, gently shaking him awake. 'I have news.'

Sürman lurched into a sitting position and groaned, looking around at the room in confusion. 'What's that?' he said, rubbing the sleep from his eyes.

Erasmus laughed at his sudden movements. 'You seem stronger,' he exclaimed, handing him a bowl of stew. 'Try and eat some more of this. You threw up most of the last bowl.'

Sürman took the food from the priest and began to eat, surprised by his own hunger. 'The last bowl?' he asked, eying the priest suspiciously. 'What last bowl?'

Erasmus chuckled. 'Don't you remember?'

Sürman shook his head, spilling a little of the broth down his stubbly chin.

'You've been here for nearly a week now, my friend,' said Erasmus. 'I thought I'd lost you a while back, but you seem to be a lot better today.' He gestured to the quickly emptying bowl. 'I'd take that a bit slower though.'

Sürman flinched as the raven flew into the room and perched at the end of the bed.

'Don't worry, Udo won't hurt you,' laughed the priest. He adopted a serious expression. 'Anyway, as I was saying, I have news.'

Sürman grunted, without lifting his face up from the bowl.

'I've been talking to my brother, Bertram, and he tells me that your servant, Adelman, is still in the village.'

Sürman paused with the spoon halfway to his mouth, and a piece of un-chewed meat hanging from between his teeth.

'Bertram is a constable of the watch, you see.' Erasmus frowned. 'I wonder sometimes if he's really the right man for the job. Some of his decisions seem a little harsh to me.' He leant forward and lowered his voice a little. 'He's not really the brightest–'

'Adelman!' snarled Sürman, sending the piece of meat flying from his mouth. 'Where is he? Where are my belongings?'

Erasmus looked blankly at him, confused for a moment. 'Oh, yes, your servant.' He frowned. 'Well, it's a sad tale, really. Thinking that you were dead, he took a room at the Bull's Head, and has been there for days, drowning his sorrows.'

'What about my things?'

'Well, according to Bertram, he arrived with two heavily laden saddlebags, and as far as anyone can tell, they've never left his room. I told Bertram not to ask too widely though, for fear of stirring up interest in the value of your possessions.'

Sürman sank back into the bed, trying to still the fevered visions that kept seizing hold of him. Erasmus had no intention of letting him live, he saw that quite clearly. The old priest would simply keep poisoning him until he passed away in his sleep. Then he would send his brother to murder Adelman and claim the relics and books for himself. He hugged his frail body and his powerlessness tormented him. A vision of Anna filled his thoughts, mocking him as she strode away from the pyre. The thought that he would die and she would live was too much. His eyes rolled back into their sockets and his muscles began to spasm as a kind of fit came over him. Suddenly, he remembered something and slipped a hand down beneath the blankets. He smiled as his hand closed around the cold metal of the knife.

'Are you alright?' asked Erasmus.

Sürman gave him a strained smile. 'Tell me,' he gasped, trying to hide his growing excitement. 'How did you heal me?'

Erasmus leant back in his chair and shrugged modestly. 'Oh, it was simple herb lore really, nothing mysterious. Long ago, before I was even an initiate, I used to dabble in such things. I just applied a poultice: a little brooklime, mandrake and figwort, and then an infusion of Queen of the Meadow. Then nothing more than rest and a light broth to keep your strength up until the fever passed.'

Sürman nodded. 'And how did you learn this "herb lore"?'

'Ah, well, my mother was,' he laughed, 'well, I suppose you'd call her a kind of wise woman. She knew all sorts of things: weird folk legends, and strange rites; you know the kind of thing.' He shook his head and looked wistfully out of the window. 'Sometimes I wonder if we've lost something, by neglecting all the teachings of the Old Faith.'

'Old Faith?' asked Sürman, continuing to smile. 'Old gods do you mean?'

'Well yes, I suppose so.' Erasmus shrugged. 'There's often a lot of wisdom in those more ancient forms of worship.'

'Sorry,' muttered Sürman, tightening his grip on the knife handle. 'Could you come a little closer, I can't quite hear you.'

Erasmus frowned. 'Are your ears infected too?' he asked, leaning towards Sürman.

Sürman's smile spread into a wolfish grin as the priest drew nearer. He slowly slid the knife up from beneath the blankets.

A terrible screeching noise filled the room and Erasmus jumped up from his chair.

Sürman cursed under his breath and slid the knife back down the bed.

'What's the matter, old girl?' cried Erasmus, dashing across the room to the raven. The bird was hopping back and forth in a frenzy and cawing repeatedly at Sürman.

Heavy footsteps pounded up the stairs and a large man blundered into the room. He was a towering, lantern-jawed brute, wearing a filthy buckskin coat that could barely restrain the proud swell of his stomach. His freckled, hairy forearms were about as wide as Sürman's waist, and the witch hunter groaned with frustration as his chance for escape slipped away from him.

'What're you playing at, brother?' the man barked at the priest. Erasmus was still trying to placate the raven, however, and not waiting for a reply, the newcomer strode past him and approached the bed. He grinned down at Sürman and enveloped his frail hand in his own meaty paw. 'Pleased to make your acquaintance, milord. Erasmus tells me you're a priest of some kind.'

Sürman's stomach knotted with anger and he remained silent, glowering up at the man from the bed.

'Don't say much, does he?' said the man, continuing to grip Sürman's hand. 'Is he a bit deaf?' He moved his broad, florid face a little closer and bellowed into Sür-man's ear. 'I'm Bertram. The village constable.' He patted a short wooden club attached to his belt. 'You might say I'm the Emperor's legal representative around here.' He loosed his grip and smiled proudly. 'I'm the one who's been investigating the whereabouts of your missing servant, Adelman.'

'Get me out of here,' gasped Sürman suddenly, sitting up in the bed and casting a fearful look at the priest. 'Your brother's trying to kill me.'

The constable paused, and frowned at his brother. 'Is he still wrong in the head?'

Erasmus gave Sürman an embarrassed smile as he stepped to his brother's side. 'I mentioned that the poultice I applied might have confused you a little. It's not that you're–'

'Take me to Adelman,' cried Sürman, grabbing Bertram's arm. 'I must speak with him as a matter of urgency.' He gave a groan of exertion and climbed out of the bed, hanging on to Bertram for support as he stood before them, trembling and naked. 'I'm surrounded by witches!' he cried, spraying spit into the constable's face. 'You must get me out of here.'

'Calm yourself, Otto,' said Erasmus, trying to usher him back into the bed.

Sürman batted him aside with surprising strength and looked at Bertram with desperation in his rolling eyes. 'I demand you take me to the Bull's Head. There's a powerful enchantress at large in this region.' He slapped the hammer on his hollow stomach. 'Anyone who fails to assist me shall be considered an accomplice.' He let go of the constable and managed to stand unaided as he levelled a finger at him. 'Are you going to help me, or should I consider you an occultist too?'

Doubt flickered across Bertram's simple face. He looked at his brother, but Erasmus looked as anxious as he did. 'Well, father,' he shrugged, 'if you really wish to leave, of course I'll help. It's just...' He looked at the bandages around Sürman's shoulder. 'Are you sure you're strong enough?'

Sürman swayed a little on his spindly legs as he turned towards Erasmus, who was hovering nervously by the doorway. 'I have my suspicions, priest,' he snapped, 'but fortunately for you, I have more important concerns at present. Fetch me some clothes and let me leave immediately, and I will try and forget your talk of "old gods" for a little while.'

Erasmus's face drained of colour, as he finally realised the nature of the man he had been treating. 'Y-Yes, of course' he stammered, rushing from the room.

Sürman's feverish mind was still lurching in and out of reality as he staggered into the Bull's Head. He peered uncertainly into the lounge of the tavern and flinched at the sight of the jostling figures moving through the smoky candlelight. Most of the villagers were crowded around a huge inglenook fireplace, warming themselves against the cold, drizzly evening that was tapping against the mullioned windows. They were simple farmers and woodsmen mostly, but to Sürman, the raging fire seemed to be melting the flesh from their faces, dripping rubbery strings of skin into their tankards. His stomach turned at the sight and he felt his legs starting to give way. He spotted a chair in a dark corner and collapsed into it, his head spinning. He closed his eyes for a few moments and tried to calm his breathing.

'Is everything alright, sir?' someone asked.

Sürman opened his eyes to see a barrel-chested man, clearly built from the same mould as Bertram. He had a long, greying beard though, and from his apron and the empty tankards in his hands, Sürman guessed he was the innkeeper.

'No,' muttered Sürman, pulling himself up in his seat and sneering at the man. 'No, it is not. My wretched servant is staying at your fleapit of an inn and every penny he's spending is pilfered from my purse.'

The innkeeper's face flushed with anger, but he refrained from acknowledging Sürman's insult. 'What name's he travelling under?'

Sürman grimaced as he noticed the man's skin growing translucent, revealing the pulsing organs and arteries beneath. He shook his head and looked again, to find the hallucination had passed. 'The useless dog is called Adelman.'

The innkeeper gave a brusque nod and stormed away.

Adelman had once been a stevedore, working on the docks in Altdorf. His neck was as thick as a tree trunk and his arms were like knotted steel, but Sürman had often wondered if he might have taken a blow to the head in his youth. As he rushed through the busy inn towards Sürman's table, his mouth was hung open with the same perpetual look of slack-jawed confusion he always wore. 'Master,' he exclaimed, dropping to his knees at Sürman's feet and hugging his legs. As he did this, his broad shoulders connected with the next table and sent it toppling over, scattering empty jugs and plates across the dusty floor.

'Watch yourself, you oaf,' hissed Sürman, batting his servant around the head until he loosed his legs and looked up at him. It always seemed to Sürman that Adelman's features had fallen into the middle of his face somehow. His eyes were nestled too close together, on either side of a small snub nose, surrounded by a vast expanse of cheekbone. And as he smiled, Adelman revealed a row of gleaming, tombstone teeth.

'You're not dead,' he said in a bass rumble.

'Quick witted as ever, I see,' muttered Sürman. 'Are my things safe?'

Adelman nodded eagerly. 'They're locked in my room. Shall I fetch them?'

Sürman shook his head. 'If you've not spent all of my money on these luxurious lodgings, would you be so good as to fetch me some food first?'

As Adelman rushed enthusiastically off to the bar, Sürman tried again to take in his surroundings. Seeing a familiar face, even one as ridiculous as Adelman's, had reassured him a little, and he felt his grasp on reality tightening. Maybe the priest's poison was finally wearing off? The woodsmen and labourers gathered round the fire were little more than shifting silhouettes, but from the raucous sound of their laughter, he could tell they had been drinking for hours. Harvest time was long past, and the woodsmen probably spent as little time in the forest as possible these days. Around the edges of the long, rectangular lounge, various other groups were huddled in the shadows, telling tales of the war and attempting to lift each other's spirits for a while.

The only group he could see clearly was sat at a table directly opposite. Several young farmhands were crowded eagerly around an older woman, who was obviously delighted with all the attention. She was dressed in a gaudy array of flowery silks and cheap trinkets, and every now and then she would lift her heavily made-up face to the beamed ceiling and burst into trilling song. She was obviously some kind of entertainer and by her odd, lilting accent, Sürman guessed that she was not from the province.

As he waited for his food, Sürman found himself listening along with the spellbound youths as she spoke. 'Obermarshall Hugo von Gryphius is the kind of man who appreciates the charms of an older woman,' she said, batting her lashes and pursing her scarlet lips, as her audience erupted into a chorus of laughter and lewd comments. 'But not only that,' she continued, adopting a more serious expression. 'He appreciates the arts in all their forms. He employs actors and musicians from every corner of the Old World.' She leant across the table, distracting the boys with a brief display of her cleavage. 'In fact, he wrote to the academy at Kleinberg, personally requesting my presence in his entourage.'

'But what's this "Obermarshall" doing in Ostland?' asked one of the farmhands.

'He sees warfare as just another one of the great arts,' she explained. 'He heard that your province was battling against a terrible foe, and he was eager to join the performance.'

The farmhands' laughter stalled as they recalled the war. 'I'm not sure it will be as much fun as he imagines,' muttered one, taking a deep swig of his ale.

Adelman reappeared with a plate of nondescript meat and some grey bread. Sürman grimaced at it, before starting to shovel down the hot food. Adelman began to speak, but Sürman signalled for him to be silent and continued listening to the singer.

'So why are you no longer travelling with his army, then?' asked another youth.

The singer curled her lip with distaste. 'He found another distraction.' She cried with disbelief. 'A priestess of Shallya no less.'

Sürman paused, with a fork of steaming offal hovering near his mouth.

'A priestess?' exclaimed one of the farmhands. 'What kind of entertainment is he expecting from her?'

The boys all burst into hysterical laughter, and the singer had to raise her voice to be heard. 'He's obsessed with her, for some reason.' She shook her head. 'And she hasn't even got any hair!'

This last comment was greeted with such howls of laughter that even the innkeeper looked over to see what was so funny.

'What happened to her hair?' asked one of the farmhands.

'Well, apparently, she fell foul of some kind of witch hunter and he tried to burn her to death.'

The farmhands' laughter tailed off again at the mention of a witch hunter. Their guffaws became quiet chuckles as they wiped the tears from their eyes.

Sürman was already struggling to his feet as the woman continued. 'Some warrior priest rescued her, but not before her golden locks had been burned clean off. She was called Anna something.'

'Fleck,' snapped Sürman, staggering up to the table and slamming his hands down on the gnarled wood.

'Eh, what's your game, mister?' cried the woman in surprise.

'Watch it,' growled the largest of the farmhands, as they all rose to their feet and stepped between Sürman and the woman. 'Just who might you be?'

Sürman managed to stand erect and jabbed a bony finger into the lad's chest. 'I'm the witch hunter you were just discussing.' He pulled open the black robes Erasmus had loaned him, to reveal the hammer burnt across his flesh.

The youths fell silent and backed away from him, suddenly feeling very sober. 'There's no reason to get yourself all worked up, mister.'

'I've done nothing wrong,' cried the woman, with a note of panic rising in her voice, as her audience all dissolved into the shadows.

Sürman gave her what he imagined was a reassuring smile and gestured to her chair. 'Please, don't be alarmed,' he said, sitting down next to her. 'I just wanted to ask you a couple of questions.'

The woman's face was pale with fear as she looked around the inn for help. The drunken farmers had started singing, however, and no one had noticed her predicament.

'Adelman,' snapped Sürman, 'fetch the lady another glass of wine.'

Once they were both seated, Sürman took the woman's hand. 'Am I right,' he asked, 'was the priestess called Anna Fleck?'

The woman was wide-eyed with terror as she replied. 'Yes, I think so.' She shook her head urgently. 'I had little to do with her though. I was simply employed as a dancer for von Gryphius. The priestess has been travelling with him for the last week or so, and I just asked her how she lost her hair.'

Sürman nodded, and squeezed her hand a little tighter. 'Is she still riding with von Gryphius?' he asked, looking hungrily into the woman's eyes.

'She was, as of this morning. I think they had planned to leave her at some kind of temple, before they encounter the enemy, but when they got there, the temple was already destroyed. When I last saw her, she seemed to have lost all reason. There's an important priest of some kind with her – a warrior priest, by the look of his armour – and she rides on the back of his horse now. She doesn't even speak, or eat, or anything. She just clings on to the priest in silence as the army heads north.' The woman eased her hand from Sürman's and frowned. 'I'm not sure she's long for this world, to be honest.'

Sürman allowed himself a little chuckle. 'You're right about that, if nothing else.' He slicked his long, lank hair into a side parting and looked at the woman thoughtfully. 'There's just one more thing,' he said, 'do you have any idea where they're headed?'

'Von Gryphius?' The woman shook her head. 'Well, north, looking for the enemy, but that could mean anywhere.'

'Think,' urged Sürman, with a hint of menace in his voice. 'It's very important. I must find this woman.'

The singer looked up at the ceiling, desperately trying to think of a place name. 'Oh, wait!' she exclaimed, grabbing Sürman's hand. 'I heard von Gryphius mention a friend. An old countryman of his. He wanted to visit his castle as they marched north. They were headed that way when I left them. It's somewhere north of Lubrecht.' Her face lit up in a triumphant smile. 'His name was Casper von Lüneberg. That's where they were headed – to Castle Lüneberg!'

Sürman leant back in his chair with a satisfied nod. Then, after a few minutes, he gave the singer a questioning look. 'Did you say you spoke with Anna?' he asked, signalling for Adelman to approach the table. 'What exactly would a dancer have to discuss with a sorceress?' He gave her a wolfish grin, as he lifted a long knife from his servant's belt. 'Unless, of course, the two of you had something in common.'

CHAPTER SIX
FAIR-WEATHER FRIENDS

VON GRYPHIUS'S SOLDIERS grimaced and pulled their thin, silk cloaks a little tighter as they rode into the bitter north. For the last week, the only change in the monotonous weather had been from cold, miserable rain to cold, miserable sleet. A grey mist lay over the tree-lined hills and the sun was no more than a silver ghost, hovering nervously behind mountainous clouds.

At the head of the long column of grumbling men, the general raised a gauntleted hand to shield his eyes against the fierce downpour and squinted down at the figure running beside him. His adjutant was jogging by the side of his warhorse, slipping through the mud and trying not to drop a silver tray piled high with small pastries. Gryphius puffed out his flabby cheeks in disgust, straining to be heard over the sound of the rain as it pinged off his winged helmet. 'I *am* making allowances, Christoff, but it's not even fit for the dogs.' He spat a mouthful into the mud. 'Is there even any sugar on there?'

There was no hint of emotion in Christoff's reply. 'I believe the pastry chef thought the raspberry jam would add sufficient sweetness, milord. Would you like to try one of the custard tartlets?'

'What's the point?' cried Gryphius in despair. He waved at the sodden musicians to his left. The ears of their animal costumes had drooped in the downpour and they made a pathetic sight as they tooted tunelessly on their waterlogged instruments. 'No one seems to be prepared to make any effort today.'

'I'll ask Chef to try again,' said Christoff, turning to leave.

'Wait,' cried Gryphius, shaking his head and grabbing a few pastries. 'I need to eat *something* this morning.'

As the general chomped unhappily on his mushy breakfast, a horse broke ranks and trotted up alongside his. Its thin, hooded rider leant over to speak to him. 'Will we reach Castle Lüneberg today, Obermarshall?'

For a few seconds the general did not reply, pouting instead at the pastry disintegrating in his hand. 'This has never been near a raspberry,' he muttered to himself, before realising he was being addressed. 'Ah, Ratboy,' he replied finally. 'Your province gives quite a welcome to its would-be rescuers,' he laughed, waving at the rain. 'It's enough to make one feel quite unwanted.'

Ratboy shrugged. 'I'm afraid this is quite normal for this far north, Obermarshall. It's only going to get worse as we approach the Sea of Claws.'

The general gave him a pastry and a smile. 'You should come with me to Averheim some time, my boy, and get a bit of southern sun on those pallid cheeks of yours.' He washed his tart down with some sherry and waved the bottle vaguely at the water-logged landscape. 'Casper's letter said he was just a few miles north of here. Next to a small town, called Ruckendorf. It should be somewhere around here.' He looked up at the rolling clouds. 'If it hasn't sunk, that is.' His eyes misted over as he remembered his old friend. 'In his youth, Casper was a very promising poet, you know. Back in Averheim, the name of von Lüneberg was often heard in the highest echelons of polite society.' An unusual note of regret entered his voice. 'It's strange the way things sometimes work out.'

He noticed Ratboy's downcast expression and shook his head, adopting his usual cheerful grin. 'Anna will recover, lad, don't you worry. She's an Ostlander.' His eyes widened with surprise as a long, rattling belch erupted from his mouth. Then he patted his prodigious belly and looked up the clouds. 'I hope Casper still keeps a well stocked larder.'

Ratboy gave a weak smile and twisted in his saddle to look back through the forest of spears and banners. Wolff and his ragtag band of followers were trailing a little way behind them, and he could just about see the figure of Anna, slumped on the back of Wolff's horse, with her head nodding listlessly in the rain. 'I'm sure you're right. She probably just needs a little time to grieve,' he said.

A shimmering figure loomed out of the rain, riding along the grass verge at the side of the road. As it came closer it gradually assumed the form of a scout. 'Ruck-endorf, sir' he cried, pointing down the road, 'around the next bend.' He paused, and shook his head. 'The enemy's already been there. The buildings are ruined.'

'Really?' snapped Gryphius in a shrill voice, clutching at the hilt of his sword. Then, remembering Ratboy was at his side, he adopted a stern expression and raised his chins proudly. 'We may not get the friendly welcome we were expecting.' He turned to one of his captains. 'Tell the men to ready their weapons. We're finally going to fight through something other than mud.'

They entered the small town through the west gate and found most of the locals waiting for them. A huge mound of bodies was piled in the market square: soldiers, woodsmen, merchants and farmers, all jumbled together in a bloody mound of twisted limbs and broken weapons. The gabled townhouses and inns were blackened and smashed and the blood of the townsfolk had been daubed across their own ruined homes.

'Sigmar,' whispered Ratboy, grimacing at the smell of rotting meat as he steered his horse slowly through the ruins. 'Is anyone in Ostland still alive?'

Von Gryphius eyed the bodies warily as he rode towards them and lifted a perfumed handkerchief to his nose. Then he nodded towards a large building on the far side of the square. Its proud pillars and wide steps must have once been the dominating feature of Ruckendorf. 'Looks like the town hall is still occupied.'

Ratboy followed his gaze and saw a few sodden figures, cowering pitifully behind a decapitated statue of the Emperor.

Gryphius led his army towards them. The horses' hooves clattered across the square as they skirted around the morbid display at its centre. For once, though, the men rode in silence, with swords and halberds at the ready as they eyed the wreckage for signs of the enemy.

'What happened here?' cried the general, as they neared the statue.

The cowering figures hesitated for a few moments, before one of them, a grizzled old infantryman, stepped out of the shadows. His jerkin was stained and torn and one of his arms was strapped across his chest in a bloody sling. His eyes were wide and unblinking as he addressed them. 'Ostland is doomed, stranger. I'd start running now if I were you. It's probably already too late, but maybe a few of you might still survive.'

'I'm an old friend of your lord,' answered Gryphius, ignoring the man's gloomy tone. 'Is Castle Lüneberg near here?'

The infantryman's face twisted into a snarl. 'An old friend, you say?' He took in Gryphius's yellow, silk breeches and high, lacy collar with a sneer of disdain. 'That would make sense.' He pointed his broken sword at the pile of corpses. 'That's what happens to old friends of Casper von Lüneberg.'

Wolf steered his horse across the square and halted next to Gryphius. 'That's no way to speak of your lord, soldier.'

The soldier glared back at the warrior priest with a mixture of fear and pride. 'I have no lord anymore, priest,' he cried, sending his sword clanging down the steps of the town hall. 'Save perhaps Morr, and I've already made my peace with him.' As he turned to leave, he waved dismissively around the side of the building. 'Keep going as you are. Meet your end with that old fool, if that's what you wish.'

Gryphius turned to Wolff with a confused expression. 'It's odd that he should be so rude. Casper always used to have such a way with people.'

Castle Lüneberg was perched high up on a rocky promontory, overlooking the town: a picturesque mass of twisting spires and gracefully arching buttresses, looming watchfully over Ruckendorf. The duke's black and white banner was still flapping bravely against the driving rain, but as Gryphius's men trudged up the steep, twisting road to its gates, their hopes gradually sank. As they approached the castle, they saw that many of the doors had been smashed from their hinges and ragged holes had been blasted through the outer wall, leaving several of the chambers exposed to the elements.

A horse and trap was hurtling down the road towards them. Its canvas sides bulged with servants and their belongings and as the driver steered the cart in their direction, a long trail of buckets and pans clattered in its wake.

At the sight of Gryphius's army, the driver pulled over to the side of the road and stared in amazement. As the troops in the vanguard marched past the cart, a row of shocked, pale faces gawped out from beneath the tarpaulin, whispering to each other and pointing at the soldiers' outlandish uniforms.

'I would have expected more of Ostlanders,' called von Gryphius, lifting his chin haughtily as his horse trotted past them, 'than to abandon their master in his hour of need.'

Most of the servants were too terrified to reply to such an august personage, but after a few seconds a buck-toothed girl popped her head out of the back of the cart. She yelled defiantly at the receding general. 'We didn't want to go nowhere, milord. The master's banished us, on pain of death. We hung on longer than most. He's swore to kill us on sight if we return. We ain't abandoning no one.'

'A likely story,' called back Gryphius. 'Why would Casper wish to be without his servants, even if the wolves *are* at his door?'

'He ain't got no need of anyone anymore,' answered the girl. 'You'll see. 'Cept perhaps some pallbearers – I guess he'll be needing them soon enough.'

Gryphius rolled his eyes at Ratboy, and led the way through the castle gates and into the courtyard. He opened his mouth to hurl another insult back at the woman, but the scene that met him stopped the words short. There were more bodies, scattered all around the central keep: sprawled across the flag-stones and slumped against broken doorframes. From their bloodstained black and white armour, it was obvious that most of the dead were state troops. There were other corpses too, though: fur-clad marauders from the north, clutching brutal-looking axes and scarred with the grotesque sigils of the Dark Gods. The whole place was stained with drying blood. As the rest of the troops filed in behind Gryphius, the eerie silence snatched the words from their lips. Even the general seemed reluctant to break it, shaking his head at the carnage as his servants rushed to help him dismount.

With a horrendous scraping sound, the flagellants dragged Raphael's litter into the castle. They were still muttering prayers to him and lashing their naked, emaciated bodies with straps as they stumbled, barefoot over the broken masonry. As Ratboy looked back at them, he winced at the sight of their prophet. Raphael's skeletal frame was arched in pain, and his anguished face was raised up to the brooding clouds in supplication, but as the litter bounced across the flagstones, his body remained frozen in a motionless spasm. His pale, scarred flesh was as rigid as the statues that lined the courtyard.

'Master,' said Ratboy, turning to Wolff, 'is that man–?'

'Hush, boy,' said Wolff, giving him a stern look as he climbed down from his horse. 'Raphael is their inspiration. He fills them with hope.' He placed a hand on Ratboy's shoulder. 'And hope is a rare thing.'

Ratboy nodded mutely as he helped Wolff lift Anna down from the saddle. She was as limp as a doll as they placed her on the ground and there was no hint of life in her eyes as Wolff gently took her arm and led her over to the general.

'Obermarshall,' said Wolff, gesturing to the destruction that surrounded them. 'This battle has already been lost. There's nothing to be done here now. I suggest we just–'

Gryphius rounded angrily on the priest. 'Lüneberg was my friend,' he cried, in a voice that cracked with emotion. 'I *must* see him again.'

An awkward silence followed his words. Gryphius saw how shocked his men were by his outburst and colour rushed to his cheeks. When he spoke again, his voice was softer. 'There are things we need to discuss. It's important that I find out what's happened to him.'

Wolff shrugged and waved at the bodies. 'Very well, Obermarshall, but I'm not sure you'll like what you find.'

A rolling, musical cry echoed around the courtyard: 'Oh, sweet, tender voice! Slicing through time's torpid veil.' Hands reached out into the rain from a vine-covered balcony above them. 'What bliss is this? Can it be that when everything seems darkest, I hear the beloved voice of Hugo von Gryphius?'

'Casper!' cried the general and his face lit up with pleasure. He stepped backwards into the centre of the courtyard to get a better view of the balcony. 'Is that really you?' He slapped a hand against his breastplate and fell to his knees. 'Old friend, I never thought I'd see you again.'

GRYPHIUS'S SERVANTS HAD quickly filled the dying castle with the illusion of life. Candlelight, song and the comforting smell of roasting meat filled the great hall for one last time. As the torches burst into flame, they gave the slashed tapestries and bloodstained walls a homely warmth, despite the broken windows that lined one side of the room.

As Ratboy stepped awkwardly to his master's side to serve him, the flickering light from the candelabras revealed his blushes. He had insisted that this duty was his alone, but as he carried the steaming food towards Wolff, he suddenly felt ashamed of his dusty travelling clothes and his simple, country manners. His stomach knotted as he looked at the grand nobles arrayed before him. Casper Gregorius von Lüneberg, Duke of Ruckendorf, was seated directly opposite Wolff, wearing a beautifully embroidered black tabard and a thick gold chain around his neck, from which dangled his badge of office: a proud, brass bull. Next to him sat his old friend, Obermarshall von Gryphius. The general had insisted on changing before dinner and was now squeezed into a plush, ruby red doublet that stretched snugly over his potbelly and tapered down towards his oversized codpiece. Gryphius had also replaced his collar with an even higher one, and as he leant hungrily over his venison, the starched lace tinkled and shimmered with tiny jewels.

As Ratboy placed the food down before his master and stood discretely behind him, he noted the priest's lack of pretension with pride. Wolff's only concession to vanity had been to let Ratboy remove his plate armour and wipe a little of the mud from his vestments, but even in such simple attire, he carried himself with a quiet dignity that, to Ratboy's mind, set him above all the other guests.

Sat silently next to Wolff was the forlorn, mute figure of Anna, and the rest of the seats were filled with Gryphius's officers, heedlessly splashing wine over their canary yellow doublets as they lunged playfully after the serving girls.

At the far end of the hall, next to a raging fire, the general's musicians launched into another frenzied jig, giving the room the feel of a joyous, rowdy tavern, rather than a doomed citadel at the edge of the world.

Casper Lüneberg was as short as Gryphius, with the same olive skin and dark, oily hair, but he carried none of the Obermarshall's extra weight. He was a slender, ethereal figure, who waved his arms like a conjuror as he spoke and let his unruly, black locks trail down to his goatee beard as he addressed them. 'Foes and maladies unnumbered; murmuring terrors and the mindless multitudes; none could touch me, in such crystal company as this!'

Gryphius grinned proudly at Wolff over the jellies and guinea fowl that sat between them. 'See? I told you he had a way with people! Such beautiful words!' He wrapped an arm around their host's shoulders, giving him a fierce hug and planting a loud kiss on his cheek. 'By Sigmar, Casper, it's good to see you!'

Lüneberg smiled wistfully. 'Your voice is like an old, beloved song, Hugo. It would rekindle my soul to see your blessed face one last time.'

The smile fell from Gryphius's lips as he looked at the bandage over Lüneberg's eyes. 'What caused this blindness, Casper? Was it old age?'

Lüneberg chuckled. 'Remember, I'm two months younger than you, old man. No, for once time was not the enemy; this veil was lowered by another hand.' The smile dropped from his face and he took Gryphius's hand, speaking so softly that Ratboy could only just catch his words over the music. 'How did we come to end our days so far from home, Hugo? What a lachrymose end to our ridiculous tragedy.'

The mood at the table changed noticeably. Gryphius's shoulders sagged and his mouth twisted into a grimace. 'Old friend,' he muttered, before lowering his gaze to the table and falling silent.

There was obviously some unresolved tension between the two men and Wolff left them to their thoughts for a while. He turned to the other diners and grimaced with distaste, as they grew loud and clumsy with drink. Eventually, he sipped from a glass of water, cleared his throat and addressed von Lüneberg. 'Tell me, Duke, when did the attacks begin?'

Lüneberg did not seem to hear the priest at first; then he shook his head. 'Sorry, Brother Wolff, what was that?'

'When did the attacks begin?' he repeated. 'You've obviously fought bravely in defence of your dukedom, and presumably with such a great castle as this came a force of some size. How it was that things started to turn against you?'

Lüneberg flicked his hair to one side, revealing a set of thick, gold hoops that dangled from his ear. 'Things were ever against me, Brother Wolff. When I came to this province I had nothing to live for.' Gryphius looked up at these words, but the duke continued, oblivious to his friend's pained expression. 'So I pitted myself against these unending hordes that plague the Ostlanders. I had some skill with a sword and plenty of money to buy and equip an army. And, most of all, I was looking for something to distract me from my past.' His words trembled with growing anger. 'And yes, you're right, I *have* fought bravely, and not just in the defence of this wretched backwater. I've marched alongside the Elector Count in countless hopeless engagements, but to what end? What was my glittering prize?' He waved at the broken windows and the pitch dark outside. 'A dukedom on the edge of sanity and the unruly damned on my doorstep. They've drunk my southern soul like an exotic wine.' He waved his hand in a theatrical flourish and his gold rings flashed in the candlelight. 'I have already passed beyond.'

Wolff leant across the table. 'Are *all* your men dead then?'

Lüneberg shook his head. 'Vanity would have finished them though, every one, if I'd let it. Even blind, I thought I could lead them to victory. Even after a thousand mindless, mournful endings I thought I could deliver them. I thought I could loose the cord around their throats, but I only pulled it tighter.'

The duke turned his head vaguely in Wolff's direction and spoke with a sudden urgency. 'But what are you doing out here, father? I know Hugo's story – it's a sad one, and his wounds run even deeper than mine. I know the bitter discontent that haunts him, but *you* still have strength left. I can hear it in your voice. Why would you squander it here? Why did you not head south, while you could? Von Raukov has assembled a great army in Wolfenberg to fight this latest abomination. A man of your faith could have been of use to him.'

Wolff was a little taken aback by the duke's words, 'I do intend to find the main force. I mean to aid the

Elector Count in any way I can,' he hesitated, 'and also, I'm seeking my brother, Fabian Wolff, who I believe is fighting in a regiment called the Ostland Black Guard.'

'But you're too far north,' cried the duke, with surprising vehemence. The rowdy officers at the other end of the table fell silent, looking over at him in surprise. 'The enemy has already swept though this whole region,' continued the duke, shaking his head in confusion. 'You must have passed them in the night somehow. Don't you realise? You're already *behind* the invasion. They marched through here two days past, slaughtering everything in their path. While my servants cowered in the cellars I threw myself at the monsters and begged them for death; but they saw that it would be crueller to let me live. My grief is a torment worse than anything they could have inflicted.' He shivered. 'There's a gentle-tongued devil leading them, a giggling grotesque that introduced himself as Mormius. The fiend charged through here so fast he didn't even wait to see his army destroy me. He did, however, pause long enough to do this.' The duke lifted his bandage briefly, to reveal two swollen lines of stitches where his eyes should have been.

Wolff grimaced at the sight of the thick, red scars. 'Why would he blind you but let you live?'

'He's utterly insane. Even by the standards of his own kind. He'd somehow heard of my love for literature, and as his soldiers tore down the walls and butchered my friends, he attempted to discuss poetry with me. I told him it was impossible that such a drooling animal could ever understand anything of beauty or the arts.' The duke shook his head. 'Something about my words seemed to amuse him – he became quite hysterical in fact. Then he threw me against the wall and gouged out my eyes with his thumbs. A day later, unable to even see my own sword, I tried to lead these poor wretches against his army as they rushed south.' His voice hitched with emotion. 'It was a shameful farce. They turned their full force against us and I ordered a retreat, but it was far too late. Half of the townsfolk had already been ripped to pieces by those dogs. What madness made me lead them into battle I'll never know.' He shook his head. 'So much death…' He lifted one of his ring-laden hands to his mouth, as though he could not bear to hear any more of his own words.

'You did what you thought best,' said a soft voice.

To his shock, Ratboy realised the words were Anna's. Tears were flowing freely from her eyes as she looked up at the blind duke. It was the first time she had spoken to anyone since Wolff had told her that the abbess was dead.

Lüneberg flinched at her words, as though she were insulting him, but he drew a deep breath and lowered his hand from his mouth, seeming to regain control of himself. He took a sip of wine and turned towards Wolff. 'I wouldn't hold out much hope of a reunion with your brother. If he's spent any amount of time in von Raukov's army, he's probably dead by now, but even if he isn't, there's no way you could reach him. You've come too far to the north-east. We're completely surrounded out here. The only way you could rejoin von Raukov's men now would be to fight back through Mormius's entire army from behind. It's impossible.'

The rest of the officers were now following the duke's words in attentive silence. At the word 'impossible' they looked towards their general for his response. Conscious of all eyes being on him, Gryphius puffed out his small chest and placed his hands firmly on the table. 'Impossible? I don't think so, old friend.' He shrugged off the gloom that had settled over him and grinned at his captains, raising his glass aloft. 'Finally, it sounds like we have a fight on our hands!'

The officers exploded into raucous cheers and whistles, banging their fists on the table and filling each other's glasses.

Lüneberg frowned. 'I understand your reasons Hugo, but there are others here who might not be so eager for the cold embrace of the grave.' He gave a grim laugh. 'Well, I suppose you would have the element of surprise though. They won't expect anything to come from this direction, other than more of their own kind.'

'Where was this Mormius headed?' asked Wolff.

'Wolfenberg,' replied Lüneberg. 'His only strategy is to race to the capital as fast as possible. But they have one last hurdle to cross before they can head south unimpeded. There's a young captain named Andreas Felhamer whose banner has become something of a rallying point. He's gathered the last of the northern garrisons together into a single force. He's quite the firebrand and his passion does him credit, but I'm not sure his judgment is sound. He's gathered all this flotsam and jetsam into an old ruined keep, named Mühlberg. The locals call it Mercy's End, in memory of its former glories, but these days the old place barely has the strength to support Felhamer's banners.'

'What of von Raukov?' asked Wolff. 'You mentioned that he's gathered a great force. Where does he intend to strike? Maybe we could join him in the counterattack?'

'He's racing north as we speak. He's heard of Felhamer's heroics and ordered him to hold Mercy's End, until the main force arrives to relieve him.' Lüneberg shook his head. 'The poor, brave child. They'll all be dead a long time before that. Mormius drives his army with a fierce determination. I've never seen anything like it. He's careless of anything but the race south. Felhamer's military career will be a short one, I'm afraid. I imagine von Raukov knows that though.' Lüneberg patted the table till he found a fork, and shovelled some food into his mouth. 'I fear that the Elector Count is simply using the captain as a sponge, to soak up some of the enemy's fury for a while, and buy him a little marching time. No one expects him to leave Mercy's End alive.'

Gryphius leant forward, so that his eyes glinted mischievously in the candlelight. 'Well, Captain Felhamer might find he has a little Averland steel to keep him company in his final watch.' He lurched unsteadily to his feet and clambered onto the table, raising his sword to his men and sending food and wine clattering across the floor. 'Tomorrow, we march to war, my friends.' The officers lurched unsteadily to their feet and drew their own swords in a solemn reply. The general took a swig of wine and grinned at them. 'But tonight, I think we need a little dancing.' He jumped down from the table and marched towards the musicians, grabbing a serving girl's hand as he went. The officers scrambled after him, laughing and shouting as they barged past Ratboy and left Wolff, Lüneberg and Anna alone at the table.

The music swelled in volume and the room filled with whirling, dancing shapes. The officers began spinning drunkenly in and out of the shifting shadows, as vague and insubstantial as the ghosts they might soon become.

Lüneberg smiled indulgently. 'He makes a good show of it, doesn't he? You'd think him quite the hero. It wasn't always so. He's not the man he pretends to be.' He winced suddenly and placed a hand over his bandage.

Anna rose from her chair and rushed to his side. She placed her hands over his and lowered her head, whispering a few soft words in his ear as she did so.

At first the duke looked irritated at being manhandled in such a way, but then a relieved smile spread across his face. 'Who is this worker of miracles?' he asked, squeezing her hands gratefully.

A faint smile played around Anna's mouth as she replied. 'No miracle worker, my lord, just someone with a little compassion for a tired old soldier.'

Lüneberg held onto her hands for a while longer. 'A Sister of Shallya, then?'

Anna frowned. 'I think so, my lord. In truth, I've been quite lost these last few days, even from myself; but hearing the pain in your voice reminded me who

I am.' She freed her hand from his and placed it on his shoulder. 'You can't carry the fate of a whole nation on your shoulders, my lord. If you hadn't led these people to war, someone else would simply have had to do it in your stead.'

Lüneberg nodded slowly and chuckled. 'It's been decades since I last saw Hugo, but he obviously hasn't lost the knack of surrounding himself with powerful women.'

Anna blushed and returned to her seat. As she stepped past Ratboy she gave him a shy nod, as though seeing him for the first time in days.

He smiled awkwardly in reply, relieved to see a little of the old determination back in her steely eyes.

'So, tell me, duke,' said Wolff, a little while later, 'how did you find yourself so far from Averland? Did you and von Gryphius set out together?'

'Ah, therein lies a tale, Brother Wolff,' replied Lüneberg with a wry smile. 'And not a happy one I'm afraid. Hugo was not always the valiant hero you see now. As a youth, his only interest was in the arts, and the idea of dirtying his hands in combat repulsed him.' He waved over to where Gryphius and his men were dancing drunkenly around the ruined hall. 'There comes a time however, when all men must fight for what they love.

'Averland is a land of rich pastures and even richer palaces. The sun smiles down on Sigmar's southern heirs with the kind of indulgence his hardy northern offspring can hardly imagine. But even in such a paradise, there are wars to be won, and enemies to repel. Hugo knew this, but his head has always been full of music and poetry.' The duke paused and tilted his head to one side, trying to reassure himself Gryphius was still out of earshot. 'He has a big heart, that one, but it is the heart of a child – easily distracted by new passions, and new ideas; sometimes he's neglectful of the things that really matter.' Lüneberg fanned out his tanned, bejeweled fingers across the table. 'These are not the hands of a natural fighter, but it was these hands that Gryphius entrusted with the safety of his young wife. Not once in his short life had he heeded the call of battle, and as bandits struck closer and closer to his ancestral home, he found an excuse to be elsewhere. The artist, Schüzzelwanst had opened a new exhibition in Altdorf and, despite the danger looming over his home, he decided he had to meet the great man, leaving me in charge of his garrison.

'Even if Gryphius had been fighting by my side, he couldn't have saved his wife, but in his heart he knows he should have been there.' Lüneberg shook his head. 'If only so he could have died by her side.'

Ratboy was so caught up in the duke's tale he forgot himself and leant across the table to speak. 'But how was it that you survived?'

Lüneberg shrugged. 'It seems to be my destiny to fail those I'm responsible for and live to tell the tale.' He lifted his clothes to reveal a thick old scar, snaking down through the grey hairs on his chest, all the way to his groin. 'They gutted me like a fish, and the pain was unimaginable,' he gave a grim laugh; 'but I couldn't bear to die until I'd seen Gryphius, and confronted him over his cowardice. To see a man's wife destroyed in such a way, when he should have been there to defend his home, gave me a bitter vitality. When he finally did return though, he blamed me for her death and we–' He paused and took a sip of wine. 'Well, let's just say, her death changed things. Our friendship was over, and neither of us could bear our pampered, pointless existence for a minute longer. We exiled ourselves from our homeland. My shame drove me north to war and Gryphius, well, he adopted the role of a rootless hedonist. He has to avoid his own thoughts at all costs, and any distraction will do: wine, food, bloodshed, fear or even death, it's all the same to him now. He just wants to be dazzled by experience, feeling everything to the full, with no concern for the consequences. He won't rest until he's ruined himself in some glorious endeavour. It's ironic, really, that we are surrounded by so much death and the one man who would welcome it has survived.'

Ratboy looked over at the general, stumbling and leaping gaily around the room. Maybe it was his imagination, but as he studied Gryphius's round, grinning face, he thought he could pinpoint a subtle hardness behind his eyes; and perhaps even a glimmer of fear.

Wolff talked to Lüneberg for a little longer, probing him for descriptions of the surrounding countryside and the nature of Mormius's army, but the life seemed to have left the duke, and eventually he rose from the table and gave them a small bow. 'Wake me in the morning, before you leave, and I'll set you on the right road,' he yawned.

'But won't you join us?' asked Anna, her voice full of dismay.

The duke shook his head sadly, as one of Gryphius's servants took his arm and began to lead him away. 'No, child, it sounds like you have a hard road ahead of you and my fighting days are long over.' He waved at the ruined hall as he shuffled away from them. 'This seems as good a place as any to meet my end. Good evening, my friends.'

Wolff and Anna retired to their rooms shortly after, but the tale of Lüneberg and Gryphius haunted Ratboy, and even after a long day's marching, he felt oddly restless. Once he was sure his master had no further need for him, he sat on a stool to watch the duke and his men dancing. The entertainment was short-lived, though. Tiredness and alcohol gradually overcame the company and one by one they slumped to the floor. Finally, there was just a single fiddle player, dressed as a goose and playing a series of discordant notes as he skipped around the room, leading the duke in a ragged, lurching jig around the hall.

The duke was still drinking heavily as he danced and something about his desire for oblivion repulsed Ratboy. He wandered out onto the battlements, to clear his head. As he stepped out into the moonlight he turned his collar up against the cold and looked down on the sleeping army. Gaudy yellow and black tents were pitched all over the courtyard and the lights of torches moved back and forth between them, as the quartermaster and his men prepared for the next day's march. The rain had eased to a fine, billowing drizzle, but it quickly seeped through Ratboy's clothes, chilling his slender limbs. After a few minutes he headed back inside to find a corner to curl up in.

As he approached the door, a strange noise caught his attention and he looked out over the other side of the tower. The scene below chilled him even more than the rain and the memory of it stayed with him for a long time afterwards. The penitent villagers from Gotburg were still awake and had crowded around Raphael's litter in prayer. They had propped up his twisted, broken corpse with a stick and as his glassy eyes stared lifelessly out over the courtyard, they called out to him for guidance and lashed themselves repeatedly with sticks, mingling their blood with the soft Ostland rain.

CHAPTER SEVEN
RIGHTEOUS FURY

THEY HEADED WEST, with the sun at their backs, looking for the war.

Ratboy gazed back over his shoulder at Castle Lüneberg, silhouetted against the dawn glow. He thought he could still just make out the lonely figure of the duke, with his hand raised in a silent farewell. 'What will become of him?' he muttered, turning to his master.

The priest replied with a hint of irritation in his voice. 'What concern is that of yours? He's made his choice and we must respect it.' He shrugged his hammer into a more comfortable position on his back and kept his gaze on the road ahead. 'Such hedonism rarely ends well.'

Gryphius's army marched behind them, carving a noisy path through the dewy forest glades, like a fast flowing river of yellow cloth and burnished metal.

Wolff, Anna and Ratboy rode at the head of the column, alongside the general and his officers. Trailing
behind the main force came the flagellants, still carrying Raphael's corpse on the slowly disintegrating
litter. Ratboy looked back at them in confusion.
'Master,' he said, 'the villagers from Gotburg – there
seems to be more of them than before.'

Wolff nodded, without turning to face his acolyte.
'Such fervour is infectious. In times such as these,
people are forever on the look out for salvation.
Raphael's new followers are mostly Lüneberg's former servants, plus some of the injured soldiers who
were still hiding out in the castle. I imagine their
numbers will continue to swell as we approach
Mercy's End.'

Ratboy shook his head in amazement, looking at
the broken body on the litter. 'But don't they realise
that Raphael has died?'

Wolff looked around with a dangerous glint in his
eyes. 'Watch your words, boy. Who knows what they
think. Some of them may believe he's in a trance,
and that he is communicating directly with Sigmar
himself. And it may even be that they see things
more clearly than you. The edifying effects of hunger,
and constant pain can have unforeseen results. Who
are you to be so mocking of their faith?' He slowed
his horse, until he was riding beside Ratboy. 'Such
scepticism does not become you. If you truly wish to
enter the priesthood you must understand how
important such fierce belief can be. It's all too easy to
let physical comfort come between you and religious
truth.'

'So you think they might be right?' replied Ratboy, incredulously. 'That he hasn't thrashed himself to death, he's just in some kind of holy sleep?'

Wolff shrugged. 'My thoughts on the matter are irrelevant. I've seen many things that defy explanation, and have learned enough humility to bite my tongue rather than make rash judgements. The only thing I'm sure of is the limits of my own knowledge. My understanding of the spiritual realm is like a single candle, flickering in the dark. There is much that I cannot see.'

Ratboy blushed and looked away from his master, feeling that he had made a fool of himself.

Wolff noticed his embarrassment and softened his voice. 'There are other considerations, too. The role of a warrior priest is to ensure the survival of Sigmar's heirs and also the survival of His doctrine. Sometimes that relies as much on tactical thought as it does on revelation. Soon, we'll need to fight our way through an army of immense size. From what the duke told me last night, Mormius's army numbers in the thousands. And somehow we must slice through that foul canker to reach von Raukov's men.'

He looked Ratboy in the eye, lowering his voice even more. 'You know that I've had doubts of my own recently. Even I began to question my purpose, Anselm. After all these years of fruitless, endless war, I had begun to doubt that I could have any effect.' He pounded his fist against the dull metal of his breast-plate with a hollow *clang*. 'But now I *know* I have a duty to fulfil. My own brother is ahead of us, marching with von Raukov's army. And I know now he's filled with corruption of the worst kind. Who can say what he intends to do, but I have to find him.' He patted the broad knife wedged in his belt. 'And stop him, somehow.'

He waved his gauntleted hand at the lurching, bloody figures trailing behind the litter. 'I have a suspicion that such fanatical faith will be invaluable. I can guarantee you that even if every man in Gryphius's army lay dead around them those villagers would still be defending their prophet. With their hands and teeth if they had to.'

After that Ratboy rode in silence, mulling over his master's words. Was Wolff saying that Raphael's followers were inspired, or merely useful? Surely they were indulging in a kind of idolatry? The litter was strewn with a strange mixture of objects, all placed there by the flagellants. Mounds of herbs and berries were draped over the corpse, and sheets of parchment were nailed to the wood, covered in manically scrawled prayers and poems. Someone had even fastened a wooden hammer to Raphael's rigid right hand, which bounced from side to side as the litter gouged its way along the forest path. Ratboy shivered. He couldn't be sure whether he was imagining it or not, but he thought there was a sickly sweet smell of rotting meat on the breeze, coming from Raphael's discoloured flesh.

The morning wore on and Ratboy's thoughts wandered onto less gruesome matters. Anna was riding a few horses ahead of him and each time she turned to give him an encouraging smile, he felt his stomach flip. Since talking to the duke she had regained a little of her straight-backed dignity and even seemed eager for the challenge ahead. Ratboy sensed that despite the horror of losing her matriarch and fellow sisters, there was still a mysterious strength in her. She fascinated him. Even riding alongside such strutting, feathered popinjays as Gryphius's captains, Ratboy found her simple white robe utterly hypnotic. He followed the cloth as it shifted up and down her pale, slender arms.

With a rush of shame, he noticed that Wolff was studying him intently. He smiled awkwardly at his master and returned his gaze to the road ahead.

There was a clatter of boots and hooves as the army crossed an old wooden bridge and left the shelter of the trees for a while, marching out across an expanse of wide, open grassland that stretched ahead of them for several miles. The musicians struck up a jaunty tune and danced around the marching troops, leaping up and down in the tall grass and trailing brightly coloured streamers behind them as they sang. As the hours wore on, Ratboy grew to hate their piping whistles and clanging bells. He glared at their painted, bestial masks, willing them to be silent, but their energy seemed boundless.

Gradually, the sun overtook the army and began to descend ahead of them, causing the soldiers to pull their helmets down a little lower over their faces and squint as they rode.

'What's this?' slurred Gryphius as a rider headed back towards him out of the sunset. The general's face was flushed from the previous night's drinking and as he leant forward in his saddle to see who was approaching, he clutched protectively at his bloated stomach.

The slender figure of Christoff made his way down the line of men with his chin lifted haughtily. It looked to Ratboy as though he imagined himself to be the Emperor himself, inspecting a trooping of the colour. He bowed almost imperceptibly to the general. 'Obermarshall,' he said, 'the scouts have spotted an abandoned farmhouse and they suggest it would make an ideal place to camp tonight. The owners have all been slaughtered, but not before they dug several trenches and fortified the outbuildings, so it will be easily defended.'

'Much good it did the previous occupants,' said Gryphius, trying to smile through his nausea. 'Very well, let's head for the farm.' He grabbed Christoff's puffed sleeve. 'Just make sure there's a reasonable meal waiting for me when I get there. No more of this northern rubbish. I want something with a little flavour, not another bucket of grey mud.'

Christoff tipped his plumed hat. 'Of course, Obermarshall.'

The army pitched its tents with the quick efficiency of men eager to get their heads down. As twilight fell over the old farm, Ratboy hunkered down next to a fire with the other servants, while Wolff and the general's captains pored over maps and discussed the impending battle. He stretched his aching limbs out across the grass with a groan of relief, and as he drifted off to sleep a strange jumble of images filled his head: Anna's delicate features morphed and decayed into Raphael's greying flesh, before being replaced by his master's flashing eyes, scowling down at him from a pulpit.

'SIGMAR'S BLOOD,' EXCLAIMED Gryphius, as he reined in his horse and looked down over the valley below. 'Is that an army or a nation?'

A silver thread of sunlight was just beginning to glimmer on the horizon and as the dawn light grew, it picked out tens of thousands of men, sprawled across the landscape, carpeting the fields as far as the eye could see in either direction. Pitched in the centre of the valley were a couple of command tents, but mostly the soldiers had just fallen where they stopped, sleeping in ditches and the hollows of trees.

Ratboy grimaced at the sight of the army. It marred the landscape like a dark, ugly scar. Severed heads dangled from their bloodstained banners and brutal, iron weapons lay scattered across the grass. A few of the soldiers were already beginning to rise; pouring filthy water over their greasy manes and flexing their fur-clad muscles as they looked across the fields towards the growing dawn.

'Down,' hissed Wolff, steering his horse back away from the brow of the hill and dismounting. 'A few more minutes and we'll be visible.'

The others followed suit, leading their horses back down the hill and then crawling back up to the hilltop to peer out through the tall grass at the marauders.

'That's it,' said Gryphius, grinning at his captains and pointing past Mormius's army to a tall, slender shape on the horizon. It was hard to see clearly in the half-light, but the general had no doubt as to the building's name. 'Mercy's End,' he hissed, drumming his fists against the ground like an excited child. 'It's the ruined castle that Lüneberg told us about. *That's* Ostland's final hope. And we're just in time to join arms with our northern brothers, before they make their last stand.' He turned to Wolff. 'We must strike now while the enemy are still rising. We could slaughter half of them in their sleep. It's all they deserve, the filthy blasphemers.'

Wolff shook his head. 'There are so many of them,' he muttered, clenching and unclenching his gauntleted hands as he looked down on the monstrous shapes. 'We'd never make it through them all.' He signalled for the others to crawl back down the hill. Once they were sure it was safe they climbed to their feet. Gryphius's captains all looked to Wolff for his guidance, a little unnerved by the brittle grin on their general's face.

'We've been very lucky, it's true,' said the priest. 'From what the duke said, this Mormius has been driving his men mercilessly for weeks without rest, but we've managed to arrive at the end of the one night they've been allowed to sleep.'

Gryphius drew his sword and held it aloft. 'I hear you, Brother Wolff. This is a unique chance. We'll take them all on. The people of Mercy's End will wake up to see a pile of corpses at their gates.'

Wolff grasped the general's arm and snarled at him. 'They outnumber us ten to one, Obermarshall, if not more. We'd never reach the citadel.'

'So what are you suggesting,' snapped Gryphius, freeing his arm and replying in a tone of haughty disdain. 'That we return to Castle Lüneberg and wait there to be slaughtered in our beds?'

'No,' replied Wolff. 'Mercy's End must endure, at least for a while, if Raukov's army is to stand any chance of halting this incursion.' He waved at the captains who were hanging on his every word. 'And an army such as yours could make all the difference, Obermarshall. But only if they aren't slaughtered before they reach the citadel.' He frowned. 'We need some kind of diversion.' He looked down the hillside at Gryphius's army, and beyond, to the ragged lines of flagellants, prostrating themselves before Raphael's corpse. 'I have an idea,' he said, and strode down the hill.

As THE SUN cleared the horizon, the flagellants descended on Mormius's army, pouring down from the hills like the end of the world.

Ratboy shook his head in wonder. The fury of their charge was breathtaking. He finally understood his master's respect for them. Raphael's cult had swelled beyond all recognition into a terrifying horde of willing martyrs. Their eyes burned with holy wrath as they ripped into the side of the sleeping army. Their screeched prayers echoed around the hills and their wiry, scarred limbs flailed up and down, hacking furiously at the confused marauders.

'Holy Sigmar,' muttered Ratboy, as he watched the carnage from the other end of the valley. 'They're going to slaughter the whole army.'

For a while it seemed he might be right. As the drowsy marauders lurched to their feet, scrabbling around for their discarded weapons and blowing their horns to raise the alarm, the flagellants tore through their ranks in a frenzy of righteous bloodlust. They wore no armour, but seemed mindless of the vicious weapons that lashed out at their naked flesh. Even from the safety of the hilltop, Ratboy found it hard to see such bloody passion heading towards him.

'What did you say to them?' asked Anna, with a note of disgust in her voice. She grimaced as the flagellants threw their naked selves into the melee, ripping at the marauders' faces with flails, clubs and broken, bloody fingernails. 'You've sent them to their deaths,' she muttered.

'We prayed together for a while,' said Wolff, ignoring the disapproval in her voice. 'And then I explained the truth of the situation.' He gestured to the litter behind them. Raphael's rotting corpse was lashed securely to the planks, which in turn were strapped to a pair of horses, in readiness for the charge ahead. 'There's only one chance that their prophet could reach the safety of Mercy's End, and it will require a great sacrifice on their part.' He rubbed his powerful jaw as he watched the shocking violence below. 'And sacrifice is the one thing they have no fear of.'

With a scrape of metal, the priest slid his great warhammer from his back and pointed it down at the battle. 'Feast your eyes on this scene, my friends. Fix it deep in your hearts for all eternity. You will never again see such a beautiful display of pure, unshackled faith.' As Raphael's followers bathed in the blood of their foes, Wolff crossed himself with the sign of the hammer and muttered a prayer for them. 'You're witnessing

Sigmar's legacy in all its unstoppable glory. These people have His blood in their veins and His strength in their hearts. While such devotion still exists, this blessed Empire will never fail.'

He turned towards Gryphius. 'Are your men ready, my lord? Our time is short. Their passion will only carry them so far. A few more minutes and the enemy will start to realise what a small force they're facing. Then things will be over very quickly.'

The general's eyes glistened with excitement as he fastened his winged helmet onto his head. He turned to his waiting army, arrayed on the hillside below. The yellow and black of their banners whipped gaily in the dawn light, and a thousand expectant faces looked back at him. 'Sons of Averland,' he cried, lifting his sword and turning his face to the sky. 'Ride for your life! Ride for the Empire! Ride for Sigmar!' With that he turned his horse and charged down the hill towards the enemy, screaming with fear and delight.

With a great thunder of hooves and armour, his troops charged after him.

'Stay close,' barked Wolff to Ratboy, as he snapped his reins and disappeared over the brow of the hill.

It was all Ratboy could do to cling desperately onto the reins of his horse as it careered wildly after the others. The general's quartermaster had buried him in armour way too big for his wiry frame: an oversized hauberk, a billowing yellow tabard and a helmet that immediately fell down over his eyes, leaving him blind and helpless as he plummeted towards the enemy.

He dared to loose a hand from the reins and lift his visor. The eyes of the surrounding horses were rolling with terror as the army plunged into the valley at incredible speed. The world rushed by in such a sickening blur that Ratboy thought he might lose his breakfast. Wolff was directly ahead, leading the charge with Gryphius, holding his hammer before him like a lance and bellowing commands as he went.

Where's Anna? wondered Ratboy suddenly, remembering that she had refused the offer of armour. He tried to look back, but it was too late. With a deafening crash, Gryphius's men slammed into the enemy troops.

Shreds of steel, teeth and bone exploded around them as they collided with the stunned marauders.

Ratboy clamped his legs tightly around his steed and ducked low in his saddle as violence erupted all around him. Horses fell and pieces of armour whistled past his face. A chorus of screams filled his ears, but in the chaos it was impossible to tell if they were war cries, or the howls of the dying.

As his horse's hooves drummed furiously beneath him, Ratboy tried to take in his surroundings. It was hard to be sure what was happening, but things seemed to be going to plan. The formation of the troops was still vaguely intact: pistoliers in the vanguard, followed by ranks of flamboyantly dressed knights and then, at the rear, the dark-skinned freelancers from Tilea. As Wolff intended, Mormius's soldiers had all been rushing towards the screaming fanatics, so this new attack had caught them unawares for a second time.

The Averlanders did not pause to press their advantage, however. They ploughed onwards at a furious pace. The plan was simple: race for the citadel; keep their heads down; pray for deliverance.

A succession of snarling faces flashed before Ratboy. They howled curses as they rushed by, barking at him in the thick, guttural language of the northern wastes. Their savage weapons clattered uselessly across his borrowed armour, but he felt far from heroic. A broadsword hung at his belt – another gift from Gryphius's armoury, but he couldn't bring himself to remove his hands from the horse's reins. Terror locked them to the leather straps. The noise and fury of the battle was like nothing he'd ever experienced. Fortunately, his steed was more experienced than its rider, pounding across the valley floor in an unwavering line and smashing straight through everything in its path.

He heard Wolff calling out from somewhere ahead. 'Raise the corpse,' he was crying, his voice already hoarse from shouting. 'Raise him up so his followers can see.'

Ratboy risked a glance up from his horse's neck and saw his master.

Wolff was still at the head of the charge, smashing through the thick press of bodies like a vision of Sigmar Himself. He was stood high in the stirrups, swinging his warhammer from left to right in great sweeping arcs, leaving a trail of splintered limbs and shattered armour in his wake. 'Sigmar absolves you,' he cried repeatedly, slamming his hammer into faces and shields with such force that his broad shoulders jolted back with the impact of each blow. Hastily fired arrows whirred towards him, clanging against his breastplate, but he rode on oblivious, dealing out

Sigmar's judgement with ten pounds of bloody, tempered steel. The priest vanished briefly behind a flash of claret, and Ratboy thought he had fallen; but then he reappeared, swinging again and again as his warhorse galloped towards the citadel.

Gryphius was next to him, laughing hysterically as he fired his flintlock pistol blindly into the rolling clouds of dust and gore that surrounded him. His wavering tenor rang out through the screams. 'For Averland! For the Emperor!'

Ratboy looked back over his shoulder and saw that they were already half way across the valley. We're going to make it, he thought with a rush of excitement. The ragged line of charging horses was unbroken. The vivid black and yellow banners had already cut a swathe right through the heart of the reeling marauders. The speed of the charge was so great that hardly a single knight had fallen. Most of the marauders were still busy with the frenzied figures at the other end of the valley. To Ratboy's amazement, he saw that dozens of the penitents were still hacking their way across the field. The fury of their attack had carried them almost to the command tents in the centre of the valley, but it looked as though their luck might soon run out. Mormius's army was finally on its feet, swirling like an ocean around the villagers; hungry for vengeance.

Hot, blood-slick hands snapped Ratboy's head back and his horse suddenly staggered under the weight of a second rider. Ratboy clasped desperately at his throat just in time to stop the blade that was shoved towards it. His hand split open like a ripe fruit and a thick torrent of blood pumped up over his face. He felt rancid breath on his ear and a steel-hard grip tightening around his neck. His attacker tried to draw the knife back for another attempt, but the blade locked between Ratboy's splintered finger bones. However furiously the knife's wielder wrenched at it, it would not come free.

The pain seemed remote and unreal. Ratboy knew he was seconds from death and clutched at his sword with his one good hand, swaying wildly in the saddle as he loosed the reins. He grasped the hilt of the weapon and began to slide it from his belt, but before he could use it, his assailant hurled him from the saddle and he slammed onto the rock-hard ground.

Agony stabbed into Ratboy's face as it crunched into the dry earth. He felt something click in his neck as the whole weight of his armoured body piled down on it. Instinct forced him to roll to one side, just in time to avoid the marauder's axe as it slammed into the ground beside him.

He lurched unsteadily to his feet, feeling as though his head was the size of a cart. His eyes were full of blood and the world swam wildly in and out focus, but he couldn't miss the figure striding towards him. It was the marauder who had destroyed his hand: a beetle-browed goliath, with a neck as thick as a tree and a great two-handed axe clutched in his meaty fingers. His scarred flesh was naked apart from a ragged loincloth and a battered iron helm topped with a long, curved tusk. 'Wolff,' gasped Ratboy, as he drew his sword to defend himself, 'help me.'

The marauder grinned down at his prey, revealing a mouthful of blackened stumps as he leant back and swung the axe at Ratboy's head.

Ratboy tried to block the blow, straining to lift his sword one-handed, but the marauder's taut, knotted muscles were the result of a lifetime devoted to war. The axe slammed the sword aside with such force that the impact made Ratboy howl. His forearms jangled with pain as the sword buckled and bounced from his grip. He staggered backwards and tumbled to the ground.

The grinning marauder advanced on him, drawing back his axe for another blow. Horses and soldiers screamed past, heedless of Ratboy's fate and he raised his hands feebly at the approaching warrior, horrified that no-one would even witness his death.

The marauder's head collapsed with a wet *crunch* as Wolff's hammer pounded into his face.

'Sigmar,' gasped the priest, dealing him another hammer-blow to the head, 'absolves you.'

The marauder swayed back on his heels and gave a bovine rumble of pain. Then he righted himself and grinned up at Wolf, snapping his nose back into place and laughing as he spat his few remaining teeth from his ruined mouth.

Wolff dropped from his horse and the two men circled each other, panting and looking for a chance to strike. There was little between them in bulk, but Ratboy could see that his master was exhausted. His breath was coming in short, hitching gasps and the joints of his armour were clogged with mud and gore.

The marauder saw a chance and swung for Wolff's legs.

The priest dodged the blow with surprising agility for such a large man, leaping high in the air and bringing his hammer down with a grunt. It thudded into the marauder's thigh and the warrior's femur disintegrated beneath the weight of the blow.

The marauder howled and fell to his knees, with vivid shards of bone erupting from beneath his leathery skin. His cry became a death croak, as a second hammer-blow knocked his head back, snapping his neck like kindling and killing him instantly. He thudded to the ground with a whistling sound, as a final breath slipped from his severed windpipe.

The momentum of Wolff's strike sent him staggering forwards into the fray and for a second, Ratboy lost sight of him. Then he lurched back towards him with a look of wild fury on his face. 'I told you to stay close,' he snapped, grabbing the whimpering acolyte's arm and wrenching him to his feet. 'You could've been hurt.'

More marauders were sprinting towards them as Wolff climbed back onto his horse and hauled Ratboy up behind him. He floored the nearest with a fierce blow to the side of his head, then charged after the Averlanders.

The pain in Ratboy's hand was growing quickly. He held it protectively to his chest, not daring to look at the damage.

'Obermarshall,' cried Wolff, banking his horse from left to right as they pursued the receding line of Empire troops. 'No!'

Ratboy strained to see around his master's bulky plate armour. He saw immediately that the situation had worsened. The Averlanders were still ploughing through the enemy at a fantastic pace, but the marauders were now massing around them in much greater numbers. Within the space of a few seconds he saw several of Gryphius's men torn from their saddles and dragged down into a fury of hacking, tearing blades. The Obermarshall's adjutant, Christoff was riding alongside Wolff when he suddenly jolted back in his saddle, clutching at his throat. He tumbled from view before Ratboy had chance to see what had killed him.

Then he saw Gryphius and understood Wolff's alarmed cry. The general had broken away from the main column and was veering off to the centre of the valley. Along with thirty or so of his men he was attempting to make a dash for Mormius's command tents. 'What's he doing?' he gasped into Wolff's ear.

'Risking everything,' grunted the priest, racing after the general. 'He's forgotten that Raphael's followers are just a decoy.' He pointed his hammer north towards a small bedraggled group, still tearing their way towards Mormius's tents. 'Gryphius thinks he can join them in beheading this invasion.' He drove his horse even harder. 'He's a damned fool, and he's going to lead his whole army to its death.'

Ratboy looked back and saw the truth of his master's words. The main column was already faltering and splitting in confusion. The soldiers didn't know whether to do as they were ordered – keep making for the citadel, or rally around their valiant general instead. As the Averlanders floundered, the marauders tore into them with renewed vigour. Howling obscenities as they dived into the confused rout.

'Obermarshall,' cried Wolff again, as they closed on the general. 'We *must* make for Mercy's End!'

The general looked back, his eyes bulging with passion and fear. 'We can take them, Wolff,' he called, blasting his flintlock into the face of another marauder. 'I know it! We can reach Mormius!'

The command tents were still several minutes' ride away, however, when the sheer volume of howling, spitting marauders slowed Gryphius and his captains to a canter. The general's battle cries took on a more desperate tone as the grotesque shapes pressed around him. The marauders here seemed even more corrupted and deformed than the others. Ratboy saw men with drooling mouths gaping in their chests, and gnarled, eyeless beaks where faces should have been. It was like descending into a nightmarish bestiary.

They had nearly reached Gryphius when the general flopped back in his saddle, clutching his side with a high-pitched yelp of pain. His horse spun in confusion and Ratboy saw the thick shaft of a spear embedded in Gryphius's side.

'Thank Sigmar,' muttered Wolff under his breath.

Gryphius's officers rallied round him, slashing frantically at the sea of blades surrounding their wounded general.

'Lead him back to the others,' bellowed Wolff, still racing towards them. As they neared the crowd around Gryphius, Ratboy saw the terror on the men's faces. They were completely encircled. However fiercely they swung their weapons, there was no way they could hack their way back to the main force. One by one the knights tumbled into the bristling mass of swords, as the marauders cut away the legs of their horses and pulled them down into the slaughter.

'Master,' cried Ratboy, as he saw that they too were completely hemmed in. Countless rows of marauders were swarming around them. 'We're trapped!'

Wolff planted his boot in the face of nearest marauder, grabbing a broadsword from his flailing hands as he toppled to the floor. 'I know,' he grunted, handing the weapon to Ratboy. 'Do something useful.'

As the misshapen figures reached out towards him, Ratboy lashed out with the crude weapon. Fear gave him strength and his blade was soon slick with blood as he hewed limbs and parried sword strikes. His mind grew blank as he fought. He was aware of nothing but the screaming pain in his muscles and his desperate desire for life. The odds were impossible though. Gradually the wall of vicious, barbed blades pressed in on them. For every marauder that fell, ten more leapt to take his place, each more fierce than the last.

Finally with an awful, braying scream, the horse's legs collapsed beneath it and Wolf and Ratboy crashed to the ground.

A tremendous roar of victory erupted from the marauders as they saw the priest drop from view.

Ratboy's sword flew from his grip as he rolled clear of the thrashing horse. He wrapped his trembling arms around his head and clamped his eyes shut, waiting to feel the cool bite of metal, slicing into his flesh.

Heat washed over him instead.

As Ratboy curled into a ball, gibbering incoherent nonsense to himself, he felt fire rush over him, shrivelling the hairs on his forearms and scorching his broken fingers. He looked up in confusion to see Wolff kneeling beside him, with his head lowered in prayer and his gauntleted hands resting calmly on the head of his warhammer. The light pouring from his flesh was so bright that Ratboy's eyes immediately filled with tears. He squinted into the incandescent halo and laughed in wonder. It was like looking into the sun, but he couldn't tear his eyes away. It was more beautiful than anything he had ever seen. Slowly, the nimbus of light expanded, washing over the confused marauders. As it touched their flesh they lit up like candles, blossoming in thick white flames that leapt from their skin and engulfed their flailing limbs. Their cheers of victory became wails of despair as their eyes exploded, bursting in their sockets with a series of audible pops.

Ratboy looked down at himself in dismay, expecting to see the flames covering his own body, but there was just a pleasant heat; no more painful than a fierce midday sun. Unlike daylight, though, this heat seemed to seep in through his pores, rushing through his veins and flooding his heart with passion. He leapt to his feet and flew at the stumbling, burning shapes; tearing into them with his broken fingers and howling in a voice he could barely recognise. As he kicked and thumped at the screaming marauders, a phrase came unbidden to his lips. The words were unfamiliar, but he howled them with such vehemence that his voice cracked. 'Every man hath heard of Sigmar,' he cried, grabbing a knife from the ground and thrusting it into bellies and faces. 'Every man hath learned to fear His blessed wrath.'

Ratboy gave himself completely to the animal rage and later, he found it difficult to say how long he had fought, or how many marauders he had butchered. It always chilled him to consider what might have happened if he had not been interrupted.

Wolff's calm voice brought him back. 'I think they've learned enough, for now,' said his master, placing a hand on his shoulder.

Ratboy lurched to a halt, looking down at his gore-splattered limbs in confusion. Then he turned to face the priest. Traces of the holy light were still streaming from his eyes and, as he smiled, it poured from between his teeth. All around them the ground was flattened and scorched, as though Sigmar had sent a comet to smite his foes. Ratboy tried to speak, but his voice was ruined and he could only emit a pitiful squeak.

Wolff nodded, as though he understood, then gestured to Gryphius's officers who were still circling around them. They were leading a riderless horse and as Wolff jogged towards it, he dragged Ratboy behind him. 'We don't have long,' he said, mounting the horse and lifting Ratboy up behind him.

Gryphius was slumped over the back of another knight's horse and as they raced back towards the main column of troops, Ratboy couldn't tell whether the general was alive or dead. Many of his men were clutching wounds of their own and swaying in their saddles, but as the marauders reeled from Wolff's holy fire, the Averlanders saw their one chance for escape and took it. Driving their exhausted horses forwards, through the charred remains, in a last, desperate charge.

The righteous fury that had washed over Ratboy gradually receded to reveal an impressive selection of pains. As he bounced weakly on the back of Wolff's horse, he realised that he was covered with dozens of cuts and grazes, but it was his left hand that worried him most of all: it was little more than a torn rag of glistening muscle and splintered bone. He gripped his master a little tighter as they left the radius of Wolff's blast and crashed back into a wall of living foes. The knights made no pretence of fighting, heading straight for the citadel in a desperate rout. Many of them dropped armour and swords as they charged, hoping to gain a little more speed over the final approach.

The ruin rose up ahead, so close Ratboy felt he could almost touch the figures watching eagerly from the battlements.

'Ride for your lives,' cried Wolff, raising his hammer and trying to drag a last burst of effort from the men. 'We're almost through.'

Ratboy looked back to see hundreds upon hundreds of marauders crossing the valley towards them. There was no sign of the flagellants, and he guessed Raphael's followers must have finally achieved the ultimate sacrifice in the name of their prophet. Raphael's corpse was gone too: dragged down to the killing floor along with the riders who carried it.

As he looked back over the desperate faces of the charging Averlanders, something caught Ratboy's eye.

Far across the valley, near the command tents, a flashing light glimmered though the early morning gloom; lifting slowly above the heads of the marauders and heading towards them. 'Master,' Ratboy croaked, but his ruined voice was lost beneath the thundering of the horses' hooves.

As the flickering shape moved towards them it picked up speed and after a few minutes Ratboy realised it was a man of some kind, covered in reflective, glassy armour and hurtling towards them with the powerful thrust of six colossal wings. Despite his fear, and the awful pain in his broken hand, Ratboy felt anger well up in him. This creature was responsible for everything; this was the reason for the slaughter at Ruckendorf and Gotburg and Castle Lüneberg; this was the fiend behind the deaths of Anna's sisters.

At the thought of Anna, Ratboy gasped. Where was she? He looked around at the riders on either side of him. She was nowhere to be seen and Ratboy's anger grew all the more as he looked back at the winged figure racing towards them.

Ragged cheers broke out ahead, as they neared the crumbling walls of Mercy's End. He turned away from the flashing figure and saw the marauders on both sides falling to their knees, pierced with dozens of black and white tipped arrows. Archers had lined the walls of the keep in their hundreds, firing great banks of arrows over the heads of the Averlanders as the towering castle gates began to slowly open.

The pain of Ratboy's countless wounds finally began to overcome him. The last vestiges of Wolff's light slipped from his throat in a tired groan as his head lolled forward against the priest's back. He was vaguely aware that up ahead hooves were clattering against cobbles, rather than blood-soaked earth, but before Wolff's horse had reached the gate, Ratboy's strength left him. He loosed his grip on Wolff's back, slid down towards the rushing ground and knew no more.

CHAPTER EIGHT
UNWELCOME GUESTS

THE SOUND OF approaching horses dragged Casper von Lüneberg from the relative warmth of his bed. He cursed as he shuffled across the bitterly cold bedchamber. 'I told them to leave me be,' he muttered, draping blankets over his royal robes as he descended the winding stairs to the great hall. 'I can't help you now,' he called out, assuming that some of his servants must have returned. Several days' worth of stubble had softened his angular features and his unwashed hair sprouted from his woolly cocoon like a collection of strange antennae. As he entered the hall, it was only the flashes of gold on his fingers that distinguished him from any other deranged refugee.

He paused on the threshold and tilted his head to one side, listening to the sound of the hooves crossing his courtyard. 'Two horses,' he said. 'Warhorses.' He stepped up to one of the broken windows and grimaced into the icy blast. 'Who's there?' he called out. 'Lüneberg is dead. There's no one here but us ghosts.'

There was no reply, but the duke heard the men dismount, drop to the ground and tether their horses. There was a clatter of metal falling to the cobbles and a furious voice rang out. 'Adelman, you oaf, be careful with that.'

A vague premonition of danger tingled in the duke's mind. There was something in the sharp, stentorian voice that worried him. 'What does it matter,' he said, with a shrug, but his words didn't quite ring true. Despite himself, Lüneberg felt a sudden lust for life. He stumbled back into the hall, grasping at chairs and walls for support.

He heard the sound of the strangers' boots as they entered the inner keep and pounded up the stairs towards him. Hearing the approach of his executioners was altogether different from picturing his death as something remote and abstract. The duke began muttering under his breath. 'Where did I leave my sword,' he said, patting the surface of the long table that divided the room. 'There must be something in here.' His fingers touched upon a variety of useless objects: cups, bowls, spoons but nothing he could use as a weapon. 'It's next to my bed,' he said, heading for the door, but as he rushed across the hall, he stumbled on a broken fiddle and fell heavily to the floor. He tried to lift himself, but couldn't seem to catch his breath.

The door flew open with a loud bang and footsteps rushed towards him. 'My lord,' cried the voice he had heard outside, 'are you injured? Adelman, help him up.'

A pair of enormous, rough hands grasped the duke, lifted him to his feet and placed him on a chair.

'Who are you?' he gasped, still struggling for breath.

'Otto Sürman, Templar of Sigmar,' replied the voice, twisting itself into a gentle croon. 'Do I have the honour of meeting Duke Casper von Lüneberg?'

The duke gripped his knees and hitched his shoulders up and down as he grabbed a few short breaths. 'Yes,' he managed to exclaim after a few minutes, 'I'm Casper von Lüneberg.' He gave a grim laugh. 'But as far as the dukedom is concerned, I fear I may be in dereliction of my duties.'

There was a pause, and the duke assumed his guests were looking around at the ruined tapestries and broken furniture.

'We saw bodies in the village, duke. Was this the work of the same Chaos force that laid waste to Strendel and Wurdorf? The marauders heading for Wolfenberg?'

Lüneberg shrugged. 'There is some kind of *thing* leading them, named Mormius. He didn't have much time to discuss tactics with me, but yes, I believe he was headed for the capital. Mercy's End still blocks their way, but I doubt it will be much of an obstacle. I've never seen such an army.'

'Mercy's End?'

The duke thrust his head towards his interrogator, as though willing his severed optical nerves back into life. 'What are you doing here? There's nothing here for you, or your god. Whichever one you profess to serve. I'm through with creeds and wars and stratagems. You can expect no help from me.' He sneered. 'I gave everything for this Empire and it spat me out like a rotten fruit.'

The duke felt a gentle hand on his, as the crooning voice replied. 'My lord, we require no help. Far from it – I simply wished to enquire after a friend of mine.'

'Which friend?'

'A priestess of Shallya, who goes by the name of Anna Fleck. I believe she's travelling in the company of one of my brethren – a warrior priest named Jakob Wolff.'

The duke blushed and shook his head, embarrassed by the harshness of his words. 'You must forgive my rudeness, Brother Sürman, I didn't realise. Any friend of that woman is a friend of mine.'

'No forgiveness needed, duke. We live in dangerous times. It's wise to be wary of strangers.'

Lüneberg heard the scraping sound of a chair being pulled alongside his, and when the soft voice spoke again, it was so close he could feel the priest's breath on his ear. 'Are you a good friend of Anna then, duke?'

The duke smiled as he remembered his encounter with the priestess. 'It seems strange to say it, after such a brief acquaintance, but yes, I feel as though I know her very well.' He leant back in his chair. 'She's of a kind though, I suppose. There are those who destroy and those who create, and I fear Anna's breed are in the minority.'

'I think I understand you, duke.' There was a slight urgency in Sürman's voice as he asked his next question. 'Is she here?'

'Oh, no, I'm afraid not, Brother Sürman. She left with Gryphius's army, two days past. She has no intention of fighting, though. They couldn't even get her to wear armour.' The duke's smile slipped from his face. 'She hopes to bring a little love to this wounded land, but I fear she might be too late for that.'

'I see. And where did Gryphius plan to go from here? South?'

The duke gave a hollow laugh. 'South? You don't know Hugo von Gryphius. He's heard that the whole weight of the Chaos realm is pressing down on Mercy's End, so he wants to be there when the hammer falls. He intends to throw in his lot with those poor, doomed souls.'

'And Anna went with him?'

'Yes, along with the warrior priest and his acolyte.'

Sürman fell silent as he considered Lüneberg's words and for a few minutes the only sound was the duke's laboured breathing.

'Tell me, duke,' said Sürman eventually, 'what happened to your eyes?'

The duke placed a protective hand over the stained bandage. 'The thing called Mormius didn't approve of my reading habits.' He shrugged. 'I'm not sure what he is, exactly, but he's indulged in the worst kind of occultism and I think it's sent him mad. His whole body has been transformed by depravity, so I suppose it makes sense that it would have warped his mind too. He has six, huge wings sprouting from his back and eyes that could flay the skin from your bones.' He shuddered at the memory. 'He treated me quite politely at first, but when I commented on his obvious heresy, he became completely unhinged.'

'So, not only did this daemonic entity enter your castle,' asked Sürman, with a slight tremor in his voice. 'You spoke with it, too?'

The duke nodded and hugged himself, suddenly remembering the cold. He waited for Sürman to continue speaking, but no words came. Instead, he felt the priest rise from the chair and step away. There was a low muttering sound as Sürman spoke to his companion, then a brief click of metal against metal.

'Tell me, duke,' said Sürman, from somewhere behind him, 'why did this child of the Old Night allow you to live?' The gentle croon had vanished, to be replaced with a contemptuous sneer. 'What perverted bargain did you make to buy your freedom?'

'Bargain? What are you talking–' The duke cut himself short with a wry laugh. 'Oh. Of course. I see.' He laughed a little harder and shook his head in disbelief. 'So this is how it finishes. What a pitiful end to a farcical life.'

'It is to the merciful justice of Sigmar that I commit you, servant of the Ruinous Powers,' replied Sürman. 'May your soul–'

'Don't waste any more of my time, you pathetic dupe,' snapped Lüneberg. 'Do whatever you imagine you must, but please don't make me listen to that puerile dogma.'

The duke barely noticed the pistol as it was pressed to the back of his head. He was already far away, in a

country of golden, rolling fields and unstained friendship. 'Hugo, old friend,' he breathed, 'forgive me.'

By the time the gunshot had echoed once around
the empty hall, Lüneberg was dead.

CHAPTER NINE
MEN OF OSTLAND

THE DARKNESS WAS all encompassing. It cradled Ratboy, caressing his damaged flesh like swaddling and easing him towards oblivion. Brutal memories tried to pierce the gloom and it was his own brutality that haunted him most of all. But for every glimpse of frenzied hands and pulsing viscera, another wave of blackness came, dragging him further and further down.

A voice interrupted his descent. 'Ratboy,' it called. The sound of his own name reminded him again of his bloody deeds and jolted him back up from the abyss. 'Stay with us.'

The soft, familiar tones gave Ratboy another memory: a brief glimpse of sunlight beside a quick, winding stream and a woman's eyes, looking into his with unashamed affection. Suddenly the darkness seemed a little less enticing.

'Try and drink this,' said the voice and he felt a cup pressed gently against his mouth, moistening his lips with warm, aromatic liquid.

He swallowed a little of the drink and opened his eyes.

For a while he only registered Anna's face, leaning over his and lit up with a broad grin. Her ivory skin was bruised and scratched, and he could see faint worry lines at the corners of her eyes that he suspected had not been there just a few short weeks ago. Her hair had grown back as a halo of glinting stubble and she had tears of relief in her eyes.

'You're alive,' he muttered.

Anna burst into laughter and leant away from him. '*I'm* alive? You're the one who vanished just as we reached our destination.' She gestured to his tightly bandaged hand. 'And you're the one who decided to grab the wrong end of a knife.'

Ratboy's nose wrinkled as he noticed a strong smell of manure. He looked around at his surroundings. He was lying on a bed of straw in the corner of a stable, surrounded by a forest of horses' legs and piles of dung.

'It was the warmest place we could find,' laughed Anna, noticing his look of disgust. 'Most of this place fell down centuries ago, but the horses do quite nicely for themselves.'

'Where's Brother Wolff?'

'Recovering, I imagine. After he rescued you, he seemed quite overcome with exhaustion. He'd barely dragged you through the gates when he collapsed. I'm not sure what he did out there – that awful light that came down on him seemed to melt flesh from men's bones.' Her eyes widened with horror at the memory of it. 'He suffered horribly for it afterwards though. His face was greyer than Raphael's corpse. I didn't think he would survive.' She gave Ratboy another sip of the tea and smiled at him as he gulped it down.

Ratboy struggled up into a sitting position with a look of concern on his face. 'So, is he asleep still? Has he recovered from his exhaustion?'

Anna pressed him gently back onto the straw. 'Don't alarm yourself. He's awake and talking to Captain Felhamer – the officer in charge of this place.' She grimaced. 'Well, I say "in charge", but the captain has quite a few egos to contend with. Everyone in here seems to have some ridiculous, vainglorious title: Kompmeister or Kriegswarden or something else that justifies their pompousness. And they all think they should be making the big tactical decisions.'

'But what of the enemy?' Ratboy's eyes grew wide with fear. 'I saw a shape pursuing us. A creature, that flew at the head of the marauders.'

Anna nodded. 'Yes, you saw the thing the duke referred to as Mormius. He said it's some kind of daemon spawn.' Her cool, grey eyes clouded over. 'It's Mormius who murdered Sister Gundram, my matriarch. And he massacred Lüneberg's men. He's the one leading the enemy against us.'

'Then are we under attack?'

'Not yet.' Anna looked at Ratboy's bandaged hand. 'It seems that our ill-advised charge may have bought Captain Felhamer and his men a little time. They were expecting the assault to begin this morning, but between us and the penitents, we left the enemy quite disconcerted.' She sighed. 'It's the briefest of respites though. Wolff and Felhamer both expect them to strike at nightfall.'

Ratboy frowned, still trying to piece together his memories of the morning's events. 'Why did you call the charge "ill-advised"? We made it to Mercy's End, didn't we?'

Anna hesitated before replying. 'Well, yes, or at least *some* of us did.' She smoothed down her white robes and looked at her long, delicate fingers. 'The Obermarshall confused things greatly by attempting to reach the flagellants. Barely half of his men reached the citadel and few of them are without injuries.' She frowned. 'And of course, every single one of the villagers from Gotburg was butchered. Just as your master knew they would be when he sent them into battle.'

Ratboy blushed at her angry tone. 'They had chosen their path before they even met Master Wolff.'

Anna shook her head, but seemed unwilling to argue the point.

'And what of the Obermarshall himself?'

Anna shook her head again. 'I've done as much as I can for him, but I couldn't remove the weapon from his side without risking more damage.' As her eyes met Ratboy's, they were full of regret. 'The most I could do was remove some of the spear and bandage the rest up. I don't expect him to see the morning.'

Ratboy nodded and fell silent. He recalled the frenzy that took hold of him during the battle and shuddered. He looked down at his chest and saw that his borrowed yellow tabard was torn and dark with blood.

Anna followed his gaze and gave him an odd, forced smile. 'Your master was pleased with your bravery. He feels that your determination did you credit.'

Ratboy closed his eyes, trying to rid himself of the awful images that plagued him. 'I'm not sure it was determination as such,' he said. 'The light that came from Brother Wolff seemed to change me. And there was so much blood everywhere, I lost track of things.' He grimaced. 'I wasn't myself.'

Anna raised her eyebrows. 'If you wish to follow in Wolff's footsteps, you'll need to accept such violence.' She shook her head. 'It's not the path I would've chosen, but the life of a warrior priest is full of such horrors. It's a path of pain, as well as prayer.'

'Of course,' replied Ratboy, a little indignantly. 'I'm not quite as naïve as you imagine, sister. My master has trained me in the martial arts as carefully as the holy texts. It's just that...' his voice trailed away and he looked down at his blood-caked hands in confusion. 'I didn't expect to find it so enjoyable.'

He looked up in time to catch the horrified expression on Anna's face. 'My motives were pure,' he said, grabbing her hand and willing her to understand. 'For a while, I felt as though I could tear down all the evil in this world. Pull it apart with my bare hands. I wanted to rip the corruption from the heart of the Empire. And as my master's light surrounded me, it seemed as though I finally could. Finally make a difference.' He shrugged, embarrassed by the passion in his voice. 'That's all I meant by enjoyable.'

She gave a stiff nod and withdrew her hand. 'Yes. I understand. I've heard such sentiments before.' She looked down at him with a smile that did not reach her eyes. 'Your master has trained you perfectly. You're already beginning to sound like him. I've no doubt that you'll make a fierce defender of the Sigmarite faith.' She rose to her feet. 'I must inform Wolff that his brave protégé is awake.'

Ratboy watched Anna's slender form as it slipped away between the restless horses. Her tone had sounded more accusatory than praising and he felt a sinking feeling in his stomach. 'Sigmar,' he muttered, looking down at the bloody lump that had once been his left hand. 'What a mess.'

DESPITE ITS CRUMBLING masonry and broken rafters, the central hall at Mercy's End was a beautiful sight. A high, vaulted ceiling reached up over a broad, circular chamber that managed to be imposing, yet light and airy at the same time, thanks to a series of tall, stained glass windows that flooded the room with coloured light. As Ratboy entered, he kept his eyes focussed respectfully on the floor, noticing that every polished flagstone was inlaid with glittering images of twin-tailed comets and the Ghal Maraz.

At the centre of the chamber was a round stone table and as he approached it Wolff rose to greet him, gesturing to the one empty chair.

'Tell us what you saw,' said the priest, placing his hand on Ratboy's shoulder, 'as we were approaching the gates.'

Ratboy looked up from the table and felt his tongue freeze in his mouth. A circle of regal, patrician faces surrounded him, and from the elaborately waxed beards and furrowed brows, he took them to be generals and captains of the highest rank. Their clothes were uniformly bloodstained and torn, but it was obvious from their thick, velvet doublets and intricately worked hauberks that they were great leaders. All of them had seen better days though. Their faces were lined with exhaustion and several of them carried fresh scars.

With a shock of recognition, Ratboy realised that one of the men was Gryphius. The Obermarshall's olive skin had drained to a sickly greenish hue and his face was contorted with pain. He nodded vaguely at Ratboy, but there was no trace of his habitual grin.

'Well, um,' Ratboy stammered, unnerved by the dramatic change in the general, 'I can't recall exactly, but–'

'What's that he says?' bellowed a silver-haired old brute, with a fierce, bristling beard and red, rheumy eyes. 'Tell him to speak up, priest.'

'I said, I can't remember too clearly,' said Ratboy, raising his voice a little. 'But I know I saw a winged creature of some kind, flying after us.'

'Winged, did he say?' barked the old soldier, looking around furiously for confirmation.

'Yes, Oswald,' snapped the man to his right – a handsome youth with short-cropped blond hair and piercing blue eyes. 'And maybe if you bite your fat old tongue for a second, he might be able to say a little more.'

The small patches of Oswald's skin that weren't covered by beard flushed red and he leapt to his feet, thrusting forward a barrel chest as broad as a shire horse. 'You're not the Elector Count just yet, Captain Felhamer,' he yelled, glowering down at the younger man. 'And it wouldn't harm you to show a little respect to your elders.'

Wolff raised a hand and all eyes immediately turned towards him. 'Gentlemen,' he said quietly, 'we don't have much time.'

Oswald continued to scowl at Captain Felhamer.

'Apologies, Marshall,' said the captain with a shrug, 'I meant no offence. Please, take your seat and let's hear what the boy has to say.'

The old soldier gave a snort of disgust and dropped heavily back into his chair.

'Please,' said the young captain, gesturing for Ratboy to continue.

'Well, that was it really. I saw a winged figure and he seemed to be made of silver, or glass, or something shiny at least. I believe it was the thing that Duke Lüneberg called Mormius.'

A babble of voices erupted around the table, as the officers turned to each other and began talking urgently.

'Gentlemen,' said Wolff, raising his hand again, and silence descended over the chamber once more. The priest turned to Ratboy. 'Did you see anything else?'

Ratboy looked down at the table's scratched stone and frowned. 'Well, I passed out soon after I saw him. But I recall that he was surrounded by soldiers who seemed larger than the others, and some that weren't even human.' Ratboy looked up at his master with fear in his eyes. 'They had so many limbs and mouths, and they scrabbled along the ground like spiders. I...' his voice trailed off as he recalled the full horror of what he saw. 'And there were other shapes following him, that were even more monstrous.' He shook his head. 'They were the size of trees.' His voice became shrill at the memory. 'They were twice the size of the marauders and they carried great clubs and axes.' He grabbed Wolff's sleeve and looked desperately at him. 'They were eating corpses as they marched.'

The man sat next to Ratboy whistled through his teeth. 'Ogres of some kind then,' he said, looking around the table. 'This is going to be some night.'

'The whole thing is madness,' cried another officer. 'We're all going to be butchered. Why aren't we pulling back to Wolfenberg, while there's still time?'

'Diterich is right,' cried a sharp-featured, beak-nosed man, wearing a monocle. He slammed his gauntleted hand down on the stone table. 'Why make a useless sacrifice of ourselves here? There's no way we can make an adequate defence of this ruin.'

'There was something else,' said Ratboy, closing his eyes in concentration.

The soldiers fell silent and waited for him to continue.

'Just before I passed out I noticed something strange about Mormius.' He opened his eyes and looked up at Wolff with excitement. 'He was injured. His right arm was all shrivelled. It looked as though there was a kind of black acid eating through his armour – stretching out like veins from his hand.' Ratboy looked down at his own bloody fingers. 'Like there was some kind of disease, or poison eating him up.'

'Tannhauser!' cried Captain Felhamer, leaping to his feet and clenching his fists with excitement. 'Maybe he reached him after all? The boy might have seen the effects of his poison. Sigmar's Blood, this could be our chance!' There was a cobalt fire burning in his eyes as he looked round the table. 'If we leave Mercy's End now they'll hunt us like rats – ripping us apart before we've gotten a mile from this valley. Our only chance is to make a stand here. If the boy's right, Mormius could be on the verge of death. Tannhauser could have reached him somehow.'

Wolff shook his head. 'Tannhauser?'

'One of my bravest captains,' replied Felhamer, his eyes bulging with passion. 'The marauders butchered his regiment as they slept, and it sent him half mad with grief. Several days ago he set out to avenge them. I tried to stop him, but he wouldn't listen.' Felhamer gave a short laugh. 'To be honest, I cursed his name at the time. Some of my best knights left with him. There was no hope of success, but he was inconsolable. He wanted to join the fight for the northern garrisons so he could try to get close to Mormius. He said he had a ring filled with some kind of poison. I thought he was raving, but from what your acolyte has described, I think he may have achieved his goal.' Felhamer laughed again. 'He was a very unusual man, Captain Tannhauser. I think I may have underestimated him.'

'But what does it matter?' cried Oswald. 'We've gathered every last vestige of our strength into one convenient slaughterhouse. Even if you're right about this lunatic, Tannhauser, which I doubt very much, the marauders have ten times our numbers. Mormius or not, we can't win here. We should be splitting our forces and choosing battlegrounds more suited to our strengths. That's the only way we can save Ostland from destruction.'

'The marauders annihilated the northern regions in a matter of days,' replied Felhamer, levelling a trembling finger at the northern wall of the chamber. 'If they're left to march any further south, there'll be nothing left to save.' He dropped back into his chair, with a despondent sigh. 'We have to hold them here for as long as we can and give the Elector Count time to bring the battle away from Wolfenberg. I have orders from von Raukov himself, requesting me to do just that.'

'So we're a sacrifice, is that it?' cried Oswald, looking at the other soldiers with an incredulous expression on his face. 'Is that all von Raukov thinks we're worth? A minor distraction, to give him time to polish his armour and rehearse his victory speech?' He drew his sword and slammed it down on the table with a clatter that echoed around the vaulted ceiling. 'I came to fight, not play games. If we stay here, we're as good as dead.'

There was murmur of disgruntled voices around the table, and most of them seemed in agreement with Oswald. Ratboy looked at his master apologetically, feeling that he was responsible for the discord.

Wolff rose from his chair with a slow majesty that silenced the debate. The light from the stained glass windows played across the iron band on his shaven head as he nodded slowly in agreement. 'It's true,' he said, 'that if you stay here and fight, it's likely you will die; if you flee, however, it's certain.' He tapped his ironclad finger against the brass hammer on his gorget. 'But, more than that, if you flee, you will have betrayed your faith, your families and your emperor.' His eyes flashed dangerously beneath his heavy brow as he looked around the table. He strode across the chamber and when he reached the nearest pillar he slammed his fist into it. The officers jumped in surprise as a cloud of dust exploded around Wolff's gauntlet. 'This is good Ostland stone,' he said. 'A little old maybe, like the rest of us, but good nonetheless. Don't let those horrors soil one blessed inch of it.' He looked directly at Oswald. 'Those afraid to give their lives in the name of Sigmar are free to leave, but I have a suspicion Ostland ran out of cowards a long time ago.'

There was a ripple of nervous laughter and even Oswald smiled, nodding in agreement as he sheathed his sword. 'It's true,' he said, 'Ostland *isn't* the easiest place to grow a few ears of corn.'

Shoulders visibly relaxed and hands were loosed from sword hilts as the tension around the room dissipated.

Wolff looked up at the crumbling masonry. 'Life is fleeting. We inhabit a tiny sliver of existence, surrounded on all sides by an endless void. We only have one chance to make a difference. One chance before we return to the endless night. Death today, or death tomorrow, what does it matter if we don't lead a life worth living?' He lifted his warhammer up into one of the shafts of light and slowly rotated it, scattering jewels of colour across the walls of the chamber and into the faces of the assembled officers. 'You're Sigmar's heirs. No one in this room was ever destined to eke out their days in a sick bed. We are the elect few, chosen for hardship and greatness. Whether it's today, or next year, your end will be glorious and godlike. And if this is your day to die, then by Sigmar make it a good day!'

Ratboy's heart swelled at his master's words and he noticed several of the officers nodding eagerly in agreement.

'I hear you, priest,' replied the beak-nosed officer, 'but your words might carry a little more weight if your friend Gryphius hadn't told me that you yourself are planning to flee south at the first opportunity.'

Captain Felhamer looked at Wolff in dismay. 'Is that true?' he asked.

Wolff nodded and returned to his seat. There was no trace of shame or embarrassment on his face as he replied. 'Yes,' he said. 'It's true. I must leave tonight.'

'Why?' cried the beak-nosed man, glaring incredulously through his monocle. 'We have need of you here. How can you advise us to hold this pile of rubble, when you yourself will not even stay to help?'

Wolff returned the officer's glare with a calm nod. 'I understand your concern, Marshall Meinrich, but I assure you, I would rather meet my end here, covered in glory, than pursue the miserable errand that waits me.'

Captain Felhamer rose to his feet, his pale cheeks flushed with colour. 'But Brother Wolff, after what you've just said, what could be more important than helping us defend Mercy's End?'

'I'll help all I can,' replied Wolff. 'There are things I can do before I leave.' He ran a hand over his shaven head and closed his eyes. 'I have a little strength left. I'll pray with your men and bless them. And I'll join you in the initial defence.' He opened his eyes and looked Felhamer in the eye. 'But I cannot neglect my duty.'

'At least tell us *why* you won't stay and fight,' said the old, bearded man, named Oswald.

'There's a traitor marching with von Raukov's army,' Wolff explained. 'He's a worshipper of the Dark Gods, named Fabian. He's a murderer and a heretic and a threat to the whole war effort. He must be stopped before he can achieve whatever perverted end he has in mind. And I'm the one person in all Ostland who could recognise him.' The priest gave a long sigh. 'He's my brother.'

Silence greeted Wolff's admission as the officers considered how exactly Wolff might stop his brother.

'If I stay here and fight,' the priest continued, 'I may be of some use to you. But in the meantime, Fabian will be free to wreak havoc on von Raukov's army. I haven't seen my brother for decades. I don't even know what name he will be using now. Who knows how high he has risen through the ranks. He may even be close to the Elector Count himself. Close enough to assassinate him maybe.' Wolff looked around the table. 'We could give our lives holding Mercy's End, only to find that von Raukov's army has been devoured from the inside.'

Felhamer shook his head and looked down at the table in despair. 'Then you must abandon us to our fate.'

'No one here is abandoned!' Wolff cried, slamming his fist against his breastplate. 'Sigmar is here, in our hearts and our swords. A priest is just a touchstone. A conduit. You don't need me to lead you. There will be a warrior god marching by your side.'

A small voice piped up from next to the Wolff. 'It's true,' said Ratboy, looking up at his master and nodding. 'This morning, during the battle, I was sure everything was lost: my hand was ruined; the enemy were all around us; but something carried me through it. I felt Sigmar, guiding me.' He laughed and looked around at the officers. 'I had no weapon and the marauders towered over me, but I still took them.' He gave a fierce grin. 'I tore them apart.'

Von Gryphius rocked back in his chair and gave a weak snort of laughter. For a brief moment his old, playful smile returned. 'If a one handed, unarmed child can fight these pigs, then I don't see what you're all so afraid of.' He climbed slowly to his feet, wincing with pain, and lifted his rapier over the table. 'Priest or not, I make my stand here. Are you all with me?'

For a few seconds there was no response. Ratboy noticed the monocled officer was studying him closely; taking in his scrawny frame and tattered, stained clothes. Finally, the man climbed to his feet, drew his broadsword and held it out over the table, so that the tip clattered against von Gryphius's sword. 'Forgive me, captain,' he said, turning to Felhamer. 'I forgot myself. It shouldn't have taken the bravery of a child to remind me of my duty, but if you'll still have me, I'd be honoured to die by your side.'

One by one the other soldiers stood and drew their weapons, creating a canopy of battered steel over the old table.

Captain Felhamer's handsome face cracked into a broad grin and his blue eyes sparkled victoriously. 'Let this Mormius make his move,' he said, rising to his feet and clanging his sword on top of the others. 'There's life in these old stones yet.'

CHAPTER TEN
MERCY'S END

As Wolff climbed up onto the ramparts, all eyes were on him. Felhamer had gathered over two thousand men beneath his banner; only a fraction of the numbers arrayed against them, but a glorious sight nonetheless. Archers, spearmen, handgunners, greatswords and engineers stood side by side with battle-hardened militiamen and stony-faced villagers, who gripped their clubs and spears firmly, despite the fear written across their faces. From high above their plumed helmets the stubborn bull of Ostland glowered down expectantly, emblazoned across a dozen rippling flags.

As Wolff reached the top step, the soldiers nearest to him dropped on one knee and lowered their heads in genuflection. The priest placed his right hand on their shoulders, muttered a quick prayer from the book held in his left hand and then strode on. As he walked along the castle wall the scene was repeated again and again, and as each of the soldiers climbed back to their feet, the fear vanished from their eyes; replaced with the fierce light of hope. As Ratboy followed behind his master, carrying his hammer for him as he blessed the troops, he recognised the light as the same force that had earlier driven him to such frenzy. He both envied and pitied the men as they crowded around his master, desperate for the touch of his hand. Many held out their swords and spears and Wolff placed a hand on every weapon that was passed his way.

As they made their way around the castle wall, Ratboy looked out over the battlements, down into the valley below. It was now mid afternoon and there was no hiding the size of the army moving towards them. The attack had already begun, he realised with a jolt. Countless rows of bare-chested northmen, were running towards the castle with shields over their heads and ladders under their arms. As Wolff continued, the captains on the wall signalled for the archers to take their positions, but Ratboy could not help wondering if they had enough arrows to take down so many men. It looked like there was a whole ocean of jagged metal and scorched wood rushing towards them. Why don't they shoot? he wondered, as the marauders raced closer and closer. They must be in range by now.

Captain Felhamer was perched at the top of a bell tower that looked down over the wall, and as the charging marauders approached, the sergeants all watched for his signal. His hand was raised above his head, ready to launch the defence, but as the marauders sprinted across the bloody ground towards the castle, he kept his hand aloft, as though waiting for some invisible sign. Finally, as the enemy were almost at the castle gates, he brought his hand down in a cutting motion.

Ratboy immediately saw the reason for his delay.

The earth around the castle collapsed with an immense explosion of mud; disappearing from beneath the feet of the charging marauders with a booming groan of collapsing boards. They toppled in their hundreds down into a broad trench, letting go of their shields as they crashed helplessly onto a bed of thick, wooden stakes. As the marauders screamed and howled with rage and panic, the archers finally launched their first volley from the castle walls.

'It's the old moat,' cried Ratboy. 'They'd hidden it!'

Wolff took a break from his prayers, to give his acolyte a short nod. 'Captain Felhamer has been preparing this wreck for weeks. I believe he has quite a few such tricks up his sleeve.'

Banks of arrows arced down into the writhing mass of stranded, thrashing figures. The dazed marauders tried to crawl back out of the moat, but the archers fired with incredible speed and accuracy, loosing arrow after arrow into the river of flailing limbs. The moat quickly became clogged with the dying and the dead.

The enemy were charging forward in such massive numbers, that the men further back had no idea what had happened at the foot of the castle wall. Waves of them rushed unwittingly towards the trench. As the first group tried to clamber back to safety, their comrades crashed into them from the other direction and the crush of bodies, spears and ladders all tumbled down into the moat, to the cheers of Felhamer's archers.

Ratboy looked down on the confusion in amazement. The scene quickly took on the appearance of a slaughterhouse as the moat filled up with broken weapons and bodies. Despite their aching arms the archers kept up the furious pace and it seemed as though the whole army was going to pour into Felhamer's trap.

Finally, Mormius saw what was happening and horns began to sound along the enemy lines, calling a retreat. The warriors nearest the castle were so enraged by the waves of arrows, that they continued trying to reach the walls, clambering over the mounds of skewered corpses and slamming their ladders against the old stone. A few of them even managed to start scrambling up towards the archers, but before they had climbed even a few feet, Felhamer brought down his hand a second time and barrels of hot oil poured down from the embrasures, sending the marauders screaming and gambolling to their deaths.

The horns continued to blow, but the northmen were now so consumed by rage and bloodlust that many of them broke ranks and continued ploughing forwards through the mayhem. The charge quickly became a directionless rout and still the endless clouds of arrows rained down on them.

Finally, Wolff blessed the last soldier in the line and turned to stand beside Ratboy. They both looked down on the massacre below. 'Barbarians,' the priest muttered, shaking his head in disgust. 'If only all our enemies were so undisciplined.' He held his hand up to shield his eyes against the light and then cried out in alarm. 'Down!' he yelled, throwing Ratboy to the ground as a cloud of arrows whirred angrily over their heads.

All along the wall, soldiers howled in pain as the enemy's arrows found their mark. Dozens of men tumbled back from the wall, spinning down towards the courtyard below, or dropping to their knees and clutching at pierced throats and chests.

Ratboy looked up at the crumbling bell tower. Felhamer and the other officers had vanished from view and he prayed they had ducked in time. His fears were quickly allayed. As the clouds of enemy arrows dropped away, Felhamer rose up and held his two-handed sword aloft, signalling for his archers to return fire.

Ratboy peered out through a loophole and saw that the marauders were finally backing away from the trench and staggering towards their own lines. Before they had got very far, the Empire archers loosed another volley down on them, dropping dozens more of the northmen in their tracks. Ratboy counted no more than fifty or so survivors who reached the safety of the main army.

A roar of victory erupted all along the walls of Mercy's End. Almost a thousand marauders lay dead or dying in the ditch below them, and only a handful of Ostlanders had fallen.

Ratboy noticed that his master did not join in with the celebrations. The priest was peering out over the battlements and frowning. 'Something else is coming,' he muttered.

Ratboy followed his gaze and saw a vague shape break away from the bulk of the enemy army and start rushing across the valley floor towards them. 'What *is* that?' he asked. The shape was charging towards them so fast and with such strange, spasmodic movements that he could not be sure what he was looking at. Strangely, as it neared the castle, the shape became harder rather than easier to define. Ratboy had an impression of limbs and maybe even faces, but rather than troops, it seemed more like a mass of pink and blue energy, rippling across the ground. Ratboy turned to his master for an explanation, but Wolff had opened one of his holy books and was leafing through the pages with such a grim look of concentration on his face that Ratboy didn't dare interrupt him.

The cheers along the wall faltered as the soldiers noticed the strange sight rushing towards them. As the pink and blue shape reached the trench, the ground seemed to warp and bulge, as though reflected in a curved mirror and even the corpses appeared to writhe and shift like smoke.

Felhamer signalled for the archers to open fire, but it was too late. The pink shape washed over the moat like quicksilver and flooded up against the castle.

'Sigmar help us,' gasped Ratboy as he finally saw what was heading towards them. The pink mass was made up of hundreds of twisted, writhing limbs and wide gaping mouths that oozed and coagulated with a peculiar elasticity. The figures giggled and snarled as they billowed upwards in a torrent of rippling flesh. Faces appeared in bellies and contorted into long arachnid limbs before bursting and reforming into other shapes. It looked like a sea of pure Chaos was rushing up towards the ramparts.

Screams of horror erupted from the Empire soldiers as the shapes flooded over the battlements and washed down onto them.

'Hold your line!' cried Felhamer, as he sliced one of the creatures in two with his greatsword. The thing immediately became two smaller shapes and leapt up at him again. He staggered backwards, wrestling frantically as the writhing mass enveloped his chest. Then he disappeared from view.

'Master,' screamed Ratboy, as one the shapes flew at him. It cackled as it latched onto his neck with dozens of slippery, grasping tentacles. Pink energy hissed around its torso and a wide mouth burst from its flesh, baring rows of serrated teeth as it struggled to press its twitching body against him.

Wolff gave no reply, but as Ratboy stumbled past him, fighting for his life, the priest rose to his feet and smashed his hammer down onto the ancient stonework. White fire erupted along the entire length of the wall, enveloping the pink creatures in a dazzling inferno of energy. As the flames touched their jerking, snapping bodies, the creatures screeched in pain and dropped to the ground, contorting as they floundered, trying to escape from the blinding light.

The soldiers needed no order from the tower. They fell on the stunned shapes with knives, spears and swords, hacking the monsters limb from limb until nothing remained but a mess of purple viscera.

The creatures' organs continued to writhe and crawl across the ground and for a few moments the only sound was the squelch of boots, grinding the remains into the stone, as the soldiers ran about, stamping on rows of snapping teeth and pulling grasping fingers from their armour.

Once the shapes had finally become still, the soldiers looked around at each other with ashen faces. They were hardened veterans of countless wars, but none of them had ever encountered anything quite so sickening as this.

Howls began to echo along the wall once more and Ratboy looked to see if there was another wave of creatures coming up the walls. It was worse than that. Some of the men who had been attacked by the monsters had begun to change. Where the creatures had gripped them for several minutes, or sunk teeth though their armour, the men's flesh had become oddly deformed: sprouting serpentine growths that quickly grew in strength and size as the soldiers looked on in horror.

One of the mutated men was standing near Wolff. The soldier groaned in disgust as the skin on his neck and face rolled and bubbled, struggling to contain the frantic changes occurring beneath. His groan turned into a muffled wail, as glistening pink tendrils rushed from behind his eyes and enveloped his face, sliding back into his head through his mouth and beginning to suffocate him.

Wolff stepped calmly forwards and slammed his hammer into the man's head. The soldier was dead before he hit the floor. Writhing shapes squirmed from his shattered skull, reaching out for something to latch onto, but Wolff stamped down on them with his iron-clad boot until they were still. Then he looked up at the horrified circle of onlookers. 'Kill the corrupted,' he said, loud enough for his words to carry all along the crowds of shocked soldiers. 'They're beyond saving.'

The soldiers whose flesh had been changed raised their hands protectively as the other men surrounded them, raising their swords but still unsure whether to strike.

Wolff leapt up onto the wall and cried out in furious, commanding tones. 'Do it now, or we all die!'

For a second, the soldiers still hesitated to kill their former friends, but then one of them screamed out in dismay as a forest of pink tendrils burst from the man nearest to him and latched onto his head, dragging him towards a gaping mouth that had suddenly opened in the mutant's neck. The soldiers attacked the men with axes and swords, slicing desperately at them before they themselves became corrupted. This was the only signal the others needed. All along the wall the Ostlanders attacked anyone who showed the merest hint of mutation, eager to save themselves from the same fate.

Ratboy reeled in horror as he watched the Ostlanders hacking at their own countrymen. To see former comrades turn on each other in this way was more than he could bear and he covered his eyes.

Wolff grabbed his hand and pulled it firmly away from his face. 'This is Sigmar's work, boy,' he gasped, glaring at his acolyte with such fury that Ratboy struggled to meet his gaze. 'Don't you dare avert your eyes.'

Ratboy nodded, and dutifully took in the full horror of the scene. The soldiers were eyeing each other warily as they backed away from the dying mutants. In just a few short minutes, they had gone from being a unified fighting force, to a collection of rabid individuals, terrified that some subtle transformation of their flesh might mark them out for execution. Rather than looking out towards the massing ranks of the enemy, they circled each other, clutching their blood-drenched swords in fear.

We're lost, thought Ratboy, watching as old friends become wary strangers and rows of drilled soldiers splintered into a paranoid mob. He looked to his master for guidance, but Wolff had slumped weakly against the wall, gasping for breath, his face drawn and grey with exhaustion. Accusations began to fly back and forth between the terrified men as they rounded on anyone who displayed even so much as a limp.

'Wait,' cried Ratboy, but his voice was lost in the general tumult. He leapt up onto the stonework and called out again. 'Wait,' he cried with more determination. 'The enemy is out there, don't do their work for them! Remember who you are, men of Ostland!'

A few faces turned to see who had spoken, and Ratboy noticed that one of them was the sharp-featured officer named Meinrich who had earlier accused Wolff of cowardice. His black and white tabard was torn and scorched, but his monocle was still firmly in place and he nodded grimly back at Ratboy.

Meinrich stretched up to his full height and his willowy frame towered over most of the men that surrounded him. 'The boy's right,' he yelled, clanging his sword on his breastplate. 'Hold your swords. Resume your positions. Man the wall!' The soldiers looked shamefully from Meinrich to Ratboy and lowered their weapons. They picked the crackling remains from their armour with distaste and stepped back into line, readying themselves for the next assault.

Ratboy dropped back down from the wall and saw Wolff, still stooped and straining for breath, but looking up at him with a grim smile. The priest nodded and gripped his arm in silent approbation, before standing up and looking out towards the enemy.

'Sigmar's blood,' he muttered, opening his prayer book once more. 'This is going to be a long night.'

Ratboy looked out over the battlements and saw another pink mass of swirling shapes rushing across the valley towards them. He gasped in horror and backed away.

Wolff was still holding his arm and pulled him close. 'I have the measure of you now, boy,' he said, squeezing his arm so hard that his metal-clad fingers bit into the boy's flesh. 'You were born for this. I thought it before and I know it now.' The priest looked deep into the acolyte's eyes. 'Keep close by my side, Anselm. Sigmar's grace is written all over you. I can see His holy wrath in your eyes.' He tightened the straps of his armour and looked up at the darkening sky. 'These fiends are no match for *two* blessed sons of the Heldenhammer.'

For the next three hours they fought wave after wave of the hideous, shifting shapes. As the crimson sun dropped slowly towards the horizon, Wolff, Ratboy and Meinrich dashed along the wall, rallying the men each time they faltered and hacking their way through the tormented shapes that poured over the walls.

The soldiers' initial terror gave way to a grim determination not to be corrupted. As the prayers of Wolff and Ratboy rang constantly in their ears, they butchered the monsters with a mute, machine-like efficiency; fighting through their exhaustion and pain until the stones were slick with the blood of their enemies.

Wolff's praise affected Ratboy even more powerfully than the holy light had done. As he strode along the battlements, his gangly frame seemed to grow in stature, and his hoarse cries rang out over the cacophony, galvanising the soldiers as they sliced furiously through the torrent of limbs and teeth.

Despite the orders yelled down from the bell tower, it was Wolff and Ratboy who became the focus of the Ostlanders' defence. Every time the line faltered, the priest and his acolyte rallied the men and fought alongside them: Wolff with his pounding hammer and Ratboy with a borrowed sword clutched tightly in his one good hand.

As the hours rolled by, the tide of corruption slowed and then finally ceased. A sanguine dusk flooded the valley as the castle's defenders lowered their weapons. They leant weakly against each other and looked down at their handiwork. Mounds of warped, broken shapes lay all along the wall and across the courtyard, but after the initial assault, only a handful more of the Ostlanders had fallen. Lamplighters picked their way through the corpses, setting torches and beacons alight in every corner of the castle. Captain Felhamer and the other officers descended from the tower, embracing the soldiers in fierce hugs and praising them for their bravery, while Wolff followed behind, anointing the battered swords and shields that were lifted up to him.

Ratboy noticed a white-robed shape flitting across the wall towards them. It was Anna, and as she moved through the ranks of tired soldiers, she held a small bottle to their lips: a restorative of some kind, he guessed, from the colour it brought to their pale cheeks.

Joining Ratboy and Wolff, Anna shook her head at the grotesque shapes that surrounded them. On Wolff's orders, the bodies were being shovelled down into the courtyard to be burned, and as a nest of twitching limbs was hurled past her, Anna recoiled. 'What are they?' she asked.

Wolff looked up from his work, and shrugged. 'Daemons of a kind,' he replied. 'Lesser minions of the Ruinous Powers.' He shook his head. 'Such things have no right to exist in our world: they're torn from somewhere beyond the corporeal realm. Only the most powerful, unspeakable magic can wrench such horrors into the mortal world. This Mormius, or someone in his service, is a practitioner of the very darkest arts.' The priest looked out across the valley at the thousands of torches that had begun to punctuate the shadows. 'He must have expended great energy summoning such unholy regiments. No doubt he will be furious that they fared so badly against the simple faith of Felhamer's garrison.'

'So you think Felhamer still has a hope?' asked Anna, incredulously.

'Of course he has hope,' snapped Wolff. 'But hope is not always enough. This is just the beginning. I doubt Mormius will have expected such fierce resistance.' He waved at the crumbling walls. 'Not from such a wreck as this. He probably thought this would be the briefest of struggles – a mere prelude to the main act – but Felhamer's men have forced him to reconsider. Mormius has wasted huge numbers by throwing his force against them so carelessly. He'll plan his next move more carefully.'

'And what of us, master?' asked Ratboy. 'Are we to stay and fight after all? What of your brother?'

The priest frowned and looked away. 'Felhamer and his men are brave beyond anything I could have expected. They're sacrificing themselves, with no expectation of survival, in the hope that others might live. They're prepared to die for the good of an Empire that will never even know their names. These soldiers are everything that's strong and pure about this land.' He sighed. 'To abandon them is a betrayal of the worst kind – a betrayal of my own vows.' He turned to face Ratboy and Anna with doubt in his eyes. For a brief moment, his fierce mask slipped to reveal the face of a tired, confused old man. 'Everything has become so clouded this last year,' he said, rolling his head back across his broad shoulders and stretching the bones in his neck with a series of audible cracks. 'Sometimes it seems that there's no clear path any more.' He looked down at his friends' concerned faces. 'Can you understand? If I leave, these men will die, but if I stay, the whole campaign will be at risk – the whole province even.'

Ratboy shook his head. 'But in the meeting earlier you said–'

'I said what they needed to hear,' snapped the priest. He took a long, weary breath to steady his voice. 'I've struck a deal of sorts with Felhamer. If I fight with his men, until nightfall, he'll show us a passage up through the hills. There's an ancient network of tunnels beneath the citadel. No one knows who built them, but they predate even the tribes of Sigmar's day. It's a maze of dead ends and impassable doors, but Felhamer has a map. With his help, we can flee Mormius's hordes and abandon these poor souls to their fate.' He looked out at the quickly sinking sun. 'Soon, I'll have fulfilled my part of the bargain and we can go.'

Ratboy felt anger and confusion well up in him as he watched Anna sneering at his master. It enraged him to see the disgust in her eyes, but he could not help sympathising with her. When his master had addressed Felhamer and the others, his words had struck a powerful chord within him. He had accepted the truth of Wolff's speech as completely as the scriptures of the Deus Sigmar; but now he saw the words from another perspective entirely. He realised that Wolff knew all along that the men had no chance of victory. His words were calculated, cynical even, intended only to shame the men who had suggested a retreat. Ratboy opened his mouth to accuse his master, but the words dried up in his throat as he saw the anguish in Wolff's eyes. He nodded in silent agreement instead.

'I must do what I can for the captain,' said Wolff, taking his hammer from Ratboy and pointing it back at the castle's central keep. 'Prepare your things and meet me by the postern gate in ten minutes.' With that, he strode off through the milling crowds of soldiers, in the direction of Felhamer and the other officers.

'As OLD AS it is, Mercy's End wasn't the first bastion to be built on this site,' explained Captain Felhamer as he led them through the deserted streets. 'When my ancestors laid the foundations, many centuries ago, they discovered the remains of an even older fortress.'

Ratboy looked away from the captain and noticed that Anna was listening to his words with a rapt expression on her face. He felt an odd rush of nausea as he saw the blushes that coloured her usually pale skin. What's so special about him, he wondered, looking at Felhamer's strong jaw, perfect teeth and tall, powerful physique. If you removed all those plates of armour and gaudy feathers he would probably look much like me, he decided.

'The architecture was like nothing they'd ever seen, or even read of,' continued Felhamer. 'The ruins were full of delicate, serpentine columns and tall arching windows – all crafted with incredible skill. Despite the obvious age of the stonework, almost all of the rooms were still intact.' The captain placed a hand on Anna's arm and gave her an excited grin. 'Imagine it,' he said, 'the handiwork of a forgotten race.'

Anna's blushes deepened and she smiled back at him, before lowering her gaze to the floor.

'People weren't so enlightened in those days, though,' he said, loosing her arm and turning to Ratboy. 'They were afraid of the strange sigils that adorned the walls, and imagined they had stumbled across some shrine to the Dark Gods.' He shook his head sadly. 'So they smashed the beautiful statues and filled the elegant rooms with rubble. Then they built Mercy's End right over the top of the old castle and forbade anyone to ever speak of it again.'

He led them into a tumbledown outbuilding and paused by a large set of trapdoors, half hidden beneath mounds of straw and dung. A group of bored-looking sentries leapt to attention as he approached, clanking their iron-clad boots and straightening their wide, felt hats.

Felhamer nodded brusquely at them, before clearing the straw away from the doors with his boot and turning to face Wolff and the others. 'For centuries the old ruins lay forgotten, until my great, great grandfather, Ernestus, ordered the building of a new well to cope with the demands of an expanding populace, and discovered this.' He reached beneath the slashed leather of his doublet and withdrew a slender knife, holding it out so that it glinted in the torchlight.

Anna gasped and stepped closer to Felhamer.

'Beautiful, isn't it?' asked the captain.

Ratboy shrugged and scowled at his feet, but Wolff answered. 'I've never seen anything quite like it,' he said, peering at the delicately engraved silver. 'Unless...' He looked closer, but then shook his head and said no more.

'Most of the relics have been lost over the years, but a few of the rooms have been unearthed.' The captain gave a proud smile. 'Many of them during my own tenure, actually. Most of the site was destroyed during the building of Mercy's End, but we've managed to clear several of the larger chambers, and we reopened a long passageway that emerges almost half a mile south of here, on the other side of the valley.' He gestured to one of the doors and a guard rushed to unlock it. 'I had a suspicion that it might come in useful some day,' he said, bending down and wrenching open one of the doors.

Wolff pulled open the other door and they all peered down into the oily blackness. The torchlight only reached the first few steps, but they were obviously made by master craftsmen, and still sound, even after centuries of neglect.

Felhamer took three torches from the walls of the outbuilding and handed them to Wolff, Anna and Ratboy. 'These should see you through to the other side,' he said, 'if you don't dawdle.' Then he took a scrap of parchment and handed it to the warrior priest. 'It's a simple map. There are only a few rooms still passable, and once you're into the main passageway, you just follow it till you reach the steps at the far end.' The captain stepped back and looked out at the encroaching darkness. His smile faltered as he remembered the task that awaited him. He shook his head at Wolff. 'Are you sure about this?' he asked, with a slight tremor in his voice. 'Is there no way you could stay? Even for a few days?' He gripped the priest's shoulder and his eyes filled with passion.

'With you to lead us, I believe we could hold back anything.'

Wolff looked away with a pained expression on his face. 'I can't,' he muttered. He handed his torch to Ratboy and placed a hand on the young captain's arm. 'Join me in prayer, for a moment,' he said. He led Felhamer to the far corner of the old barn and they knelt together on the straw. Ratboy could not hear their words, but as the priest led Felhamer in a series of muttered catechisms, the air began to hum with a tangible energy that tingled deep in his bones and raised the hairs on his arms. The torches spat and flickered oddly, and a sense of foreboding filled the room, as though a great storm were brewing. Ratboy saw that Anna and the guards had noticed it too; they were looking around nervously at the lurching shadows and had placed their hands on the hilts of their weapons, as though expecting an attack.

After a few minutes, Wolff and Felhamer rose to their feet and returned to the top of the steps. The captain's face was transformed. The fear had vanished from his eyes and there was a stern, determined line to his jaw. As he gripped Wolff's arm, his hand was trembling with emotion. 'Good luck, Brother Wolff,' he said. 'I shall not forget what you did for us here today. Whatever unholy powers your brother has allied himself to, I doubt they'll be a match for such unshakable faith as yours.'

Wolff nodded but his eyes were full of doubt. He gave no reply as he stepped down into the darkness.

CHAPTER ELEVEN
THE WARRENER

'STAY CLOSE,' MUTTERED the priest as he trotted quickly down the steps. As his boots clattered across the ancient stone, the sound was swallowed by the thick gloom. The light from their torches only reached a few feet either side of them, but every now and then Ratboy glimpsed pale, delicate columns, rearing up into the blackness.

'Who could have built these rooms?' he whispered, afraid to disturb the centuries-old silence.

'Who can say?' replied Wolff, without breaking his stride. 'The world is old beyond reckoning. Man was certainly not the first race to inhabit these northern regions. Older, stranger folk came here long before we did.' As he turned to face Ratboy and Anna, the flickering light threw deep shadows across his brutal features. 'Some say that it was the dabbling of those ancient peoples that unleashed the winds of magic on the world;

that they unshackled the Ruinous Powers and gave them access to our realm.' He shrugged and turned away. 'But if such a people ever did inhabit this place, they fled long ago, leaving us to deal with the consequences of their hubris.'

Wolff paused as they reached the bottom step, and held his torch over the map Felhamer had given him.

As the priest frowned at the scrap of parchment, Ratboy held his own torch aloft, peering into the gaping void that surrounded them. His light revealed nothing but rat bones and a few pale spiders that scuttled quickly back into the shadows. The air seemed different this far down though, and his throat grew tight at the thought of all the earth above their heads. A thousand childhood tales nagged at the edge of his memory: tales of creatures that lived below the earth. Were these chambers really uninhabited, he wondered?

'This way,' barked Wolff as he strode off to the left.

Ratboy and Anna had to move quickly to keep pace with the priest's broad strides, but they were keen not to lose sight of his torch. Without a map, it would be all too easy to get lost in the maze of archways and tunnels. They rushed through a succession of ornately carved doorways and Ratboy sensed from the echoes of their footfalls that each room they entered was slightly smaller than the last. As they crossed the third room, a flash of light caught his eye. Something was reflecting the glare of their torches. He guessed it was only a few feet away and veered off from Wolff's light for a minute to get a closer look.

'Ratboy,' snapped Anna, from behind, 'what are you doing?'

Her voice echoed strangely through the darkness and Wolff stopped immediately to see what was happening.

'There's something over here,' replied Ratboy, lowering his torch towards the glittering object. As the light washed over the dusty stone, a pale face grinned up at him and Ratboy yelped with shock.

'What's that?' cried Wolff, dashing over to his side and thrusting his torch towards the object. A skeleton lay sprawled across the flagstones. It was fractured, ancient, and obviously not human. The limbs were unnaturally slender and the skull was elongated in a way that none of them had ever seen before. Clutched in its hand was a slender, curved sword. Most of the blade was hidden beneath centuries of dust and cobwebs, but a tiny section of the hilt flashed merrily in the shifting firelight.

Anna staggered back from the bones with a look of horror on her face. 'Don't touch it,' she gasped, 'it's some kind of daemon.'

Ratboy didn't hear her. The glittering metal entranced him and before Wolff could stop him, he reached down and grabbed the sword.

'Let me see that,' growled the priest, snatching it away from him. He wiped away the dust and muck and held the sword up to his face. The blade flashed in the torchlight, scattering lances of brilliance around the chamber and revealing tantalising glimpses of the crumbling architecture. The sword itself was a thing of incredible beauty, and of a similar design to the knife Felhamer had showed them earlier. Delicate scrollwork ran along its entire length, depicting astrological symbols, and a series of long, sculpted characters were entwined around single red stone embedded in the hilt. Wolff peered at the sword for a few minutes, turning it slowly in his hands. Then he shrugged, and handed it back. 'This is no ordinary weapon,' he said, looking closely at Ratboy, 'but I can't see anything *unnatural* about its manufacture.' He watched as Ratboy cradled the sword in his trembling hands. 'It seems strange that it's lain here for all these centuries, hidden from everyone and yet the second you entered the room, you noticed it.'

Ratboy boy's eyes were wide with excitement as he ran a finger along the edge of the blade. He snatched his hand away with a gasp and placed his finger in his mouth. 'Still sharp,' he muttered, 'after all this time.'

Wolff nodded. 'It's a good sword.' He placed a hand on Ratboy's shoulder. 'Just be sure to tell me if you notice anything strange about it.' He looked at the twitching shadows that surrounded them. 'Well made is one thing, but an aspirant priest should always be on the look out for any signs of sorcery or occultism.'

Ratboy's face flushed with pride at the suggestion he could even aspire to being a priest. As they marched out of the chamber, he felt as though he had discovered two prizes in the dark beneath Mercy's End.

They passed into another chamber that smelled strongly of damp and rotting vegetation. Ratboy frowned at the overpowering stench and, after slotting the sword securely in his belt, he held his hand over his mouth to try to block out some of the stink. He looked back at Anna and she twisted her face into an exaggerated grimace.

They reached a doorway so wide that even when Ratboy stretched his arms out to their full extent, he couldn't touch the sides. It led into a broad, empty passageway that continued onwards, arrow straight for as far as they could see. 'This is the central route that leads up into the hills,' said Wolff, pausing for a moment so that they could catch their breath. He removed one of his vambraces and massaged the bruised muscles of his forearm. 'The next attack will have already begun,' he said in a voice tinged with regret. 'And I fear we hadn't seen the half of what Mormius had in store for Felhamer.'

Anna shrugged. 'I don't think we saw all that Felhamer had in store for the enemy either. There's a strength in him that won't be easily broken.'

Wolff nodded as he pulled his armour back on and strode forwards. 'You're right, sister,' he said, as they rushed after him. 'But I can't help feeling I've sent a good man to his grave. Many good men, in fact.'

Anna gave a hollow laugh that echoed strangely around the passageway. 'Isn't that your job, Brother Wolff?'

They walked in an awkward silence for a while, each lost in their own thoughts. After a while, the passageway began to slope upwards and the atmosphere grew a little less oppressive.

'This must be it,' said Wolff after nearly an hour had passed. Their torches lit up a pair of massive stone doors at the end of the passageway. 'If Felhamer was right, they should open out onto the far side of the valley.' As he reached the doors, he pressed his shoulder against them and shoved. The hinges groaned and the doors moved, but only an inch or so, and Wolff gave a bitter laugh. 'They're locked,' he said, peering through the gap. 'There's a chain on the other side.' He stepped back and lifted his warhammer from his back. 'Stand clear,' he said, as he prepared to smash it against the stone.

'Wait,' cried Anna, grabbing his arm. 'You must be joking. Those doors are a foot thick. You'll break your arm.'

'Master,' said Ratboy, rushing up to the door and drawing his new sword. 'Let me try.'

Wolff drew breath to speak, then shrugged and stepped back.

Ratboy peered through the gap and then slid the slender blade carefully through it. After a moment's pause, he lifted the sword and then brought it down with a grunt of exertion. It sliced downwards with a flash of sparks and clattered on the flagstones. Ratboy turned to give Wolff a mischievous grin before gently pushing the doors open to reveal the star-laden heavens beyond. The chain dangled at the edge of the door, sliced neatly through the middle. 'Well made indeed,' he said, proudly twirling his sword as he strode out into the cool night air.

As Felhamer had promised, they emerged nearly a mile away from Mercy's End. The door was cut into the far side of a small hollow, and the Forest of Shadows was spread out below them, for as far as the eye could see. They closed the doors carefully behind them and replaced the nettles and branches that grew over them. As they stepped out onto the hillside, Ratboy noticed with surprise that the doors had completely disappeared from view. He remembered his master's instruction to be vigilant for signs of sorcery, but bit his tongue. If the doors had remained hidden for all these centuries, he did not think he should be the one to ask why.

They clambered up to the top of the hill, savouring the cool night air and the open sky above their heads. Once they had reached the summit, they looked back towards the castle. It was adrift amongst an ocean of flickering lights and even from this distance there was something sinister about the fires. Greens and blues mingled with the more natural yellows and every now and then great gouts of flame would erupt from one of the lumbering, indistinct shapes that towered over the crush of smaller figures.

'They're still holding on,' said Wolff, with a note of awe.

Ratboy peered at the castle and saw that his master was right. Fire had spread all along the battlements, but Felhamer's banners were still flying. The black and white designs were tinged a sickly green by the daemonic fires raging beneath them, but they were a clear sign that the citadel had not fallen.

'What happened to Gryphius?' exclaimed Anna suddenly. 'Is he still down there?'

Wolff nodded. 'I think I may have underestimated him. I took him for a mere dilettante, but he has proved himself to be much more than that.' He turned to Anna and noticed the tears that suddenly glistened in her eyes. 'There's nothing to be done for a man such as that, sister. His wounds are old and deep. But I assured him that he will find peace at last in this battle – whatever the outcome.'

'Peace in death, you mean?' she snapped. 'Do you really think the only way to ease a broken heart is to stop it?'

Wolff shrugged. 'We should keep moving,' he said, ignoring her question and turning away from the besieged ruin. 'We aren't safe travelling in such a small group. The sooner we can find von Raukov's army the better.'

With that he jogged down the hill towards the trees, leaving his acolyte to bear the brunt of Anna's fury.

'Pig-headed hammer hurler,' she muttered, scowling at the priest's back. She turned on Ratboy. 'Why do you people always believe bloodshed is such a cure-all?'

Ratboy shrugged, in unconscious imitation of his master and moved to follow him.

'Wait,' said Anna, grabbing his arm. 'How's your hand?'

Ratboy paused as she removed the bandages.

'Improving a bit, I think,' she said, in the same angry tones. She unclasped a small bag that was slung over her shoulder, and removed a large dried leaf. As she pressed it onto the wound, Ratboy's eyes widened with pain. 'Don't be such a child,' she said as she replaced the bandages and rushed after the quickly disappearing Wolff. 'It will do you good.'

As they reached the edge of the trees, Wolff paused and looked up at the shadow moon, Morrslieb. It was hanging unusually low in the sky and seemed to be almost resting on the black, shifting peaks of the forest. As Ratboy and Anna approached, gasping for breath, he turned to them with an odd smile. 'What a choice,' he said, gesturing to the trees. 'Take our chances beneath these malign boughs, or risk the open country.'

'I've spent my entire life crossing this forest,' replied Anna. 'The trees themselves are no more dangerous than a field of corn.' She shrugged. 'And wise travellers know how to move without calling too much attention to themselves.' She waved at the hills that surrounded them. 'Mormius will doubtless have many more recruits heading this way. I think it would be safest to use the cover of the trees.'

Wolff nodded. 'You're right, of course.' He glanced up at Morrslieb again and frowned. 'Let's tread carefully, though.'

Their feet sank deep into the loamy, grey soil as they crept beneath the sombre boughs of the forest. Countless tiny creatures scampered away at their approach. Aspens and pines reached up over them, fracturing the lurid moonlight and scattering it across the ivy, bracken and brambles that carpeted the ground.

They moved forward in a watchful silence, slipping lightly through the shadows and over the fallen leaves and branches. Ratboy shivered and pulled his cloak a little tighter. Ostland was rarely warm, but as they moved onwards through the dewy groves the trees seemed to amplify the autumnal chill.

Anna seemed quite at home in the forest and scouted ahead, creeping quickly through the thicket and pausing every now and then to unearth toadstools and seeds and drop them in her bag. As she reached the edge of a small clearing, she paused and crouched low to the ground, pressing her hands down onto the springy turf. She turned back to Wolff and Ratboy and raised a finger to her mouth as they approached.

They stooped down beside her to see what she had found. At first Ratboy could see nothing in the pale moonlight, but Anna traced her finger around a series of shapes embedded in the grass. It looked like the tracks of a large, hoofed animal, but as Anna glanced nervously around the clearing, Ratboy guessed these were no natural tracks.

Anna's eyes were wide with fear as she rose to her feet and pressed her finger to her mouth again, before skirting around the edge of the clearing. They re-entered the trees and continued on their way, but Anna was now moving much slower and with even more care than before. After ten minutes or so, she crouched behind a tree trunk and signalled for them to approach quietly.

Wolff and Ratboy crept up beside the priestess and followed the direction of her gaze. Down below them was a small gulley, cutting through the trees, and a column of figures was hurrying silently along it. Ratboy felt a rush of fear as he watched the shadowy procession. There was something dreamlike about the scene. It was hard to see clearly in the dark of the forest, but they were clearly not human. Their broad, naked chests were covered with a thick hide of fur and their bestial heads were crowned with gnarled, vicious horns. Talismans and fetishes dangled from their massive, tattooed arms and cruel, ugly weapons hung from their belts. An acrid, animal stink came from them that was so powerful the three travellers instinctively covered their noses. Beastmen, thought Ratboy, clutching his sword with fear. He had encountered such creatures of Chaos before, but had never become accustomed to them. He looked up at his master, wondering what they would do.

Wolff's face was filled with disgust as he watched the creatures rushing by, but as he caught Ratboy's questioning look he shook his head and gestured for them to back away.

They crept with painstaking slowness away from the gulley, and only after several minutes, did anyone dare to speak.

'We're safe for the moment,' whispered Anna. 'We're downwind from them,' she explained, with a grimace at the awful smell that had followed them from the gulley. 'And they seemed to be in quite a hurry.' She frowned. 'In fact, they were oddly disciplined for beastmen. From what I know of their nature, they rarely behave like that.'

'They were probably headed for Mercy's End,' replied Wolff. 'Mormius must have great power at his command to bring order to such rabble.'

'Is there nothing we can do to stop them?' asked Ratboy. 'Felhamer has so many men pitted against him already. Maybe we could set up some kind of ambush?'

Wolff shook his head. 'There are far too many of them. We can't risk it. And anyway, even if we could stop this one small group, what difference would it make? Remember why we left Mercy's End. I have to find out what part my brother has to play in all this.'

Anna nodded eagerly, keen to stay as far away from the beastmen as possible. 'If we keep to the higher ground, they won't even know we were here,' she whispered, and started clambering up a steep escarpment that led away from the gulley.

After five minutes or so they reached a wide, moon-lit plateau that reared up above the treetops and gave them a clear view over the surrounding forest. Far behind them, they could make out the silhouette of Mercy's End. The ruin was still bejewelled with the strange lights, but it was impossible from this distance to see how the battle was progressing. Ratboy took comfort from the fact that there was clearly some kind of movement along the castle walls.

At least it hasn't been burned to the ground, he thought.

'What's that?' asked Anna, pointing in the opposite direction.

West of the plateau, was another collection of lights, nestling in the northern foothills of the Middle Mountains. 'Is that Ferlangen?' she asked, peering through darkness.

Wolff shook his head. 'We're still too far east.' He frowned as he studied the lights. 'There are no cities in that direction. It must be an encampment. And a large one at that.'

'Von Raukov?' asked Ratboy, hopefully.

The priest nodded. 'Let's pray that it is.' He looked down at the forest that lay between them and the distant lights. 'If we make good speed, we could reach them by tomorrow night.'

Ratboy looked around with disappointment at the soft turf that covered the hilltop. 'I suppose that doesn't leave any time for a quick rest?'

Anna shook her head in disbelief. 'Have you forgotten what we just saw? These trees are probably crawling with those creatures. Would you really be able to shut your eyes with such horrors for bedfellows?'

'Quite,' said Wolff, answering for him. 'We keep moving.' He waved back towards Mercy's End. 'Felhamer's garrison could be defeated at any time, and this whole region will be overrun with Mormius's horde.'

They spent the rest of the night rushing through the trees in complete silence. After the sight of the beastmen, none of them wanted to risk drawing any attention to themselves and Ratboy had to bite his tongue on several occasions, as his imagination painted horned shapes on the sombre shadows. The threat was not always in Ratboy's mind, however. On one occasion they were forced to clamber into a ditch as a band of mounted marauders broke from the trees, heading north to join the battle. It was only Anna's keen sense of smell that saved them. Noticing an odd scent on the wind, she herded Ratboy and Wolff into the ditch, just seconds before the horsemen charged by. The priest was forced to give her a grudging nod of respect as they dragged themselves back up from the bed of damp, rotten leaves.

Gradually, as dawn approached, the trees began to thin out, interspersed with large areas of scrub and bracken. The sky behind them shifted from black to a deep azure, and a chorus of birdsong erupted from the branches. Wrens and nuthatches scattered at their approach, trilling petulantly as the heavy-footed interlopers hurried past.

As the first rays of sunlight began to warm the backs of their necks, the scattered trees were replaced by featureless moorland, and Wolff began to pick up the pace, urging his already exhausted companions into a brisk jog.

'Look,' hissed Anna, as they approached a long, winding hawthorn hedge. 'It's one of the creatures.'

Wolff and Ratboy stumbled to a halt as they saw what she was referring to. Something was curled up beneath the hedge. It was mostly hidden from view by the thick mass of leaves, but the grubby fur on its twisted, hunched back was clearly visible and as they slowly approached, a croaking snore rang out.

Wolff and Ratboy cautiously drew their weapons as they approached the hedge.

They were within a few feet of the sleeping figure, when it sensed their presence and lurched up out of the hedge, staggering towards them with its arms raised.

Wolff raised his hammer to strike, but Anna grabbed his arm and cried out in alarm.

'Wait,' she cried. 'He's human.'

'Sigmar, you're right,' gasped Wolff, lowering his weapon and looking down at the creature with amazement.

But as the man shuffled towards the three travellers, rubbing the sleep from his eyes, Ratboy wondered if Anna might be mistaken. His spine was so hunched and twisted that his face barely came up to Ratboy's chest, and he had to wrench his head awkwardly onto one side to look up at them. His whole misshapen body was wrapped in a stinking mass of old, mangy rabbit skins and strange contraptions of metal and wire that clattered as he moved. Ratboy guessed that some of the metal objects were traps, but there were many other things he couldn't identify: clumps of feather, tied together with thick cords of grass, little idols made of shell and animal bones that rattled as he reached his crooked arms out towards them. His loose, wet lips sagged down in a duck-like pout, but as he looked up at Wolff, they spread into a grin of recognition, revealing a single, large tooth. 'Priest,' he said in a thick, phlegmy voice.

Ratboy flinched at the sight of the man's face. Dozens of warts and growths had warped his pale, pockmarked flesh so that he almost resembled the mutated creatures they had fought on the walls of Mercy's End.

Anna noticed Ratboy's disgust and gave him a quick scowl of disapproval before stooping to speak to the strange man. 'Who are you?' she asked gently, taking his gnarled hand fearlessly into her own.

'Helwyg,' grunted the man, gripping her hand tightly and licking his wide, drooping lips in excitement. 'The warrener.' As he spoke to Anna, his large, watery eyes kept flicking to Wolff and he seemed eager to speak to him.

'Your names?' he asked, struggling a little to force the words from his deformed mouth.

'Anselm, Anna and I'm Brother Jakob Wolff,' replied the priest, stepping closer. 'What are you doing out here alone? These forests are crawling with the enemy. It's not safe to walk alone.'

'Soldiers need food,' said the little man with a grin, licking his lips again. 'They sent the warrener for coneys.' He shrugged. 'But Helwyg is no hunter.' He gestured to the hedge. 'Got tired. Sat down.' He chuckled. 'Fell asleep.'

'Soldiers, you say?' asked Wolff. 'Whose army are you travelling with?'

'Iron Duke,' replied Helwyg with a moist lisp. He shuffled towards Wolff and pawed at his scarlet robes. 'The saviour,' he explained, spreading his arms with a rattle of springs and bones, 'of the Empire.'

'The Elector Count, you mean,' asked Wolff, frowning. 'Are you talking about von Raukov?'

Helwyg shook his head.

'Is it Ostlanders you're marching with?'

Helwyg gave a vague nod, but his attention seemed to have wandered. He was fingering the thick chains that fixed Wolff's holy texts to his cuirass and eyeing the gold filigree that decorated the edges of his gorget. 'Mighty priest,' he muttered. 'Jakob Wolff.'

Wolff nodded impatiently and backed away from the strange, hunched figure. 'Can you lead us to the army?' he asked, trying to hide his disgust as the man's grasping fingers followed him.

The warrener grinned, and began to stroke the objects that were strapped across his furs, eying Wolff's armour the whole time. 'Yes,' he said. As he turned and began lurching slowly away, he clapped his hands with excitement. 'Priests are better than coneys.'

After the race through the tunnels, Helwyg's awkward, shuffling gait seemed painfully slow, but from what little they could see of him, beneath the layers of grubby fur, his legs were as ruined as the rest of him. Ratboy, for one, was glad of the slower pace, and took the opportunity to examine his new sword a little more closely, tracing the strange runes on its hilt with his finger and wondering what they might mean.

After a couple of hours, Anna grew impatient with Helwyg's tortuous slowness. She began scouting ahead and peering into the growing light to see if she could spot the army. Finally, as the sun reached its zenith and a light rain began to waft across the fields towards them, she called back from the top of a small incline. 'They're here,' she cried, pointing in the direction of some low, quick-moving rain clouds. 'We've found them.'

The others rushed to her side and looked down over a wide plateau. A huge army was spread out before them, camped under a dazzling panoply of banners bearing not just the bull of Ostland, but the emblems of several other provinces too. The rain was coming down harder with every minute, and it was hard to see the encampment clearly, but Ratboy guessed there must be thousands of men down there, cleaning their weapons and preparing for battle.

'Thank Sigmar,' said Wolff, turning to the others. 'These must be von Raukov's men. And they're not much more than a day's march from Mercy's End.' He lifted one of the books that hung at his side and kissed it. 'My brother must be down there somewhere.'

'Brother?' asked Helwyg, shuffling towards him.

Wolff gave a brusque nod, but said no more on the subject as he strode off down the hill.

CLOSE UP, THE scale of the army became utterly bewildering. As they entered the encampment a crush of figures barged blindly past them: soldiers, swineherds, blacksmiths, ostlers, merchants and messengers, all dashing through streets of gaudy canvas as the army prepared to decamp. Ratboy had never seen such a gathering of humanity and without Wolff to lead him, he would have cowered beneath the first available cart. The mouth-watering aroma of frying sausage meat mingled with the tang of unwashed bodies and the sweet stink of infected wounds. His master strode purposefully onwards through the pandemonium. He picked out a black banner, emblazoned with a golden griffon and headed straight towards it.

Helwyg strained his neck to look at the distant banner and grinned. 'Priest has priestly friends?' he asked, hobbling after Wolff and clutching at his burnished armour.

Wolff gave a brusque nod. 'It's unusual to see Knights Griffon so far from Altdorf,' he said.

'Knights Griffon?' asked Ratboy.

Wolff gave a sigh of annoyance at being asked so many questions. 'Yes, Knights Griffon. They're closely linked to my own order,' he snapped. 'As you should well know.' At the sight of Ratboy's blushes, he softened his voice a little and gestured to the crowds of soldiers that surrounded them. 'A familiar face might be useful if we want to find out what's happening here.'

As they neared the banner, Ratboy saw flashes of polished steel glinting between the tents; then, as they turned a final corner, he saw the Knights Griffon revealed in all their glory. Seemingly blind to the chaos that surrounded them, the knights were lined up in calm, orderly ranks as their captain rode slowly between them, carefully inspecting their gleaming armour and their impressive array of weaponry. Ratboy had never seen such an obvious display of wealth and power. Everything about the knights, from their polished, plumed helmets, to the scalloped barding on their destriers, was intricately worked and lovingly polished. Even the dour Ostland rain only added to the effect, as it washed over the oiled steel of their visors.

The captain was a grizzled old veteran, whose short, silver beard seemed as hard and glinting as his fluted helmet. At the sight of Wolff, his leathery face split into a broad smile and he threw his arms open in greeting. 'Brother Jakob Wolff, as I live and breathe,' he said, with a voice like the rumble of thunder. 'What an unexpected blessing.'

The captain dismounted and the two towering figures embraced with a clatter of armour. Then they stood back and peered into each other's faces.

'I seem to remember a little black amongst the grey,' said Wolff, nodding to the knight's fringe of silver hair.

'Well, yes, some of us *were* young once, Jakob. Unlike your good self of course – I'm reliably informed that you left the womb with a shaven head and the Holy Scriptures in your fist.'

A strange growling noise came from Wolff's throat and after a few seconds Ratboy realised it was laughter. It was a sound he'd never heard before and he turned to Anna with a bemused look on his face.

The priestess rolled her eyes.

'Maximilian von Düring,' sighed Wolff, visibly relaxing at the sight of his old friend. 'It's good to see you, Baron. I have much to ask.'

Maximilian dismissed his knights with a wave of his hand and gestured for Wolff to follow him to his tent. 'If your squires speak to my quartermaster, he'll find them some food,' he said.

Anna's eyes flashed with indignation and Wolff shook his head. 'Ah, no, Maximilian, let me introduce–'

He paused as he noticed the expectant face of Helwyg looking up at him. 'Thank you for your help,' he said, nodding to the warrener. 'You may return to your work.'

Helwyg looked a little disappointed at being dismissed, but nodded all the same. 'Always glad,' he slurred, before shuffling away into the jostling crowds of lackeys and liegemen.

'As I was saying,' continued Wolff, 'this is my noviciate Anselm, who goes under the name of Ratboy, and our travelling companion is Sister Anna Fleck, of the Order of the Bleeding Heart.'

Maximilian frowned and gave a deep bow. 'Apologies,' he said. 'I should have noticed your clerical robes. This miserable Ostland weather paints everything a muddy brown.'

Anna gave a brisk nod, but Ratboy mirrored the baron's deep bow and his face lit up at being greeted so graciously by a knight of such high rank.

'Let's get out of this rain for a minute,' said the baron and gestured to his tent. 'Mobilising a force of this size takes a while. We still have an hour or two at our disposal, I should think.'

The baron's tent had the austere look of a monk's cell. Beyond a few sheets rolled up in the corner there was just a small table and a couple of books. The four of them sat on the ground, just inside the door, as the rain drummed on the canvas stretched above their heads.

'Something has changed in you since we last met,' decided Maximilian, once they had finished exchanging the usual pleasantries. He peered closely into Wolff's eyes. 'And I don't just mean a few extra grey hairs.'

Wolff looked a little awkward under his friend's intense stare and seemed unsure how to reply to so direct a statement. He glanced at Ratboy, as though ordering him to bite his tongue. Then he shrugged. 'The last year or so has been difficult for everyone. I imagine we're all a little changed.'

The baron nodded, slowly. 'That's true, Jakob, but you of all people know how to find comfort in the sacred texts and scriptures. Your belief has been a constant inspiration to me whenever I felt afraid. I know the strength of your faith: it is as immovable as the earth beneath our feet; but I see some kind of doubt in your eyes that wasn't there before.' He leant forward. 'Tell me, old friend, what's brought you here, at this precise moment?'

Wolff examined the back of his gloves, spreading his fingers thoughtfully and then clenching his fists, before meeting the baron's gaze. 'I entered the church at a very young age,' he said quietly, 'as you know. But I only intended to become a sacristan or an archivist of some kind. My interest was chiefly in the study of holy tracts and sacred artefacts, rather than in the martial aspects of our faith.'

A look of surprise crossed Anna's face and she moved to speak, but Wolff continued.

'I only decided to devote myself to the life of a mendicant warrior priest as penance for what I believed was a terrible betrayal,' he lowered his voice even more, 'of my own parents.'

Wolff paused, seemingly overcome with emotion at the memory.

His three listeners waited patiently for him to continue.

'However,' he continued, looking up at Ratboy, 'penance can only carry one so far. I've failed and abandoned so many stout-hearted friends that I began to feel a fraud. I felt as though my faith was built on foundations of sand.' The baron shook his head urgently, but Wolff continued. 'And then, to top it all, I recently discovered that the crime was never mine to pay penance for. It was another man entirely who betrayed my parents.' He shrugged. 'But, in a way, that discovery gave me a new resolve. The man I speak of is a cultist of the worst sort.' He looked desperately at Maximilian. 'And I believe he's right here, marching in von Raukov's army.'

The baron shook his head. 'This army is von Raukov's in name only. The Elector Count was seriously injured during the recent defence of

Wolfenberg. He'll be bedridden for weeks, if not months.'

'Then who's leading you?'

The baron smiled. 'A great general indeed,' he answered. 'They call him the Iron Duke. He shares your surname, actually,' he said with wry smile. 'His name is Kriegsmarshall Fabian Wolff.'

HELWYG SHUFFLED SLOWLY though the crowds as pavilions toppled all around him, crumbling to the ground in great billowing piles of muddy canvas. Even the thick hides that enveloped him could not hide the odd, jerking nature of his movements. The soldiers were too busy checking their weapons and readying the horses to pay him much attention, so he was able to snake undisturbed through the encampment. After nearly an hour, he reached the command tents: towering, bunting-clad behemoths that loomed over everything else. As he lurched towards the largest tent, the Iron Duke's honour guard eyed him with distaste from beneath their lupine, sculpted helmets, but made no move to prevent him entering.

Once inside, Helwyg fastened the doors behind him and looked around the tent to make sure it was empty. Then he approached an ornate throne, silhouetted against a row of torches at the back of the tent. He fell awkwardly to one knee and lowered his head respectfully, then climbed to his feet again and began to remove his grubby furs. They dropped to his feet in a stinking pool of sweat and mud and he stepped to one side, completely naked. Deprived of its protective covering, the extent of his body's deformity was revealed. His limbs were crooked and twisted almost beyond recognition and the serpentine curves of his spine were clearly visible beneath his filthy skin.

He began to scratch at the greasy strands of hair that crowned his head, digging his fingers deep into his scalp with such force that streams of dark blood began to flow quickly over his face. He showed no sign of pain though, and as his dirty fingernails sliced under the skin, he pulled it away from the bone. A thick flap of scalp came free with a soft tearing sound. He pulled it forwards, down over his face, to reveal a mass of blood-slick feathers beneath. The streams of blood became rivers as he wrenched open his chest cavity, spilling his organs across the ground in a steaming mass, revealing his true form: a small, willowy man, covered in blue iridescent feathers that shimmered as he moved. He stretched to his full height and sighed with relief. 'I've found him,' he said, with a proud smile spreading across his thin, avian features.

'Are you sure?' came a low voice from the throne.

'Yes, my lord,' piped the creature. He stepped closer, wiping the blood and sinew from his feathers. 'It was your brother. I heard his name quite clearly: Jakob Wolff.'

A tall, slender knight rose from the throne and stepped slowly into the torchlight. His face was long and aristocratic. The flames were reflected in his coat of burnished mail, and in the jewels that adorned a leather patch over his left eye. He stepped towards the feathered man and took his head in his hands, stooping to plant a passionate kiss on his bloody forehead. 'Then your soul is assured its place alongside mine in eternity, Helwyg.' He twirled his elegant, waxed moustache between his fingers and turned away from his servant. 'How did you discover him? Is his presence widely known?'

Helwyg skipped lightly after him. 'In all truth, lord, he found me. I'd given up the search. I was planning to return this very morning and inform you that you must be mistaken. Then, as I took a brief nap, just outside camp, he stumbled across me, looking for a guide.'

Fabian's shoulders shook with laughter. 'How delicious are the devices of our master?' He looked down at Helwyg. 'And who knows of his presence?'

'As you predicted, Kriegsmarshall, he made straight for the Knights Griffon and has approached no one else.' He shrugged, 'Wolff is a common enough surname, and in a gathering of this size, no one will guess at any connection. He wouldn't be foolish enough to openly accuse you. Apart from maybe to his pious friend, Maximilian; but what could they do alone? Who would believe them? After all your glorious victories, these men would slit the throat of anyone who spoke against you. And how could Jakob prove you're his brother?' Helwyg looked up at his master. 'You don't even look alike.'

Fabian nodded and a smile lit up his hawk-like features. 'It's true, I always did take after mother.' He returned to his throne and sat down. 'You've done well, Helwyg. I now have my brother exactly where I wanted him. Whatever he has planned, it's safest that I keep him close to me. Watch him closely. At *all* times.' He looked up at his servant. 'You can't leave like that though, Helwyg,' he said, nodding to the shimmering feathers.

Helwyg's narrow shoulders slumped dejectedly and he pouted. 'I've been limping around in that warrener's body for weeks,' he said, wrinkling his nose. 'And he stank even before I killed him.'

Fabian narrowed his eyes.

'Very well,' muttered Helwyg, peevishly. He scoured the shadows of the tent and after a few moments he pounced, flying across the room in a blur of talons and feathers. There was a muffled squeak and then a rat scampered out of the darkness. It nodded its head once at Fabian and slipped away, through a small gap at the bottom of the tent doors.

Fabian leant back in his throne with a sigh of satisfaction. Then, he lifted his patch to reveal a running black sore where his eye should have been. The scab glistened with moisture and it swelled and bulged as a shape began to move beneath it. After a few seconds, the scab parted like a small mouth, dangling strands of white pus over a black, featureless orb. 'O Great Schemer,' said the general, 'guide me.' The orb began to roll in its socket, as it perceived a torrent of shapes and colours. For a while the general could not discern anything beyond the vaguest outlines and textures, but soon he began to make out specific images: tall, crooked trees, looming over a gloomy forest path; an ancient grove, throbbing with eldritch light; a narrow defile, clogged with weeping, dying men and finally, a glittering, winged knight bearing down on him with a long sword in his hand. A breeze slipped beneath the canvas walls and became a whisper, calling to Fabian from the shadows. 'Deliver me from Mormius,' it said. 'Send him to the abyss. I will raise you up in his place.'

'But master,' replied Fabian, gripping the arms of his throne. 'What of my brother?'

There was no reply, and as suddenly as they had come, the visions ceased. Fabian replaced the patch and sat back in his throne with a frustrated sigh. 'Oh, Jakob,' he breathed. 'A promise is a promise, no matter how many years have passed. How can you dare to approach me, even now?' He closed his uncorrupted right eye, and cast his mind back through the decades, to a distant summer's day and a room in his father's house.

CHAPTER TWELVE
BLOOD TIES

'FABIAN,' CALLED A thin, musical voice. 'Come and say hello to your brother.'

Fabian stared morosely through a wide bay window onto the secluded valley outside. He was only fourteen, but already felt as though life had betrayed him. He pressed his face to the warm, leaded glass and as he looked out at the sunlit idyll of his parents' estate, he wept. A glorious jumble of orchards and wildflower meadows lay sleepily across the hillside, surrounding the long drive that led down to the gatehouse, where the servants were unloading his father's coach. He lolled back into a mountain of damask cushions and wiped away hot, angry tears. 'I'm busy,' he replied, picking up a book of folk tales that lay forgotten on the table next to him.

An azure cloud of embroidered silk bustled into the drawing room. 'Fabian,' scolded his mother, frowning at him through her pince nez. 'Don't pout. We haven't seen Jakob for months. Brother Braun said in his letter that he's done exceptionally well in his studies.'

'Really,' replied Fabian, nonchalantly turning a page and refusing to look up from the book. 'You *do* surprise me.'

'Fabian…' repeated his mother in a stern voice, gesturing to the open door.

'Very well,' he replied, accepting defeat and snapping the book shut. 'Although I really don't see why everything must stop at merest mention of the word "Jakob".'

He followed his mother out through the carpeted reception rooms and into the garden. The verges and borders were ablaze with colour and he immediately felt his nose tingle at the scent of the honeysuckle that trailed over the house's pink-grey stone. He held a handkerchief to his face, in the hope it would give him some protection.

The façade of Berlau house was covered with dozens of tall windows, and as the new arrivals approached, they had to shield their eyes against the inferno of light reflected in the glass.

'Jakob,' cried his mother, unable to contain her excitement at seeing her firstborn. She dashed across the small courtyard and threw her arms around the youth, smothering him with kisses. 'I swear you look even taller,' she exclaimed, hugging him tightly.

'Margarethe,' said the elegant, elderly gentleman next to Jakob. 'Really – you'll suffocate the poor boy.' Even dressed in his mud-splattered travelling clothes, Fabian's father looked every inch the nobleman. The nostrils of his long, aquiline nose flared at such a gaudy display of emotion and he ground his heel angrily into the cobbles. Despite his annoyance, though, he could not hide the proud gleam in his eye as he placed a hand on Jakob's shoulder. 'Let him change, at least, before you drown him in syrup.'

Margarethe stepped back, and allowed the boy to head inside. 'You are cruel to me, Hieronymus,' she said, giving her husband a coy smile. Then, she nodded to the old priest waiting patiently next to her husband. 'Brother Braun,' she trilled. 'It's good to see you.'

The man nodded his tonsured head. 'Frau Wolff,' he said, kissing the fingers she dangled before him. 'The pleasure is all mine, I assure you.'

'Come inside,' she said, taking his hand. 'You must be tired out in this heat. I'll order us some drinks and you can tell me your news.'

As the priest entered the house, he bowed to Fabian, who was slouched just inside the entrance hall.

Fabian nodded slightly in reply but did not return the priest's smile.

'Busy as ever, I see, Fabian,' said Hieronymus, as he approached his son.

Fabian gave his father an ironic grin, before sauntering back into the house and following his brother upstairs.

He found Jakob in the library, replacing a few books he had taken at the start of the summer. Unlike the rest of the house, the library was swathed in a cool gloom, and as Fabian approached his brother he squinted, purblind, at the texts. '*The Relations of Matter and Faith*,' he read. 'Sounds gripping.'

'Hello, Fabian,' replied Jakob, continuing to slide the books back into the dusty spaces on the shelves.

Fabian studied him. Since his revelation a few years earlier, Jakob's passion for all things ecclesiastical had transformed him. Not just spiritually, either. His burgeoning faith seemed to have fed his adolescent body too. He now towered over his slender young brother, and there was a wholesome robustness about him that nauseated Fabian. He was a vision of perfect Ostland youth: even, white teeth; thick, black hair; broad, muscled shoulders and clear, intelligent eyes. Everything about him seemed designed to show the slight, bookish Fabian in an unfavourable light.

'What's dragged you back amongst us weak sinners?' he asked, dropping into a chair. 'I thought you'd end your days in that draughty ruin.'

'Brother Braun's temple *is* a little ramshackle,' replied Wolff, coming to sit next to Fabian and starting to unlace his muddy jerkin. 'But too many home comforts can be a distraction from contemplation.'

'I'm quite fond of my home comforts,' said Fabian, before breaking off into a series of hacking coughs. 'Wretched flowers,' he wheezed asthmatically, sitting bolt upright as he tried to calm his breathing.

Jakob eyed his brother with concern. 'Can I help?'

Fabian shook his head and took a few more whistling breaths before replying. 'You could pray, maybe,' he gasped. Once he had wiped his streaming eyes, Fabian looked at his brother. 'Tell me,' he said. 'While you're contemplating, do your thoughts ever include the shameful state of your own family?'

'Shameful? The name Wolff is a well-respected one,' replied Jakob, frowning in confusion. 'It has been for centuries.'

Fabian gave a hollow laugh. 'You've been away a long time, brother. Things have changed.'

'I'm not sure I understand you,' replied Jakob, rising to his feet and eyeing his brother suspiciously. 'But I can see at least one thing that hasn't changed. You're as angry and ungrateful as ever. Look at you – born into the lap of luxury and as bitter as a starving orphan. What have you got to complain about?'

'Our father's become a laughing stock, Jakob,' said Fabian, flushing with anger. 'Even a dullard like you, with your head full of prophets and miracles, must be aware of it. He thinks of nothing but the Sigmarite Church. While the stewards rob us blind, marauders are running unchallenged across our estates. The whole of Ostland is almost overrun and the Elector Count needs every sword he can get, but our father spends all his time praying.' He clenched his fists. 'And signing away our inheritance to charitable causes.' He levelled a finger at his brother. 'And all because of the sycophantic drivel Braun pours in his ear. He can't think about anything useful since that senile old fool convinced him you're some kind of holy protégé.'

Jakob's lip curled in a sneer of disgust. 'Maybe if you didn't spend your whole time reading ridiculous novels, *you* could achieve something with your life. Then you might not be so consumed with jealousy.'

Fabian leapt to his feet and squared up to his brother; undeterred by the fact that his face barely reached Jakob's broad chest. 'The bailiffs all laugh at him behind his back, Jakob. They take wages for soldiers they sacked months ago, and leave the gatehouses unmanned. They pocket the profits from the harvest and tell him the crops all failed. But the old fool won't believe me when I tell him what a bunch of crooks they are. Berlau is barely defended at all these days. But father just tells me about the new chapterhouse he's funding or shows me a sketch of some new chancel in Wolfenberg that Braun has convinced him to pay for. He's pissing all over our family name, Jakob. He's forgotten his heritage. Another few years of this neglect and Berlau House will be as ruined as Braun's temple.'

'I'm not in the mood for this rubbish, Fabian,' said Jakob, turning to leave. He paused at the door and glared back at his brother. 'You're not a child anymore. You should learn to be a bit more respectful when talking about our father. He's a good man.'

'Really?' replied Fabian, striding after him and jabbing a finger into his chest. 'You think you can come back here, after spending months peering into your navel, and tell me what kind of man our father is?'

Jakob grabbed his brother's shoulders and slammed him back into the bookshelves. 'Watch yourself,' he whispered as leather-bound volumes thudded to the floor around them. 'Sigmarite doctrine doesn't tend to preach forgiveness.' He pushed Fabian back against the shelves, so that the boy grimaced with pain. 'Don't take me for a pious sop. I'm still a Wolff.'

For a few seconds the boys stood there, glaring at each other with complete hatred. Then Fabian flared his nostrils and twisted his face into an exaggerated frown. 'The blood of a Wolff runs true,' he said, in note-perfect imitation of their father's low, booming voice.

Jakob held his brother for a few more seconds, scowling furiously, then the tension suddenly exploded from his lungs in a bark of laughter. He stepped back, shaking his head and started to giggle 'The blood of a Wolff,' he gasped, in the same ridiculous low voice Fabian had used, 'does indeed run true.'

'Boys,' came their mother's voice. 'Stop playing and come down for a drink. We're in the Long Gallery.'

The two brothers were still chuckling as they marched obediently down the stairs.

'There's only so much I can teach him,' Braun was saying as they entered the room. He was stood in front of a window that looked out onto a sun-dappled orchard and as he spoke he dabbed repeatedly at his face with a damp handkerchief. 'He's already surpassed me in several areas,' he explained, waving at Jakob. 'Your son can recite *The Life of Sigmar* in its entirety as easily as I can recall a simple prayer.' He shook his head in wonder. 'I've never seen anything quite like it, to be honest. I've already allowed him to perform some important ordinances and observations, and he executed them with startling success. For instance, only last Wellentag he recited the most beautiful threnody for a recently deceased goat.' He paused, and closed his eyes, seemingly holding back tears. 'Old Man Göbel loved that animal more dearly than his own children and your son's eloquence was a great comfort to him.'

'Then what are you suggesting?' asked Hieronymus. There was no trace of emotion on his stern face, but a slight tremor in his voice betrayed his excitement. 'Is the boy ready to be fully ordained into the church?'

Braun shrugged. 'It's always hard to gauge such things. One must be wary of subjecting a noviciate to the trials prematurely, but he certainly shows unusual promise. I've been corresponding with an old friend of mine in Altdorf, Arch Lector Lauterbach, regarding the matter, and he has requested that I bring your son to the capital, so that he may test him more thoroughly in the Cathedral of Sigmar.'

Hieronymus could control his features no longer. His eyes bulged as he looked from Jakob to Braun. 'An Arch Lector? I had no idea you had been discussing the matter with such senior figures.' He placed a hand on Jakob's shoulder and allowed himself a slight smile. 'Of course you can take him to Altdorf, Brother Braun. It would be a great honour for us.' He puffed out his chest and dusted an imaginary piece of fluff from his jacket. 'In fact, it is a long time since I visited the capital myself. If it would be of use, my wife and I should be glad to accompany you.'

Braun raised his eyebrows in surprise. 'Well, no offence to your lordship, but I had really imagined it would just be Jakob and myself.'

Hieronymus's face remained impassive, but Fabian noticed the slight tightening of his jaw that usually preceded an explosion of anger. 'I imagine the priests would be keen to meet such a generous benefactor as myself, Brother Braun,' he said in carefully controlled tones.

Braun opened his mouth to speak, but then seemed to reconsider. He gave a wide smile and bent his frail old body into a low bow. 'Of course, that's absolutely right your lordship. And it would be a perfect opportunity for you to see some of the work you've contributed to. I would be delighted if you and Frau Wolff could accompany us.'

'Excellent,' said Hieronymus, clapping his hands down on his thighs. 'Then we'll leave as soon as possible.'

Fabian backed cautiously towards the door.

Hieronymus grabbed him by the shoulder. 'You too, boy. It will do you good to see a little of the real world, instead of wasting your time on all those infantile myths you seem so obsessed with.'

'But father,' whined Fabian, 'the priests have no interest in meeting me.'

Hieronymus gave a short bark of laughter. 'You think I'd take you to the cathedral? And let you ruin your brother's future with some petulant remark?' He loosed Fabian's shoulder and shook his head in disbelief. 'I think not. But I won't leave you here to wreak havoc in our absence. I dread to think what we'd return to. And you may even be able to make yourself useful in Altdorf. You'll stay with my cousin Jonas, and if you value your hide, you'll do as he asks. Spending time with an educated gentleman such as Jonas might give you a little of the intellectual ballast you seem so sorely lacking in.'

'Altdorf,' murmured Margarethe, looking nervously up at the religious plasterwork that decorated the ceiling. She took her husband's arm. 'Is it wise to travel at the moment, Hieronymus? Altdorf is such a long way from here and the roads are so dangerous.'

Hieronymus nodded his head firmly. 'A journey to the very heart of the Empire is just what these boys need.' He noticed Margarethe's concerned expression and took her hand. 'Don't worry yourself unduly. We'll take guards. There won't be a problem.'

Servants bustled into the room and handed out slender glasses of wine. Brother Braun took a tiny sip and placed the glass carefully on a table. 'There's actually another small matter I wished to discuss with your lordship,' he said, taking the seat that was offered him. Once he was settled, and the others had taken their seats too, he continued. 'There has been some concern over the last couple of weeks that…' he paused, unsure how to continue. He was suddenly unable to meet Hieronymus's eye and as he continued, he fixed his gaze carefully on the elaborate wallpaper behind the noble's head. 'Well, some of the villagers feel that they've been somewhat abandoned.'

Braun noticed the expression on Hieronymus's face and hurried to finish before he was interrupted. 'It's not that they mean to criticise your lordship's management of the estate in any way, it's just that at this particular time they would be grateful–'

'What *exactly* is the problem?' interrupted Hieronymus.

Braun took a deep breath and frowned. 'It's one of my own brethren, I'm afraid,' he said. 'Well, at least I believe he's a lay brother of some kind. I'd been turning a blind eye to his eccentricities, but now he's taken it on himself to pass a very harsh judgement on one of your villagers.'

Hieronymus shrugged and sat back in his chair. 'Surely I have men to deal with this kind of thing, Braun. Do you really need to bother me with such matters?'

'There are no men, father,' snapped Fabian, his voice squeaking with excitement. 'I've already told you: your stewards have been lying to you for months. The militia's almost non-existent. We're left open to every fraud and charlatan who wants to fleece the good people of Berlau. In fact just last–'

Hieronymus silenced his son with a raised hand and a glare. 'Who is this lay brother, Braun, and what exactly is he trying to punish?'

'His name's Otto Sürman,' answered Braun. 'I know very little about him. When he arrived last summer, I took him for a devout man of learning. He attended a few of my services and asked if he could make use of my library. To be honest, I had suspicions from the first, but I could see no reason to be rude to the man, and I let him stay. Recently, though, it seems he's assumed the role of judge, jury and executioner. I'd heard several rumours from my congregation and dismissed them as idle fancy, but now I've seen an example of his cruelty with my own eyes.'

Hieronymus nodded for him to continue.

'There's a boy in the village who goes by the name of Lukas. He's a little simple maybe, but nothing more than that as far as I can see and Sürman has accused the poor lad of the most terrible crimes. He claims he has been communing with the gods of the Old Night.'

'And has he?' asked Margarethe, her face filled with concern.

Braun shook his head. 'The boy's a bit of a loner that's all, but I hear that Sürman's had his eye on him for a while. Lukas is not so bright and maybe a little odd, so the other villagers tend to steer clear of him. His only real friends are a bunch of carrier pigeons he keeps in a small cage. They're a mangy bunch, and useless as messenger birds, but he dotes on them.'

'Where's the crime in that?' asked Hieronymus.

'There's no crime that I can see, but this Sürman character noticed the boy talking to the birds and claims they were responding to his commands – as though he was talking to them in their own language. He decided that such behaviour – along with Lukas's other eccentricities – marks him out as a witch of some kind.'

'How ridiculous,' exclaimed Hieronymus. 'I believe I even know the boy. There isn't an ounce of evil in him. What has this lay brother done to the poor soul?'

Braun grimaced. 'He told the villagers that Lukas is possessed by some kind of bird spirit. They're a superstitious lot, but even they found that a bit hard to swallow, so Sürman offered to prove the boy's guilt with a trial. He got the carpenter to construct a huge birdcage, then he locked the boy inside it and had him hoisted up thirty feet from the ground.'

Margarethe gasped. 'What on earth does he intend to prove by doing that?'

'The cage is open-topped but there is no way the boy could reach the pole to climb down. He'd break his neck if he even tried. Sürman has convinced the villagers that if they leave him up there long enough, the daemon will be driven mad by thirst and hunger and break free from Lukas's flesh. He claims it will fly to freedom – thus freeing the boy from possession.'

'And the villagers have allowed this to happen?' asked Hieronymus, shaking his head in disbelief.

Braun nodded. 'You must understand, lord, they're all terrified of Sürman. He's told them he works for the church as a witch hunter, so they're desperate not to anger him in any way.'

At the words 'witch hunter', Margarethe raised a hand nervously to her throat and looked at her husband. 'Perhaps we shouldn't become involved in a dispute like this. If he believes this boy is possessed, maybe he is. Who are we to deny the will of Sigmar?'

'The man is nothing to do with Sigmar,' replied Braun, shaking his head. 'I've made enquiries, and there's no record of him ever being ordained.' He placed a hand on Margarethe's knee. 'The countryside is overrun with such charlatans, my lady. In dark times such as these, simple rural folk are easily swayed. Their paranoia robs them of good sense.'

'Still,' replied Hieronymus, frowning, 'if he has the will of the people behind him, it might be dangerous to stir up trouble. Maybe my wife is right.'

'Father,' cried Fabian, leaping to his feet. 'Remember who we are! We are Wolffs. Are we to hand over control of our estates to any witless vagabond who wanders across our borders?'

'Watch your manners, boy,' snapped Hieronymus and Fabian sat down again with a sigh.

'Very well,' said Hieronymus. 'Let us make a compromise. I have no desire to delay our journey and get caught up in some petty legal dispute, but for once I think my son may have a point. This kind of bullying will lead to trouble if left unchecked.' He rang a little bell that was hung on the wall near to his head.

After a few minutes, an ancient hunchback shuffled into the room. Conrad Strobel had been the Wolffs' retainer since the time of Hieronymus's grandfather. Despite the heat, and his advanced years, Strobel was dressed for war. A thick leather jerkin enveloped his frail torso and his pinched, shrew-like features were almost completely hidden beneath a battered old helmet. 'M'lord?' he asked.

'How many of my personal guard are on duty today?' asked Hieronymus.

The old man's rheumy eyes grew even more clouded and he began to mutter under his breath.

'What was that?' asked Hieronymus.

'Three,' Strobel replied, raising his tremulous voice.

Colour rushed into Hieronymus's face, but he refused to acknowledge the smug expression directed at him by Fabian. 'Three units, do you mean?'

Strobel slowly shook his head. 'Three men,' he replied. There was a hint of accusation in his voice as he continued. 'I did inform His Lordship when I was forced to lose Ditwin and Eberhard.'

Hieronymus's eyes widened and his cheeks darkened to a deep purple, but he replied calmly. 'Of course. Have the three of them ride into the village would you, Strobel? There's a man by the name of Sürman who's causing a bit of trouble.'

'Should they arrest him?' asked the retainer.

Hieronymus stroked his long chin and thought for a moment. 'No, just have them free the boy he's imprisoned and then banish Sürman from my estate. Tell him that if he ever returns, I'll have him up before the magistrate.'

'Very good,' replied Strobel and left with the same chorus of sighs and wheezes that accompanied his arrival.

'Is it wise to antagonise these people, my dear?' asked Margarethe, obviously uncomfortable at the thought of banishing a witch hunter.

'I'm not antagonising him, I'm removing him,' replied Hieronymus sharply. 'Now, I'd rather not spend the whole afternoon discussing such tedious matters. Brother Braun – let's retire to my study and plan the route to Altdorf.' As he rose to his feet his eyes were gleaming with excitement. 'Imagine it, a personal invite from an Arch Lector.' He looked down at his sons. 'And your first visit to the capital. Believe me boys, you'll barely recognise yourselves by the time you return to Berlau. Altdorf is a city like no other. Nobody who passes through those hallowed gates is ever the same again.'

CHAPTER THIRTEEN
THE UNKNOWN HOUSE

'Is THAT THE drains or the locals?' asked Fabian, wrinkling his nose in disgust as they drove into the Königplatz. His impression of the city had so far been less than favourable. Their coach had approached the great north gates at a painful crawl, as the driver steered carefully through the flea-ridden lake of slums and refuges that had besieged Altdorf. Pock-marked fingers had reached up to them as they passed, begging for alms or passage into the city, and the driver had been forced to fend off hordes of naked, filthy orphans who clambered onto the roof and pleaded for food. It had been a miserable end to a miserable journey.

Once through the gates, things hadn't got much better. Fabian baulked at the confusing maze of crowded, narrow streets and tall, teetering townhouses. The filthy, cramped buildings of the city grew more bloated with each wonky storey, so that by the third or fourth floor their half-timbered facades were almost touching the houses opposite: arching over the bustling streets like bridges and plunging the flagstones below into a constant gloom.

There was a brief glimpse of blue sky overhead as they entered the Königplatz, but the broad square was no less crowded than the streets that led onto it. As Fabian tried to climb down from the coach, grinning, shouting hawkers clutched at his clothes, thrusting their wares into his face and vying aggressively for his attention.

'Fabian!' cried his father. 'Back in the coach, now! They'll have the shirt off your back if you give them half a chance.'

Fabian climbed back inside and looked in amazement at his parents. 'What a hellish place,' he muttered. 'And what *is* that smell?'

To his annoyance no one seemed to hear him. They were all peering through the windows, engrossed by the mayhem outside. Despite his loud sighs, they continued to ignore him, so he followed their example, squeezing his face next to Jakob's and looking out through the coach window.

Every form of life was parading through the square. The coach rocked constantly as the crush of bodies barged past it and the hawkers outside pressed dolls and clothes to the glass. A few feet away a man was driving a train of cages through the crowd and each one was filled with a menagerie of incredible creatures, half of which Fabian couldn't even name. Birds with dazzling, rainbow-coloured feathers dozed on their perches and giant cats with ragged, white manes gazed idly out from their prisons. Further into the square, rows of striped awnings shaded produce from every corner of the Old World: fruit, livestock, fish and leather passed over the heads of the jostling figures as they haggled and joked with each other. Further still, in the heart of the square, ranks of crumbling statues towered over everything; made faceless and nameless by the elements, they watched the turmoil at their feet with a regal, patrician disdain, marred only by the thick layer of bird muck that coated their faces.

Fabian fastened a handkerchief over his nose and settled back in his seat. The thick odour seeped through the cotton. It seemed to be a powerful mixture of horse piss and rotting fish, with a persistent, acrid bass note that he guessed was coming from the open sewers.

'There's our man, cried Braun, pointing out a young priest fighting his way through the crowds towards them. 'I'd never forget that face.'

Fabian raised his eyebrows as the slender youth neared the coach. The boy's appearance certainly *was* memorable. His head was shaven, as with any other novitiate, and his vestments were simple and unadorned, but his face seemed to have slipped to the sides of his head. His broad, watery eyes were closer to his ears than his wide crooked nose, and his broad mouth was so big it seemed to hinge his whole head as it broke into a broad smile.

'Brother Potzlinger,' cried Braun, shoving the door open and fighting his way down to embrace the youth. 'It's *so* good to see you.'

Potzlinger gave a hyena laugh and patted Braun's back enthusiastically. 'And you too, brother.' He turned his head to one side with an odd, bird-like movement and looked up at the Wolffs with one bulging eye. 'Welcome to Altdorf,' he cried, struggling to make himself heard over the cacophony.

Hieronymus climbed down and took his hand. 'It's good to meet you, Brother Potzlinger,' he said waving his hand back at the coach. 'This is my wife Margarethe, and our sons Fabian,' he paused for dramatic effect, 'and Jakob.'

'Ah, yes, Jakob,' said Potzlinger, reaching up to take the boy's hand. 'We've learned so much about you from Brother Braun's letters. I feel as though I already know you.' He looked around at the square and grimaced. 'We should find somewhere better to speak though. Königplatz is like this every Aubentag. I'm not sure what the river wardens do with their time, I'm really not – it seems like we let any old riffraff into the city these days.' He shrugged. 'Well, we may as well make straight for the cathedral. We can have a little peace there. I believe the Arch Lector has arranged some accommodation for you.' He held a hand up to Margarethe. 'It's probably easier if we walk. Your boys will see more of the city that way anyway.'

'Oh no, Fabian isn't accompanying us,' explained Hieronymus hurriedly. 'He'll be staying with his Uncle Jonas. The driver knows the way to the house.' He narrowed his eyes as he put his head back inside the coach. 'Just sit tight until you get there, Fabian. We'll only be gone for a few days I should think, so try keep your head down and not cause your uncle any trouble.' With that he slammed the door shut, cutting out at least a little of the racket from outside.

Fabian watched his family struggling across the square, as Brother Potzlinger pointed out the various landmarks to his wide-eyed brother. Then, as the coach began to edge cautiously back towards the narrow streets, he sat down and hissed through his teeth. 'What a place,' he said, pressing the handkerchief to his face and shaking his head in disgust.

He soon lost track of their route as the coach bounced and clattered through the labyrinthine maze of streets. The houses pressed closer and closer overhead and just as there seemed barely enough room for the coach to squeeze any further, they reached their destination. They had left the noise of the market place far behind, and as Fabian climbed down onto the grimy cobbles, he felt oddly nervous. The townhouses that surrounded him were all four or five storeys tall and as they leant out over his head, leaving just a narrow slit of sky, their small, deep-set windows peered down hungrily at him.

'It's that one,' muttered the driver, nodding towards the last house on the street. It was even taller and more asymmetrical than the others. A mixture of architectural styles had been piled on top of each other to create a haphazard column of crumbling render and gnarled timbers. It looked to Fabian like a stiff breeze would send all five of its crooked, gabled storeys tumbling to the ground. There was a sign over the gate, beautifully painted in gothic script that announced enigmatically: The Unknown House.

'Are you sure this is the right place?' asked Fabian, turning back to the coach, but the driver just gave him an odd smile as he dropped the luggage at the gate and climbed back onto the coach.

Fabian sighed, hefted his bag onto his back and climbed up the flagged path to the front door. There was a large iron knocker in the shape of a snarling wolf, and he clanged it three times, before stepping back to wait for a response.

No one came, and after a few minutes he pressed his ear to the door and listened for footsteps. He heard another sound instead: a mournful, unearthly moaning that throbbed gently through the wood. Fabian felt a tingle of fear. No mortal being could make such a noise. He stepped back again and turned to speak to the coachman, but he was gone. The coach was already turning a corner and disappearing from view. I wonder if I could find the cathedral, he thought, looking back down the winding street.

With a screech of rusted hinges, the door opened.

The eerie droning sound flooded out onto the street and Fabian turned to face a towering, fur-clad giant of a man, who had to stoop to fit his broad shoulders out through the doorframe. 'What do you want?' he growled, through a long, shaggy beard. He spoke in such a thick Kislev accent, though, that it sounded more like: 'Vwaht do you vwant?'

'Uncle Jonas?' asked Fabian, doubtfully.

The giant's eyes narrowed beneath his thick brow. 'I'm no one's uncle, child,' he said. 'I'm no one's anything, thank the gods.' He eased his massive bulk back in through the doorframe and stepped to one side, signalling for Fabian to step into the gloomy interior. 'Jonas probably won't return until tonight. You'd best speak to his wife, Isolde. Come inside.'

Fabian hesitated, looking wistfully back over his shoulder at the street, before stepping into the house. He found himself in a muddle of narrow corridors, cramped staircases and sombre, dark panelling. The Kislevite had to remain stooped as he led the way beneath the low, beamed ceilings. Strange objects pressed in on them, crowding the shelves and cupboards that lined the walls: china dolls and stuffed birds crowded every available space and crooked pictures shook on the walls as the man stomped across the uneven floors. The whole place was filled with the odd, whirring buzzing sound and as they approached a door at the far end of the hallway, it grew louder. The only light came from a single, filthy window, and it was hard to see clearly, but Fabian thought he could make out two large sentries flanking the door. As they reached it, however, he realised he was mistaken. The bulky figures were actually the stuffed carcasses of two massive bears. They were an imposing presence, despite their dusty, moth-eaten fur and Fabian found it hard to look at their snarling faces as he hurried though the doorway.

They had entered another narrow hallway that ended in a rickety spiral staircase. The Kislevite waved one of his meaty fur-clad paws at it. 'She'll be in the Tapestry Room. Second on the left.'

Fabian nodded, and squeezed past the man towards the stairs. 'Thank you...' he said, waiting for the man to supply his name.

The giant gave a low chuckle and nodded back. 'Kobach,' he said, in an amused rumble, before stomping away.

'Kobach,' repeated Fabian quietly to himself; not sure if it was a name or an insult. The stairs shifted unnervingly beneath his feet as he climbed up to the next floor. There was another door at the top, and as he pushed it open and stepped onto the landing, the droning chorus grew even louder. As Fabian looked down the long, twisting hallway, he thought he could discern some kind of melody in the noise, as though the house were humming a lullaby to itself.

As he passed the first door, he noticed that it was open and squinted through the gloom to see if the room was empty. It wasn't. His pulse quickened as he realised at least two of the shadows in there were alive: a couple of hooded monks were sat close together, whispering to each other in hurried, urgent tones. They looked up angrily at Fabian's approach and one of them leapt to his feet and slammed the door shut. Fabian only caught the briefest glimpse of his face, but it was enough to unnerve him even more. The man's pale, narrow features were beaded with sweat and his bloodshot eyes were running with tears.

He hurried onwards, towards the awful sound. Finally he reached the next door. There was something strange about the frame. At first he struggled to see what exactly it was in the half-light, but after a few seconds he realised the entire structure was carved from the jaw of some monstrous leviathan. With a grimace of disgust, he saw that its bleached teeth were still in place, surrounding the door with rows of jagged canines.

This close, the sound was really quite terrifying and Fabian looked back down the corridor, wondering if even now it might be possible to escape. He could imagine how amusing his brother would find it though, if he arrived at the cathedral, having been too scared to wait in his own uncle's house. I'd never hear the end of it, he decided and after taking a long, hitching breath he tapped gently on the door.

The noise stopped immediately, as though the house were holding its breath.

The door opened slowly, flooding the hallway with smoke and warm, yellow light. A beautiful woman looked out at him with sleepy, half-lidded eyes. Her pale skin was flushed with warmth, or alcohol and her thick black tresses were tousled and unkempt, as though he had woken her from a deep sleep. She gave him a languid smile and stooped to place a long, moist kiss on his forehead, as though they were old, intimate acquaintances. As she leant back again, Fabian's eyes rested briefly on the expanse of ivory cleavage straining at the emerald-green velvet of her dress. He blushed as he realised she had noticed the direction of his gaze and the woman's smile broadened as she stepped back into the room and signalled for him to follow.

It was a large room, but every inch of it was crowded with crates, chests and piles of books. The walls were lined with thick, faded tapestries depicting a gaudy multitude of creatures, both mythical and real. There was a large, canopied bed in one corner and next to it an oil lamp was quietly hissing, filling the room with soft, shifting shadows. The light also picked out a haze of scented smoke that was hovering at about the level of Fabian's face. He couldn't place the aroma, but as he inhaled the fumes he felt a pleasant heaviness in his limbs and suddenly realised how tired he was.

'Take a seat,' said the woman in a soft voice, waving vaguely at the jumble of furniture that cluttered the room. Then she yawned, reaching up in a slow, feline stretch, obviously conscious of how flattering the light was as it played across her curves. As the light shimmered over her hair, Fabian noticed it was bejewelled with dozens of tiny, yellow flowers. Once she had finished stretching, the woman curled up in a large, leather chair and rested her chin on her hands, gazing through the smoke at Fabian's discomfort with obvious amusement.

He finally found a chair and perched awkwardly on the edge of it, looking everywhere but at the woman. 'Your servant told me it was best to wait here,' he muttered, 'until my uncle returns.'

'Of course,' she replied, nodding sagely. 'And who is your uncle?'

Fabian frowned and finally met her eye, wondering why on earth she had kissed him so fervently if she had know idea who he was. 'My… my uncle is Captain Jonas Wolff,' he stammered, wondering if he had come to the wrong room.

The woman flicked her ebony hair back from her face and looked up at the ceiling as though trying to recall something. 'Jonas Wolff is my husband's name too,' she said, seeming a little confused. 'How odd.'

Fabian waited for her to continue, but she just frowned up at the ceiling in silence. He took the opportunity to admire the long, pale curve of her neck and as he did so, he noticed a silver chain that pointed enticingly to the neckline of her dress. The chain ended in a small, ivory figurine of some kind, but Fabian could not quite make it out through the heady fug. After a few minutes, the silence began to seem a little odd. 'Then, are you Isolde?' he asked.

The warm smile returned to her face and she looked back at him. 'Of course I am, silly boy.' She rummaged down by the side of her chair and lifted a strange contraption up onto her lap. It looked like an oversized violin, but it had a cranked wheel attached to it and the soundboard was covered with a row of small teeth-like keys. 'Are you a fan of the wheel fiddle?' she asked. Before he could reply, she began to turn the handle, filling the room with the awful whining buzz he had heard earlier. As she played, the woman closed her eyes and mouthed a stream of silent words. She seemed to quickly forget all about her guest.

As the droning notes washed over him, Fabian felt his head growing lighter and his eyelids growing heavier. He tried to keep himself awake by studying the animals depicted on the tapestries, and to his delight he realised they were moving, dancing across the walls of the room in time to the music and fluttering gaily across the ceiling. Scale seemed to have no meaning for the crewelwork creatures. Rats pounced viciously on horses, wrestling them to the ground with their teeth, and monkeys rode on the back of goldfinches, waving little flags above their heads as they circled the light fittings and skipped around the doorframe. Fabian laughed to himself, thrilled to think that Jakob had missed out on this incredible carnival, just so that he could be lectured by a bunch of sour-faced old priests. The music eddied and swelled, enveloping his thoughts with its odd, serpentine phrases. After a while, he slipped gratefully into unconsciousness, dragging the creatures down with him into his dreams.

'Isolde, what have you done?' cried an angry voice and Fabian woke with a start. For a moment he could not place his surroundings. The oil lamp had burned itself out and the only illumination was a few shards of moonlight knifing through the gaps in the wooden shutters. He saw the dark-haired woman curled up on her chair, fast asleep, but still clutching the strange instrument to her chest. With an inexplicable feeling of guilt, Fabian remembered what had happened and lurched up from his chair. His head spun sickeningly and he felt as though the floor was giving way beneath him. He turned towards the door, to see the owner of the voice.

An elderly gentleman was stood in the doorway, and Fabian immediately realised it must be his uncle. He had the same regal bearing and aquiline features as his father, but if anything, they were even more refined. He was obviously much older than Hieronymus: in his late seventies possibly, and he had to support himself on a long, delicate cane; but his clothes were perfectly tailored. His doublet, jerkin, and hose were all jet black and embellished with delicate silver needlework, and he wore a high, ermine-lined collar, ribbed with sparkling leaves of silver. His long, grey moustache was waxed in a flamboyant curl and as he took in Fabian's slender form, he dipped his head in a graceful bow. 'Fabian, I presume?' he said, annunciating each syllable with the soft, precise tones of a poet.

'Yes, my lord,' gasped Fabian stumbling through the chaos and taking the man's hand. 'I was instructed to wait here by your servant, but I was tired after the journey and–'

'I can imagine what happened, child,' interrupted the old man, giving Fabian a kind smile. He eyed the sleeping woman with concern. 'My wife has been a little unwell of late.' He placed a hand on Fabian's shoulder and looked deep into his eyes. 'Don't give any credence to anything she might have told you. The poor thing has become slightly confused. She inhabits a strange fantasy land half the time.' He gestured to the wheel fiddle. 'She finds it helpful to indulge her passion for music.' He chuckled. 'But it's not always so helpful for everyone else.'

He steered Fabian out of the room and quietly closed the door behind him. 'As you have no doubt guessed, I'm your Uncle Jonas,' he said, leaning on Fabian's shoulder for support as they headed off down the corridor. 'I had hoped to be here to meet you, but I got caught up in a dispute with some rather disreputable foreigners.' They entered a smoky, book-lined study. A small, cast iron fireplace filled the room with light from its merry, crackling blaze and Fabian helped the old man into a seat beside it.

'Did you mention a servant?' asked Jonas, signalling for Fabian to sit next to him and handing him a small glass of thick, ruby liquid.

Darius Hinks

Fabian eyed the glass suspiciously, still feeling unsteady from his unexpected nap. 'Er, yes,' he replied. 'Your butler, I think. A large Kislevite man. He showed me to your wife's chambers. I think he was called Kobach.'

Jonas leant back in his chair with a snort of amusement. 'So, Kobach Ivanov has returned to Altdorf!' He shook his head. 'That man is bound for either greatness or the executioner's block, but I wouldn't like to bet which.' He noticed Fabian's look of confusion and patted his knee reassuringly. 'I'm sorry, lad – I'm not laughing at you. You should learn not to make such quick assumptions though. If Kobach had realised that you mistook him for a servant, I wouldn't like to imagine where you'd be now. This house is a refuge for some of the city's more interesting visitors; many of them are very powerful men in their own countries, but they're all a little dangerous in their own way.' He drained his glass and waved at the drink in Fabian's hand. 'Drink up, son. We have a whole city to explore and you'll need little fire in your belly to survive your first night in Altdorf.'

Fabian looked out through a small leaded window at the darkness outside. 'We're going out now?' he asked.

Jonas shrugged. 'Well, you can retire to your bed if you wish. There's one all made up for you if you'd like an early night.' He leant forward, so that the flames flashed mischievously in his eyes. 'I just have a feeling you're a little more adventurous than that.'

No adult had ever spoken to Fabian in such conspiratorial tones before and he was unsure how to respond. He realised that despite the physical similarities, this man was nothing like his father. There was a hint of danger in the old man's voice that both troubled and excited him. It did not take him long to make up his mind. He emptied the glass with one hungry gulp and as the potent drink filled him with warmth he grinned. 'I'm not really *that* tired,' he replied.

'THEY CALL THIS the Street of a Hundred Taverns,' explained Jonas as they fought their way through the jostling crowds of revellers. He was leaning heavily on Fabian for support, but his eyes sparkled with excitement as he waved his cane at the array of inns and clubs that surrounded them. Despite the late hour, the street was ablaze with light and crammed with people: lame beggars grasped at their legs as they passed; drunken dockhands hurled red-faced abuse at each other; nobles barged past in gaudy, flamboyant palanquins and sinister, hooded figures watched attentively from the ill-lit side streets. Despite his fear, Fabian felt more alive than he could ever remember feeling before.

'This is the vital, pounding heart of the city,' continued Jonas, tapping his cane on the filthy cobbles. 'The whole Empire even.' He pointed out an incredible array of characters to Fabian, from infamous crime lords and legendary war heroes, to distinguished plutocrats and revered musicians, all crushed together in a whirling mass of drunken faces and raucous song. 'Anything worth knowing is being discussed right here, right now. There are deals being struck in these taverns that will influence military strategy in every corner of the Empire. Kingdoms have been toppled as a result of a chance remark uttered in the back alleys and cellars that surround us.'

He shouldered his way towards a narrow, anonymous-looking door, tucked away beside a rundown theatre. He tapped firmly with the knocker and after a few minutes a shutter snapped to one side and a pair of suspicious eyes glared out at them. 'Ah, Captain Wolff,' came a voice. 'Back so soon?' There was a *click clack* of locks being turned and the door opened inwards onto a surprisingly plush interior. Candles lined the walls of a wood-panelled hallway and a liveried butler bowed graciously at them, waving for them to enter.

'Thank you, Vogel,' said Jonas, handing the man his hat and cape as he entered.

The butler was a flame-haired youth, whose pale, freckled face split into a grin at the sight of Jonas. 'Always a pleasure, Captain,' he replied. After hanging the hat and cloak in a side room, he leant close to Jonas and whispered conspiratorially in his ear.

Jonas laughed and clapped him on the back. 'Ah, yes – I thought as much. I'm not afraid of a few half-soaked Tileans though, Vogel,' he said. 'Anyway,' he continued, nodding at Fabian, 'I have some muscle with me tonight.'

The butler laughed and waved them down the hall.

At the far end was another door, much grander than the first. It was a broad, venerable thing, made of polished oak and elaborate brass hinges. There was a large letter R engraved in the central panel, framed within a cartouche of writhing serpents. Jonas gave Fabian a sly wink and shoved the door open to reveal a wide, carpeted drawing room, lined with tapestries and curtained booths. Deep, high-backed chairs were scattered around the room and several distinguished-looking gentlemen were sat reading books or talking. There was a haze of pipe smoke that made it hard to discern the club's patrons very clearly, but as Fabian caught glimpses of their exotic clothes and heard snatches of their foreign accents, he deduced that many of them were not from the Empire. The place throbbed with an undercurrent of danger and he looked nervously at his uncle, but Jonas placed a reassuring hand on his shoulder and grinned. 'Welcome to the Recalcitrant Club,' he said proudly.

'Jonas,' said an unfeasibly obese gentleman, as he waddled slowly towards them. He wore his dark hair slicked back from his jowly face in a greasy bob, and his small, porcine eyes nestled behind a pair of round, wire-rimmed glasses. Blue robes billowed around him as he embraced Jonas and placed a kiss on his cheek. He studied the noble's slender physique. 'The years have been kind to you,' he said, in a creamy, effeminate voice. 'I doubted I would ever see your dear face again. What a delightful surprise.'

Jonas smiled and squeezed the man's shoulder. 'I only saw you this morning, Puchelperger,' he replied, 'so I'd hope I've not worn too badly.' He looked down at the man's vast, trembling paunch. 'I see times haven't been too hard for you, either.'

Puchelperger raised his eyebrows. 'I endeavoured to keep myself hale and hearty in the hope of your eventual return.' He gestured to an empty booth. 'Let me buy you a drink and you can introduce me to your new friend.'

They settled back into plush, leather couches and a waiter discretely deposited three tall glasses on their table.

'This is my cousin's son, Fabian,' said Jonas, smiling paternally, and patting the boy on the shoulder. 'It's his first time in Altdorf.'

'Ah, an innocent,' said Puchelperger with a glint in his beady, black eyes. 'Well, my boy, you couldn't have wished for a better guide.' He gestured to the tall glass in front of Fabian. 'Please, I insist,' he said.

Fabian's thoughts were already a little muddled from his previous drink and he looked at his uncle with a worried expression.

Jonas laughed. 'It won't harm you, boy,' he said, taking a swig from his own glass. 'I'm not sure how they do things in the country, but I think you're old enough to sample a few of life's more cosmopolitan pleasures.'

Afraid of appearing a fool in front of his urbane new friends, Fabian emptied the entire glass in one swallow. He felt a sudden rush of euphoria followed by an equally sudden rush of gas. He grinned at his uncle, as an explosive belch ripped through his throat.

The two men burst into raucous laughter.

'Ah, yes,' cried Puchelperger, clapping his chubby hands, and causing the table to rock as his belly jiggled up and down. 'He's a Wolff alright!' He leant as far forward as his stomach would allow. 'Tell me though, boy – what brings you to this noble city?'

The smile dropped from Fabian's face. 'My brother,' he muttered. 'He's some kind of *wonderful* student. The priests wanted to interview him at the Cathedral of Sigmar.'

Jonas noted Fabian's sullen tone with interest. 'And you? Have you studied the holy texts?'

Fabian gave a harsh laugh. 'No, uncle, to be honest, I find all that stuff as dull as ditchwater.' The rush of euphoria was still growing in his head and he felt his shyness slipping away. He raised his eyebrows disdainfully and his voice rang with a new-found confidence. 'I find it a facile ideology at best. I've read many of the older, epic poems and they seem to me far more interesting.'

Jonas and Puchelperger both fell silent at these words and Jonas continued to study Fabian intently.

'Interesting,' said Puchelperger, giving Jonas a knowing look as he emptied his own glass. 'Well, I'm sure you won't find it dull spending an evening in the company of your uncle.'

Jonas smiled. 'I have a few interesting diversions in mind.'

'Jonas Wolff,' barked a harsh voice and Fabian turned to see a leathery, olive-skinned rake, wearing a colourful gypsy bandana and scowling at Jonas with evident rage. 'I was hoping to see you in here,' he said in a strange, lilting accent. The man was slender, but with the taut, sinewy physique of a dancer or an acrobat, and as he leant over the table, Fabian noticed he was clutching a long, needle-thin knife. A group of similarly flamboyant men were stood behind him, all holding knives of their own.

'Calderino,' replied Jonas, with an amiable smile. 'What charmingly rustic manners you have. And it's always such a delight to hear your interpretation of our language.'

The man's teeth flashed, bright white against his tanned skin as he snarled his reply. 'We had a deal, Jonas. I secured the books for you.' He grabbed Jonas by his tall collar and pulled him across the table. 'Where's my money?'

Jonas slapped the man's face with such force that he loosed his grip and stepped back, holding his hand to his cheek in shock. 'Not in the club, Calderino,' Jonas hissed, gesturing to the red-haired butler, Vogel, who was watching them from the doorway with an anxious expression on his face.

Calderino looked around to notice that the room had fallen silent and all the other club members were watching him over their papers, scowling with disapproval. He took a deep breath and removed his hand from his face. 'Well, whatever happens Wolff, I *will* have my payment,' he whispered, levelling his slender knife at Jonas. Then, with a flamboyant flourish of his short, silk cape he stormed out of the room, leaving his friends to hastily finish their drinks and rush after him.

Jonas smiled apologetically at the butler and settled back in his seat. 'The books were all forgeries,' he explained to Puchelperger, loud enough for the rest of the club to hear. 'And not even good ones.'

Puchelperger shook his head and sighed despairingly at Fabian. 'See what I mean?' he said. 'Whatever else he might be accused of, your uncle is rarely boring.'

For the next hour or so, Fabian listened respectfully as the two men exchanged anecdotes and discussed the state of the Empire. Another drink appeared mysteriously before him, but he drank this one a little slower, already feeling as though he might need to borrow his uncle's cane when it was time to leave. As the conversation turned to politics, his mind wondered to Jonas's strange young wife. She could not have been more than thirty, and she was strikingly beautiful, yet she was attracted to a man of Jonas's advanced years. He wondered if he could ever learn to be as witty and assured as his uncle. How different he was from his pious, bumbling father. Fabian shook his head as he considered how much more there was to life than the simple, god-fearing dogma his brother had adopted.

'I sense we're boring you, Fabian,' said Jonas, finishing his drink and rising from his chair. 'I find it all too easy to while away the hours in this genial haven, but there's so much more I'd like to show you tonight.'

Puchelperger bade them an enthusiastic farewell and as they headed for the door, several of the other club members gave Jonas their regards and commented on the poor manners of the foreigner who had accosted him.

As they left the warmth of the club, the cold night air left Fabian reeling. He felt his uncle's steadying hand on his arm though, and quickly recovered his composure.

'Are you alright, son?' asked Jonas, with an amused smile.

'Yes, uncle,' said Fabian with a manly cough, but as they re-entered the crowded street he found it difficult to focus on the multitude of shapes and colours rushing by.

As they made their way south down the Street of a Hundred Taverns, the constant stink of the city became more focussed. The smell of the sewers and livestock was eclipsed by the overwhelming stench of fish and brine. And beneath the calls of beggars and drunks, Fabian thought he could make out a vague sloshing sound.

They reached the end of the road and Fabian gasped. A broad expanse of moonlit water lay stretched out before him, carving right through the heart of the city, and dotted with small islands, all linked by a myriad of crowded bridges.

Dozens of galleons and barges were moored up at the quayside and even at this late hour, crowds of sailors and stevedores were rushing to-and-fro along the gangplanks, laden with exotic goods and yelling commands to each other in a wonderful variety of accents and languages. Fabian looked up at the nearest ship in awe. Its mountainous, barnacle-encrusted hull reared up over him, and he felt a cool spray landing on his upturned face as the sails snapped and boomed over his head. On the far side of the river lay the rest of the city: a teeming mass of spires, roofs, domes and bridges. The combination of the alcohol rushing through his veins and the incredible panoply arrayed before him left Fabian's heart racing. He suddenly felt as though he might burst into tears at the sheer spectacle of it all.

'Quite a sight, isn't it?' said Jonas, looking out over the water. 'It's best to keep moving though,' he said, steering Fabian back into the flow of people. 'The docks aren't the safest place to be at night.'

Fabian did not really need his uncle's warning. Most of the figures rushing by looked as though they would slit his throat as easily as asking him to step aside. He saw hostile eyes watching from every alleyway and violence filled the air as palpably as the stink of fish. He shuddered and stepped a little closer to his uncle.

'Watch yourself,' laughed Jonas, as a pile of brawling drunks scattered across the cobbles in front of them. With surprising agility, he dragged Fabian around the mass of flailing limbs and turned up a quiet back street. It was so steep and narrow that they had to walk in single file as they clambered up past the shuttered warehouses and dingy archways. As they reached the summit, Fabian noticed a light was flickering through the window of one of the buildings. A small, battered sign was hanging above the door, in the shape of an open book.

'Those dusty old fools in the university district will tell you they're the keepers of Altdorf's entire reserves of knowledge,' said Jonas, pausing outside the shop. 'But there's much more to be learned in this city, for those willing to look.' He tapped on the door and stepped back into the street to wait for a response.

After a few minutes the door squeaked open and an elderly woman peered myopically out at them through the thick, scratched lenses of her spectacles. Her skin was as shrivelled as a dried fig and her back was so hunched by age that she was barely four feet tall.

'Frau Gangolffin,' exclaimed Jonas, giving the old lady a gracious bow. 'I hope I didn't wake you.'

'Don't be cruel, Jonas,' she replied with a voice like sandpaper on gravel. 'You know perfectly well how little sleep I get.' She peered up at Fabian and shook her head. 'At my age I'm lucky if I can close my eyes for so much as an hour.' Without another word, she shuffled back into the shop, leaving the door swinging open behind her.

Jonas smiled mischievously at Fabian and ushered him inside.

Every inch of the shop was crammed with crooked, heaving bookshelves and teetering piles of dusty, leather-bound folios. The comforting smell of old paper was almost enough to mask the stink of the river and Fabian took a deep, grateful breath. There was an oil lamp sat on a desk at the foot of a narrow staircase and the glow of the shifting flame danced across the rows of foiled spines. Fabian sighed as he took in the wealth of obscure bestiaries and ancient poetry anthologies. He reeled from shelf to shelf, unsure where to look first, dazzled by the wealth of esoteric learning on display.

He noticed that Jonas was chuckling softly. 'It's quite something, isn't it?' he said. 'Choose any book you want and consider it a gift.' He nodded to the old woman, who seemed to have already forgotten them. She was hunched eagerly over a parchment on her desk, peering at it through a large magnifying glass. 'I have an account with the old dear,' he said.

'Frau Gangolffin,' said Jonas, waving to the narrow stairs. 'Do you have the books I ordered?'

The old woman still had the magnifying glass in front of her face as she looked up, giving her the appearance of a confused, whiskery cyclops. 'Ah, yes,' she croaked, with a look of recognition. She placed the lens back on the cluttered desk and started climbing very slowly up the stairs. 'They did arrive, I think, with the last Estalian shipment. They should be up here somewhere.'

'Take your time, my boy,' said Jonas, waving at the bookshelves. 'Who knows when you'll be here again.' With that he followed the woman upstairs.

Fabian immersed himself in the books, comforted by the creak of the floorboards overhead and the muffled sound of his uncle's voice as he chatted to the old woman. Finally, after nearly an hour had passed, Jonas climbed back down the stairs with a pile of books under his arm. 'Find anything of interest?' he asked.

Fabian held up a handsome volume, bound in white leather, with a gold knife foiled on the front. 'Is this too expensive?' he asked hesitantly.

'Almost certainly,' replied Jonas with a smile and called up the stairs. 'And a copy of Lang's *Dooms and Legends*, please Frau Gangolffin.'

There was a croak of acknowledgment from the old woman as she climbed slowly down the stairs.

'And about the other matter?' asked Jonas, giving the bookseller a strange smile.

She nodded to Fabian. 'Is he to be trusted?'

'Of course.'

'Very well. Check the street,' she muttered, glaring at Fabian. 'And shut the door.'

Fabian leapt to obey, peering up and down the alley-way. 'No one there,' he said, closing the door behind him with a *clunk*.

The old woman turned to her desk and started to shove it across the floorboards with a horrible scraping sound. Before she had moved it more than a couple of inches however, she was gripped by a coughing fit that was so violent Fabian rushed to her side and began patting her back.

She batted him away with a grunt of irritation and, after wiping the spittle from her chin, gestured to the floor beneath her desk.

Fabian noticed that table's movement had disturbed a rug and revealed the edges of a trapdoor. With the old woman waving him on, he shoved the table a little further until the trapdoor was completely exposed, and then stooped down to lever it open. Hidden beneath the floorboards was a small shelf holding three books. Each one was carefully wrapped in oilskin and fastened with a thick, knotted cord.

Jonas moved Fabian to one side and gazed lovingly at the small, innocent-looking bundles. 'Which one?' he whispered.

Frau Gangolffin backed away from the books; watching them carefully from a few feet away, as though they might leap for her throat at any minute. 'The middle one,' she muttered, with a note of fear in her voice.

Quick as a flash, Jonas snatched the book, secreted it in a pocket and slammed the trapdoor shut.

As he signalled for Fabian to move the table back into place, the boy noticed that his uncle was flushed with excitement.

Jonas took a deep, relieved breath, and smiled at Fabian. 'Don't mention what you've seen, my boy. Frau Gangolffin has some particularly disreputable competitors, and they'd all dearly love to know about that trapdoor.'

Fabian nodded in reply.

'I believe that's everything,' said Jonas, giving the old woman a stiff bow. She was already climbing slowly back up the stairs though, and if she heard him she gave no sign of it.

'Well, Fabian, we're almost done,' Jonas said as they stepped out onto the street. 'I just have one last call to make, and then we can head home.'

Fabian suddenly realised how exhausted he was. He nodded sleepily and stumbled after his uncle, making no pretence of supporting the elderly gentleman as he tottered back towards the quayside. Before they reached the river, Jonas veered off down another narrow winding street and after a few lefts and rights, Fabian gave up trying to work out which direction they were heading in. The routes criss-crossed and doubled back on themselves in a mind-boggling confusion of pitch dark side streets and crooked, sombrous alleyways. Tiredness added to Fabian's bewilderment and he began to feel as though everything that had happened to him since his father left him in the coach had been nothing more than a strange dream.

A predawn glow was just beginning to lift the gloom a little when Jonas led them onto a street full of narrow tenements, huddled together against the wall of a large park. Cheerful lights flickered in many of the small, square windows, and figures flitted hurriedly in and out of the open doorways.

Fabian pointed out an iron bench, just outside the entrance to the park. 'Wait there for a while, lad,' he said. 'I have one last bit of business to attend to.'

Fabian eyed the tall, crooked building with concern. 'Will you need my help climbing the stairs?' he asked.

Jonas grinned and ruffled his hair. 'Bless you, son, no. I have friends in there who will be more than happy to take my hand.'

Fabian blushed, as he realised what kind of house it was. 'Oh, of course,' he muttered

Jonas began to walk away and then hesitated, pursing his lips as he looked up and down the street. He came back to Fabian and placed a hand on his shoulder, stooping so that their eyes were level. 'Best keep yourself out of view,' he said, frowning. 'Altdorf at night is, well...' He stumbled over his words, looking a little anxious. Then he shrugged and his mouth split into a broad grin. 'You'll be fine,' he said patting Fabian's shoulder. 'Anyway, I won't be long.' With that he hobbled off into the darkness.

Fabian rushed over to the bench and did his best to become invisible. As he sat there, trying desperately to stay awake, Fabian saw a stream of people rushing by: ne'er-do-wells of every class and creed, from rowdy, drunken dockhands to sinister, hooded nobles, none of whom seemed to notice him as he crouched sleepily by the park gate.

After a few minutes had passed, Fabian began to get the unnerving feeling he was being watched. He studied the faces of the passers-by, but everyone he saw was intent on either getting in or out of one the houses as quickly as possible. None of them were paying him any attention at all. So why was his skin crawling so unpleasantly? A movement caught his eye in an alleyway directly opposite. He peered into the shadows, but it was still too dark to see very clearly. Was that a barrel, or a crouched figure, he wondered? Despite his best instincts, he rose from the bench and started walking across the street towards the alleyway. As he neared the hunched shape, it suddenly leapt from the ground and dashed silently back up the alley, quickly disappearing from view. Fabian's fear grew, as he realised his suspicions had been correct: someone *had* been watching him. The idea horrified him and he looked anxiously up at the house Jonas had entered, praying he would not be left alone for much longer.

Fabian passed another awful fifteen minutes on the bench, crippled by fear and flinching at every shape that rushed past. Finally, he saw a tired Jonas step back out onto the street and head towards him, leaning heavily on his cane and finally looking as old as Fabian knew he must be.

'Is everything alright?' asked Jonas with a yawn, as he saw the fear in Fabian's eyes.

'Yes, of course,' he replied. 'I'm a little tired, that's all.'

'Of course you are, my boy. We should get you home. Isolde will be expecting us.' He nodded to the wide, moonlit lawns of the park. 'We can cut back through here.'

A flagged path dissected the park, lined by tall, noble oaks, and low, serpentine yews. In the grey calm just before the dawn, it was one of the few places in the city that Fabian hadn't felt claustrophobic. The path was broad, straight and silent and it seemed that for the briefest of moments that Altdorf was asleep.

They had just spied the gates on the far side of the park when Jonas paused and frowned at Fabian. 'Did you hear that?' he asked.

Fabian shook his head, but something in his uncle's tone reminded of him of the figure he saw fleeing up the alleyway.

Jonas stayed stock still, listening carefully. After a few minutes he curled his lip in disdain. 'It seems that the evening's entertainment isn't over.' He reached beneath the black velvet of his doublet and withdrew a long knife. He flipped it in his hand and held it out to Fabian, handle first. 'Just in case,' he said, with a wry smile.

The sound of running feet came from behind them and Jonas and Fabian turned to see five slender figures sprinting towards them out of the darkness. Fabian recognised the gypsy bandanas that covered their faces from the men in the Recalcitrant Club. A cold fury replaced his fear, as he pictured the treacherous Calderino murdering his frail old uncle. He finally felt as though he had a relative who understood him and these dogs were going to butcher him.

With a howl of rage, Fabian dropped his book and charged at the masked figures, brandishing his knife as though it were a lance. Every heroic tale he had ever read flooded through his mind as he leapt at the first runner, planting a well-placed boot in the man's face and sending them both tumbling backwards onto the grass. Without a pause for breath, he climbed to his feet and threw the knife with all his strength at the second runner. It spun through the air, flashing in the moonlight before embedding itself deep in the man's thigh.

He screamed in pain and tumbled to his knees, clutching at the blade and spitting out a stream of insults in a language Fabian did not recognise.

Fabian flew at the man and pounded his fist into the side of his head, sending him sprawling across the flagstones. 'The books were forgeries!' he cried, his voice cracking with emotion. 'Keep your hands off my uncle!' Then he gasped in pain as his face suddenly slammed against a flagstone. He realised vaguely that someone had just punched him, but as the stars whirled over his head, he could not quite work out how to operate his legs.

A furious, swarthy face snarled down at him. 'Stay out of this, you ridiculous child,' cried Calderino, ripping the bandana from his face and spitting on the path. 'I'd be quite happy to slit your throat too.'

Fabian tried to climb to his feet, but his legs collapsed beneath him and his stomach emptied its contents noisily across the path. He could do nothing but watch in helpless, mute despair as the men drew their knives and stepped towards his defenceless uncle.

CHAPTER FOURTEEN
KINDRED SPIRITS

FABIAN WRITHED ACROSS the ground, still retching as the men circled Jonas. All his strength had vanished and a terrible nausea twisted his guts as he realised his uncle was about to die.

Calderino and his men tossed their slender blades from hand to hand as they closed in on the old man, hurling mocking insults as they prepared to strike. Even the man Fabian had injured managed a grin as he limped towards his prey.

Jonas, however, seemed quite calm. He placed his books carefully on the ground and raised his slender cane, as though intending to use it as a weapon. Then he shook his head sadly. 'You've wasted a lot of my time today, Calderino. Thanks to you I was unable to greet a very important guest, and the lies you told about those books will set my studies back months. But as a club member, I was prepared to forgive your lack of professionalism. Despite my better judgement, I was willing to write the whole thing off to experience.'

Calderino's wiry body shuddered with fury. 'You owe me my money, Wolff!' he screamed. He looked around at his men and pointed his knife at Jonas's head. 'Kill the bastard, quickly. I can't bear to listen to his stupid, pompous voice.'

The man nearest to Jonas sprang, cat-like, bringing his stiletto down towards his face with lightning speed.

Jonas rocked back on his heels with the practiced ease of a dancer. His agility shocked the knifeman and he stumbled past him in confusion. Jonas drew a long, slender sword from within his cane and slid it neatly through the man's ear so that it emerged on the other side of his head in a bright fountain of blood.

The man twitched and lurched for a few seconds, dangling puppet-like from Jonas's sword, then the old man withdrew the blade and the attacker slumped lifelessly to the floor.

Fabian stopped trying to climb to his feet and lay down again in shock. His uncle's movements had been faster and more graceful than any swordsman he had ever seen. He noticed something else, too: as Jonas fought, his lips had moved as fast as his limbs, mouthing strange, silent words and phrases.

Calderino's three remaining men took one look at each other and leapt at Jonas with their blades flashing.

The old man rolled to the ground in a fluid, elegant movement, so fast that the first man to reach him tripped awkwardly over his hunched frame and toppled heavily onto the path. Jonas then rose smoothly to his feet and skewered him through the back of his neck with a quick thrust of his rapier, leaving him gasping horribly for breath and clutching at his severed windpipe.

The second man to reach Jonas jabbed his stiletto at the small of the old man's back, but Jonas simply rolled forward out of harm's way and the knifeman's own momentum sent him crashing to his knees. He had barely cried out in pain before Jonas spun around in a delicate pirouette with his sword held at just the right angle to sever the man's head from his shoulders and send it bouncing away down the path.

At the sight of such formidable skill, the third man tried to halt in his tracks, abandoning his attack and turning it into an attempt to flee, but his leg still had Fabian's knife embedded in it, and as he turned it collapsed beneath him. He slipped on his heels and fell backwards with a cry of fear. Jonas had no need of any more acrobatics. The man was so petrified, Jonas simply took one step forward and, with an artistic flourish, jabbed his sword quickly in and out of the man's left eye, puncturing his brain and leaving him to thrash around for a few seconds like a landed fish, before finally lying still.

Jonas raised his hand to stifle a yawn as he turned to face Calderino. 'That's even more effort I've wasted on you,' he said, taking a languid step towards him. 'You're running up quite a debt.'

Calderino shook his head in horror and backed away into the shadows. 'You're a witch,' he hissed, before turning to sprint away across the silvery lawns.

Fabian looked up at his uncle in awe as he loomed over him. 'I can't believe what you just did,' he groaned, struggling not to vomit again. 'You moved so fast. It was incredible. Even men half your age aren't so agile.'

Jonas looked down at him with a sad smile. 'It's true,' he said, placing the tip of his sword against Fabian's throat.

'What're you doing?' asked Fabian, trying to twist his neck away from the blade.

The smile slipped from Jonas's face, to be replaced by humourless frown that Fabian had not seen before. 'I could never have learned such techniques from any normal swordsman,' he continued. 'And unfortunately, on the rare occasions I'm forced to use them, I must ensure there are no witnesses. It's nothing personal, you understand. It's just crucial that nobody can tell the world of my special talents. Calderino may have eluded me for the moment, but his days are numbered. I'll see to him shortly. You, however, are a different matter.'

'I don't understand,' croaked Fabian, hoarse with panic. 'You're going to kill me?'

Jonas sighed heavily and nodded. 'It *is* most unfortunate,' he said. 'I've already grown quite fond of you. I particularly liked the way you attacked a gang of vicious hired killers without the remotest chance of surviving.'

'Uncle, I beg you,' cried Fabian, grabbing his uncle's leg. 'Don't do this!'

Jonas narrowed his eyes. 'I wonder,' he muttered, pressing the tip of his sword a little harder into the soft flesh under Fabian's chin. The boy whimpered as he felt a thin trickle of blood run around his trembling neck and begin to pool on the ground beneath his head. 'Tell, me Fabian,' said Jonas, lowering his voice to a whisper. 'What do you crave most of all in the world? What do you dream of?'

A host of possible answers filled Fabian's mind. He saw that his life depended on choosing the right one, but which was it? What did his uncle wish to hear? That he wanted to be an honest, law-abiding man, or an infamous villain? Or that he wished to be a great scholar and author, or an artist even? What could it be? He sighed and let his head fall back to the ground, realising that it was hopeless. What ever he said would be wrong. 'If I weren't about to die in this filthy, fish-stinking, cesspit of a city,' he said finally, 'my dream would have been to reinstate my family's honour. And to see a Wolff at the head of the Empire's armies once more; leading us to glorious victories, as my ancestors did, instead of poring over prayer books and building even more temples.' He glared up at Jonas. 'And who knows, maybe if I hadn't been betrayed by such a lying, ungrateful maggot of an uncle, I could have reminded my father that Jakob isn't his only son.'

Jonas continued to frown at him for a few seconds, then a smile spread slowly across his face. He tilted his head back and began to chuckle. Then his chuckles became great, heaving guffaws and he dropped his rapier to the ground with clatter. 'Lying, ungrateful maggot,' he gasped through his laughter. 'Oh, I like that.' He fell to the ground, next to Fabian, still shaking with laughter. 'We truly are kin, you and I,' he said, blinking away a stream of tears.

An overwhelming feeling of relief washed over Fabian as he realised he'd somehow stumbled across the right answer. As a grey dawn crept nervously over the convoluted spires of Altdorf, it found the two Wolffs laughing and rolling hysterically across the park, surrounded by blood and the spread-eagled corpses of their foes.

As THEY ARRIVED back at the door of the Unknown House, blackbirds were trilling from its eaves and sleepy-eyed merchants were already hurrying past on the way to market.

Isolde was waiting for them: leaning against the doorframe with her arms folded and a despairing look on her face. 'I see you've already introduced our guest to the dubious pleasures of Altdorf's nightlife,' she said with a wry smile.

As his uncle placed a kiss on her outstretched hand, Fabian could hardly believe it was the same woman. Her hair was tied back in a neat, intricate plait, and her eyes were bright and alert. She was no less beautiful, but all trace of her earlier feyness had vanished. She shook her head in reply to Jonas's wry smile and held out her hand to Fabian.

'I doubt Jonas has found time to mention me. I'm Isolde, his wife. It's a pleasure to meet you, Fabian.'

Fabian frowned in confusion, but Jonas's raised eyebrows and fixed smile implied that Fabian should say nothing about their previous encounter, so he simply kissed her hand and gave a low bow. 'The pleasure's all mine, Frau Wolff. Uncle told me you were beautiful, but you surpass even his most enraptured descriptions.'

Isolde pursed her lips in disbelief. 'Hmm. I see he's been giving you lessons in flattery, too.' She gave a good-natured chuckle as she waved them inside. 'Come in. Come in. I doubt he remembered to offer you anything as mundane as food. I thought you'd come scurrying back at first light, so I've rustled you up some breakfast.'

The house was just as gloomy and labyrinthine as the day before, but with Isolde waltzing through its maze of halls and antechambers, humming a merry tune as she went, the atmosphere seemed far less oppressive. She led them to a dining room crammed with suits of rusting armour and dusty, stuffed animals, bears mainly, who crowded around the long table like hungry dinner guests. Fabian shoved a mangy badger from the seat he was offered and began to eat. Isolde had prepared a platter of cold meats, sour bread and scrambled eggs and as soon as Fabian took his first bite he realised how hungry the night's adventures had left him. For a few minutes he forgot everything else in his eagerness to wolf down the food.

After a while he sat back in his chair and found that Isolde had left them. He could still hear her nearby, whistling and bustling around the house, and the sound comforted him for some reason.

'So,' said Jonas, pouring him a cup of tea. 'Where does this leave us, you and I?'

Fabian leant across the table and looked imploringly at his uncle. 'I would never talk of what I saw. You must believe me.'

Jonas nodded and twirled his waxed moustaches thoughtfully. 'And just what exactly *did* you see?'

Fabian shrugged. 'I saw a man too old to walk properly, suddenly become the most agile, deadly swordsman I've ever seen. I saw him slay four trained assassins with no more effort than if he were combing his hair.' He paused, recalling the incident. 'And I saw him utter strange, whispered sentences that seemed to aid him in some way – almost as though the strength and speed of the attack were linked to the force of the words.'

Jonas nodded. 'You've a sharp mind, and you've already guessed at far more than I would usually be comfortable with. However, as I said earlier, I feel we share more than just a bond of blood. Your ambitions remind me very much of my own adolescent dreams.' He took a sip of tea and sat back in his chair, eyeing Fabian carefully.

'I'm a collector of curiosities, Fabian,' he explained. 'Curiosities and antiques of all kinds, and I'm not just talking about physical relics. I'm a kind of archaeologist of ideas, as much as anything. I've spent my whole life digging beneath the oppressive, facile foundations of our universities and colleges, looking for older, broader forms of knowledge. However,' he said, waving at his lined face, 'I'm even more ancient than I look, believe it or not, and I sometimes wonder what will happen to all this accumulated wisdom when I finally grow tired of life. I've no children, you understand.'

He looked around at the rows of glassy eyes that surrounded them. 'I inherited the Unknown House from my great grandfather, Johannes Wolff. I know very little about him, but I believe he may have shared the same desire for strength and glory that burns in the two of us. I'm not sure of his profession, but his house was full of oddities even before I took possession of it, and I also inherited many of its odd guests. They continued to arrive, unannounced, long after Johannes had died, still expecting an unquestioning welcome at the house of a Wolff.' He shrugged. 'So, in exchange for various gifts and pieces of information, I let them keep coming. This house has countless rooms and half of the time I couldn't tell you who's staying in them. But my guests have proved to be an invaluable source of knowledge. Many of them have travelled from the furthest corners of the Old World and are prepared to provide me with the most incredible artefacts in exchange for nothing more than hospitality and discretion. My one condition is that only the most interesting people are admitted. If there's one thing I can't bear, it's a dullard.'

Fabian leant across the table towards Jonas, his eyes wide with excitement. 'Share your learning with me, uncle, I beg you. I've already spent long hours in the library at Berlau, reading of the days before Sigmar. I know much about the Old Faith that preceded our current church.'

'There are things I could show you,' conceded Jonas. 'There are certain techniques and methods that might help you realise your ambitions.' He took a silver chain from around his neck and placed it in Fabian's hand. Fabian recognised it as being identical to the one he saw around Isolde's neck. In the hazy light of the dining room, however, he could now discern the small figurine that hung on the end of it: it was the head of a wolf, carved intricately from a piece of bone. Jonas closed the boy's hand over the pendant and squeezed, until the icon pressed painfully into the flesh of his palm. 'You must swear an oath of secrecy, though, Fabian,' said Jonas, gripping even more tightly. 'And if you ever break this oath, a curse of the most violent, terrible magnitude will come down on you and your family.'

Fabian did not hesitate for a second. 'I swear,' he said. 'I swear I would never tell a soul. Even if it meant my life or the life of my parents.'

Jonas gripped Fabian's hand for a few seconds longer, peering into his eyes as though looking for something. Then he nodded, withdrew the pendant and hung it back around his neck. 'Do not take that oath lightly, my boy,' he said, with a deep sigh. Then, after finishing his tea, he rose to his feet. 'You should probably bathe and get a little sleep,' he said, in stern, serious tones. 'We may only have a few days before you leave and there is much to learn before then.'

Fabian did as he was instructed. Isolde made him a hot bath and showed him to a small attic room that looked out over a noisy, wooden dovecote and a sun-lit yard at the back of the house. He was exhausted from the night's exertions, but he still only managed to sleep for a couple of hours. His dreams were filled with visions of his uncle's brutal acrobatics; but it was his own face that was muttering the strange words as he plunged a glinting rapier into the bodies of count-less, reeling foes.

He awoke well before midday and leapt from his bed, tingling with excitement at the thought of what awaited him. Jonas was in his study, reading a letter. He didn't look up at Fabian's approach, but acknowledged him by beginning to read out loud. 'The Arch Lector would like to consult a few of his brethren before making a firm commitment, but as you can imagine, we are all very proud that Jakob would even be considered for ordination at such a young age. It is a great honour for our family. As a result of this good news, the Arch Lector has graciously invited us to stay in the cathedral for another week or so. I hope Fabian is not making too much of a nuisance of himself, and look forward to seeing you and making the acquaintance of your wife. Yours, etc, etc, Hieronymus Wolff.'

As he reached the end of the letter, Jonas looked up from his cluttered desk. 'Good. We have a little longer than I expected then. There's something I'd like us to discuss with Puchelperger this evening at the Recalcitrant Club, but before then I think I should introduce you to a few basic martial concepts.' He shook his head. 'It was undoubtedly brave of you to defend me from those Tileans last night, but I've no idea what you thought you could achieve by throwing yourself at them like that.'

Jonas looked around at the crowded shelves that lined the room. Skulls, books, leering painted masks and jars of pale, cloudy liquid filled every available inch of space. 'There's a lifetime of study in this room, Fabian,' he said, rummaging in the drawers of the desk, 'which can make it a little hard to track things down. Ah!' he exclaimed, spotting a small wooden box sat on the desk in front of him. 'Just the thing.' He handed the box to Fabian and turned to look inside a large trunk next to his chair. 'Put it on,' he said, with his head buried in the chest.

Fabian sat next to the fireplace in the same chair he'd used the night before and carefully opened the box. He sighed with pleasure as he saw a silver chain just like his aunt and uncle's, complete with the same wolf's head pendant. He placed it over his neck and relished the feel of the cold metal on his skin.

Jonas's head popped up again and when he saw the chain in place he peered anxiously at Fabian, as though waiting for some kind of adverse reaction. Then he nodded. 'Good, good,' he said and rose from behind the desk with a long needle and a bottle of ink in his hand. 'Now, take off your right shoe.'

'My shoe?'

'Yes, your shoe child – as quick as you like.'

Fabian could not help but feel a little nervous as his uncle crouched before him and took his foot in his hand.

Jonas dipped the needle in the ink and held it a few inches from the sole of Fabian's foot. 'This may hurt a little,' he said before piercing the tough skin of his heel. The old man muttered something under his breath as he worked the ink into Fabian's flesh. It sounded like some kind of tune, but as Fabian winced in discomfort, he could not quite make out the words. 'There,' said Jonas after a few minutes, rising to his feet with a wheeze and a creak of protesting joints. 'All done.' He stepped up to a terrible portrait of Isolde, which hung behind his desk and moved it to one side, revealing a small safe embedded in the wall. He unlocked it and withdrew a sheaf of papers. Then, after closing the safe and sliding the painting back in front of it, he sat down at the desk again.

'Let me see,' he muttered, leafing through the crumbling old parchments. He gave a grunt of satisfaction as he found the one he wanted. 'Right,' he said, taking a stick of chalk from his desk and stepping into the middle of the room. He kicked aside a rug to reveal the dusty floorboards beneath. Fabian noticed that a palimpsest of faded chalk marks covered the wood, where dozens of geometrical symbols has been drawn, erased and redrawn. Jonas crouched down with the chalk in one hand and the paper in the other, and began to transcribe an intricate series of shapes from the parchment to the floor. The symbols and numbers were mind-boggling in their complexity, and Fabian felt the first stirrings of doubt.

'Uncle,' he said, frowning at the shapes.

'Yes?' replied Jonas, with a hint of irritation in his voice as he concentrated on the drawing.

'Is all this, well…' Fabian stumbled over his words as his uncle looked up at him. 'Well, there's nothing heretical about what we're doing, is there?'

'Pah!' snapped Jonas, returning to his work. 'Such words are open to interpretation. Your parents would no doubt think so – and your brother too by the sounds of him. But such prejudice only reveals the paucity of their education – and its blinkered, narrow focus.' He climbed to his feet and gestured to the grotesque scrawl he had created. 'This is science, lad, nothing more, nothing less. But it's a wisdom that stems from an older, more holistic world view than the simple, crude tenets of the Sigmarites.' He pointed to a circle in the centre of the drawing. 'Place your right foot there, and don't move it until I say you can.'

Fabian did as his uncle ordered and noticed that a mixture of blood and ink began to mingle with the chalk marks. After just a few seconds a peculiar warmth began to spread across the sole of his foot. He looked at his uncle in surprise, but the old man simply gave him a brusque nod, before turning to rifle through his books. The heat spread quickly up his legs, though his groin and into his stomach, where it grew in strength and rushed through his chest and into his arms and head. The heat was not unpleasant, and something about Jonas's calm, matter-of-fact demeanour infected Fabian so that he remained unconcerned, even as the chalk marks began to smoke slightly. Fabian beamed as he felt a fierce vitality rush through him. He flexed his muscles and sighed with pleasure as he felt a new strength blossoming in them. He suddenly felt as though he could tear the whole house down with his bare hands if he wanted to.

Jonas heard his sigh and turned away from the bookshelves. He raised his eyebrows at the sight of Fabian's broad grin and the smoke trailing up around his legs. 'That's enough,' he snapped. 'Step back, Fabian.'

Fabian reluctantly lifted his foot out of the circle, but to his delight a vestigial glow of the heat and strength remained in his muscles as he stepped back. He had to stifle the urge to punch something.

'Stand by the door,' said Jonas, seeming slightly annoyed, 'and we'll get down to work.' He grabbed a pair of foils from the wall and stood next to Fabian with a large book in his hand. 'If you're ever going to make something of yourself, you must learn to master the Circle of Defence and the geometrical principles propounded by the Old World's greatest swordsman, Agilwardus.'

'I've never heard of him,' said Fabian, frowning at the intricate diagrams his uncle was holding up to him.

'Of course you haven't. He was burned as a heretic three hundred years ago, simply for being a little ahead of his time. There are only three copies of this wonderful treatise still in existence and they're all in this room.' Jonas placed the book on a lectern, gave Fabian one of the swords and raised his own into an en garde position. 'Remember,' he said with a lupine grin, 'this will hurt me a lot more than it will hurt you.'

As THEY SET out towards the Street of a Hundred Taverns, Fabian was moving even slower than his elderly uncle. He carried bruises on almost every part of his body and the fire in his muscles had been replaced by the dull, throbbing ache of exhaustion. They had trained until well after nightfall, without even a break for food or water, and all he wanted to do now was to collapse onto a bed.

The streets were just as crowded as on the previous night, but Fabian was blind to the figures that swarmed around them. His mind was spinning with a wealth of new information. As his uncle had lunged and parried, he had yelled out a stream of commands. Some of them in languages Fabian never heard before: musical, lilting phrases, or harsh, guttural barks, but he had understood the meanings behind them quite clearly. The energy from the chalk marks had not just filled him with strength, but also a strange intuition. As his blade flashed back and forth in a desperate attempt to fend off Jonas's attacks he had felt his skill growing with each word his uncle hurled at him. When they finally stopped sparring, both of them had collapsed to the floor, gasping for breath and covered in sweat. Fabian had crawled up into a chair, feeling like his head was some kind of strange pupa, bulging and writhing as it struggled to contain an entirely new Fabian, who was straining to burst free from behind his eyes.

Now, as he stumbled after his uncle, Fabian still felt the mass of information twisting somewhere in his head, but it seemed to be biding its time, waiting patiently at the back of his thoughts until it was called upon. He felt its presence as clearly as he felt the weight of the rapier his uncle had tucked in his belt as they left the house.

Jonas left the boy to his thoughts as they made their way to the club, but every now and then he would cast a discreet sidelong glance at him, as though watching for something.

'It's good to see you again, Captain Wolff,' said the flame-haired butler as he welcomed them in out of the heaving throng.

'Thank you, Vogel,' said Jonas, handing him his hat and cloak. 'Has Puchelperger arrived yet?'

Vogel shook his head with a cheerful grin. 'I'm sure he'll be here soon though. I passed on your note myself, and he seemed delighted at the prospect of spending another evening in your company.'

'Very good,' said Jonas, stepping into the lounge and taking the same table as on the previous night. 'Strange,' he said, taking a sip of the drink that appeared before him. 'Puchelperger is usually here well before midnight.'

Fabian gave no reply, still struggling with his thoughts as he took a deep, grateful swig of his own drink.

They waited in a tense silence for nearly an hour, with Jonas drumming his fingers angrily on the table and sighing every few minutes.

'Terrible business with those Tileans last night,' said a ruddy cheeked, whiskery old general, pausing at their table.

'How do you mean?' asked Jonas, a little nervously.

The general shrugged. 'Shouting like that, in the club. It's really not what one expects in an establishment of this quality.'

'Oh,' said Jonas, visibly relieved. 'Quite.'

'If I had my way, anyone as ill-mannered as Calderino would be barred.' He sniffed disdainfully. 'I saw the villain this morning, actually. Practically knocked me over he was in such a hurry.'

'Really?' asked Jonas, taking another sip of his drink and trying to look uninterested.

'Yes. I was leaving Puchelperger's house and the blackguard barged past me on the way to the gate.' He shook his head in disapproval. 'What a scoundrel. He didn't even acknowledge me.'

Jonas lowered his glass carefully to the table. 'Are you sure it was Calderino?' he asked.

The general frowned. 'I may be retired, Wolff, but I've not lost control of my faculties just yet. It was Calderino, I tell you. Whoever recommended that man for membership must be a bloody fool.'

'Well, General Rauch, it's always a pleasure, but I've just remembered I promised Isolde I'd get the boy home a little earlier tonight.' Jonas drained his glass and stood. 'Come, Fabian,' he said striding towards the door.

Fabian smiled apologetically at the general as he rushed after his uncle.

As soon as they were out in the street, Fabian let out a groan of despair. 'This is bad,' he muttered, hobbling away as fast as his old legs would carry him. 'Very, very bad.'

'Do you think Calderino meant to harm Puchelperger?' asked Fabian, taking his uncle's arm and trying to support him a little.

Jonas looked at Fabian in disbelief. 'I think you could probably answer that yourself, don't you? General Rauch is exactly right – the man's a scoundrel. He's too afraid to approach me after what happened last night, so he's turned on my friends.'

Jonas led the way through a baffling sequence of lefts and rights until yet again Fabian had absolutely no idea where they were. They eventually emerged on a wide moonlit avenue, lined with tall plane trees and large, handsome townhouses. Most of the windows were filled with light and the elegant silhouettes of Altdorf's great and good, but there was a house near the end of the avenue that was utterly dark and lifeless. It was this house that Jonas rushed towards. As they approached the spiked iron gate, they saw that it was swinging on its hinges, and as they rushed up to the front door, Jonas pushed it inwards with a gentle shove. 'Unlocked,' he muttered. As the door swung open, the moonlight washed across the polished floorboards and picked out a large crumpled shape lying at the foot of a grand, sweeping staircase.

They rushed towards the prone figure, but before they had got within a few feet of it, they could see the ink black lake that had pooled beneath it.

'Ah, old friend,' groaned Jonas, lifting the corpse's head and revealing an ear-to-ear gash beneath Puchelperger's rolls of fat. 'Whatever you may have done, you did not deserve to die like this – at the hands of a petty criminal.'

Fabian looked nervously up the gloomy stairs. 'Do you think he might still be here?'

Jonas shook his head as he climbed slowly to his feet. 'No, there's no need to be afraid, boy. He's long gone. Probably on his way to butcher someone else dear to me.' Jonas's eyes widened and he staggered backwards, as though someone had slapped him. 'Oh, by the gods,' he muttered. 'Isolde.' He clutched his face in his hands and let out a terrible wail of anguish. 'I'm probably already too late. He knows what time I leave for the club.' He grabbed Fabian's shoulders and looked desperately into his eyes. 'You might make it though boy,' he hissed. 'Run as fast as your young legs will carry you.' He saw the doubt in Fabian's eyes as he pictured himself fighting the Tilean swordsman. 'It will all come back to you,' hissed Jonas. 'Everything I showed you today – even the strength from the sigils, it will all come back when you need it most. But you must be quick,' he cried, pushing him back towards the door.

'But which way do I go?' yelled Fabian in reply. 'I'll never find my way back alone.'

Jonas's face twisted into a mask of fury and for a second Fabian thought he would strike him. Then he took a deep breath to calm himself and looked around the house. His eyes came to rest on the pool of blood that surrounded them. 'Hold out your hand,' he said, stooping to the floor and dipping his finger in the cold, thick liquid.

'Left at the top of this avenue,' said Jonas, drawing a crimson line across Fabian's palm. 'Then a right, then two lefts, two rights and another left.' He stepped back and looked at Fabian with desperation in his eyes. 'Go, I beg you.'

Fabian looked at the crude, sticky map on his hand, and nodded once, before turning and dashing from the house. Fleet with fear, he pounded across the flagstones: barging past drunks and leaping over walls and hedges. As he ran, the map trailed across his skin, gradually losing all its definition and finally, with one turn still remaining, the lines of Puchelperger's blood blurred into a shapeless smear.

'Where now?' gasped Fabian in horror, as he reached a wide junction at the end of a row of tenements. He had no idea which way to turn. His heart was pounding in his chest as he looked up and down the two roads that lay before him, straining to remember the last direction. He groaned in despair. Then, something familiar caught his eye: the large dovecote that sat beneath his bedroom window. He gave a howl of delight and sprinted towards it. After a few seconds he saw the narrow street that led to the Unknown House and dashed up it.

As he ran towards the gate, he saw that just like Puchelperger's it was swinging on its hinges and to his horror, he saw that the front door was ajar too. 'I'm too late,' he panted, stumbling down the path.

He froze as he saw Calderino's face looming out of the darkness towards him. He drew the rapier his uncle had given him, but then he paused. There was something odd about Calderino: he was much taller than Fabian remembered him and his tanned, gaunt face was knotted in fear.

Fabian squinted into the darkness of the hall and slowly made out a second, much larger figure, stooped behind Calderino. The colossal shadow stepped forward into the moonlight and Fabian gave a laugh of relief. Calderino was dangling helplessly in the grip of one of Kobach Ivanov's massive hands. Fabian stepped aside as Kobach hurled the cursing Tilean out of the door. Kobach gave Fabian a brief nod of recognition before turning and closing the door firmly behind him.

Calderino leapt to his feet, spitting insults in his own language and pulling a stiletto from beneath his cape as he stepped towards Fabian. 'If I can't have his whore, you'll do instead,' he hissed, before lashing out with the needle-thin blade.

A stream of droning words fell from Fabian's mouth and the world seemed to slow. He watched the Tilean's blade moving towards his face with a feeling of cool dispassion and stepped easily out of the way. As Calderino tumbled into the space where Fabian had just been standing, the boy casually extended his leg and sent the Tilean sprawling across the path. The man crashed to the flagstones with a grunt and his knife clattered away into the darkness.

The world resumed its usual pace and Calderino clambered to his feet, turning to face Fabian with a look of horror on his face. 'You're just like him,' he gasped, backing away towards the gate. 'You're sorcerers, the pair of you.'

Fabian raised his slender sword, and levelled it at the man's head. 'You should leave,' he said calmly.

Calderino cursed as the gate flew open and Jonas staggered, gasping, onto the path.

'I think not,' said Jonas, grabbing the Tilean's shoulder and ramming his sword up through his chest.

Calderino stiffened with pain as the weapon emerged between his shoulder blades, then he slumped lifelessly in Jonas's arms. The old man laid his body down onto the path and looked back down the street to see if they were being watched. Once he was sure they were alone, he sheathed his sword and stepped towards Fabian, grasping his hand and nodding enthusiastically. 'You see? You've begun a great journey, my boy.' He looked down at Fabian's clean, unused blade and shook his head. 'You've still much to learn though.'

CHAPTER FIFTEEN
SECRETS AND LIES

'HE'S BECOME UNBEARABLE,' said Fabian, steering his horse through the powdery snow.

Winter had come early to Ostland and the Berlau estate was a kingdom of ivory, frozen ponds and heavy, glittering boughs. 'He was never the most rational soul,' continued Fabian, as his charger picked its way carefully through the waist-high drifts, 'but since we returned from Altdorf, he seems determined to prove his holiness at every turn. Mainly by labelling everyone around him as morally suspect.' He pulled the collar of his fur-lined coat a little tighter, as a fresh flurry of snow rolled across the hills towards them. 'Sigmar knows why they ordained him at such a young age, but it's made him even more in love with his own myth. I dread to think what he wants to talk to me about. I imagine he intends to announce his impending godhood.'

The young man riding beside Fabian threw back his hood to reveal a face that looked like it had been carved from granite; his features had a crude, brutal quality to them and his eyes were as flat and lifeless as a corpse's. He grunted in disgust. 'So why are we running back to the house with our tails between our legs?' He patted the bleeding mass of fur and teeth hanging from his saddle. 'The hunting is good at this time of year.'

Fabian shrugged. 'I hear you, Ludwig, but Jakob's been ensconced in the temple with Brother Braun since the summer, so I suppose even I'm a little interested to know what his news is. But, more than that, for the first time in my life, my father is actually allowing me some leeway.' He clutched the waxed, fur-clad sheath that held his sword. 'My new-found military prowess has achieved the impossible and actually impressed the old man, so I'm determined not to do anything to upset him.' He looked over at his friend. 'Finally, I'm able to remind people that the Wolffs are a family with a proud history – a family not to be trifled with.' He gestured at the grizzled head that was fastened to his saddle. 'Father would never have let me roam the estates like this, marshalling the watch, and cleansing the woods of filth, if I hadn't proved to him that I have skills as impressive as Jakob's. How wonderful it is to finally be able to reinstate some order.'

'And dispatch transgressors,' said Ludwig, leaning forward with a hungry grin on his face.

Fabian looked over at his friend a little nervously. 'Yes, that too I suppose. Although it might be best to keep that under our hats for now.'

Ludwig's head snapped to one side a couple of times in an involuntary twitch. 'They deserve everything they got. The idiot peasantry only understand brute strength, Fabian. We were absolutely right to kill them. It will be a long time before anyone dares to poach from the Berlau estate again.'

Fabian continued to watch Ludwig from the corner of his eye. He was his oldest childhood friend and had been very useful during the months since he had returned from Altdorf, but he was beginning to wonder if he had been a little too open with him. 'Remember, Ludwig,' he said, placing a hand on the reins of the man's horse and bringing it to a stop, 'we should not mention any of my uncle's training techniques either. Father knows my new-found skill is due to Jonas's teachings, but he has no idea of the methods involved. And I don't think he would understand. Such ancient, unorthodox practices could easily be misconstrued by people less cultured than ourselves.'

Ludwig nodded eagerly, continuing to grin. He stretched out his arms, tensing and relaxing the muscles with obvious delight. 'We wouldn't want everyone to have such skills anyway – we'd lose the advantage.' He laughed. 'I imagine that's why your uncle made you swear that ridiculous oath of secrecy – to limit the number of people who might be able to face him in single combat.'

Fabian flinched at the mention of the oath. With so many miles between him and Altdorf, it had seemed no great crime to share what he had learned with his closest friend; but every now and then, he felt a chill of doubt. 'You're probably right,' he muttered, steering his horse onwards down the hill. 'But nevertheless, I'd rather no one else knew.'

He smiled to himself as he remembered the other reason he was happy to visit Berlau: there was a parcel waiting there for him. Since their training sessions in Altdorf, Jonas had sent several packages containing fencing manuals, military textbooks and other, more unusual items. In his most recent letter he had mentioned some dolls, acquired through one of his guests at the Unknown House. They were things of incredible antiquity, believed by Jonas to have originated in far Cathay. The letter explained that despite their grotesque appearance, the dolls contained great power. Jonas claimed that if Fabian placed a single strand of a man's hair beneath the wax skin of one of the dolls, he would be granted unnatural power over the flesh of that man. Fabian had thought immediately of how easy it would be to pluck a hair from his brother's pillow.

They crested the brow of the next hill and saw the white folds of the valley spread out before them. 'Someone's burning the welcome feast,' said Ludwig, nodding to a thin column of black that was snaking up towards the bright, pregnant clouds.

'Odd,' muttered Fabian. The smoke was coming from near the house and it gave him an unpleasant sense of foreboding. He kicked his horse into a canter and cut through the deep snow with as much speed as he could manage.

As they approached the sprawling mass of the house, the source of the smoke became clearer: a pyre had been constructed not far from the gatehouse.

Fabian peered through the eddying banks of snow and made out a group of figures, silhouetted against the whiteness. 'What's this?' he muttered, with growing impatience at his horse's slow progress.

His agitation grew as he neared the figures. A loose circle of servants, soldiers and officials was scattered around the smouldering pyre and at the head of them was Brother Braun with his head bowed in silent prayer. Next to the priest was a small, stocky figure, swaddled in a mountain of furs and bright, ceremonial robes. Fabian recognised him immediately as Tischer, the local magistrate, but there was another man by his side he could not place: a wiry, fanatical-looking priest of some kind. Fabian's gaze passed quickly over the stranger and came to rest on a shape near to the pile of charred wood. Jakob was lying a few feet from the pyre, curled up on the snow in a foetal position and shuddering violently.

Fabian reined in his horse as a row of ashen faces turned towards him. At a nudge from the magistrate, Braun looked up from his prayers and saw Fabian riding towards them.

'Fabian,' called Braun, with a look of panic on his face. He began clambering up the hill towards him, but Fabian had now looked beyond Jakob and fixed his eyes on the pyre. His head felt oddly light as he focussed on two corpses fastened to the top of the wreckage. They were burned beyond recognition, but from Jakob's shuddering sobs, he had no doubt who they were. The brightness of the snow seemed to grow suddenly, lancing painfully into his eyes and the whole scene began to spin around him as though he were drunk. He gripped the neck of his horse in an effort to stop himself falling.

'What have you done?' he whispered under his breath, steering his horse down the hill towards his brother. 'What have you done?' he repeated a little louder as he neared Braun who was still clambering up the hill. 'What have you done?' he howled, as he kicked his horse into a gallop, leaving a cloud of snow behind him as he charged down the hill.

'Wait, Fabian,' gasped Braun, reaching out in desperation as the horse thundered past.

'What have you done?' screamed Fabian, leaping from his horse and planting a ferocious kick into Jakob's side.

Jakob spun across the snow and clambered to his feet. His eyes were red raw from crying and he looked across at his brother in confusion.

Fabian strode forward and punched Jakob with such force that his head snapped back with an audible click of bone, sending a spray of red across the crisp, white snow.

Jakob reeled backwards but managed to stay on his feet. The blow seemed to clear his head slightly and he looked at Fabian with a spark of recognition in his eyes. 'Occultists,' he slurred through bloody teeth, trying to explain.

Fabian's face flushed a dark purple and he howled with inarticulate rage, before drawing a long hunting knife from his belt and rushing at his brother.

'Wait,' cried a piercing voice.

Fabian paused to see the wiry priest striding towards him, closely followed by the magistrate and a group of militiamen. The priest had odd, pale eyes that bulged out of his thin face as he approached. 'Jakob only did what he had to,' he said. 'Your parents were engaged in the most depraved, heretical activity. Who knows what havoc they would have wrought if your brother hadn't reported them to me. You should thank him.'

Fabian shook his head in disbelief. 'Who are you?' he gasped, noticing that the guards lined up behind the man were drawing their weapons.

'My name's Otto Sürman,' he replied, 'and I'm a Templar of Sigmar.' He nodded to the guards and officials that surrounded him. 'You should think very carefully about what you say.'

'Sürman's telling the truth, Fabian,' said the magistrate, anxiously rubbing his hands together and cowering behind the priest. 'You know how fond I was of your parents, but there was very convincing evidence. I'd never have sanctioned this if there had been any doubt.'

'Wait a minute,' growled Fabian, ignoring the magistrate and pointing his knife at the witch hunter. 'I recognise your name. You're the man my father banished from his estate, just a few months ago. You locked a village idiot in a cage because he spoke to his birds.' His whole body was trembling with fury as he strode towards Otto. 'I see what this is,' he said, his voice sounding strained and unnatural. 'My father made a fool of you, and this is your vengeance.'

The witch hunter was about to reply when Jakob cried out. 'No, brother, that's not how it is. I found the evidence. They were involved in something terrible.' His voice cracked with emotion as he turned to face the pyre. 'But I didn't realise the punishment would be so...' he placed his head in his hands.

Fabian shook his head in disbelief. 'How could you betray our parents to this charlatan?' As his eyes filled with tears, he let out another keening wail of despair. 'They were starting to notice me. Finally. After all those years in your shadow.'

Sürman cautiously stepped closer to the weeping Fabian and the magistrate signalled for the guards to ready their weapons.

'Your brother's not to blame,' said Sürman as he emptied a small bag onto the snow at Fabian's feet.

'What's that?' snapped Fabian with a dismissive sneer. 'Something you planted on them, no doubt.' As he stooped to examine the objects, the colour drained from his face. They were small, wax dolls; ugly, deformed little things, but there was no disguising their heretical nature. Fabian recognised them immediately from the description in his uncle's letter.

Sürman was just a few feet away and as he saw Fabian's look of recognition, he frowned in confusion. 'Do you–?' he began. But as the magistrate stepped to his side, the witch hunter clamped his mouth tightly shut and said no more.

Fabian's legs folded beneath him and he crumpled silently into the deep snow.

Jakob stepped to his side and looked down at him. 'There's nothing we could have done, brother. They brought this on themselves.'

'No, they didn't,' spat Fabian, 'you did. You and your obsession with holiness.' He climbed back to his feet and leant towards Jakob until their noses were almost touching. 'If you weren't so wrapped up in your own twisted idea of virtue, our parents would still be alive. You've murdered them as surely as if you lit the fire.'

Jakob shook his head in desperate denial, but could think of no words to defend himself.

Fabian's rage returned to him and he drew back the hunting knife.

Before he could strike, the soldiers rushed forward and grabbed his arms, knocking the knife from his grip and dragging him away from his brother.

Fabian slipped, eel-like from their grasp, leaving them stumbling through the snow in confusion. He reached down to retrieve the knife, but then, noticing the dolls at his feet he paused and glanced nervously at the witch hunter. He left the knife where it was and turned to face his brother. 'Just go,' he said, trying to control his breathing. 'You've destroyed everything. The Wolffs are ruined. Don't make me a murderer too.'

Jakob shook his head in a pitiful, mute plea.

Fabian pointed at the bodies. 'Look at what you've done,' he cried. 'You must leave Berlau. If I avenge them, I'll be ruined too.' He nodded at the surrounding whiteness. 'Take your wretched prayers away, Jakob. Be anywhere but here.'

Jakob looked from his brother to the charred corpses of his parents and his face twisted with anguish. Then his shoulders slumped in defeat and he gave a slight nod. 'If it's what you wish,' he muttered, giving his brother one last pleading glance.

Fabian was still trembling with anger and refused to meet his eye. 'If I ever see you again, I won't be responsible for my actions,' he hissed, sounding close to tears. 'But if you swear never return to Berlau, I won't hunt you down.'

Jakob swayed, as though slapped, but gave another weak nod as he turned away. He stumbled off through the valley like a dying man and after just a few minutes his stooped, lonely figure disappeared behind the whirling banks of snowflakes.

CHAPTER SIXTEEN
MASSACRE AT HAGEN'S CLAW

THE IRON DUKE, Kriegsmarshall Fabian Wolff, surveyed his vast army with a long sigh of satisfaction. 'Have you ever seen anything so beautiful?' he asked the grey-haired captain riding beside him.

The old knight's head jerked sideways in a series of involuntary twitches, then he looked back at the men behind them. 'Never,' he replied as he studied the sea of rippling banners.

Fabian had begun the campaign with a force of considerable size, but over the months, it had grown even larger, becoming an unwieldy host of epic proportions. As the seriousness of the incursion became known, von Raukov had sent reinforcements from every corner of Ostland in support of his beloved protégé. It would be impossible to say exactly how many men were now marching behind him. They numbered in the tens of thousands though, certainly: knights, engineers, spearmen, pistoliers and greatswords, all eager to serve under such a revered general. Fabian's exploits had already become the stuff of legend. After three decades of combat, his mind was as fast as his sword arm; in fact, he was almost as deadly in real life as he was in the tales his agents had spread across the province. The officers under the Iron Duke's command followed him with a fanatical devotion and the Elector Count had placed complete trust in him. He had achieved almost everything he had ever desired.

'The scouts have returned from Mercy's End, Kriegsmarshall,' said the captain. 'Felhamer's run of luck has finally ended. Mormius didn't even stop to pursue the survivors. They just torched the ruins and continued marching south.'

Fabian nodded. 'His only interest seems to be reaching Wolfenberg as quickly as possible. Was there any news of Felhamer himself?'

'None, although I doubt he would have fled with the survivors.'

'No, I imagine you're right, Ludwig – from what I hear, the captain was as honourable as he was stupid. He'll have held out until the very last minute.' As they rode up out of the valley, he raised a hand to shield his eyes from the late afternoon sun and looked down across the rain-drenched hills and forests of Ostland. 'We should meet them very soon,' he said, with a slight tremor in his voice. 'The moment I've waited for, all these years, has finally arrived.' He lifted a pendant from beneath his polished cuirass and studied it closely. It was the ivory wolf's head his uncle had given him all those years ago in the Unknown House. 'After this battle, the name Wolff will never be forgotten,' he said, turning the pendant slowly in his fingers. He lowered his voice and smiled at Ludwig. 'And once my master has accepted the wonderful gift I'm bringing to him, I'll become the mightiest warrior the Old World has ever seen.'

Ludwig shook his head. 'I can understand why the Ruinous Powers would wish you to bring them such a great sacrifice – to lead so many soldiers into their grasp is truly a wondrous gift, but there's something I can't understand.'

Fabian looked around to see if any of the other officers were near enough to overhear. Then he leant closer to Ludwig and nodded for him to continue.

'If you're taking this great army to your master as a sacrifice, will Mormius know not to strike you down, as he has done so many others. Does he understand the bargain you've struck?'

Fabian leant back in his saddle and stroked his moustache. 'I imagine he knows nothing of me, or my true purpose. My master won't care which of us triumphs – either result will amuse him. If I can defeat Mormius and his rabble, and make my great sacrifice, he'll reward me in ways I'm only just beginning to comprehend. But, if I fail, and Mormius lays waste to Wolfenberg, the power I sought will be bestowed on him. We're playthings, nothing more – just an amusing diversion for the Great Deceiver. Mormius will only see me as an obstacle on the road to glory.' Fabian clutched the hilt of his sword and smiled. 'He should make a worthy opponent.'

Ludwig nodded, and rubbed his cold, lifeless eyes. 'Well, whatever the outcome, it will be good to finally reach him. We seem to have been marching for decades.'

ALMOST HALF A mile behind Fabian and his officers, rode Baron Maximilian von Düring, at the head of his squadron of Knights Griffon. Beside him rode Jakob, Ratboy and Anna.

'Can you be sure we're talking about the same man?' asked Ratboy, looking at the group of banners at the head of the army. 'Do you really think that's your brother up there?'

Wolff nodded. 'There's no other explanation. I was filled with dread at the thought of my brother marching with this army and now I find he's the man leading it.' His brow was creased in a thunderous scowl. 'It's much worse than I anticipated. Fabian's not the hero these men think he is. His master isn't von Raukov, but some unspeakable, unholy force. I can't imagine what he has planned for this army, but it's certainly not victory.'

'But it makes no sense,' said Maximilian. 'I've been hearing tales of the Iron Duke's victories ever since I first arrived in Ostland. He's driven back countless invasions. Why would he have done that if he's some kind of pawn of the Dark Powers?'

Wolff looked over at his old friend. 'He's playing for higher stakes. All he's ever dreamed of is to be a great hero – the *greatest* hero in fact. As a child, he pictured himself as a valiant knight, torn straight from the old lays and ballads. He always wanted to march at the head of a great Empire army such as this one. He's been carefully biding his time and gradually winning the trust of the Elector Count, and now he's leading the largest force in the province.'

'Then we should confront him,' cried Ratboy, brandishing his graceful sword. 'We should reveal him as the heretic he is.'

Maximilian shook his head. 'You'd never get within thirty feet of him, boy – unless he wanted you to. His personal honour guard watch him constantly. He calls them the Oberhau and their swordsmanship is legendary. They wield greatswords as easily as if they were rapiers.' He frowned. 'They wear fearsome helmets, fashioned in the shape of a snarling wolf and are famed for their ruthlessness. Rumour has it that the Iron Duke trains each of them personally; but, if your suspicions are correct, maybe there's more to the training than meets the eye.'

Wolff nodded. 'To reveal myself now would be a mistake. Fabian has an entire army fawning at his feet. He'd simply have me arrested. I imagine these Oberhau would have no qualms about executing me, if Fabian ordered them to.'

'Then what will you do?' asked Anna, looking around anxiously at the ranks of marching soldiers that surrounded them.

'Bide my time,' replied Wolff. 'Ostland's on the edge of ruin. Even if I could convince these men that their general is a traitor, I'm not sure I should. It's only Fabian that's holding them together.'

'But if he's a cultist of some kind, he's probably leading them all to their deaths,' she gasped, anxiously stroking the velvety stubble that covered her scalp.

Wolff nodded. 'All I can do is watch and wait.' He turned to Maximilian. 'We should move a little closer to the command group.'

Maximilian nodded and urged his horse into a canter, signalling for the other knights to pick up their pace too.

After a few hours, Maximilian nodded at a large hill that sat at the end of a long, narrow defile. It was topped with five odd, slender towers of stone. 'There's Fabian's destination,' he said, 'Hagen's Claw.'

Wolff peered at the distant hill. 'Have you spoken to my brother then?'

'Not personally, no, but two nights ago, I met with his closest advisor, the captain of the Oberhau.' Maximilian pursed his lips, as though tasting something bitter. 'His name's Ludwig von Groos and apparently he's Fabian's oldest friend, but there's something about the man that made my skin crawl.'

'Von Groos?' muttered Wolff, frowning. 'The name *does* sound familiar, but I spent most of my childhood in a temple. I never really knew my brother's friends. Why did you find this von Groos so unpleasant?'

Maximilian shrugged. 'Hard to say, really. I knew him by reputation anyway. He's considered unusually brutal, even by the standards of the Oberhau, but it wasn't that – there was something in his manner that made me feel on my guard. His words were quite deferential and his tone was perfectly reasonable, but I still felt as though he was mocking me somehow.'

'I see. But he explained Fabian's strategy to you?'

'Yes, although not in any detail. He simply told me the same as he told the other senior officers. The Iron Duke wants to reach an old burial site named Hagen's Claw and have time to dig in before the marauders arrive. His judgement has been sound on every previous occasion, so I simply thanked von Groos for the information and ushered him out of my tent as quickly as I could.' He shuddered at the memory. 'He started leafing through one of my tactical manuals with a ridiculous grin on his face – poking fun at the techniques and asking if I really used them. If I'd not found an excuse to shove him out of the door, I think we might have come to blows. Fabian's plan seems quite logical though. The hill's steep and topped with ancient monoliths, so there'll be plenty of cover and places to position the guns. There's also an unusually narrow valley behind it, so if things go badly, we'd be able to inflict *very* heavy losses on Mormius's men as we withdrew.'

Ratboy watched the smouldering, red sun as it sank behind the hill, silhouetting the towering obelisks that guarded the valley. There were four intact stones and a fifth that was broken and leaning to one side like a thumb. 'Whose tombs are they?' he asked. 'They're like nothing I've ever seen before.'

Maximilian shook his head. 'I've no idea, friend. I know they're old beyond reckoning, but other than that I've only heard rumours and legends. Maybe one of the Ostlanders would know,' he said, waving at the ranks of black and white troops that surrounded them. 'I think even they might struggle though.'

As the sun sank lower, bathing the landscape in scarlet light, the army reached the summit of the hill and began planting their standards between the strange columns. Half of the fifth stone had fallen, to be eagerly embraced by the shrubs and long grass beneath, but those that still stood reached even higher than Ratboy had expected. As he rode between them they seemed to bow over his head, so great was their height. 'Who was Hagen?' he asked in hushed tones, eyeing the obelisks with suspicion.

'I believe he was some kind of tribal warlord – a contemporary of Sigmar's – who met his end here,' answered Maximilian. The polished steel of his visor flashed red as he raised it to get a better view of the stones. 'The Ostlanders tell all sorts of gruesome tales about him. Allegedly, when he suspected one of his men of coveting his wife, he accused him of being no better than a wild scavenger, tied him to one of these stones and pierced his side with a knife. Then he left him to the mercy of the wolves that roam hereabouts.'

Ratboy looked up at the sombre columns with even more suspicion, wondering if it were shadows or dark stains he could see on the lichen-covered stone.

'How did Hagen die?' asked Ratboy.

'Well, if the legends are true, his power corrupted him and eventually he became a disciple of the Dark Gods. Sigmar heard stories of his strange behaviour and travelled out here to confront him. He found Hagen attempting to use the stones as part of some unspeakable rite, so they fought,' Maximilian gave Ratboy a wry smile, 'and Hagen died.'

Wolff saw the concern on Ratboy's face and gave Maximilian a disapproving shake of his head.

The old knight chuckled through his thick, silver beard. 'Very well,' he said. 'I suppose I shouldn't fill your head with legends and ghosts. You'll soon have plenty of mortal foes to keep you busy.' He shrugged. 'Anyway, odd as it is, the Iron Duke had this site in mind right from the start of the campaign. He sent scouts up here weeks ago to prepare for this battle. We're going to engage the enemy *exactly* where he planned to. Whatever your master thinks of him, Fabian is no fool. He must have had good reason to drive us so hard, and ensure that we fought here rather than any other spot.' He waved his men over to one of the few areas of hillside not already swarming with soldiers. 'That seems as good a place as any. Let's prepare ourselves.'

Once they'd reached the spot, Ratboy dropped from his horse and helped his master down from his. Then he perched on one of the pieces of fallen stone and, following the example of the Knights Griffon, began to polish his weapon in preparation for the battle. As he did so, he noticed Wolff looking anxiously through the bustling crowds that covered the hillside. Ratboy followed his gaze and saw the Iron Duke's standard, snapping proudly at the summit: a wolf and a bull, rearing side by side on a black background. He tried to imagine how Wolff must feel, to be so close to his brother, after all these decades.

'I wonder what he'll do, when the time comes to act,' said a voice at his ear.

Ratboy turned to see Anna, watching Wolff too. He dusted down a patch of moss and she sat next to him on the stone.

'A brother is a brother,' she said, sitting next to him. 'Whatever's happened in the past.'

Ratboy shrugged. 'He's been so concerned with tracking Fabian down, but I don't think he ever actually worked out what to do when he found him. I've never seen him so subdued. I suppose he imagined he would be dealing with a soldier, not the head of an army.'

Anna shrugged. 'How's your hand?' she asked, peeling back the bandages. The wound was beginning to heal up, but his fingers had set in a crooked, useless fist. She shook her head and frowned. 'It looks like I managed to stave off any infection, but I doubt you'll ever be much of a musician.'

Ratboy smiled. 'I don't think I was ever destined for artistic greatness.' The pain had been growing worse and he grimaced as he flexed his scarred, bent fingers. 'Some of the movement has returned already,' he said, trying to hide the extent of his discomfort. 'I may even be able to use this fancy sword properly, one day.' He raised the blade in his left hand, so that the metal caught the sun's dying rays. 'I've almost got the hang of using my other hand now anyway.' He looked over at Anna. In all the excitement of the last few days, he had almost forgotten her loss. 'How are you feeling?' he asked.

She continued studying his hand for a few seconds, frowning with worry. Then she placed it back in his lap and studied a ring on her finger. It was the one

Wolff had brought from the temple: the one that had belonged to the abbess. As she spoke, she traced her finger over the dove that decorated it. 'The sisters were my only family,' she said. 'I only pray that some of them managed to flee before...' She paused and closed her eyes. When she opened them again, they were bright with tears. 'I doubt a single one of them would have abandoned the people in their care.'

Ratboy took her hand. 'There were soldiers in there with them. They may have evacuated some of the sisters before the fighting started.'

Anna nodded. 'It's possible,' she said, with little conviction. She squeezed Ratboy's hand and took a deep breath. 'I don't feel completely alone now though. You've shown me great kindness.' She met Ratboy's anxious gaze with a smile, then looked out across the gloomy landscape. 'I may not have to wait long before I meet my sisters again, anyway. It seems that nothing can stop this Mormius, or his hideous creatures.'

Ratboy recalled the battle of Mercy's End with a shudder. 'I wonder if Gryphius, or Captain Felhamer escaped,' he said.

She shrugged. 'Felhamer knew those tunnels as well as anyone. Gryphius was carrying a terrible wound though. I don't think we'll see him again.'

Ratboy nodded and looked deep into her eyes. 'And what about you, Anna? You're not seeking a glorious end. What is there here for you? Mormius's hordes will arrive any time now. Who can say what will happen, but I doubt many of us will survive. Shouldn't you head back towards Wolfenberg? You could find other members of your order. I imagine there's much healing to be done in the capital. You should leave while you still can.'

'And would you come with me, Ratboy? This is no place for a young, inexperienced acolyte. A desperate battle won't help to complete your training. You could leave with me, head south and present yourself at the first chapterhouse you find. In a year or so, you'd be a fully trained warrior priest, just like your master. Think how much more use your life could be, if you didn't end it here, as a novice.'

Ratboy shook his head fiercely. 'I would *never* abandon Brother Wolff.' His face flushed with colour and he turned away from the priestess, embarrassed by the passion in his voice. 'He'll need me tonight, more than ever before and if it means my life, then I'll be proud to die by his side.'

Anna nodded and loosed his hand. She gave him a sad smile and climbed to her feet. 'I know,' she said quietly. 'I owe you my life, and if there's anything I can do to aid you, I'll be here to do it.' She looked around at the rows of pale, nervous faces rushing past them. 'And I imagine you won't be the only one who'll need my help.'

Ratboy stood and pulled her towards him. His eyes were wide with emotion, but before he could speak, a chorus of shouts erupted from the surrounding soldiers. The troops' preparations suddenly became much more urgent. Valets and equerries sprinted past and sergeants began barking commands at their men. 'What's happened?' said Ratboy turning from Anna and looking out into the darkness of the surrounding meadows.

'Listen,' said Wolff, stepping past them both and climbing up onto the stone. He looked out across the rippling pools of grass and shadow.

Ratboy held his breath and heard an odd sound on the breeze. He climbed up beside his master and followed his gaze. He could see nothing, but as the wind shifted slightly to the east, the noise suddenly swelled. He heard a horn of some kind, but it was playing no melody he could recognise. The thin, plaintive sound simply undulated slowly up and down, like the baleful song of a wading bird.

There was a clatter of armour as the surrounding men formed themselves into orderly ranks. The dark, feral helmets of the Oberhau could be seen all over the hill, dashing back and forth as they directed regiments into the formations Fabian had requested. The squadrons of knights and pistoliers took up positions near the bottom of the incline, while every man with a bow was ordered up to the summit, to stand alongside the engineers and their bizarre assortment of black-powder weapons. As the eerie, surging sound grew louder, the archers arrayed themselves in a long line across the top of Hagen's Claw and began to ready their weapons.

'We should take our positions,' said Wolff, placing a hand on Ratboy's shoulder.

They climbed down from the stone and, with Anna in tow, rushed back over to where Maximilian was inspecting his men.

The knights had already mounted their chargers, and as Maximilian looked them up and down he nodded with satisfaction. Despite the panic and noise erupting all around them, the Knights Griffon sat calmly in their saddles, with straight backs and raised chins. To Ratboy, they looked as immovable as the monoliths that towered above them.

'We don't have long,' said Maximilian, turning from his men and facing Wolff. 'Would you do us the honour of giving us your blessing, old friend?'

Wolff paused, dragging himself from his reverie with visible effort. Then he nodded slowly and stepped before the rows of gleaming knights. He unclasped a book from his cuirass, signalled for the men to lower their heads and muttered a quick prayer. To Ratboy, though, his words sounded oddly flat. The passion that usually filled his voice was gone, and he recited the words with a vague, distracted air.

> *Where there is weakness give us strength,*
> *Where there is lowliness, give us majesty,*
> *Where there is death, give us eternity.*

Then he moved along the ranks of men and placed his hand on each of their swords in turn, muttering a blessing as he went:

> *Fill this heart with faith undying,*
> *Gilt this sword, with strength unceasing.*

Once he'd reached the final knight, Wolff climbed up onto his own horse and positioned himself at the front of the squadron, next to Maximilian. There was a look of bleak despondency on his face.

The old knight gave Wolff a concerned glance. 'This isn't the first time we've faced such a foe,' he said, nodding to the row of flickering lights that had begun to appear on the horizon.

Wolff shook his head, but did not look up from where his hands were resting on the pommel of his saddle. 'It's not what's out there that worries me, Maximilian,' he muttered.

Maximilian lowered his voice and leant closer to his old friend. 'I have faith in you, Jakob, even if you do not. Whoever and whatever you face tonight, I know you will emerge victorious.'

Wolff lifted his eyes, and Ratboy saw agony and doubt burning there. The priest opened his mouth to answer Maximilian, but the words were lost, as Hagen's Claw exploded into an inferno of sound and flame.

All along the hillside, rows of canon and mortar boomed into life. Ratboy flinched and gripped his horse's reins in terror, taken by surprise as the guns unleashed hell on the vague shapes massing below. With the sound of the guns still ringing in his ears, he looked around and saw to his shame that Wolff, Maximilian and Anna were all sat quite calmly, peering through the growing darkness to see the effect of the volley.

'The range of these things is amazing,' said Maximilian as some of the lights below them flickered and died.

The enemy was still far from the foot of the hill and it was hard to see anything very clearly, but the droning horn faltered for a few seconds and several of Fabian's regiments burst into spontaneous cheers.

'It's a little early to begin victory celebrations,' said Anna, giving Ratboy a wry grin. 'I'm going to move back up the hill, there's nothing I can do in the thick of the fighting. I'll see if I can find the surgeons and wait for the wounded to arrive.' She placed a hand on Ratboy's arm and opened her mouth to say something. Then she changed her mind and simply nodded at him.

He gave her a mute nod in reply and watched her ride away between the ranks of stern-faced soldiers. As she disappeared from view, he felt an almost overwhelming urge to rush after her, but a look at his master's troubled face give him new resolve and he drew his sword instead.

'Here they come,' said Maximilian, snapping his visor down.

Ratboy saw that the tides of light below were now rushing towards the hill at great speed. The drone of the horn shifted up a key, becoming a shrill scream and he began to make out individual figures at the head of Mormius's army. He frowned. There was something odd about the men sprinting towards them. They were clad in crude, brutal armour, tatty shreds of hide and helmets crowned with vicious tusks, but it was not their dress that made him frown. There was something about their proportions that confused him. He turned to Wolff with a question on his lips, but his master was engrossed in his own thoughts and barely seemed to register the army hurtling towards them.

As the men moved closer, other marauders emerged behind them and it was then that Ratboy realised what was so strange about the warriors in the vanguard: they were colossal. The marauders behind them were obviously well built, but they barely reached the waists of the warriors in the front line. As the giants pounded across the field towards them, Ratboy noticed that their faces were as grey as month-old corpses and their canines were grotesquely enlarged – jutting from their drooling mouths like boar tusks. 'What are they?' he gasped.

'Ogres of some kind,' replied Maximilian, his voice ringing oddly through his helmet. 'They're a fearsome breed, from what I've heard. Fond of human flesh.' He raised his sword in silent command and there was a scraping of steel behind him as the ranks of knights all drew their own weapons in perfect unison.

Maximilian gestured to Ratboy's sword. 'That should serve you well, son.'

Ratboy nodded and lifted the ornate weapon higher, but as he saw the haunted expression on Wolff's face, doubt filled him. Just then another, even louder explosion of artillery erupted behind them and Ratboy's horse flinched violently, almost throwing him from the saddle.

'Steady,' said Maximilian, as the first rows of marauders started to dash up the hill towards them, led by the huge, lumbering ogres. As the creatures grew closer, Ratboy realised he could hear their hoarse, grunting breath beneath the wailing of the horn. He looked at Maximilian, wondering what he was waiting for. In a few more minutes the monsters would be all over them. The baron was faceless behind the polished steel of his helmet and did not acknowledge him.

Just as Ratboy was about to speak, a dark shape passed overhead. The archers at the top of the hill had finally loosed their arrows and the dusk grew even deeper as the lethal cloud filled the sky. The marauders were so close by this point that even the fading light could not obscure their outlines. Thousands of black and white-flecked arrows thudded into their thick hides.

Countless ranks of marauders fell screaming back down the hill, clutching at their throats and chests as they went, but the ogres barely stumbled. They hardly seemed to notice the arrows that sank into them. With a chorus of derisive grunts and snarls they simply snapped the shafts and continued rushing up the hill.

'They're unstoppable,' muttered Ratboy, looking around to see if the other soldiers would hold their ground in the face of such a horrendous foe.

'Watch,' said the baron, gently turning Ratboy's face back towards the front line.

The grunting, stomping mass of corruption was only a few feet from the vanguard of Fabian's army when, at the bark of a captain, the soldiers in the frontline raised an impressive array of pistols, muskets and crossbows. The men did not fire however, watching for the captain's signal as the ogres lurched towards them. Soon, they were so close that Ratboy could smell the thick, meaty stink of their flesh.

At the very last minute, the captain stepped out to meet them. It was one of the wolf-helmed Oberhau, and as the first ogre approached him, the captain calmly fired his flintlock pistol into the monster's head, tearing the skin from its skull with a fierce blast of gunpowder. As the report of the pistol echoed across the hillside the creature finally paused. It raised its hands to the pulpy mess where its face had been and gave a grunt of confusion. Then it toppled lifelessly back down the hill.

The captain dropped to one knee, lowered his head and pointed his sword at the enemy. At this silent signal, the entire frontline fired their weapons. The noise of so many guns blasting in concert was incredible and the hillside lit up in a brief, sulphurous flash. It was so bright that for a second the ogres' faces resembled those of grotesque actors, leering out into the footlights of an infernal theatre. Then the lead shot ripped the flesh from their bones and left gaping, blackened holes in their chests. Even in death, though, many of them seemed incapable of halting; stumbling forwards even as viscera spilled through their hands and their legs collapsed beneath them.

As a second thunderous volley tore into them, most of the ogres finally ground to a bloody halt: only one actually managed to blunder, half-blind, into Fabian's army. It was even larger than the others and its misshapen head was crowned with a thick, white mohican. The left side of its face was hanging down around its neck like a glistening scarf, revealing its long teeth in a fierce rictus grin as it stumbled, bellowing, up the hill. Black and white ranks of soldiers crowded around the towering figure, trying to block its way, but the thing's rage and momentum powered it through them. Its only weapon was a rough-hewn piece of sharpened iron, but the crude blade was taller than any of the men who pressed around the ogre and the monster cut them down as easily as grass, pausing only to tear at their faces with its gleaming, exposed teeth.

The ogre wove a spiralling, confused path through the soldiers and Ratboy realised with a rush of dismay that it was heading towards the Knights Griffon. Dozens of blades rose and fell against it, but to no avail. Then, with a crash like waves against rocks the full force of the marauder army ploughed into the Ostlanders. The battle began in earnest and the ogre was forgotten.

A cacophony of screamed commands engulfed Ratboy as the surrounding regiments began charging down the hill, howling with fear and bloodlust as they rushed towards the enemy. Meanwhile, clouds of arrows were still swarming overhead and the *phut phut* of mortar fire had begun, sending whistling, iron balls down into the approaching hordes, where they exploded into fragments of white-hot metal.

Ratboy looked at Maximilian and saw to his surprise that he was still sat utterly still. Watching with calm disdain as Hagen's Claw descended into a riot of fear and pandemonium. Behind the baron, his knights waited, equally patient and at the baron's side, Wolff seemed unaware of the fighting. His huge, armour-clad shape remained motionless, as he studied his hands with a perplexed frown on his face.

The injured ogre was now only a few feet away, hammering its brutal weapon through ranks of men, utterly oblivious to the countless wounds that networked its calloused flesh. With a roar of frustration the thing slammed its huge shard of metal into a row of spearmen attempting to block its way, sending them reeling backwards in a shower of splintered wood and bone. The men screamed in horror and pain as the ogre trampled maniacally over their bodies, crushing ribs, lungs and hearts as it continued up the hill. Then, with a confused snort, the beast found itself facing a dazzling sight: Maximilian and his knights.

Wolff finally looked up from the back of his hands to see a bleeding colossus staring directly at him. The ogre seemed enraged by the priest's air of devotion. Ignoring the knights it made straight for Wolff, raising the huge piece of metal above its head with a belching roar.

Wolff and the surrounding knights scattered their horses just in time as the hunk of iron sliced deep into the soft turf. Anger flashed in Wolff's eyes and as his horse circled the beast, he drew the warhammer from his back, testing its weight as though he'd never held the weapon before.

Ratboy saw the muscles tighten in his master's powerful jaw and wondered if the priest's anger was at the sight of the monster or at the thought of his own inaction.

'Sigmar,' bellowed Wolff, with such fury that everyone within earshot paused and looked in his direction. Even the ogre hesitated, lowering its guard for a second and turning to face the priest with a slack-jawed grunt. 'Absolves you,' continued Wolff, slamming his hammer into the thing's knee. The *crack* of breaking bone rang out, audible even above the gunshots further down the hill.

The ogre's leg folded backwards, sending it crashing to the ground and the last traces of doubt vanished from Wolff's eyes. Dismounting, he grasped the hammer in both hands, strode towards the dazed creature and slammed the weapon into its face. As he did so, the rekindled flames of his devotion rushed from his flesh and into the metal, so that as it connected with the monster's jaw, the head of the hammer was throbbing with white, holy radiance.

The ogre's skull detonated in an explosion of blood and light and it sprawled backwards across the scorched grass.

Wolff looked around at the soldiers charging down the hill with surprise on his face. Then he clambered back onto his horse and turned to face Maximilian, Ratboy and the knights. His ornate, iron cuirass was drenched in the ogre's blood and his face was flushed with exertion but, as he wiped the gore from his shaven head, he smiled at his friends. 'We've work to do,' he said, nodding at the carnage below.

The initial wave of ogres had been replaced by a crush of human marauders so great that the Ostlanders were already being forced to concede ground. A chorus of grunts and screams had replaced the sound of gunfire as the two armies locked together in a heaving, flailing forest of limbs and spears.

Maximilian nodded in reply and signalled for his standard bearer to raise their colours. As the cloth unfurled in the breeze, the baron snapped his reins and began riding down the hill at a slow trot. Behind him, the ranks of knights followed suit, maintaining their neat, orderly lines as they made their way through the battle.

As they neared the bottom of the hill, Ratboy realised that despite the size of Fabian's army, the tide had already turned against them. Marauders were flooding out of the darkness like a plague. The horizon had vanished behind a sea of pale, muscled flesh and scaled, mutated limbs. Ratboy saw horsemen, with long, drooping moustaches and others with helmets fashioned from the skulls of great beasts. Behind them marched blue-eyed tribesmen wearing human pelts and bearded, screaming goliaths with chains woven through their tattooed flesh. Despite their initial display of firepower, the sheer volume of the enemy was now overwhelming the Ostlanders. Guns were useless in close combat and the bare-chested marauders hacked and clawed their way through them in an orgy of bloodletting.

Ratboy swallowed hard as he neared the frontline. The din of clanging swords and screaming wounded was horrendous and as the last traces of sun vanished the slaughter became a strange, gruesome, tableau. The rows of grim faces looked suddenly flat and unreal as silver moonlight threw them into sharp relief.

The crush of bodies was so great that before Ratboy and the others could reach the marauders, their horses ground to a halt, hemmed in by clanking, serried ranks of Empire soldiers, several feet away from the fighting. The heaving mass of shields and spears was rocked by tides of movement, lurching and stumbling from left to right and Ratboy's horse strained beneath him, struggling to keep its balance in the tumult. Despite his fear of the marauders, Ratboy found it worse to be stranded like this, so close, but unable to act.

'What do we do now?' he called to Wolff. The priest was right next to him, but he had to yell to be heard over the clamour.

Wolff was looking back up the hill at the banners that surrounded the command group. There was no sign that Fabian and his officers were going to join the fighting. At the sound of his acolyte's voice, Wolff turned to face him with a frown of confusion. 'What?' he yelled back, leaning forward and cupping his ear.

'What do we do?' repeated Ratboy, raising his voice to a hoarse yell.

Wolff pointed his hammer at the advancing ranks of marauders. Their numbers were quickly overwhelming the Empire soldiers. 'Wait,' he replied, making the sign of the hammer over his chest. 'And pray.'

They did not have to wait long.

Far down in the valley, there was a flash of silver, as a winged figure lifted up over the heads of the marauders. From this distance it was barely more than a glittering speck, but Ratboy thought he could make out multiple pairs of wings, shimmering in the moonlight as it flew towards them. 'It's Mormius,' he gasped, leaning forward in his saddle to try and see more clearly. The din of battle drowned out his words, but he assumed he was right. As Mormius approached, Ratboy saw him raise a long, tapered horn to his lips and the awful, undulating sound echoed around Hagen's Claw again.

At the sound of Mormius's horn, his army surged forward with renewed vigour. They seemed utterly consumed by passion, howling furiously and throwing themselves against the Ostlanders with complete abandon.

The captain of the Oberhau tried to rally his men, swinging his greatsword with such phenomenal speed that a circle of headless corpses quickly built up around him. As the marauders pushed the other Empire troops slowly back up the hill, the captain found himself alone in an island of calm at the heart of the enemy vanguard. As the rows of muscled, mutated barbarians crowded around him the captain's strikes grew so fast his movements were hard to follow. Only the wolf mask of his helmet was visible, seeming to snarl with delight at the constant supply of fresh blood. Finally, inevitably, the circle closed in on him as the marauders used the sheer mass of their bodies to stifle his blows. Ratboy saw the lupine snout of his helmet one last time before it vanished under a tsunami of swords, axes and spears.

As Mormius's horn pealed out across the battlefield, driving his men onwards, Ratboy's concerns about reaching the frontline evaporated. The Ostlanders were now falling in droves and the fight was moving towards him with alarming speed. A nearby group of halberdiers dropped their weapons in panic and tried to scramble back up the hill, but they were blocked by the dignified, immovable presence of the Knights Griffon. The marauders made short work of the stranded men: hacking at their backs with broad, iron axes and ripping out their throats with crab-like claws.

As the last of the halberdiers fell to the ground, Maximilian's knights finally had room to manoeuvre and he waved them on with a twirl of his sword. As their chargers leapt forwards, Ratboy's horse followed suit and he found himself flying towards the screaming, blood-drenched marauders, with Wolff's broad, armoured back just ahead of him.

The knights fought with vicious, carefully drilled efficiency. Their swords rose and fell in graceful arcs, quickly cutting a path through the enemy and leaving a trail of broken claws and splintered shields. Wolff seemed to forget his brother for a moment and let the heat of battle consume him, swinging his hammer with brutal effectiveness and screaming out blessings as he pummelled and crunched his way through the marauders.

Ratboy tried to imitate the knights' unruffled precision, but as the sneering marauders crowded around him, his horse reared in panic and Ratboy lashed out in a desperate frenzy. The strange sword felt light and swift in his hands and his frantic blows were surprisingly effective. Few marauders made it past Wolff's pounding hammer, but those that did met a blur of flashing steel.

Across the hillside, other knightly orders were entering the fray and for a while the enemy's advance slowed. The winged figure of Mormius was still gliding towards Hagen's Claw and as he approached, his horn rang out once more. The wavering note was now so loud that several of the Ostlanders had to clamp their hands over their ears to block out the trilling sound. The marauders exploded into action – driven onwards by the close proximity of their general's rallying cry. Even Maximilian's knights struggled to defend themselves against such unhinged aggression. The bare-chested barbarians threw themselves at the polished armour of the knights with no thought for their own safety. For every one that fell, gutted, to the bloody ground, a dozen others clambered up onto the horses, their eyes rolling wildly as they wrenched and hacked at the men's armour.

The crush of bodies slowly halted the knights' advance. In fact, as the horn drove them to even greater fury, the marauders began to push them back up the hill. As the marauders swarmed over them, Ratboy saw one of the knights dragged from his charger. A crowd of enemy soldiers had grappled and shoved at his horse with such fury that it eventually toppled onto its side, thrashing and kicking in fear as the marauders plunged knives beneath its scalloped armour. The knight rolled clear of the horse and continued to fight with calm dispassion, but down on the ground he stood little chance against the seething mob. The other knights showed no sign of recognition as he vanished beneath a flurry of blows; they simply closed ranks and continued to fight with a quiet dignity as they were forced slowly back towards the monoliths.

A furious roar echoed across the hillside as the marauders greeted the arrival of Mormius. He dropped gracefully down amongst them and folded his flashing wings behind his back. Ratboy found it hard to look directly at him. It seemed almost as though a fragment of the bright, gibbous moon had broken away and fallen to earth. He could see quite clearly how tall the man was though; he was almost as big as the ogres that had led the attack. But as he strode towards the Empire troops, he showed none of the ogres' animal simplicity. He sauntered casually through the carnage, as though promenading into a ballroom, flicking his red hair back from his face as he drew a long, two-handed sword.

The first Ostlanders to face him were so paralysed with fear that Mormius simply ignored them, strolling past the rows of shocked faces and leaving the marauders that followed in his wake to hack them to the ground.

Two of Fabian's honour guard attempted to rally the Ostlanders, charging at Mormius with their two-handed swords above their heads and calling furiously for the ashen-faced onlookers to follow. As they neared the winged colossus, a detachment of swordsmen grudgingly shuffled after them, wide-eyed and trembling in the face of such an unholy vision. As the wolf-helmed Oberhau reached Mormius, they dropped into a low crouch and edged slowly towards him.

At the sight of the two officers, Mormius revealed his perfect teeth in a broad smile. His regal gait became a lurching, twitching stagger, as a fit of laughter gripped him; but then his pretty face twisted with anguish. 'Be calm,' he hissed, in a desperate voice, shaking his head furiously as the soldiers approached. 'It's not funny.' He took a deep, calming breath and his crystal wings spread out behind him, creating a flash of moonlight so powerful that it temporarily blinded the Oberhau. They faltered, raising their hands to try to block the glare and, with a casual flick of his wrist, Mormius lopped their heads from their shoulders.

The swordsmen baulked in the face of such incredible speed and as the giggling, cursing champion stepped towards them they backed away, raising their shields defensively against the glare of his glimmering breastplate.

Mormius continued up the hill. As the terrified Empire soldiers shuffled back, they created a broad path ahead of him, leading straight towards the distant banners of the command group. The only possible danger to the champion seemed to come from himself; as his expression alternated from a leering grin to an agonised scowl, he began slapping his armour-clad fists against the side of his head, punching himself with such force that blood began to flow from his ears.

'We must stop him,' cried Wolff, leaping back up into his saddle. 'If he reaches Fabian something terrible will happen, I can feel it.'

Maximilian nodded and with a wave of his sword, ordered his men to abandon their futile attempt to advance. He led them sideways across the hill, through the moonlit jumble of corpses and broken guns. The crush of bodies was just as great in that direction though, and they soon found themselves mired once more in the mass of struggling soldiers. The knights hacked and shoved with all their strength, but the marauders seemed endless. Ratboy's face and hair were slick with blood and his voice was hoarse from screaming. He paused, mid strike, as a familiar face looked out at him from the heaving throng. He could see no more than a pair of pale eyes, glaring at him from behind the flailing mass of swords and limbs, but something about the face chilled him. He had no time to dwell on it though, as another lumbering brute lashed out at him, swinging a battered sword straight at his head. He parried the blow and kicked the marauder to the floor and when he looked again, the face in the crowd was gone.

Wolff suddenly gave a howl of frustration and Ratboy looked over in alarm, surprised by the desperation in the priest's voice. Wolff's face was purple with rage and his scarlet robes were drenched with sweat and blood. His inability to reach the champion seemed to have driven him to distraction. There was a feral look in his eyes that Ratboy had never seen before.

Wolff leapt from his horse, diving face first into the enemy. His heavy frame hit the northmen with such force that a whole row of them toppled backwards under his weight. Before they could clamber to their feet, Wolff grabbed the nearest one by his greasy hair and slammed his warhammer into his face. 'Bow down before Sigmar!' he screamed, pounding the weapon repeatedly into the man's shattered head and shaking him violently back and forth, even though he was obviously already dead. 'Receive His judgement!'

Ratboy watched in horror as his master ripped and pounded his way through the struggling men. He seemed unhinged; inhuman even. As he bludgeoned his way towards Mormius, the priest was no longer taking heed of who crumpled beneath his bone-crunching hammer blows. Ratboy saw several Empire soldiers, smashed to the ground by his blind, uncontrollable rage. The sight of such untrammelled fervour reminded him of someone and with a sickening rush of fear, Ratboy realised who he had seen in the crowd. It was the witch hunter, Sürman: alive and here with them on Hagen's Claw. He must have trailed them right across the province, but for what purpose? He looked around but could see no sign of the frail old man amongst the crowds of struggling warriors.

Ducking beneath a spear thrust, he dropped from his horse and ran to his master's side. On approaching him, he paused. As Wolff screamed a tirade of furious blessings into the pulped faces of his victims, he suddenly seemed indistinguishable from Sürman. Is that what I will become, wondered Ratboy, lowering his sword in horror. A vision of Raphael's corpse filled his head, surrounded by his adoring crowds of penitent followers, tearing their flesh for the glory of Sigmar. Where were they now? Broken and forgotten on a muddy field. Sacrificed on a whim of his master. Anna's intense, grey eyes suddenly filled Ratboy's thoughts and he looked back up the hill, wondering if he had made a terrible mistake. I can't do this, he suddenly realised, blanching at the sight of so much bloodshed. He turned away from his master and began to climb back up the hill.

Rough hands grabbed him beneath the shoulders and hoisted him up onto a horse. He found himself sat behind Maximilian. The knight's helmet was gone and his steel grey beard was splattered with blood, but he had a fierce grin on his face. 'We'd best keep up with your master, eh lad?' he said, giving Ratboy a suspicious look. 'A wolf needs his pack around him at a time like this.'

Ratboy flushed with embarrassment and nodded, gripping his sword a little tighter.

Wolff's frenzied attack had cleared a path across the hillside, and as Maximilian rode after him, Ratboy got his first clear glimpse of Mormius. The champion was only about two-dozen yards away, and he noticed again that some of his crystal armour was stained and dark. The black shadow had now spread from his left hand all the way down to his waist, and, from the awkward, one-handed way Mormius held his sword, Ratboy guessed he was in a lot of pain.

'He's wounded,' he yelled into Maximilian's ear, pointing at the champion's arm.

The knight nodded as he steered his horse around the struggling figures, closing quickly on Wolff. 'Doubtless his corruption is eating him up from the inside. Should make our job a little easier.'

As they reached Wolff's side, there was no sign of his wrath diminishing. He was fighting towards the gleaming champion with jerking, spasmodic movements that reminded Ratboy of a marionette or an automaton. As he shouldered and punched his way into the clearing around Mormius, the priest's robes were hanging in tatters from beneath his dented armour, but he still had his warhammer grasped firmly in both hands, and it was glowing with a light almost as dazzling as Mormius's armour. 'Blasphemer,' he gasped, slamming his hammer against one of the stone columns with a dull *clang*.

Mormius paused at the sound and looked back. He met Wolff's bloody scowl with a wild grin. 'A priest, a priest, a warrior priest,' he sang, strolling back down the hill towards him. 'Have you come to pray for me?' He gave out a thin shriek of laughter and looked around at the rows of terrified faces that lined his path. 'I think you may be a little late.' His laughter grew so hard that tears welled in his eyes and as he neared Wolff, his face was flushed with colour. 'Your congregation seems to have already written me off.'

'Speak carefully,' yelled Maximilian, as his horse crashed through the rows of cowering soldiers, a little further up the hill. As they rode down towards the champion, Ratboy's pulse began to throb painfully in his temples. Mormius's towering shape was essentially human, but corruption seemed to pour out of him. Ratboy found it impossible to meet the giant's eyes as he turned towards them.

'What's this?' asked Mormius, leaning heavily on his sword as the battle raged around them. He wiped the tears from his eyes and shook his head. 'A welcoming committee? Finally. I was beginning to feel quite snubbed. Anyone would think you people had forgotten your manners.'

Maximilian's horse tossed its mane nervously as the knight rode towards Mormius and Wolff. As they approached him, Ratboy realised that his master, well built as he was, barely reached the flashing plates of Mormius's chest armour.

'You abomination,' muttered Wolff, wiping the gore from his shaven head and striding forwards. He pounded his gauntleted fist against the hammer device on his chest armour. 'Sigmar denounces you, with every muscle, heart and sinew of His Holy Empire.'

The champion's laughter faded as he saw the passion burning in Wolff's eyes. 'I see no muscle here,' he replied, waving his sword nonchalantly at the rows of petrified onlookers. 'Maybe Sigmar has tired of His snivelling, bastard offspring. Maybe He's forsaken you, little priest.'

Wolff gave no reply, but broke into a sprint, raising his hammer to strike as he raced towards Mormius.

Mormius turned slightly so that the crystals of his armour flashed in the moonlight and presented Wolff with an image of his own, livid face.

The priest stumbled in confusion and lowered his hammer.

Mormius stepped to one side and sliced his greatsword at Wolff's neck.

The blade hit Maximilian's sword with a ringing sound. With Mormius distracted by Wolff, the knight had managed to approach the champion and was now just a few feet away. He had extended his sword just in time to parry the blow and save Wolff's life, but Mormius's strength was such that the knight's weapon flew from his hand, spinning across the battlefield towards the crowds of onlookers. The old soldier cried out, clutching his arm.

Mormius rounded on Maximilian and Ratboy with a sardonic smile on his plump lips. He strode towards them, but then stumbled and winced. Ratboy noticed again that the crystals on his left arm were dark and lifeless. In fact, now that he saw it a little closer, he realised that his whole side was atrophied and twisted.

There was a rending metallic crunch as Wolff's hammer slammed into the small of Mormius's back. The champion's eyes widened in shock and he stumbled towards Maximilian's horse. As he fell past them, Ratboy lashed out with his sword and a flash of red erupted from the champion's face. Mormius slammed to the ground like a felled tree.

Wolff strode forwards and struck again, but Mormius rolled to one side and the blow pounded harmlessly against the ground.

The champion lurched to his feet and turned to face his three attackers, batting his long eyelashes in shock and pouting as he clutched his bleeding cheek. Then his mouth set in a determined line as he saw several other Knights Griffon fighting their way through the carnage and lining up behind Maximilian with their swords raised. He lowered his hand from his face, allowing the blood to flow freely down his pale neck and grinned. Then, he rocked back on his heels, rolling his eyes at the moon and letting out another burst of hysterical laughter. 'Little friends,' he gasped, waving his sword at the scene behind them. 'Your determination is commendable, but can't you see? It's already over.'

Wolff and the others turned to see that marauders were now flooding the hillside in such numbers that the Empire troops had no option but to retreat. Huge crowds of the black and white clad figures were rushing back towards the banners at the top of the hill. Trumpets were blaring in several places as the sergeants ordered their men to retreat.

Mormius spread his wings to the breeze that was buffeting the hillside and lifted himself up over the heads of his opponents. 'I've no time to entertain you,' he called, apologetically, as he flew up the hill towards the command group. As he glided over the soldiers, he lifted his long horn from his back and the mournful, undulating sound washed across the hillside once more, driving the marauders to new levels of ferocity as they rushed after him.

Wolff vaulted up onto his horse and without even pausing to acknowledge his friends he raced up the hill.

Maximilian and the other knights charged after him, led by the flashing shape of Mormius. The retreat was quickly becoming a rout. A second wave of ogres had swelled the ranks of marauders and as they grunted and stomped their way into the fray, the Empire soldiers fled for their lives.

As they thundered back up the hill, Ratboy saw that the enemy had even overrun the command tents, trampling the striped canvas to the ground as they chased their prey. 'Where's Fabian?' he called.

Maximilian shook his head and gave no reply as they raced towards the tents.

As they reached the summit, Ratboy saw no sign of the Iron Duke, or his officers. The tents were empty and as the Ostlanders saw they had been abandoned to their fate, they screamed in fear and confusion, before fleeing down into the narrow valley behind Hagen's Claw. Thousands of them were already scrambling and tumbling into the ravine, leaving a trail of broken weapons and banners as they went.

Mormius was flitting back and forth like a carrion bird, searching desperately for Fabian and lashing out at the fleeing shapes in frustration. His great wings were silhouetted against the moon as he landed on top of one of the stone columns and looked down over the battlefield. Even from such a high vantage point, his enemy eluded him and the champion howled and gibbered at the stars, as though the heavens themselves were responsible for Fabian's escape.

Without their general to lead them, the Empire army lost all sense of order and its neat ranks collapsed into an unruly jumble of beleaguered knights and panic-stricken foot soldiers. Ratboy scoured the confusing scene for any sign of his master, but it was impossible to make out individual figures in the riot of plumed helms and tattered banners. This is it, he decided. This is the moment my master feared. Fabian has abandoned his army to its doom. He's led them here to die.

The ringing of swords filled his ears and he turned to see that Maximilian's knights were now a lone island of purity, surrounded by a host of screaming, grotesque brutes. The marauders were clambering over each other in their desperation to attack the knights and Ratboy saw immediately that they were about to be overwhelmed. 'We must flee with the others,' he cried. 'Into the valley.'

Maximilian shook his head and hissed with frustration, lashing out at the clutching fingers trying to drag him from his horse, unwilling to show weakness in the face of such a barbarian rabble. Within seconds of Ratboy's cry, however, the whole front rank of knights collapsed with a scream of twisting metal and injured steeds.

'Retreat,' cried the baron in a despairing voice, as several of his men were dragged to the floor and butchered right before his eyes. 'Pull back into the valley.' He turned his horse up the hill and led his men in a desperate charge away from the advancing hordes.

Even then, on the very edge of defeat, the knights carried themselves with a quiet dignity that belied the hopelessness of their situation. As they reached the summit of the hill, they slowed to a canter and formed themselves back into neat, ordered ranks.

Maximilian and Ratboy looked back to see a myriad of grotesque shapes teeming over the hillside: towering, slack-jawed ogres, sinewy, broad-shouldered barbarians and lumbering, unnatural shapes, all heeding the call of the winged monster perched on top of the obelisk.

'My master's probably down there,' cried Ratboy, straining to be heard over the din and pointing down into the crowded valley on the other side of the hill. 'He'll be trying to find his brother.'

Maximilian had regained his composure and nodded calmly at the acolyte. 'We'd not last a minute up here on our own anyway. And down there we can at least defend our countrymen as they retreat.' He signalled to his men with a flourish of his sword and led them down the hill after the fleeing Ostlanders. 'Whatever Fabian's motives,' he cried as they rode down the hill, 'he was right about this ravine. The pass is so narrow, the marauders will find themselves in a bottleneck as they try to attack. Their numbers will work against them in such a confined space. Mormius will pay dearly for every foot he advances.'

Ratboy nodded vaguely, but he was only half listening to the baron. As they raced down the hill, with the enemy hordes at their backs, he scoured the crowds of fleeing soldiers for any sign of a white-robed girl or an old man with pale, staring eyes.

If there were any officers left alive, Ratboy saw no sign of them as the reached the valley floor. The Ostlanders were less an army than a terrified, demoralised mob. For months, Fabian had been the cornerstone of their faith: the incredible luck and charisma of the Iron Duke had made the impossible seem possible, but now he was gone the full horror of their situation had hit home. Handgunners, swordsmen and halberdiers all piled together in a desperate, headlong stampede through the narrow valley. The Knights Griffon brought up the rear of the fractured army, but all they could do was flee with the others as Mormius swooped down into the ravine at the head of his daemonic host.

'They must stand and fight,' snarled Maximilian, as they raced after the receding army. 'Where's that wretched traitor, Fabian? If no one turns this army around, they'll just spill out onto the plains and be butchered. At least in here we've *some* a chance of seeing the dawn.'

Ratboy nodded weakly, but could think of nothing to say in reply. He had scoured the terrified faces that surrounded them, but had seen no sign of Wolff or Anna. His oath to protect Wolff, whatever the cost, had been proven worthless and he had failed the priestess too. He looked down at his beautiful sword with disgust. What use had it been, in the end? As they fled from Hagen's Claw, all his earlier doubts returned to him. The Empire had raised an army of incredible size, thousands of good men had abandoned their lives in the name of Sigmar and what had it achieved? What began as a noble crusade was about to end as a pitiful farce. He realised his dreams of following in Wolff's footsteps were nothing more than a romantic fantasy. As the army neared the end of the valley, he shook his head in despair and let the sword slip from his hand.

A rolling boom, like the sound of thunder filled the ravine. The horrified Ostlanders looked back over their shoulders to see what fresh horror had been summoned to assault them. The whole army stumbled to a halt and gawped in shock. The far end of the canyon was collapsing in on itself. The walls were engulfed in smoke and dust as a curtain of crumbling rock hurtled down onto Mormius's men. The champion flew clear of the explosion, beating his wings in a desperate attempt to escape the avalanche, but the great host beneath him vanished, as the walls of the valley slid downwards in a lethal, deafening storm of granite.

As the dust and stones settled, the Ostlanders stared in bewildered silence at the huge, silvery cloud rippling towards them. Then a movement far above it caught their eye. All along the sides of the ravine, rows of soldiers began to appear, led by a proud, slender figure clad in dark plate armour and wearing a helmet styled to resemble a wolf's head. Behind him fluttered a black and white banner, showing a wolf and a bull.

A chorus of shocked voices erupted from the men around Ratboy. 'It's the Iron Duke,' they cried. 'He hasn't abandoned us.'

Maximilian tugged at his stiff, silver beard and gave out a bark of laughter. 'The old devil must have planned this. He intended for us to retreat into this ravine.'

Ratboy peered through the thinning smoke and saw the surviving marauders climbing from the rubble. They made a pitiful sight as they dragged themselves clear on twisted, broken limbs while howling up at their champion to save them. Grey dust covered their bodies, giving them the appearance of ghosts, or revenants, crawling from a rocky grave. 'But how could Fabian have predicted the avalanche?'

'He didn't predict it, he created it,' replied Maximilian with a nod of grudging respect. 'I thought it was scouts he sent out here all those weeks back, but they must have been engineers.' He waved along the top of the canyon, where the ranks of soldiers had appeared. 'This whole area must have been lined with black powder, primed and waiting for us to lead the marauders to their doom. And meanwhile Fabian kept back a reserve of soldiers, waiting here to strike.'

He shook his head at the pitiful state of the Ostlanders that surrounded them. 'He really must be made of iron though. Rather than let his men know the plan and risk it being discovered by spies, he let them fight on, oblivious to his intentions, until so many had died they were forced to pull back in a genuine retreat.'

Ratboy gasped at the brutal logic: to sacrifice so many men on a gamble made his head spin. What if they hadn't retreated? What if the explosives hadn't detonated? Then he remembered: Fabian would have no qualms about sacrificing Empire soldiers if he was worshiping at the altar of some dark, ancient power.

As Mormius flitted back and forth above his screaming, broken wreck of an army, Fabian led ranks of fresh men down into the valley. With a pounding of drums and hooves they charged into the crowds of wounded marauders.

The soldiers around Ratboy lifted their tired heads and cheered. Then, forgetting their fear and exhaustion, they rushed back down the gully, eager to join the slaughter. Maximilian led his men after them in a slow, stately trot.

At the sight of Fabian, Mormius let out a strangled wail and dived towards him. His wings blurred and he drew his greatsword from his back as he fell. He smashed into the ranks of the Oberhau with the force of a comet, sending a plume of dust from the side of the ravine. For a few minutes, Ratboy struggled to make out what was happening. Then, as the haze cleared, he made out the two men, locked in a fierce duel on an outcrop of rock. The colossal, winged champion dwarfed Fabian, but as he swung his greatsword at him in a flurry of wild, furious blows, the Iron Duke danced easily out of the way, wielding his own sword with calm, controlled skill.

As the lines of fresh, eager-faced soldiers charged down towards them, the surviving marauders turned and fled, limping and clambering back up towards Hagen's Claw. Many of them were too crippled to run and the vengeful Ostlanders fell on them with undisguised glee.

As the clouds of dust folded and banked through the moonlit canyon, Ratboy caught brief glimpses of the carnage. Most of the Empire soldiers had thought themselves as good as dead, and their relief now manifested itself in an orgy of bloodletting. Swords and knives plunged into the struggling marauders as they reached up pathetically towards their embattled champion.

As the Knights Griffon approached the bloody scene, Ratboy saw a familiar face and cried out with delight. The broad-chested shape of his master was striding purposefully though the clouds of dust, still screaming his litany and pounding his two-handed warhammer into the crumpled bodies of his foes.

'Master Wolff,' cried Ratboy, leaping from his horse and sprinting towards him.

At the sound of his acolyte, Wolff looked up from his work with a fierce expression on his face. The ornate scrollwork of his cuirass was glistening with blood and his dark eyes were burning with rage. As he saw Ratboy his eyes cleared a little and his expression softened. He looked down at his gore-splattered chest and limbs in confusion. Then he lowered his hammer to the ground with a *thud* and took in the shocking brutality that surrounded him. In their fury the

Ostlanders had become as bestial as the marauders, tearing through the wounded northmen like rabid dogs. As Wolff's fury waned, so did his strength. He had only taken one step towards Ratboy when his legs collapsed beneath him. He dropped to his knees with a grunt of exhaustion.

Ratboy rushed to his side and, taking his arm, helped him to his feet. 'We've won,' he gasped, trying to sound cheerful despite the horrific sights that surrounded them. He gestured to the crowds of figures scrambling back up towards the obelisks. 'The marauders are retreating.'

Wolff's face remained fixed in a grim scowl. 'Where's my brother?' he croaked, through bloody teeth.

Ratboy pointed up to the duelling figures, lunging and slashing at each other on the rocky outcrop. It was an incredible sight. They seemed to Ratboy like gods, locked in a contest to decide the fate of all humanity. Even at this distance though, it was obvious that Mormius was struggling. The whole of his blackened left side looked twisted and deformed and his leg kept buckling beneath him as Fabian forced him closer to the edge of the precipice.

Wolff's amour rattled as he fought through the bloodthirsty mob, trying to get a better view. He and Ratboy both gasped as they saw Fabian plant his boot into the champion's deformed leg and send him stumbling back towards the chasm. Mormius's wings thrashed one last time as he crumpled to the floor, but before he could lift himself, Fabian turned on his heel and sliced his sword cleanly through his neck.

The soldiers ceased their butchery for a moment and an eerie silence descended over the canyon; then, there was an explosion of cheers as Fabian strode calmly into view, with Mormius's severed head dangling from his upraised fist.

CHAPTER SEVENTEEN
SHADOWS AND GHOSTS

ANNA AWOKE WITH cool liquid trickling into her throat. She swallowed it thirstily but immediately gagged. It was thick and tasted of iron and she realised her mouth was filling with someone else's blood. She groaned and struggled to rise, but a heavy weight held her firmly in place. Upon opening her eyes she found that the weight was a dead marauder. The full mass of his stinking flesh was pushing her down onto a wooden floor that was jolting and bouncing painfully against her back. She gasped in disgust. The man's pale, clammy face was pressed right against hers and she could see his eyes rolling in their sockets. His limbs were cold and already stiffening and she guessed she had been trapped under him for some time.

As Anna wrestled with the dead man, a low, guttural voice rang out nearby and she froze. The words meant nothing to her, but she immediately recognised the fierce language of the northern wastes. A second voice replied in the same language, but this one whined in a higher register than the first, speaking in a babbling torrent of bleats and snorts.

The first voice replied with an angry, dismissive grunt and they both fell silent.

Fear crippled Anna. The voices had sounded very close: just a couple of feet away at most. She lay still for a second and tried to calm her breathing. She was surrounded by broken limbs and weapons but through a gap in the corpses she saw a tiny square of sky and realised she was moving. Low, moonlit clouds were rushing overhead and she guessed from the lurching movement beneath her that she was on some kind of cart. As she listened more carefully, she heard the sound of creaking wheels and horses' hooves and the loud, heavy breathing of the two marauders.

The wheels bounced up over a ridge and as the vehicle slammed back down onto the ground, the corpse's head knocked against Anna's, spilling a fresh load of semi-congealed blood over her face. She groaned and rolled quietly to one side, finally freeing herself from the weight of the corpse. Other bodies lay over her, but she managed to carefully disentangle the mass of torsos and limbs and brought her face up to the surface, gasping for air like a tired swimmer. Luckily for her, the moonlight was too weak to illuminate most of her fellow passengers, but from what little she could make out, the scene resembled an immense butcher's slab. Ostlanders and marauders lay where they had fallen in a confused jumble of broken bones and severed arteries.

Other shapes were travelling beside the cart, slipping through the darkness like ghosts. With a thrill of horror she saw that she was surrounded by marauders: some riding ferocious-looking steeds and others sprinting on foot, but all racing with grim determination from the distant silhouette of Hagen's Claw.

We must have won, thought Anna with a shock. This is no victory parade – they're running away. She nestled back down into the pile of damp bodies, relieved to be unnoticed for the moment. As the cart bounced wildly over the uneven turf of the valley, she saw that huge crowds of northmen were fleeing from the stone towers with no pretence of order. It was a complete rout and Anna's head reeled. The last thing she could remember was fleeing for her life as the hordes of enemy soldiers overran the command tents. She had tried to escape down into the canyon with the others, but as she dashed between the struggling soldiers something had cracked against the back of her head. She must have dropped into the back of this cart and then been gradually covered by the dead and dying.

The hopelessness of her situation suddenly hit her. If she stayed where she was, the marauders would carry her to whatever ungodly destination they were racing for, but if she tried to escape, she would be seen immediately. She shuddered, wondering why the marauders had not detached the cart. What foul purpose did they have in mind for the bodies?

The higher, whining voice cried out again and she felt hands pressing down near her head. She realised one of the drivers must be looking back over her, towards the hill. She froze, doing her best to look like a corpse. The marauder whined again, pointing to something as he leant over her. His face was so close to Anna's that she could smell his rancid breath. Then the other marauder bellowed furiously and wrenched him back onto the driver's seat.

Anna looked cautiously where he had pointed and saw that several of the marauders were dropping to the ground. As she strained to see more clearly, she saw flashes of black and white moving amongst them: Ostlanders, pursuing the defeated army and hacking them down as they fled.

She dropped back with a sigh of relief. It looked like it would only be a matter of time before all of the marauders were overtaken and slaughtered. As long as she remained hidden beneath the bodies until then, she should be safe.

As she shrugged herself back down beneath the corpses, she felt a movement that didn't seem to come from the wheels below. She looked around and saw a large rat, perched on the face of one of the bodies and watching her intently. There was a spark of intelligence in its eyes that she found a little unnerving, but she decided it was too small to have been the cause of the movement.

She turned the other way and saw that one of the marauders was also staring at her. His plaited hair was slick with blood and she could tell by the black, clotted line around his neck that his throat had been cut. As she watched the man, trying to discern whether it was he who had moved, he suddenly spread his teeth in a wide leering grin and pulled himself towards her.

Anna stifled a scream and squirmed away from him, but she quickly felt her back press against the side of the cart and realised she was trapped.

As the marauder crawled slowly towards her, he opened his mouth wider in an attempt to cry out, but all that emerged from his ruined vocal chords was a faint, liquid croak that was lost beneath the sound of the rattling cart. He freed his legs and lunged across the cart.

Anna tried to worm herself away from the man, but his eyes were fixed on hers with a fierce hunger and as he moved across the mounds of damp, ruptured flesh, he wrapped his hand around the hilt of a broken sword. The blade gleamed with the same cold fire as the marauder's eyes and he jabbed it at her face with a gurgle of amusement.

The two embraced in a silent struggle. Anna gripped his shoulders and shoved with all her strength, but he would not give up. Gradually his grinning face bore down on hers as he forced the shard of metal towards her throat.

Anna fought the urge to scream and reached around for something to use as a lever. Her hand came to rest on a piece of metal and she realised it was the hilt of another sword. Confusion and terror mingled in her head. She had sworn countless oaths to cherish life in all its forms, but as the marauder's broken sword pressed up against her throat, she could not believe it right to simply submit. Everything in her rebelled at the idea of hurting another being, but the psychotic glee in the man's eyes disgusted her. She screamed in despair as a warm fountain of blood washed over her neck.

It was only as the marauder began thrashing about in pain that she realised what she had done. Her trembling hand was still clutching the long sword she had buried in his neck. She had murdered him. Anna closed her eyes and groaned in revulsion as he jerked and twitched violently back and forth. In her horror, she seemed unable to loose the sword, and as the man's struggles grew weaker, she felt every last one of his pitiful, gurgling breaths. Finally, he grew still and, forgetting the danger, she screamed in despair. In that one second everything she knew about herself collapsed. She felt as though she were suddenly trapped inside the mind of a stranger.

Anna did not have long to wallow in her guilt. Her scream had alerted the cart's drivers to her presence and as she shoved the marauder's body to one side, she saw a sinewy, fur-clad youth grinning down at her. His knotted flesh was networked with serpentine, self-inflicted scars and his greasy topknot was dyed a deep, henna red. As he stood up in the driver's seat, he drew a long, curved knife and let out a whooping howl of pleasure.

Anna tried to pull the sword from the corpse, but her terror had jammed it so deep into the flesh that it would not move. She raised her hands in front of her face as the marauder lifted his sword to strike.

There was a staccato thudding sound as four arrows sank deep into his chest, leaving a row of black and white flights buried in his thick furs. He spun his arms for a few seconds, trying to maintain his balance, then he toppled beneath the wheels of the cart. His lifeless body jammed in the axle and the cart lurched out of control. The remaining driver roared in pain as the wheel shattered and the reins sliced through his fingers.

The cart tipped and Anna flew through the air in a shower of weapons and body parts. The air was knocked from her lungs as she slammed down into a clump of long grass. Screams and howls surrounded her as the marauders nearby fought for their survival. Everywhere she looked, Ostlanders were charging out of the shadows, riding down the enemy with swords, lances and spears and howling victoriously as they trampled the northmen underfoot.

Anna looked away from the slaughter and studied the blood on her hands. As struggling figures tumbled past her, she tried to clean her fingers, rubbing them desperately against her white robes, but the more she rubbed, the more blood-stained she became and after a few minutes she let out a low murmur of despair. 'Murderer,' she whispered under her breath.

'Sister,' cried a young, wide-eyed soldier, spotting her sat amidst the carnage. 'Watch yourself,' he yelled as he steered his horse to her side and dismounted.

She flinched at his touch and looked him up and down in terror, taking in his bloody sword and battered breastplate. Then, seeing the concern in his eyes, she relaxed a little and accepted his helping hand. 'Murderer,' she muttered as he pulled her to her feet.

He shook his head in confusion, shaking the tall white plumes on his helmet. 'Who's a murderer?' he asked, looking round at the violence that surrounded them.

'I killed him,' she answered, staring at the young soldier with an intensity he found unnerving.

'Aren't you the priestess who was travelling with the Knights Griffon?' he asked, struggling to meet her eye.

Anna nodded vaguely and continued trying to wipe the blood from her hands.

The young soldier nodded back, relieved at the thought she might be someone else's problem. 'They're still making their way down from Hagen's Claw,' he said lifting her up onto his horse. 'Let's get you back to them.'

As they rode back towards the monuments on the hill, fighting against a tide of victorious soldiers, Anna saw the Iron Duke leading a pack of wolf-helmed Oberhau. They thundered through the heart of the other soldiers, bellowing commands at them as they charged past. Fabian himself had flung back his visor and she caught a brief glimpse of his gaunt face and glittering eye patch. 'They're heading for the forest,' she heard him scream as he rode past her.

As he made his way up the hill, the soldier spotted the unmistakable squadron of Knights Griffon. Despite everything that had occurred that evening, they were still riding with their shoulders thrown back and their chins raised to the heavens. Even the blood of their foes seemed ashamed to stain the knights' armour and it still gleamed and sparkled in the moonlight.

'It's Anna,' cried Ratboy, as he saw the soldier's horse trotting up the hill towards them. Wolff was riding next to him and nodded in reply, but did not slow the speed of his horse as he charged down the hill. Ratboy reined in his own steed and allowed Wolff and the Knights Griffon to race on ahead, so that he could greet the young soldier and his passenger. 'She's alive,' he gasped as the soldier approached.

Recognition flared in the priestess's eyes at the sight of Ratboy and she held her stained hands up to him like a guilty child.

'What's happened?' he cried, grabbing her arms and noticing that her gaze seemed even more passionate than usual.

Anna gave no reply and simply hung her head in shame, but she grasped Ratboy's arms as tightly as he held hers.

Ratboy gave the soldier a questioning look.

'I found her next to a wrecked cart,' he said. 'It looks like some of the marauders had been trying to use it to escape in.' He shook his head. 'It's a bloodbath down there. I thought she would be safer up here with her friends.' He looked at the blood that covered her hands and robes. 'I'm not sure how she got mixed up with the enemy retreat.'

Ratboy frowned in confusion, but nodded all the same. 'Thank you for finding her,' he said, dismounting. He helped Anna down onto the ground, steadying her as the ranks of Ostlanders charged past, screaming for bloody vengeance.

'Anna,' he said, taking her head in his hands in an attempt to make her focus on his words. 'You must stay here. My master and Maximilian are in pursuit of the duke and I must follow, but it's not safe down there. The marauders won't die without a fight.'

Anna's eyes opened even wider as she realised Ratboy meant to abandon her. She shook her head fiercely and threw her arms around him.

The soldier chuckled. 'Looks like she has other ideas.' He looked around at the brooding stones that covered the hillside. 'She's probably no safer up here anyway. Not all of the marauders will have fled.'

Ratboy looked down at the massacre below and grimaced. 'How many are still alive?'

The soldier shook his head and followed Ratboy's gaze. 'Impossible to say. It's even darker down there in the shadow of the forest. Hundreds of them have already fled beneath the trees. The ogres are all dead and the riders from the Steppe vanished as quickly as they came. They seem to have lost their fighting spirit,' he laughed. 'The Iron Duke is determined that none should survive to reach their own borders though. He's ordered the whole army to pursue them into the forest.' He laughed again, obviously a little light-headed after their unexpected victory. 'I've a feeling some of our more experienced veterans may have taken the opportunity to slope off. The battle is obviously won, so who can blame them, really. We'd all be making for the nearest town to start the celebrations if it was up to me.'

'So, *is* the battle over?'

The soldier shook his head. 'No, not really, I suppose. I'm only talking about a few people who were a little too eager to return home. The bulk of our men are following the duke into the forest.' He raised his battered sword and grinned enthusiastically. 'After all – there's more than one way to celebrate a victory.' The grin dropped from his face as he remembered something

Ratboy had said. 'Did you say that your master is in *pursuit* of the duke?'

Ratboy sneered. 'Yes!' he snapped. 'My master must stop–' he paused as he noticed the frown on the soldier's face. 'Well, yes, of course' he continued, in a softer voice. 'He wishes to assist the duke in any way he can.'

The soldier's eyes narrowed with suspicion, then he gave a curt nod. 'Good luck, friend,' he muttered, snapping the reins of his horse and disappearing down the hill.

Ratboy shook his head at his own stupidity and hoped that no harm would come of his indiscretion. Then he helped Anna up onto his horse and climbed up after her. 'Well, sister,' he said, taking the reins. 'Let's see if we can keep ourselves out of any more trouble.' With that, he rode after the distant, sparkling helms of the Knights Griffon.

'I've killed a man,' whispered Anna into his ear.

Ratboy reined in his horse and looked back at her in confusion.

'Earlier on.' she said, holding up her bloody fingers and shaking her head at him. 'I put a sword through his neck and watched him die.' She groaned in horror at the memory. 'What right had I to take another's life? He would have had parents and children. How could I do such a thing? I was a Sister of Shallya, but what am I now?'

Ratboy lowered her hands. 'Alive.'

Anna simply stared at him.

'We must move fast, if I'm going to catch up with my master,' he said, afraid of the despair in her eyes. He steered his horse down the hill and tried desperately to think of something more useful to say.

Beneath the eaves of the forest, the darkness was almost total. As Fabian's men left behind the open, moonlit fields, they slowed their horses to a walk and peered nervously into the shifting gloom. The Iron Duke's army still numbered in the thousands, but as the ancient trees engulfed it, the host fragmented. Something of the forest's wildness seemed to infect them and as they hunted down the fleeing marauders, the Ostlanders ignored the commands of their officers and blundered wildly through the undergrowth, even abandoning their horses as the slender pines gave way to low, twisted yews and ugly, knotted oaks.

It was only by the flashing armour of Maximilian's knights that Ratboy was able to find his master in the shadows. 'Lord,' he gasped as he climbed down from his horse and rushed after him with Anna following close behind. 'How will you find Fabian in this darkness?'

Wolff looked back and Ratboy saw that his face was still twisted in an animal snarl. Ratboy blanched at his master's fierce glare, feeling that he was looking into the eyes of a stranger. 'I'll find him,' growled the priest.

After a few minutes, as they entered a small hollow, one of the knights grunted in pain and stumbled backwards with a spear jammed under his breastplate.

The rest of the party paused and raised their weapons, scouring the small clearing for any sign of the attackers as the injured knight dropped, wheezing, to his knees.

'There,' cried Maximilian, pointing his sword at a group of figures emerging from the trees.

Ratboy gasped in disgust as the vague shapes entered the pool of moonlight at the centre of the clearing. Most were the same bare-chested northmen they had faced on the hillside, but there were other, stranger things with them. He realised that they were the creatures he had seen before: men with deformed, bestial heads, cloven hooves and thick, greasy hides.

At a signal from Maximilian, the knights fell on the creatures with a flurry of sword strikes.

Wolff launched himself at the marauders with a terrifying combination of hammer blows and scripture. As the knights pushed the other warriors back towards the trees, the priest grabbed one of the beastmen by the scruff of its neck and slammed its head into a tree trunk. The creature collapsed, with a bellow of pain and Wolff placed a foot on its chest and crunched his hammer down into its face. The priest's fury only seemed to grow as the creature stopped breathing and as its dark blood rushed over the roots of the tree, he kept swinging the hammer: pounding the metal into the broken body with spasmodic, jerking blows.

Ratboy saw the look of horror on Anna's face as she watched the priest and he rushed to Wolff's side. The other attackers were already fleeing or dead and as the knights resumed their positions they were also eying Wolff with unease. 'Master,' said Ratboy, placing a hand on the priest's shoulder. 'He's dead.'

Wolff spun around. His face was white with passion as he glared at the acolyte. 'Yes,' he muttered, looking down at the corpse with a slightly confused expression.

He staggered back from the dead beastman and raised his dripping hammer towards the heart of the forest. 'We must keep moving,' he gasped, breathlessly.

Maximilian looked at Wolff's pale, blood-splattered face with concern. He stepped after him and placed a hand on his arm. 'Brother Wolff, rest yourself for a moment, I beg you. Your zeal does you credit, but the battle is won.' He looked with distaste at the crumpled mess Wolff had made of the marauder. 'Do we really need to hunt down every last one? My hatred of these beasts is as great as yours, I assure you, but this forest is fey, and unpredictable. I have a feeling that the deeper we go, the stranger it will become. Why not let the stragglers crawl back to their own lands? It would be no bad thing if a few of them lived to spread the word of our decisive victory.' He waved at the calm faces of his knights. 'I've no desire to sacrifice my men in a pointless game of cat and mouse.'

Wolff's black eyes flashed. 'Do as you wish,' he growled, 'but I must continue. Listen,' he said. The surrounding trees echoed with the noise of the victorious army, clattering and hacking their way after their general. 'Fabian's leading these men into the forest for a reason. I don't know exactly what it is, but I know it's going to end in more bloodshed. As you say, the battle's won, but my brother was never interested in victory – he's brought these men here for some dark purpose of his own.' He gripped Maximilian's shoulders. 'I think he means to use them as some kind of sacrifice. I'm not sure how, but I think he's going to use their blood to buy the favour of his dark masters.' He shook his head. 'It's not the marauders I'm pursuing, it's my brother.'

Maximilian turned away with a sigh. 'Tell me, Jakob – how can you be sure Fabian is so evil? He's just led this army to another glorious victory. You saw how he dealt with Mormius.' The baron looked back at Wolff. 'Maybe he's just a brilliant tactician who's eager to protect his homeland?'

Wolff gripped the baron's shoulders even more tightly and glowered at him. 'I know my own brother, Maximilian. I think that deep down I've had my suspicions for decades, but guilt clouded my judgement. As soon as I heard the truth from the witch hunter, Sürman, I knew it had to be right.'

Maximilian shrugged. 'Could this Sürman not have been mistaken?'

Ratboy suddenly gasped and rushed to Wolff's side. 'He's here,' he gasped. 'I saw Sürman's face in the battle. He's followed us.'

Anna let out a groan of dismay, wrapping her arms around herself and looking around at the mass of ancient, winding boughs.

Wolff shook his head at Ratboy. 'I doubt it very much, boy. I hammered a stake into his chest.'

Ratboy gripped his master's arm with an urgent expression on his face. 'I'm sure it was him – I'd never forget those peculiar eyes of his.'

Maximilian took a deep breath and freed himself from the priest's grip. 'Old friend,' he said, still watching Wolff with concern. 'When this witch hunter denounced your brother as a heretic, was it before or after you attacked him with a piece of tree?'

Wolff strode after the knight with a furious expression on his face. 'I *know* Fabian's guilty, Maximilian.

He spent his whole childhood dreaming of military glory, but he was useless with a sword and could barely ride a horse. The closest he ever came to battles was reading about them in old folk tales. Then, around the same time as I discovered occult objects in our family home, he suddenly became a deadly warrior.' He shook his head in disgust. 'I was so wrapped up in my own guilt over summoning the witch hunter, it never occurred to me that there might really be a cultist in our family, but now I have no doubt about it at all. I don't know exactly how this will end, but I think this whole campaign is just a way for Fabian to somehow gain even greater strength.' He leant closer to the knight. 'Come with me Maximilian. I *must* find him.'

Maximilian gave a long sigh. He looked around the clearing at the rows of expectant faces. 'Well,' he said finally, 'I'm not sure I really follow your logic, but I don't like the idea of leaving you to go on alone. Your brother's still surrounded by those swordsmen of his, the Oberhau.' He nodded at Wolff's dripping hammer. 'And whether you're right or not, I'm sure they'll defend their lord fiercely. I doubt even you could take them *all* on.' There was a metallic *clang* as he patted Wolff's shoulder and turned to his knights. 'Looks like we still have a little work to do.'

The priest gave a barely perceptible nod of thanks, before turning on his heel and heading off into the trees.

As Maximilian predicted, the deeper they moved into the forest, the stranger it became. Ratboy struggled to keep up with his master's brisk pace as the moonlight began to play tricks on him. Dawn was still several hours away but, as they rushed after the rest of Fabian's army, pale lights flickered at the corner of his vision, only to vanish when he tried to focus on them. He shivered and tried to keep his eyes on the bear-like silhouette of the priest as he shouldered his way through the trees. It was tough going. The forest floor was sloping slowly upwards, and after the exertion of the battle, Ratboy soon grew short of breath.

'Are you sure it was him?' whispered Anna, looming out of the darkness and gripping his arm.

'What?'

'Are you sure it was Sürman you saw on the hill?'

'Oh, yes,' he replied, without slowing his pace or taking his eyes off Wolff. 'I couldn't forget a face like that. He was watching me, I'm sure of it.' He let his eyes flick briefly in Anna's direction. 'I think he must have followed us here.'

Her eyes widened and she clenched her blood-stained hands together. 'How could he have survived such an injury?' she muttered.

Ratboy shook his head as he vaulted a low branch. 'Who knows? I imagine old mendicants like that are hardened by all those years of travel. Maybe he's not as frail as he looks.'

'I knew he'd come for me,' whispered Anna, tightening her grip on Ratboy's arm. 'The day you rescued me I knew it. As soon as I saw he had escaped from your master, I knew he would hunt me down.'

Ratboy frowned. 'He might not be here for you, Anna. He could be after any of us. Wolff's the one who injured him. I can't imagine he'll forget that in a hurry.' He shrugged. 'Anyway, I might be wrong. Maybe he didn't follow us. He might have just seen me in the crowd and wondered where he knew my face from.'

Anna shook her head. 'He's come for me, I can feel it.'

They ran on in silence for a few minutes and then noticed that the trees were thinning slightly and the soldiers ahead of them were slowing their pace.

Up ahead, Wolff reached the top of the wooded slope and paused at the edge of a large clearing. As Ratboy and the others huffed and clattered to his side, Wolff turned and raised his hand, signalling for them to stop at the edge of the trees. 'They're making camp,' he announced, with an incredulous expression on his face.

Ratboy looked past him and saw that it was true. Hundreds of the Ostlanders had gathered on the plateau at the top of the slope, and none of them looked happy to be there. The fervour that had driven them into the forest was fading quickly. There was a tangible feeling of menace about the place that made them wonder if they had been acting entirely under their own volition. They had huddled together for protection and there was a hum of nervous conversation as they eyed the surrounding trees. The wolf-helmed officers of Fabian's honour guard were moving amongst them, and as the nearest one caught sight of Wolff and the Knights Griffon, he strode over and gave Maximilian a stiff bow. 'The Kriegsmarshall has granted you all a few hours rest,' he said, waving to the treetops spread out below them. 'The marauders have already hidden themselves throughout the forest. You'll need some sleep before we start the long job of hunting them all down.'

Maximilian looked around at the dismal clearing. 'He wants us to rest here?'

The officer's only reply was a nod and his helmet made it impossible to see his expression.

'Very well,' said Wolff stepping to the baron's side. 'If the Iron Duke wishes it.'

The officer studied Wolff in silence for a few seconds; then he gave another brisk nod and moved on.

'We're completely exposed up here,' said Maximilian, turning to Wolff with a frown. 'Why on earth would we sit out the night in a strange place like this?' He waved at the crowds of tired soldiers flooding into the clearing. They were watching the trees fearfully as they spread out on the long grass. 'If these men are meant to be hunting the marauders, why wait until the morning? They can obviously sense there's something odd about this place and anyway, if they don't move soon, the enemy will be long gone.'

'I expect most of the marauders have already made their escape,' replied Wolff, drumming his fingers on the haft of his weapon. 'My brother didn't bring these men up here to fight. He brought them up here to die.'

'Is he even here though?' asked Ratboy, scouring the hilltop. 'I can see his banner over there with the Oberhau, but I can't actually see the general anywhere.'

They looked over at the tattered black and white standard and the soldiers milling around beneath it. Ratboy was right: there were dozens of Oberhau, cleaning their long, two-handed greatswords and snapping orders at the other Ostlanders, but there was no sign of the general himself. As they watched, a young soldier crossed the clearing and approached Fabian's honour guard. Ratboy felt a chill of fear. He recognised the man immediately as the soldier who had discovered Anna. The young officer spoke urgently to one of the guards and then, after a few minutes he gestured over towards Ratboy and the others. Several of the Oberhau crowded round, quizzing him intently and turning to look at Maximilian and Wolff.

'This looks interesting,' said the baron, tugging at his short silver beard as he watched the exchange. He turned to Wolff with an ironic grin. 'I'm not sure we'll be getting that much rest after all.'

Ratboy gave a nervous cough and looked up at the pair of hoary old veterans. 'I think I might have spoken to that man earlier,' he muttered with a shame-faced expression. 'And accidentally mentioned that we were pursuing the general.'

Wolff's nostrils flared with anger, but when he spoke it was in clipped, controlled tones. 'Was it him, or not?'

Ratboy looked again and nodded. 'It was him – I'm sure of it.'

Wolff grimaced with frustration and closed his eyes for a few seconds to think. Then he turned to the baron. 'Whatever happens,' he said, 'I need to find my brother. I can't die here; not without confronting him.'

'I understand,' replied Maximilian with a stern nod. He looked at his men. It was hard to believe they had just survived a fierce battle. During the whole engagement, only six of their number had fallen and those that remained looked as calm and lethal as if they had just emerged from their chapterhouse. They stood in neat, gleaming rows at the edge of the trees and each of them had their hands folded in exactly the same way across the hilt of their swords. 'We can hold off Fabian's swordsmen for as long as you need us to,' said Maximilian. He waved at the crowds of Ostlanders still shuffling fearfully into the clearing. 'I can't guarantee what everyone else here will do though and even we couldn't hold off an entire army.'

'Leave that to me,' replied Wolff.

The Oberhau finished talking to the young officer and dismissed him. Then, the most senior amongst them huddled together, looking repeatedly towards the Knights Griffon as they talked. Finally, they came to some kind of accord and drew themselves into ordered ranks, before marching over towards Maximilian and his men. All across the clearing, the groups of resting soldiers watched the scene with interest and several of them rose to their feet to get a better view.

The knight at the head of the Oberhau was slightly larger than the others and looked to be their captain. He wore the same dark, burnished armour, but his wolf-shaped helmet and two-handed greatsword were a little more ornate, and a pair of huge, black and white feathers topped his sculpted helmet. Upon reaching Maximilian and Wolff he threw back his visor with a *clunk*. His eyes looked out from the dark metal with a dispassion that Ratboy found utterly chilling. There wasn't a trace of humanity in them. 'Good evening, baron,' he said, nodding at Maximilian. 'I must congratulate you and your men on their work this evening.' He spoke in flat, neutral tones and stood with the casual poise of a relaxed athlete. 'I noticed you were amongst the very last to retreat into the valley.'

'Thank you, Captain von Groos,' replied Maximilian with a deep bow. 'It's a pleasure to–'

A flash of movement interrupted Maximilian's reply. It was so fast that for a few seconds Ratboy struggled to work out what had happened. It was only when Maximilian staggered backwards that the acolyte saw there was a greatsword, buried deep in his chest. Von Groos had shoved it through the baron's cuirass with such force that the blade had sliced through the metal and emerged between his shoulder blades. As he dropped to his knees, Maximilian tried to speak, but all that emerged from his mouth was a thick torrent of dark blood. As he collapsed into his men's arms, with a confused expression on his face, he was already dead.

Von Groos wrenched the blade free with a screech of grinding steel and stepped back.

For once, the Knights Griffon forgot their training. With a chorus of despair and rage, they launched themselves at the Oberhau. Ratboy just managed to drag Anna aside as they slammed into the swordsmen.

There was an explosion of limbs and swords as the Oberhau defended themselves against the vengeful knights. Captain von Groos was already on the floor. Wolff had him by the throat and as Ratboy looked over, he saw the priest slam his forehead into the captain's face, shattering his nose with an audible *crunch*.

The captain muttered a stream of indecipherable words and writhed snake-like from Wolff's grip. As he leapt to his feet, he turned lightly on his heel and brought his two-handed sword down towards the priest's head.

Wolff was nowhere near as fast as his opponent and before he could dodge the blow, the blade slammed into his neck. His ornate gorget took most of the impact, but the edge of the blade scraped across the side of his face, sending up a thin arc of blood and causing him to bark in pain. He rolled forward and rammed his head into the captain's stomach.

Von Groos's breath exploded from his lungs and Wolff lifted him up over his shoulders. The priest draped one arm over the captain's neck and the other over his legs and before von Groos could raise his sword for a second strike, Wolff jerked his elbows downwards and snapped the captain over his broad back, cracking his spine in two. As the priest let him slide down his back onto the floor, von Groos whispered pitifully, then, after a final, rasping breath he fell silent. Wolff glared at the corpse for a few seconds, disappointed he could only kill the man once.

The rest of the Oberhau were faring a little better. Despite their expensive armour and years of training, the Knights Griffon could not seem to lay a single blow on their opponents. As they fought, the Oberhau whispered strange, arcane words and danced easily out of reach with lightning-fast movements.

Wolff backed away from von Groos's corpse and raised a hand to his scarred face to gauge the damage. With a nod of satisfaction he turned his attention to the fight. The combatants were well matched. The Oberhau whirled and slashed with incredible speed, but so far they had been unable to break the proud fury of Maximilian's knights.

Other soldiers had begun swarming around the fight, speechless with shock and unsure what to do. None of them were willing to enter the fray without being sure whose side to take.

Wolff wiped the blood from his cheek and rose up to his full height. He looked out at the gathering crowds and raised his warhammer. 'Men of Ostland,' he cried, loud enough to be heard over the sound of the fighting. 'I'm Jakob Wolff: Templar of Sigmar and brother of Fabian Wolff, your Kriegsmarshall.'

A crowd immediately formed around him.

Blood flew from Wolff's face as his booming voice filled the clearing. 'Is that natural?' he cried, waving at the Oberhau. 'Who can fight with such speed?' His voice rose even louder. 'Other than the damned?'

At the sound of Wolff's words, several of the Oberhau tried to break free and rush towards him, but Maximilian's stern-faced men blocked their way.

The soldiers surrounding Wolff looked at each other with confused expressions. A young pistolier stepped forwards. His armour was dented and torn and there was a bloodstained bandage over one side of his face, but he pointed defiantly at the Oberhau. 'They're the Iron Duke's own men,' he cried. 'He's taught them to fight as well as he does.'

'And where do you think your Iron Duke learned such incredible skill?' snapped Wolff, glaring at the pistolier. 'He's my brother, but I won't defend him.

Only the Ruinous Powers give such unnatural strength.'

'He's an Ostlander,' the pistolier cried back, looking around at his comrades for support. 'One thing we've all learned to do well is fight.'

A ragged cheer met his words and several of the soldiers raised their weapons in agreement.

Wolff grabbed the man by his jerkin, pulled him close and roared into his face. 'Fight for what?' he cried. He waved at the surrounding trees. 'What are you doing here? The battle is won. Why has the Iron Duke led you to the black heart of this forest? To a place where the enemy has all the advantage? I know Fabian Wolff. He's led you here as a sacrifice. You're a gift. An offering to the very enemy he claims to be hunting.'

There was a chorus of jeers and boos. 'Never,' cried the pistolier, freeing himself from Wolff's grip with a shocked expression on his face. 'How could you accuse him of such a thing?'

'Tell me,' replied Wolff, looking out over the crowd. 'Where's your general now?'

The soldiers looked nervously around the clearing, but the pistolier was undaunted. 'He's most likely scouting the surrounding area, looking for the enemy.'

Wolff shook his head. 'Mormius is dead. His army is already defeated. Those that survived have already fled. Fabian has abandoned you.' He waved at the sinister, twisted trees that surrounded them. 'Here, in this wretched forest.'

A fierce debate broke out amongst the crowd. Some of the soldiers already felt unnerved by their frenzied journey through the trees. It almost felt as though an external force had been driving them onwards. Many of them had been eager to head home even before they reached the clearing and its ominous atmosphere. Wolff's accusations had only made them more anxious to leave. The quarrel quickly grew louder. The men were tired and scared and Wolff's speech had put a name to their fear. There was rattle of swords being drawn and the crowd fragmented into a morass of snarling faces and furious insults.

As the arguments became fights, Ratboy noticed that his master had turned away from the troops. He was peering at something just outside the clearing and Ratboy stepped to his side to see what it was. It was too dark beneath the trees to see very clearly, but Ratboy thought he could make out a face, watching them. 'What is it?' he asked, looking up at the priest. 'Is that Sürman?'

Wolff frowned. 'No, I don't think so. I'm not sure it's even…' his words were lost beneath the din of the battle as he strode off towards the edge of the clearing. He paused briefly at the edge of the trees and looked back at the confusion he had created. The soldiers' frenzy had returned, but now it was directed at each other. It would be several minutes before they remembered the priest who had caused their disagreement. Wolff gave a nod of satisfaction and vanished from view.

Ratboy rushed after him, with Anna close behind. As they plunged into the damp, arboreal gloom they had to reach out and feel their way through the network of roots and shrubs, but Wolff rushed ahead, oblivious to the twigs and branches that lacerated his flesh. Ratboy saw his prey: it was a small deer of some kind, skipping easily through the trees.

'What's he doing?' asked Anna. 'His friend has just been butchered and he decides to go hunting.'

Ratboy shook his head in confusion and cried out. 'Master, where are you going? What about Maximilian's men?'

Wolff ignored his acolyte and blundered on through the trees, chasing the terrified animal. They reached the banks of stagnant pool and the deer paused, knee deep in the moonlit water, looking back at them expectantly. 'Look at it,' gasped Wolff, stopping to catch his breath.

Ratboy peered at the motionless creature. Now that he could see it more clearly, he noticed that there was something very strange about it. Its limbs were crooked and its hide bulged in places where it should have been smooth. It reminded Ratboy of some of the stuffed animals he had seen in Castle Lüneberg. Its eyes were not those of a dumb animal and they gazed back at him with a cool, human intelligence.

'What's that along its back,' whispered Anna, trying not to scare the animal.

Ratboy followed her gaze and saw that all along the deer's hunched, undulating spine there was a flash of iridescent blue, bursting up from under its skin. 'Are they feathers?' he asked.

At the sound of Ratboy's question, the deer bolted. It moved with lightning speed but Wolff was almost as quick, splashing through the water and disappearing back into the trees.

As Ratboy raced after him, he quickly realised that the growth beyond the pool was even more gnarled and closely packed. He and Anna did their best to clamber after the priest, but they felt as though the branches were deliberately lashing out and pressing their ancient weight down on top of them. The strange lights also began to reappear in the corner of Ratboy's vision: flickering sprites that vanished as soon as he tried to pinpoint them. As they struggled deeper and deeper into the brooding heart of the forest, his eyes began to play other tricks on him too. Branches slipped out of reach as he reached for support and leering faces appeared in the knotted trunks, only to vanish when he looked a second time.

'What's that sound?' asked Anna, panting and grunting as she fought through the undergrowth.

Ratboy paused for a second and noticed that beneath the sound of his own laboured breathing, there was a low throbbing noise. It was barely perceptible, but it seemed to emanating from all around them, as though the forest itself were groaning with fear. He shook his head and stumbled onwards after Wolff, terrified at the thought of being left alone in such a place.

After a few minutes, he noticed there was a pale green light pulsating through the trees ahead. He turned to Anna and guessed from her frown that she had seen it too. As they neared the light, the throbbing sound grew louder and Ratboy's nervousness increased. He could no longer see his master, but as they scrambled through the undergrowth he began to make out the source of the strange radiance. There was a grove up ahead that seemed quite distinct from the rest of the forest. An arcade of tall silver birches led proudly towards it, before forming themselves into a perfect circle around the small, raised clearing. The light was bleeding between the gaps in the sentry-like birches, so Ratboy stumbled onto the avenue and raced up towards the clearing. The light was so bright in the grove that he had to shield his eyes as he ran into the dazzling circle of trees.

CHAPTER EIGHTEEN
THE SACRED GROVE

THE GROVE WAS filled with blinding light. The glare was so intense Ratboy struggled to see for a few seconds. When his vision cleared, he saw that Wolff was stood just ahead of him, silhouetted against the brightness and watching the deer as it trotted across a carpet of mossy turf. Ratboy saw that the animal's movements had become even more erratic. It lurched into the centre of the grove and dropped to its knees before the hollowed-out bole of an old oak tree. As it fell, its internal organs slipped from beneath its skin in a steaming mess, spilling onto the grass like stew from a pot, to reveal a small, humanoid shape crouched within the hide.

'Sigmar,' whispered Ratboy, as the figure discarded the animal's remains and climbed, gasping, to its feet. 'What's that?'

The creature stretched its slender arms above its head and let out a sigh of satisfaction. As the rest of the deer's innards slid down its back, they revealed a coat of blue feathers that shimmered in the throbbing light. 'Kriegsmarshall,' it said, bowing towards the tree stump, 'the other two are close behind.'

'They're already here, Helwyg,' replied a low voice from somewhere within the inferno of light.

The feathered creature turned to look back at Ratboy and Anna in surprise. His eyes were bright yellow and widened in fear at the sight of them. He dashed away from the sodden remains and vanished into the light.

'Master,' cried Ratboy, rushing towards Wolff but, before he had gone more than a few feet, he froze. The light that washed over his skin felt thick and tangible and it rooted his feet firmly to the spot. He moaned in fear as he felt it entwining his limbs and snaking through his clothes. Within seconds, his entire body was paralysed. The most he could do was roll his eyes from side to side in terror. As he did so, he saw that Anna was frozen too, just a few feet to his left. Tendrils of light snaked between the two of them and Wolff, making a crackling, glimmering triangle. He tried to scream, but even his vocal chords refused to obey. His horror mounted as he realised that he had not seen Wolff move an inch since he and Anna entered the grove. They were all paralysed.

'It's been a long time, Jakob,' said Fabian in an imperious voice, stepping out of the light. His regal features were flushed with pride as he surveyed his handiwork. In his left hand he held an old, battered book, bound in white leather, with a gold knife foiled on the front. Several of its pages were missing and scraps of mismatched parchment had been sewn clumsily into the jacket, but its power was unmistakable. Waves of emerald light were leaking from the paper, rippling through the grass and glittering in the stones on Fabian's eye-patch. 'But I'm sure you remember the promise I made you,' he continued. 'I swore not to hunt you down, but you've brought yourself to me. And I warned you that if we ever met again, I'd have no choice but to kill you.'

The priest tried to answer, but he was completely shrouded in light, and as he strained to escape, the only sound he could make was a strangled groan of frustration.

Fabian strolled slowly towards his brother, still holding the book before him. In his other hand, he held a small black object. As the old general stepped closer, Ratboy realised he was holding the beak of a carrion bird, long and gleaming as he rolled it between his thumb and forefinger.

'You're so old,' muttered Fabian as he reached his paralysed brother. He looked with fascination at Jakob's weather-worn features and ran a finger slowly across his face. 'You've lived a whole lifetime that you didn't deserve.' Fabian's one good eye was the only hint of their shared heritage. Where Jakob was broad and heavy-set, Fabian was slender and graceful; they were as opposite as two men could be, but his eye was as black and dangerous as his brother's. 'Your destiny has finally caught up with you,' he said, pressing the beak into the side of the priest's neck.

Wolff tried to pull away, but the dancing light held him firmly in place and as the curved, filthy beak slipped beneath his skin it sent a dark stream of blood rushing down his thick neck. Fabian gave a low chuckle. 'Bless you, brother. I had my doubts that this would work. My lord had complete confidence in your naiveté, but I thought after all these decades you might have developed a little more insight.'

He stepped back to watch as Wolff's blood pooled on the ground. As soon as the liquid touched the grass, it fanned out into a series of thin, viscous strands, each one twisting and spiralling as though alive. The lines of blood traced around the priest's feet in a complex set of circles, framing him within an elaborate, glistening design.

Fabian shook his head at his brother's confused expression. 'It must be wonderful to see the world in such simple terms – to divide everything along crude fault lines of good and evil, but it does leave one a little blinkered.'

He sighed as he watched his brother struggling. Then he waved at the slender, blue creature watching nervously from the edge of the clearing. 'My eyes have been on you for a long time, Jakob. I've waited and waited for you to realise the truth, but you never did. Your head's still so full of righteousness. Even after all these years, it robs you of sense. You knew I was coming here to make a sacrifice.' He leant forward, so that his face was just inches away from his brother's. 'But not for a minute did you consider that the sacrifice might be you.' He savoured the mute agony in Wolff's eyes. 'Yes, you see it now. Now that you've sent so many innocents to their deaths, believing I was interested in a horde of meat-headed soldiers. I've led you a merry dance, brother, but you embraced the role with enthusiasm. I think you can take credit for all the bystanders you've dragged down with you.' He shrugged. 'To be fair, the idea wasn't mine. I *did* originally intend to buy immortality with the blood of my men. But my master's taste is far more particular. Only a very choice morsel is good enough for such an imaginative appetite.' He raised his hands to the star-speckled heavens and cried out in a dramatic voice. 'Not just the blood of a powerful Sigmarite, but the blood of my own brother! How delectable!' He shook his head. 'I never dreamt you would be so stupid as to bring yourself to me – trotting meekly into my master's own house, but he had faith; he had the vision I lacked.'

The veins in Wolff's neck looked ready to burst as he pulled against the light that enveloped him. Finally, with an incredible effort, he managed to let out a feeble word. 'No,' he croaked.

'Yes,' replied Fabian with a broad smile. 'Yes, yes, yes! You're my gift, Jakob. The whole campaign was nothing but a joke, with you as its moronic punchline. Two entire armies sacrificed, just to make a fool out of you – just to see if you'd take the bait. Everything was leading to this moment. Do you really think it's so easy to stroll from behind the lines of such an army as Mormius's? I thought you would see through the ruse though, I really did. I thought you would spot the handiwork of the Architect of Fate. How could you not recognise the artifices of the Great Beguiler.' He shook his head and his smile became a laugh. 'I could maybe understand your cynical abuse of the flagellants' faith, but what happened at Mercy's End, Jakob?

I felt sure you would see sense then. How could you think it was right to abandon all those men? You let Mormius rip the heart out of this province, just so you could pursue a personal vendetta. Don't you see? With you by their side, they would have won. Was there ever such a proud display of Ostland grit as Felhamer and his garrison? How could you just leave them all to die? How could you think that was right? You abandoned every article of your faith when you left those men to be butchered.'

Wolff's struggles grew weaker with each word. His shoulders slumped and his chin dropped, until it seemed as though the light was all that was keeping him on his feet. He looked utterly destroyed.

Fabian stepped over towards Anna. 'And what strange company you keep, brother. What a wretched collection of apostates.' He looked down at Anna's bloodstained robes with obvious amusement. 'A murderous Shallyan – who ever heard of such a thing? How quickly we abandon our beliefs in the face of pain.' As Fabian leant closer to the priestess, her body bucked away from him, lurching violently within the prison of light. 'Did you enjoy it, Anna,' he whispered, as he pressed the beak into the side of her neck, 'when you felt him struggling for life?' Anna moaned in horror as blood rushed from her throat, mingling with that of her victim. 'Did you relish the power, as you stopped his heart?' Fabian stepped back to watch as the blood danced around Anna's feet, before writhing across the ground and linking with the pool at Wolff's. 'Did you really think you were left alive in that cart by mere chance?'

He nodded with satisfaction and then moved over to Ratboy. 'And this one, brother' he chuckled. 'Did you know he tried to forsake you?' He sneered with disgust. 'While you were fighting to preserve his homeland, this wretched turncoat was planning his escape. Can you believe that? After everything you've done for him, he tried to abandon you to save his own worthless skin. He wouldn't even be here if the Knights Griffon hadn't caught him trying to worm his way to safety. He lacks your faith, brother. He lacks the faith to kill.'

Ratboy's eyes filled with tears. The truth of Fabian's words cut through him. Fabian was right. The battle had terrified him, but not as much as the sight of Wolff's animal frenzy. That was what he had been fleeing – the fear of such inhumanity. His chest shook with great, heaving sobs. He had pictured many endings to his life as a novice, but never this one: to die by the side of his master after such awful betrayal. Ratboy's desolation was complete. He barely noticed as Fabian slid the beak into his throat and sent a spray of blood down his filthy hauberk. The liquid quickly merged with the morass of crimson symbols on grass.

Fabian turned away from him and flicked through the pages of the book. He muttered a few incoherent lines under his breath and the light grew in brilliance. The tears in Ratboy's eyes fragmented the brilliant display, so that he saw dozens of Fabians stride back up to the ancient tree stump and remove their eyepatches.

As the light grew, so did the throbbing sound. The birches surrounding the grove began to bow and creak with the force of it. At the same time, the strands of blood formed ever more complex shapes around the three captives: eyes merged into fish and flames formed into skulls and all with such frenetic purpose that the liquid seemed to possess an awful, animal sentience.

Ratboy's mind reeled in the face of such an onslaught and he felt his reason slipping away. The trees at the edge of the clearing were now undulating and throbbing in time to the pulses of light, twisting themselves into strange, serpentine shapes. Ratboy gave Wolff a final despairing look, but the priest was hanging like a limp doll, tossed back and forth by the currents of his brother's magic. Ratboy closed his eyes but the awful visions simply burned through his eyelids and flooded his broken heart.

CHAPTER NINETEEN
THE BLOOD OF A WOLFF

ENVY NEVER DIES, thought Anna as Fabian's sorcery pawed and scratched at her flesh. Where had she heard those words? For the life of her she could not remember, but as she watched the old general, muttering feverishly over his book, she realised why she had thought of them. In an instant, her mind stripped away the decades and she saw a small boy stood behind the shattered oak; a child consumed by jealousy for his older brother. Her despair began to be replaced by anger. Had so many men really been sacrificed to assuage the petty hatred of a child? Was she really going to die here for such a pathetic reason? Whatever she had done, whatever mistakes she had made, she could not bear to be sacrificed on the altar of some paltry sibling rivalry. She strained her muscles one last time, testing the strength of her bonds, but the column of light that surrounded her was now a furious hurricane of glyphs and visions and there was no way she could break through. As Fabian's incantation droned on in the background she began to seethe with fury. The lattice of energy had lifted the three of them several feet off the ground, coursing through their bodies with such force that they jolted back and forth like branches, battered by a storm.

A movement caught her eye and she twisted her head back over her shoulder. There was a pair of men crouched in the avenue of trees that led up to the grove. They were stood in the darkness beyond the luminous display and she couldn't quite make out their faces, but as the smaller of the two edged forwards, she saw his pale, staring eyes and felt a shock of recognition.

Sürman had finally found her.

Thoughts tumbled through her head. Death, or something worse, was only seconds away. Would the witch hunter do anything? She peered into his strange eyes and flinched at the hatred she found there. She could see that, even now, as unholy energy arced and flashed around the clearing, he was desperate to come to her. If there was ever an ounce of sanity in him it had long gone. She saw a profound madness in his thin, jaundiced features. The only thing keeping his ruined body alive was his hunger for her blood.

She looked around the grove. Fabian was completely lost in rapture. His working eye had rolled back in its socket and his flesh was incandescent with power. The strands of blood and magic that linked her to Wolff and Ratboy were coruscating wildly in time to the rhythm of his words. The throbbing was now so loud she could barely hear him, but the imploring tone was unmistakable: he was using their vitality to summon something. At the heart of the circle of light a nimbus was forming in the bole of the old oak tree. It was too bright to look upon directly, but Anna thought she could see movement stirring deep within it: a foetal shape, twitching and straining for life. Whatever it was, the links between her and the others were feeding it, she was sure of it.

An idea began to form in her mind.

With all her remaining strength, Anna raised her hands above her head and twisted her face into a victorious grin. As she turned towards Sürman, she felt the light playing around her fingertips and laughed with pleasure.

Sürman's eyes bulged at the sight of Anna's ecstatic movements. It was more than he could bear to see her relishing the power that surrounded her. His worst suspicions were confirmed. She was obviously a witch of unbelievable power. He clutched his head in dismay and stumbled into the light, lurching towards her as though dragged by invisible hands.

His companion grabbed him by the shoulder, trying to pull him back to safety, but the witch hunter shrugged him away with a cry that was lost beneath the throbbing hum of Fabian's magic.

Anna twisted her hands into a series of vaguely mystical shapes, trying to ignore the pain that was eating into her limbs and assuming the role of an unrepentant sorceress.

Finally, with a storm of invectives Sürman broke into a run and launched himself at Anna. He grabbed hold of her legs and they both slammed down onto the muddy grass.

The triangle of light collapsed and arcs of power thrashed wildly around the grove, like the flailing limbs of a dying animal. The throbbing ceased immediately and Wolf and Ratboy dropped heavily to the ground.

A hiccupping scream echoed around the clearing.

Anna looked up to see that all of the light had turned back in on its source, pummelling into Fabian's body with such force that it had pinned him to the ground. The book fell from his hand and smoke began to rise from his clothes as the power rippled over his prone body. 'Gods, what have you done?' he screamed at Sürman, as the witch hunter struggled with Anna, attempting to drag her from the clearing.

'Help me Adelman, you oaf,' hissed Sürman, looking back at the hulking figure stood beneath the trees. The man looked at the wild directionless power lashing across the grass and shook his head, white with fear. 'Quick,' said Sürman, wrapping his wiry arms around Anna's legs as she tried to drag herself away.

Anna had almost pulled herself free of the old man's grip when his servant finally plucked up the courage to come after her. He lumbered across the grove and levelled a crossbow at her. Two bolts were loaded in its breach and Anna yelped in pain as the first sank deep into her thigh. As she clutched at the wound, gasping in agony, Adelman lifted her easily over his shoulder and began to carry her back towards the trees, with the grinning witch hunter following closely behind. Anna's screams echoed around the grove, but both Wolff and Ratboy were still spread-eagled on the grass and gave no sign of hearing.

They had almost left the clearing when Adelman stumbled to a halt. He looked down at his chest with an expression of dog-like stupidity. There was a smouldering hole where his chest should have been.

'What are you doing?' snarled Sürman. 'Why've you stopped?' Then he noticed the wound and his eyes widened in fear. As Adelman toppled to the ground, vomiting thick blood across the grass, Sürman and Anna saw the source of his injury. Fabian had struggled to his feet, still enveloped in the green light and was lurching drunkenly towards them. His right hand was extended and crackling with power.

'Leave her,' he said, with light sparking off his teeth.

'She's mine!' screamed Sürman, pinning Anna to the floor and glaring back at him. 'She escaped my justice once but not–'

Fabian silenced the witch hunter with a single flick of his wrist. Light poured from his veins and slammed into the frail old man.

The witch hunter barely had time to cry out in pain before the flesh melted and shrivelled from his face. As he collapsed on top of Anna, his head was little more than a mass of charred bone and smouldering hair.

'Actually, she's mine,' said Fabian, pulling Sürman's smoking remains off Anna and grabbing her arm. The power in his fingers scorched her skin and she cried out in pain. 'I won't be stopped,' he growled, pulling her face towards his.

For the first time, Anna saw Fabian's left eye and she gasped in disgust. The scab had opened and the huge black orb was rolling excitedly in its moist, pus-lined socket. She felt a malign intelligence studying her through the bloated lens and turned away in fear. There was a smell of cooking meat coming from Fabian and she noticed that where the light was leaking through his pores, his skin was blistering and cracking. His determination seemed to blind him to his pain though and, despite Anna's screams and kicks, she found herself being dragged slowly back towards the shattered oak.

Anna gasped as she saw that the foetal shape had already doubled in size. Birdlike talons had erupted from its skin and were scrabbling at the wood in an attempt to climb free. Its flesh was rippling and twitching as it tried to settle on a fixed shape and as they approached it Anna heard the wet, laboured sound of the thing's first breath.

As she struggled to escape, Anna noticed that Wolff had climbed to his knees and was praying to his warhammer. His head was bowed and he was muttering furiously under his breath. The ornate tracery that decorated the head of the weapon was glimmering slightly with a light of its own: not as dramatic as the green fire that was devouring Fabian, but enough to give Anna a fierce rush of hope.

Fabian followed the direction of her gaze and hissed with frustration. He threw her to the ground and stretched out his hand towards Wolff. 'This is my destiny, Jakob,' he shrieked, as light exploded from his arm and hurtled across the clearing towards the priest's head.

Wolff calmly raised his hammer to meet the blast and a deafening explosion filled the grove.

The flash was so bright that for a second Anna was blinded. When her vision cleared, she saw that all traces of magic had vanished. The forest had been plunged back into darkness and Fabian was sprawled, gasping on his back. The bole of the tree was empty once more and there was no sign of the grotesque foetus that had been forming within its bark. Anna's ears rang with the sudden silence as she climbed to her feet. She had forgotten the bolt lodged in her thigh and she cried out in pain, dropping heavily to her knees again.

At the sound of her voice, Fabian lifted his head and gave a weak groan of despair. With the light gone, he saw how scorched and ruined his flesh was. 'What have you done?' he croaked, peering though the darkness at the tree trunk, then turning to look at his brother.

Wolff was still knelt in prayer.

'You can't stop me,' howled Fabian, managing to stand 'Not now, after all my work.' He stumbled across the grove, with burnt clothes and skin trailing behind him like a bridal train. 'You. Can. Not. Stop. Me,' he said, punctuating each word with a punch to Wolff's head.

Jakob took the blows with unflinching stoicism, before rising to his feet and glaring down at his smaller brother. 'This is wrong, Fabian,' he said calmly. 'Whatever has passed between us, you must know I *can't* let you do this.' He adopted a fighting stance and gripped his warhammer firmly in both hands. 'I have to stop you.'

Fabian let out a long, bitter laugh. 'I'm not a child anymore, Jakob,' he said, drawing his sword and mirroring the priest's pose. 'And father isn't here to save you this time.' As he spoke the word 'time' he lunged forward with surprising speed, jamming his blade through a gap at the top of Wolff's vambrace.

Wolff staggered backwards, clutching his arm in shock and trying to stem the flow of blood that rushed down his forearm. He quickly recovered and swung his hammer towards Fabian's head, but the Iron Duke was already gone. Wolff's weapon connected with nothing but air and the priest's momentum sent him crashing to his knees.

Fabian laughed again as he planted a boot into his brother's back and sent him sprawling across the grass. 'So slow,' he chuckled. 'So old.'

Wolff leapt to his feet, gasping for breath. 'You're a Wolff,' he cried. 'Think what that means. Think of your heritage.'

The smile dropped from Fabian's gaunt face and his mouth twisted with rage. 'What would you know of being a Wolff?' he screamed, sending trails of spit from his scorched lips. 'How can you dare to speak of our heritage?' His anger overwhelmed him and he threw back his head, pulling at his own hair and screaming at the stars. 'You ruined everything! I was going to place our family back at the heart of history, where we belong.' His voice cracked and squeaked as he glared at Wolff. 'And you destroyed us. You and your church and your pathetic devotion. You killed our parents, Jakob.' He lurched across the grass with tears of rage flooding down his cheeks. 'How can you dare to even speak to me?' he cried, placing a fierce kick into the side of Wolff's head.

Wolff climbed to his feet and pounded the haft of his hammer into Fabian's breastplate, so that he reeled backwards towards the tree stump. '*I* killed them?' cried Jakob in a voice that sounded as strangled as his brother's. 'What are you talking about? I simply discovered your guilt.' He levelled a finger at Fabian. '*You* brought shame on our family, brother, not me. You diluted our bloodline with heresy and lies.'

Fabian was trembling with fury and his elegant fighting stance was completely forgotten as he ran wildly back towards Wolff. 'You're nothing but a puppet, Jakob,' he cried. 'A puppet of a dying creed.' He lashed out wildly with his sword.

Wolff was faster. His hammer smashed the sword aside and connected with Fabian's head.

The general's neck snapped backwards and he let out a gurgled moan, before toppling backwards into the bole of the tree.

Wolff placed one foot on the tree trunk and raised his hammer for the killing blow.

He paused.

Beneath him, Fabian was trying to speak. His head was horribly misshapen where his skull had cracked and his hair was dark with gore, but he still had the strength to reach out: pawing at his brother's robes in a final, desperate plea: trying to form words with his slack, blood-filled mouth.

Wolff scowled and raised his hammer a little higher, but still he couldn't strike. 'What?' he muttered finally, stooping so that he could place his ear next to his brother's mouth.

Fabian's eye was full of fear, but as he repeated the words, a faint smile played around his mouth. 'The blood of a Wolff runs true,' he whispered, gripping Jakob's shoulder.

The priest flinched. To hear their childhood joke, after all this time, filled him with horror. The years fell away and he saw that the bloody wreck before him was still Fabian. This awful fiend was still his brother. 'I can't do it,' he groaned, amazed by his weakness. He freed himself from Fabian's grip and dropped his warhammer to the grass. Then he stumbled backwards and sat heavily on the ground, with his head in his hands.

Fabian lay there for a few moments, watching his brother with an odd, pained expression on his face. Then, with a gurgling cough, he pulled himself out of the tree trunk and began to limp towards the far side of the grove.

He had only taken a few steps, when a crossbow bolt thudded into his back. He stumbled on for a few more feet, reaching out towards the gloomy boughs, then collapsed onto the grass with a final, ragged breath.

Ratboy approached with the crossbow still in his hand. He stooped and whispered into the corpse's ear. 'I've regained my faith, general,' he said.

CHAPTER TWENTY
PENITENTS

Jakob lay on his back watching the endless Ostland rain. It billowed and swept across the forest in great columns, falling with such force that dozens of rivulets had begun rushing down the hillside, washing over the priest's battered armour and heading down towards the valley below. A couple of miles away, the ragged fingers of Hagen's Claw pierced the downpour, reaching up towards the dark belly of the clouds like a drowning man. Jakob narrowed his eyes. Even from this distance he could see figures moving beneath the granite columns. Without their general to drive them onwards, the army was dispersing. The soldiers were making their way back to their families and homes, keen to forget the strangeness of the forest. In a few months the crows and other scavengers would have removed any trace of the dead that were left behind. In time, even the broken weapons would disappear beneath the grass and there would be no sign that the battle had ever taken place.

Wolff saw faces in the clouds rushing overhead. His brother's mainly, filled with anguish as he begged for mercy, but there were others too, a whole army of dead souls, all gazing down at him with hatred in their eyes. 'Sigmar forgive me,' he muttered.

'He's waking up,' came a voice from somewhere nearby.

Wolff lifted his head and wiped the rain from his eyes. Ratboy and Anna were sat watching him. They both looked awful. Their rain-lashed faces were white with exhaustion and pain. As Anna climbed to her feet and hobbled towards him, Wolff saw that the crossbow bolt was still embedded in her thigh and the lower part of her robe was black with blood. Ratboy was sat just a few feet away and Wolff guessed it was his voice he had heard. He was rocking back and forth, cradling his damaged hand, but there was a look of fierce determination in his eyes that the priest had never seen before. Wolff could hardly recognise him. He seemed to have aged a lifetime in an evening.

Wolff looked at them both in silence for a few seconds, unsure what to say. He felt somehow naked, ashamed of what they had witnessed during the night. Ashamed that they now knew so much about him. They had not only heard every word of his disgraceful confrontation with Fabian, but they had also seen his weakness and stupidity. It appalled him to think that without Ratboy's courage, Fabian would have escaped. His brother had made him a fool. 'How can I have been so blind?' he said, lowering his head in shame.

'He fooled us all, Jakob,' said Anna, reaching his side and placing a hand on his shoulder.

Wolff winced at the pity in her voice. She had never had any love for him, or his beliefs, so her sudden kindness made his skin crawl. What a pathetic figure he must have become if even Anna felt sorry for him.

'None of us could ever have dreamt that he would engineer a whole campaign – a whole war – just to ensnare his own brother,' she continued. 'That's the thinking of a lunatic. How could we have guessed he was working to such an insane plan? To sacrifice so many innocents,' she stumbled over her words and closed her eyes for a second, 'beggars belief.'

'I should have seen it,' said Wolff, recoiling from her touch. 'I knew him. I should have known.' He threw himself back on the grass. 'And everything he said about me was true. I was blinded by rage. I left all those men to die. I've betrayed everyone: you, the flagellants, Felhamer, Maximilian, Lüneberg, Gryphius – the entire army. Everyone.'

'Nothing he said was true,' replied Ratboy, shaking his head fiercely. 'His whole existence was a lie.' He climbed to his feet and looked down over the sodden trees. 'I *did* lose my nerve for a minute,' he said, with a note of shame in his voice. 'I couldn't recognise you for a while, as we fought through the marauders. I saw something in your face that terrified me.' He rushed to Wolff's side and looked at him with panic in his eyes. 'But Fabian lied. I would never have betrayed you. It was a moment of fear, nothing more.' He dropped to his knees and looked imploringly at his master. 'Even if Maximilian hadn't stopped me, I would've come back. As soon as I came to my senses.' He shook his head. 'I know I wouldn't have abandoned you. That's how I saw that he was nothing more than a cheap trickster. That's how I knew I had the strength to kill him.'

Wolff took Ratboy's hand. 'I never doubted your courage, Anselm. You've nothing to be ashamed of. In fact, you were right to fear me. I could think of nothing but revenge and murder. And even in that one, simple task I failed.' He turned his face to the rain and closed his eyes. 'In the end, I couldn't kill him. If you hadn't been there he would have gone free. It was my faith that failed, not yours.'

For a while the only sound came from the rain, drumming against the hillside. None of them even had the strength to crawl back towards the trees, so they just sat there in a disconsolate silence, letting the water soak through their clothes. Wolff was still staring up at the clouds, and still haunted by his brother's face. In those final seconds, when he saw the fear in Fabian's eye, a kind of awful epiphany had stayed his hand. It was his own religious zeal that had driven his brother down his dark path – he had suddenly seen that quite clearly. What an unbearable child he must have been: always so perfect, always so pious. Who could blame Fabian for rebelling? Who could blame him for attempting to find his own form of devotion?

After a while, Anna looked over at him. 'I think you're wrong, Brother Wolff.'

The priest looked over at her with a frown.

'I don't think it was a lack of faith that stayed your hand,' she continued. 'I think it was your humanity.'

She looked at the blood that still covered her hands. 'We're just frail mortals, all of us: nothing more, nothing less. But maybe that's what makes us worth saving?'

'But my brother was a monster! To let him live would have been to loose a great evil on the world. Don't you see? Every decision I've made has led to bloodshed.' He groaned and clutched his head in his hands. 'I'm no better than a dumb animal. I don't even remember half of the battle. In fact, I'm just the same as Fabian. I've been deluding myself all this time that I have to save the Empire from his evil, but in reality, I'm no better than he was.'

Anna shook her head. 'No, Jakob, Fabian was a monster.' She grabbed his hand. 'And the very fact that you let him live proves that you're not. He had become inhuman but, in the end, after everything, you were still just a man. *That's* the difference between the two of you.' There was an intense urgency in her voice and Ratboy suddenly realised why: she was desperate for Wolff to forgive himself, so that she could do the same.

As Wolff looked back at her, a tiny glimmer of hope flashed in his black eyes. They held each other's gaze for a few seconds and then, briefly, the harsh lines of his face relaxed. He gave a barely perceptible nod and squeezed Anna's hand in gratitude. He closed his eyes and muttered a quiet prayer of thanks that was lost beneath the sound of the rain. Then, when he opened his eyes again, he noticed Anna's wounded leg and gave her a brusque nod. 'Let me see if I can I can help,' he said, spreading his hands over the wound.

As a soft, healing light began to leak from the priest's fingertips, Anna looked over at Ratboy with tears in her eyes and a faint smile playing around the corners of her mouth.

CHAPTER TWENTY-ONE
REMEMBRANCE

THE GREAT POPPENSTEIN would not be missed. In the few months since his arrival, the villagers of Elghast had quickly grown tired of his tatty costumes and amateurish tricks. Maybe he had been telling the truth when he boasted of his years in the Tsarina's circus, but if so, his age and alcoholism had long since robbed him of any real skill. His hands had trembled as he had performed even the most basic illusions and his juggling had been positively dangerous. When the conjuror's body was discovered, half eaten in the back of his bright red cart, no one was much surprised. The bear, Kusma, seemed destined for better things, and the villagers did not really blame him for wanting to dispose of his less talented partner.

The rain had turned the gardens of remembrance into a treacherous swamp of half-submerged headstones and slippery, flower-strewn paths. A few mourners had turned up, in the vain hope of seeing some of Poppenstein's celebrated circus friends, but they had soon hurried away again when they realised he had misled them about that too. With war continuing to rage across the province, funerals had begun to lose their appeal as a spectator sport. There was hardly a day that passed without some poor wretch being crammed into the packed cemetery.

Erasmus gave a grunt of exertion as he stamped the final mound of sod into place. Mud oozed over his sandals and between his toes and he grimaced in disgust. Then he leant back with his hands on his hips until his back gave a satisfying *crack*. 'Udo,' he called to the raven perched on a nearby headstone. 'Let's get back inside. This weather will be the death of us.'

It was already nine, but there was no sign of sunlight breaking through the low clouds. For weeks now, the village had been smothered in a perpetual gloom. News of the Iron Duke's victory in the north had been greeted with little enthusiasm. Few doubted that it would be long until the next incursion. Even the rumours of his mysterious disappearance held little interest for people so concerned with their own survival. Times were hard and the villagers of Elghast had long since lost their appetite for war. As the priest made his way back through the headstones towards the small temple he pulled his robes a little tighter and gave a long, weary yawn.

The raven remained perched on the stone and let out a peevish croak.

Erasmus paused and looked back over his shoulder. 'Come on, old girl,' he said, peering through the downpour at the huge bird. 'I've not even had my breakfast yet. Let's get inside. If I don't eat some porridge soon, my stomach will digest itself.'

The bird refused to follow Erasmus, but skittered from side-to-side across the top of the stone instead, letting out another harsh cry.

'Udo!' snapped the priest as he stomped back through the ankle-deep mud. 'What on earth's the matter with you?' His robes were now completely soaked and he shuddered as several icy trickles ran down his back. Upon reaching Udo he held out his arm and glared at the bird in an angry silence.

It was only after a few seconds of scowling that he realised they were not alone. There was a figure: a young man, or a boy even, cowering beneath the eaves of a large mausoleum and watching them intently. Erasmus squinted through the rain but could not make out who it was. The mourner was hooded and small, but beyond that he couldn't make out any details. Elghast was barely more than a hamlet and Erasmus knew most of the villagers by name, but this boy did not look familiar. 'Were you a friend of the deceased?' he called to the robed figure.

There was no reply, so he stepped towards him. 'I'm afraid the service is over. Is there anything I can help you with?'

The mourner remained silent.

Erasmus gave an irritated sigh and walked a little closer. 'Are your parents in the village?' he asked, stepping under the roof of the mausoleum.

As he reached the mourner, Erasmus realised his mistake. The stranger was not a boy at all, he was just incredibly hunched and frail.

The man lurched forwards and threw back his hood, revealing a gleaming mask of burnt flesh. 'Heal me,' he whispered. His lips had been burned away, leaving his mouth in a permanent grin and the rest of his face was scorched beyond all recognition. Erasmus had no doubt who the man was though. Despite the awful scarring that covered his skin, his colourless eyes were unmistakable.

'Sigmar help me,' gasped Erasmus, staggering backwards as the witch hunter grabbed hold of his robes. 'Sürman.'

Udo finally launched herself from the headstone, letting out another croak as she headed back towards the temple, leaving the two men struggling desperately in the shadows.

ABOUT THE AUTHOR

After a music career so disastrous it landed him in court, **Darius Hinks** decided a job in publishing might be safer. Since joining the Black Library he's worked on such legendary titles as *Inquis Exterminatus* and *Liber Chaotica* as well as writing *The Witch Hunter's Handbook* and short stories for several of the Black Library's anthologies. Rumours that he still has a banjo hidden in his loft are fiercely refuted by his lawyers.

WULFRIK ~ CL WERNER

WARHAMMER HEROES

UK ISBN 978-1-84416-892-7 US ISBN 978-1-84416-893-4

SWORD OF JUSTICE ~ CHRIS WRAIGHT

WARHAMMER HEROES

UK ISBN 978-1-84416-876-7 US ISBN 978-1-84416-877-4

SWORD OF VENGEANCE ~ CHRIS WRAIGHT

WARHAMMER HEROES

UK ISBN 978-1-84970-020-7 US ISBN 978-1-84970-021-4